Cindi Myers is the [author of ...] novels. When she's [not ...] she enjoys skiing, gardening, cooking, [...] daydreaming. A lover of small-town life, she lives with her husband and two spoiled dogs in the Colorado mountains.

Julie Miller is an award-winning *USA Today* bestselling author of breathtaking romantic suspense—with a National Readers' Choice Award and a Daphne du Maurier Award, among other prizes. She has also earned an *RT Book Reviews* Career Achievement Award. For a complete list of her books, monthly newsletter and more, go to juliemiller.org

MOUNTAIN CAPTIVE

CINDI MYERS

SPECIAL FORCES K-9

JULIE MILLER

MILLS & BOON

First Published in Great Britain 2024
by Mills & Boon, an imprint of HarperCollins*Publishers* Ltd
1 London Bridge Street, London, SE1 9GF

www.harpercollins.co.uk

HarperCollins*Publishers*
Macken House, 39/40 Mayor Street Upper,
Dublin 1, D01 C9W8, Ireland

Mountain Captive © 2025 Cynthia Myers
Special Forces K-9 © 2025 Julie Miller

ISBN: 978-0-263-39695-9

0125

This book contains FSC™ certified paper and other controlled sources to ensure responsible forest management.

For more information visit: www.harpercollins.co.uk/green

Printed and Bound in the UK using 100% Renewable Electricity at CPI Group (UK) Ltd, Croydon, CR0 4YY

MOUNTAIN CAPTIVE

CINDI MYERS

Chapter One

Rand Martin had built his reputation on noticing details—the tiny nick in an artery that was the source of life-threatening blood loss; the almost microscopic bit of shrapnel that might lead to a deadly infection; the panic in a wounded man's eyes that could send his vitals out of control; the tremor in a fellow surgeon's hand that meant he wasn't fit to operate. As a trauma surgeon—first in the military, then in civilian life—Rand noticed the little things others overlooked. It made him a better doctor, and it equipped him to deal with the people in his life.

But sometimes that focus on the small picture got in the way of his big-picture job. Today, his first call as medical adviser for Eagle Mountain Search and Rescue, he was supposed to be focusing on the sixty-something man sprawled on the side of a high mountain trail. But Rand's attention kept shifting to the woman who knelt beside the man. Her blue-and-yellow vest identified her as a member of the search and rescue team, but her turquoise hair and full sleeve of colorful tattoos set her apart from the other volunteers. That, and the wariness that radiated off her as she surveyed the crowd that was fast gathering around her and her patient on the popular hiking trail.

"Everyone move back and give us some space," Rand ordered, and, like the men and women he had commanded in his mobile surgical unit in Kabul, the crowd obeyed and fell back.

SAR Captain Danny Irwin rose from where he had been crouched on the patient's other side and greeted Rand. "Thanks for coming out," he said.

"Are you the doctor?" Another woman, blond hair in a ponytail that streamed down her back, rushed forward.

"Dr. Rand Martin." He didn't offer his hand, already pulling on latex gloves, ready to examine his patient. The blue-haired woman had risen also, and was edging to one side of the trail. As if she was trying to blend in with the crowd—a notion Rand found curious. Nothing about this woman would allow her to blend in. Even without the wildly colored hair and the ink down her arm, she was too striking to ever be invisible.

"My dad has a heart condition," the blonde said. "I tried to tell him he shouldn't be hiking at this altitude, but he wouldn't listen, and now this has happened."

"Margo, please!" This, from the man on the ground. He had propped himself up on his elbows and was frowning at the woman, presumably his daughter. "I hurt my leg. It has nothing to do with my heart."

"You don't know that," she said. "Maybe you fell because you were lightheaded or had an irregular heartbeat. If you weren't so stubborn—"

A balding man close to the woman's age moved up and put his hands on the woman's shoulders. "Let's wait and see what the doctor has to say," he said, and led Margo a few feet away.

Rand crouched beside the man. He was pale, sweating and breathing hard. Not that unusual, considering the bone sticking out of his lower leg. He was probably in a lot of pain from that compound fracture, and despite his protestation that nothing was wrong with his heart, the pain and shock could aggravate an existing cardiac condition. "What happened?" Rand asked.

"We were coming down the trail and Buddy fell." This, from another woman, with short gray curls. She sat a few feet away, flanked by two boys—early-or preteens, Rand guessed. The boys were staring at the man on the ground, freckles standing out against their pale skin.

"I stepped on a rock, and it rolled," Buddy offered. "I heard a snap." He grimaced. "Hurts like the devil."

"We'll get you something for the pain." Rand saw that someone—Danny or the blue-haired woman—had already started an intravenous line. "Do you have a medical history?" he asked Danny.

The SAR captain—an RN in his day job—handed over a small clipboard. Buddy was apparently sixty-seven, on a couple of common cardiac drugs. No history of medication allergies, though Rand questioned him again to be absolutely sure. Then he checked the clipboard once more. "Mr. Morrison, we're going to give you some morphine for the pain. It should take effect within a few minutes. Then we're going to splint your leg, pack it in ice to keep the swelling down, and get you down the mountain and to the hospital for X-rays and treatment."

"But his heart!" Margo, who'd shoved away from the balding man—her husband, perhaps—rushed forward again.

"Are you experiencing any chest pain?" Rand asked, even as he pulled out a stethoscope. "Palpitations?"

"No." Buddy glanced toward his daughter and lowered his voice, his tone confiding. "I had a quadruple bypass nine months ago. I completed cardiac rehab, and I'm just fine. Despite what my daughter would have you believe, I'm not an idiot. My doctor thought this vacation was a fine idea. I'm under no activity restrictions."

"Your doctor probably has no idea you would decide to hike six miles at ten thousand feet," Margo said.

Rand slid the stethoscope beneath Buddy Morrison's T-shirt and listened to the strong, if somewhat rapid, heartbeat. He studied the man's pupils, which were fine. Some of the color was returning to his cheeks. Rand moved to check the pulse in his leg below the break.

"Chris, come hold this," Danny called over to the young blue-haired woman after he had hooked the man's IV line to a bag of saline. She held it, elevated, while he injected the morphine into the line. Rand watched her while trying to appear not to. Up close, she had fine lines at the corners of her eyes, which were a chocolatey brown, fringed with heavily mascaraed lashes. She had a round face, with a slight point to her chin and a Cupid's bow mouth with a slightly fuller lower lip. It was a strikingly beautiful face, with a mouth he would have liked to kiss.

He pushed the inappropriate thought away and focused on working with Danny to straighten the man's leg. Buddy groaned as the broken tip of the bone slid back under the skin, and the gray-haired woman let out a small cry as well. Margo took a step toward them. "What are you doing?" she asked. "You're hurting him!"

"He'll feel a lot better when the bones of the leg are in line and stabilized," Rand said, and began to fit the inflatable splint around the man's leg. Once air was added, the splint would form a tight, formfitting wrap that would make for a much more comfortable trip down the mountain on the litter.

The splint in place, Rand stood and stepped back. "You

can take it from here," he told Danny, and watched as half a dozen more volunteers swarmed in to assemble a wheeled litter, transferred Buddy onto it, and secured him, complete with a crash helmet, ice packs around his leg and warm blankets over the rest of his body.

While they worked, another female volunteer explained to Buddy's family what would happen next. In addition to the family and the search and rescue volunteers, a crowd of maybe a dozen people clogged the trail, so each new hiker who descended the route was forced to join the bottleneck and wait. The onlookers talked among themselves, and more than a few snapped photographs.

Danny moved to Rand's side. "It's a little different from assessing a patient at the hospital ER," Danny said.

"Different from the battlefield too," Rand said. There was no scent of mortar rounds and burning structures here, and no overpowering disinfectant scent of a hospital setting. Only sunshine and a warm breeze with the vanilla-tinged scent of ponderosa pine.

"Thanks for coming out," Danny said again.

"You could have handled it fine without me," Rand said. He had heard enough from people around town to know Eagle Mountain SAR was considered one of the top wilderness-response teams in the state.

"The family calmed down a lot when I assured them we had a 'real doctor' on the way to take care of their father," Danny said. He glanced over to where Margo and her mother were huddled with the balding man and the two boys, their anxious faces focused on the process of loading Buddy into the litter. "But I won't call you except in cases of emergency, if that's what you want."

"No. I want you to treat me like any other volunteer," Rand said.

"You mean, go through the training, attend the meetings, stuff like that?"

"Yes. That's exactly what I mean. I like being outdoors, and I need to get out of the office and the operating room. I'm in good physical shape, so I think I could be an asset to the team, beyond my medical knowledge."

"That's terrific," Danny said. "We'd be happy to have you. If you have time, come back to headquarters with us, and I'll introduce you around. Or come to the next regular meeting. Most of the volunteers will be there. I'll give you a training schedule and a bunch of paperwork to sign."

"Sounds good." Rand turned back to the crowd around the litter as it began to move forward. He searched among the dozen or so volunteers for the woman with the blue hair but didn't see her. Then he spotted her to one side. She stood in the shadow of a pine, staring up the trail.

He followed her gaze, trying to determine what had caught her attention. Then he spotted the man—midforties, a dirty yellow ball cap covering his hair and hiding his eyes. But he was definitely focused on the woman, his posture rigid.

Rand looked back toward the blue-haired woman, but she was gone. She wasn't by the tree. She wasn't with the volunteers or in the crowd of onlookers that was now making its way down the trail.

"Is something wrong?" Danny asked.

"The volunteer who was with Mr. Morrison when I arrived," he said. "With the blue hair."

"Chris. Chris Mercer."

"Has she been a volunteer long?"

"Off and on for four years. Her work has taken her away a couple of times—she's an artist. But she always comes back to the group." Danny looked around. "I don't see her now."

"She was just here," Rand said. "I was wondering where she went."

"There's no telling with Chris. She's a little unconventional but a good volunteer. She told me she was hiking about a mile down the trail when the call went out, so she was first on the scene," Danny said. "She's supposed to stick around for report back at the station. Maybe she's already headed back there."

"Looks like she left something behind," Rand said. He made his way to the spot where she had been standing and picked up a blue day pack, the nylon outer shell faded and scuffed. He unzipped the outer pocket and took out a business card. "'Chris Mercer, Aspen Leaf Gallery,'" he read.

"That's Chris's," Danny said. He held out his hand. "I'll put it in the lost and found bin at headquarters."

"That's okay. I'll take it to her." Rand slipped one strap of the pack over his shoulder.

"Suit yourself," Danny said. He and Rand fell into step behind the group wheeling the litter. Morrison's family was hiking ahead, though the daughter, Margo, kept looking back to check on their progress. Every twenty minutes or so, the volunteers switched positions, supporting the litter and guiding it down the trail or walking alongside it with the IV bag suspended. They continually checked on Mr. Morrison, asking him how he was doing, assessing his condition, staying alert for any change that might indicate something they had missed. Something going wrong.

Rand felt the tension in his own body, even as he reminded himself that this was a simple accident—a fall that had resulted in a fracture, free of the kinds of complications that had plagued his patients on the battlefield, and the motor vehicle collision and gunshot victims he often met in the emergency room where he now worked.

Heavy footfalls on the trail behind them made Rand turn, in time to see the man in the dirty yellow ball cap barreling toward them. The man brushed against Rand as he hurried by, head down, boots raising small puffs of dirt with each forceful step. "Hey!" Rand called out, prepared to tell the man to be more careful. But the guy broke into a run and soon disappeared down the trail.

"Guess he had somewhere he needed to be," Danny said.

"Guess so," Rand said, but the hair on the back of his neck rose as he remembered the expression on Chris's face as she had stared at the man.

She hadn't merely been curious or even afraid of the man. She had been terrified.

Chapter Two

Chris prowled the bedroom of her apartment above the art gallery, throwing random items into the suitcase on her bed, her mother's voice on the phone trying, but failing, to soothe her jangled nerves. "I'm sure the man was only looking at you because you're so striking," April Mercer said.

Chris stepped over her dog, Harley, who raised his head and looked at her with brown eyes full of concern. The Rhodesian ridgeback mix had picked up on her mood as soon as she entered the apartment, and he refused to be more than a few inches away from her. "I don't think so," Chris told her mother. "He looked familiar. Do you remember that guy who used to stand at the back of the room, glaring at everyone during Sunday-night meetings? Jedediah?" Chris grabbed a handful of socks and stuffed them into the side of the suitcase. A shudder went through her as she remembered the man on the trail.

"Oh, honey, I'm sure it wasn't him," April said. "It's been so long. I'm sure all of those people have forgotten about you by now."

"Do you really believe that, Mom?"

Her mother's silence was all the answer she needed. Jedediah and the others hadn't forgotten about Chris. That hadn't been her name back them, but that wouldn't matter to them.

"Would you really remember what he looked like after all these years?" April asked finally.

It wasn't the man's features that had been so familiar to her, but the look in his eyes. So full of hate. "He sure acted as if he recognized me."

"How could he?" April asked. "You changed your hair and had that nose job. And you were twelve years old. You were a child when he saw you last."

"I know." She swallowed down the rising panic and forced herself to stop and breathe deeply. "I just... The way he looked at me."

Harley stood and leaned against her. She bent and rubbed behind the dog's ears, finding solace in his solid presence.

"He's just a creep," April said. "There are plenty of them out there. If you really think he's a threat, tell the sheriff. Didn't you tell me he's a decent guy?"

"Yes. I mean, I've only interacted with Sheriff Walker on search and rescue missions, but he has a good reputation." Still, how would he react if she told him someone she had last seen when she was twelve had been glaring at her? And did she really want to reveal that whole sordid story to anyone here?

"You know you're always welcome to stay with me for a while if it makes you feel better," April said.

"I know." But Chris had already hidden out at her mom's place three times in the past two years. And at least one of those times had been a false alarm. She had heard the talk from other search and rescue members about how often she was out of town. Everyone seemed understanding, but that was probably because they thought her work as an artist was taking her away for weeks or months at a time. "I'm tired of running away," she said.

"Oh, honey."

The tenderness in April's voice might have broken a weaker woman. But Chris had had years to develop a hard shell around her emotions. "I was just wondering if you had heard anything about Jedediah. If you knew if he had a reason to be in this area."

"No," April said. "I try to keep tabs on people, but I have to rely on the few friendly contacts I still have, and they're understandably reluctant to reveal too much. But Colorado and Jedediah have never come up in our conversations."

Chris nodded, even though she knew her mother couldn't see her. "Okay, that's good. I guess."

"I'm sorry this happened to upset you," her mother said. "But I don't think it has anything to do with what happened all those years ago."

"You're right." Chris let go of the dog and turned to stare at the suitcase, into which she had apparently packed a dozen T-shirts and eight pairs of socks but no underwear or pants. "I'll just...keep my eyes open, and if I see anyone suspicious or threatening, I'll tell the sheriff."

"That sounds like a good plan," April said. "But know you can come stay with me anytime."

A knock on the door set her heart racing. Was it Jedediah? Had he managed to find her? "I have to go now, Mom."

"I love you," April said.

Harley was already moving toward the door. He hadn't barked or even growled, but the ridge of hair along his spine stood at attention.

"I love you too," Chris whispered. She slid the phone into her pocket and tiptoed toward the door, careful not to make a sound. Holding her breath, she peered through the peephole with Harley pressed against her side, his body taut.

Chris exhaled in a rush as she recognized the man on the other side. She unfastened the security chain and dead bolt and eased the door open a scant two inches. "Hello?"

"Chris Mercer?" The doctor who was now working with search and rescue asked. She couldn't remember his name, but she wasn't likely to forget his face anytime soon. Blue eyes, curly dark hair, cleft chin—he had definitely made her look twice when she had first seen him.

"What do you want?" she asked.

He held up her day pack. "You left this behind on the trail. I thought you'd want it back."

"How did you find me?" She didn't like the idea that a stranger—no matter how good looking or well intentioned—could walk right up to her front door.

"There's a card for the gallery downstairs in the outside pocket of the pack," he said. "I asked and the woman at the register told me you were upstairs."

Chris frowned. She would have to have a talk with Jasmine. "Thanks." She opened the door wider and reached for the pack. Thoughtless of her to have left it, but that showed how shaken up she had been.

Harley shoved forward and stuck his head out the door. He glared at the doctor, a low rumble vibrating the air.

The doctor took a step back. "Hello, there," he addressed the dog.

"That's Harley. He won't hurt you." Not unless she told him to. The dog was trained to protect, though most of the time he was a genuine sweetheart. "Just hand me the pack."

The doctor—why couldn't she remember his name?— held it out of reach. "Are you okay?" he asked.

"I'm fine. Can I have my pack, please?"

He handed it over. "You left the trail in a hurry," he said. "We didn't get a chance to meet. I'm Rand Martin."

"Thanks for returning my pack, Rand." She tried to close the door, but he caught the frame and held it.

Harley's growl intensified, his body rigid. Rand glanced down at him but held his ground. "First, I want to make sure you're okay," he said. "You looked really upset back there on the trail. You still look upset."

"I'm fine."

"Who was the man watching you?"

Her breath caught. "You saw him too?"

"Yes."

"Do you know him?" she asked.

"Why don't I come in, and we'll talk about it?"

Just then, Jasmine, a petite woman with short red hair and white-rimmed glasses, appeared at the top of the stairs at the end of the hall. "Is everything okay, Chris?" she asked. Her gaze shifted to Rand, then back to Chris, eyes bright with curiosity.

"Everything is fine." Chris signaled for Harley to stand down and opened the door a little wider. "Come on in," she said to Rand. At least if he turned out to be a threat, Jasmine would be able to identify him. Not that there was anything particularly threatening about the doctor. He was older than Chris—early forties, maybe—but he was fit and strong. He exuded calm, and he struck her as someone who would be good to have on her side should Jedediah, or whoever that man had been, decide to show up.

He moved into her apartment, and she shut the door behind him. Harley stayed between them, silent but wary. Rand stopped in front of a painting beside the front door, an eight-by-ten canvas depicting a young girl crouched beside a pool in a mountain stream. A face was reflected in the water—a much older woman meant to represent the girl in her later years. "One of yours?" Rand asked.

"Yes." She dropped the pack onto the floor beside the sofa. "Do you know the man who was watching me there on the trail?"

He shook his head. "No. But you looked like you recognized him."

"I thought I did, but I was wrong."

"Then why were you afraid?"

"I wasn't afraid." The lie came easily. She was practiced at hiding that part of herself.

"You were terrified." He spoke with such certainty, as if he knew her and her innermost thoughts. But he wasn't saying the words to use her emotions against her as a weapon. If anything, his expression telegraphed understanding. As if he, too, had felt terror before and knew its paralyzing power.

She turned away from him. "I'm a single woman," she said. "I don't appreciate when a man I don't know takes such an intense interest in me." Would Rand take the hint that he, himself, should leave her alone?

"For what it's worth, I looked for him on the way down the trail, but I didn't see him again." He looked around her place. "I take it he didn't follow you here?"

She shook her head. She had made sure she was alone before she risked coming here. "Thanks for returning my pack," she said. "I really have things to do now." Unpack her suitcase, for one. Maybe do a little research online and try to find out what happened to Jedediah. Could she dredge up his last name from memory? Had she ever known it?

"Would you have dinner with me?"

The question startled her so much her mouth dropped open. She stared. Rand stared back, his lips tipped up at one corner, blue eyes full of amusement. Was he laughing at her? "What did you say?" she asked.

"Would you have dinner with me?"

"No." Absolutely not.

"Why not?"

"I don't date."

"Why not?"

"I just… I'm not interested in a relationship."

"Neither am I," he said.

"Why not?" She hadn't meant to say the words out loud, but seriously, the man was gorgeous. A doctor. He appeared to have a decent personality.

"I'm a trauma surgeon. I have a terrible schedule. I can't even get a dog, my hours are so unpredictable. Any woman in my life invariably ends up feeling neglected and resenting me."

"Then why ask me out? I don't do one-night stands either."

That little barb didn't faze him. "Everyone can use a friend," he said gently.

She hugged her arms across her chest. "You don't want to be friends with me."

"Why not?"

"I come with a lot of baggage."

He laughed. A loud, hearty guffaw. The sound elicited a sharp rebuke from Harley.

"It's okay," Rand said to the dog. He crouched and offered his hand for the dog to sniff. Harley approached cautiously, then allowed Rand to pet his sleek side.

Chris glared at him. "What's so funny?"

"Show me a person over twenty who doesn't have baggage, and I'll show you someone not worth knowing," he said. "Come on. Have a burger and a beer with me."

The offer tempted her, if only for the chance to have an evening outside her own head. She took a step back. "No. I think you need to leave now."

She expected him to argue, to turn charming or pleading. Instead, he only stood and took a card from his wallet and offered it to her.

She stared at it but didn't take it. He laid it on the table beside the sofa. "That's my number, if you need anything." He shrugged. "In case that guy shows up, for instance."

"What are you going to do if he does?"

"I could probably persuade him to leave you alone."

From anyone else, the words might have come across as a brag. From Rand, they rang true. He wasn't an overly big man, but he had a wiry strength, and the attitude of someone who wouldn't back down from a fight. "Thanks," she said. "But I'll be fine."

He nodded and left, letting himself out and shutting the door softly behind him. She locked up, then leaned against the paneled surface of the door. If Rand could find her so easily, Jedediah could too. The thought ought to have renewed the terror she'd felt earlier, but instead, the idea annoyed her. She had told her mother the truth when she said she was tired of running away. Jedediah had been powerful and threatening when she had known him before, capable of hurting her. But she wasn't a child anymore. And she knew the truth behind the lies he and others had told. She didn't have to keep running. She could stay and resist.

This time, she might even win.

Chapter Three

The parking lot at Eagle Mountain Search and Rescue head-quarters was full by the time Rand pulled in Thursday evening. He had just had time to grab a quick shower and a sandwich before leaving for this first training meeting. His adrenaline was still revved when he stepped into the cavernous garage-like space and studied the group arranged in an assortment of chairs and old furniture angled toward the front of the room.

He spotted a few faces familiar to him from the previous Saturday's rescue, but found himself searching for Chris. He spotted her in a far corner, at one end of a sofa, her dog, Harley, at her feet. He took the empty seat beside her. "Hello," he said.

She eyed him coolly. "Hey."

Harley approached and Rand petted the dog. He wanted the animal to trust him, even if his mistress didn't. "How are you?" he asked.

"Fine."

She wasn't exactly unfriendly, just…guarded. Which only made him want to break through her reserve more. "I saw some of your paintings at a restaurant in town," he said. "I really like your work."

"They're all for sale."

"I might buy one. I've always enjoyed landscapes, and yours are beautiful—but they're also complex." He glanced at her arm and the artwork there. She wore a sleeveless blouse, revealing a tapestry of colorful flowers and birds from shoulder to wrist on the arm closest to him. Columbines, bluebells, foxglove, a bluebird, and a gold finch. The scene reminded him of one of her paintings. And yes, there, just above her elbow, half-hidden between a dragonfly and a sunflower, a woman peered out with large dark eyes, hiding and watchful. "Mysterious."

"Hmmm. Not that I don't like it when people say nice things about my work, but it's not going to convince me to go out with you."

"Can't blame a man for trying." He smiled.

She looked away.

"Let's get started, everybody." Danny spoke from the front of the room, and the chatter died down. "I'll start by introducing our newest team member. Some of you already know Dr. Rand Martin, who assisted with our rescue of the injured hiker on Saturday. In addition to serving as our medical adviser, Rand has decided to join as a full-fledged volunteer."

Scattered applause from the gathered volunteers. Rand nodded. Danny continued, "Just so you know, Rand's a rookie, but he has a lot of experience. He served with a mobile surgical unit in Afghanistan and is the new director of emergency services at St. Joseph's Hospital in Junction."

More applause, and a few shouts of "Welcome!"

"You can introduce yourselves at the break," Danny said. "Now, let's get down to business." He consulted the clipboard in his hand and read off a list of upcoming training opportunities, certification deadlines and local news. "The sheriff asked me to remind everyone that the annual Back-country Base Camp rally is August 1 through 4. There's also a scout group from Denver planning a wilderness-skills camp up on Dakota Ridge starting August 5. Both of those groups could mean more calls for us."

"A bunch of kids playing with fire and knives?" a big man near the back of the room said. "What could go wrong?"

Danny smiled and waited for the chuckles to die down. "I'm going to turn it over to Tony now for our training unit on wilderness searches. For some of you this will be a re-view, but pay attention, because we have some new pro-tocols based on the latest research. And for you newbies, know that you could be called to put this into practice any day now. We have a lot of wilderness we're responsible for, and it's easy for people to get lost out there."

Rand pulled out a notebook and pen and settled in as a tall, thin man, his blond hair and goatee threaded with silver, moved to the front of the room. Chris passed Rand a sheaf of handouts. "Pretty much everything is on these," she said.

"Thanks."

He pretended to study the first sheet of the handout, but he was really focused on her. She was more relaxed than she had been Saturday, but she still had the hyperawareness he recognized from his time in Afghanistan. In a war zone, chaos could break out at any second, even in the middle of dinner or when you were trying to sleep after a hard battle. Soldiers lived on high alert, and being in constant fight-or-flight mode took its toll physically and psychologically.

But Chris wasn't in a war zone. So why so tense?

The room darkened and Tony began his presentation. Rand forced himself to concentrate on the lesson. Appar-ently, people who became lost tended to behave in estab-lished patterns depending on their age, gender and history.

"Knowing these patterns doesn't guarantee we'll locate them," Tony said. "But it helps us establish a search plan and can increase the odds of finding them."

Rand underlined phrases on the handout and wrote notes in the margin. And here he had thought his training would consist of learning to tie knots and reviewing how to administer first aid. He was so absorbed in the material he had to shake himself out of a kind of trance when the lights went up again. He checked his watch and was surprised to find over an hour had passed.

"We'll break for ten minutes, then finish up this unit," Tony said.

Chairs slid back and the hum of conversation rose. Rand turned to address Chris, but she was already out of her chair and moving across the room. Danny waylaid her, and the two fell into earnest conversation. Curious, Rand worked his way toward them but was stopped by other volunteers who wanted to introduce themselves. He made small talk, all the while working his way over to Chris and Danny, who stood in the hallway outside the restrooms.

Rand positioned himself in front of a bulletin board around the corner from them and listened. "I'm sorry," Chris said. "I know I shouldn't have disappeared like that, but it was an emergency. I got a call from my mom. She's okay now, but I thought at first I was going to have to rush to her."

"I'm sorry to hear that," Danny said. "I've been in that position myself. But next time, let someone know. Send a text or something."

"I will. I promise."

"Are you sure that's all that's going on?" Danny asked.

"Of course." Rand thought he recognized a forced cheerfulness in her voice. He moved over to get a better look, and Chris collided with him as she came around the corner.

"Sorry," he said, steadying her with one hand but immediately releasing her. She was skittish as a wild colt, and he didn't want to upset her.

She stared up at him, eyes wide, then moved away. Rand watched her cross the room, half believing she would leave altogether. Instead, she stopped by a table of refreshments and began filling a plate.

She didn't return to her seat until Tony had resumed the lesson. She slid onto the sofa beside him just as the lights went down, as if she had timed her arrival to avoid further conversation.

When the evening ended, Rand started after her but was halted by a trio of men, including the big guy who had made the remark about the scouts. They introduced themselves as Eldon Ramsey, Ryan Welch and Caleb Garrison. "Have you done any climbing?" the big guy, Eldon, asked.

"Only a little," Rand asked.

"It's a skill that comes in handy on a lot of the rescues we're called out on," Ryan said. "You'll have training opportunities, but any time you want to get in some practice on your own, give us a shout."

"We're climbing in Caspar Canyon most weekends during the season," Caleb said. "Come on out and join us anytime."

"Thanks," Rand said. "I'll do that."

The instructor for the evening, Tony Meisner, introduced himself next, along with Sheri Stevens, Jake and Hannah Gwynn, Grace Wilcox, and several others whose names Rand couldn't remember. Everyone was friendly and offered to help him in any way they could. By the time the building emptied out, Rand had accepted that he wasn't going to talk to Chris tonight. She would have left long ago.

Except, apparently, she hadn't. He spotted her and Harley walking across the parking lot and headed after her while trying to appear as if he wasn't in a hurry. She glanced over her shoulder at his approach but said nothing. The stiffness in her shoulders told him she was a few breaths from telling him to get lost. No sense wasting the opportunity with small talk. "Have you seen any more of the man who was watching you Saturday?" he asked.

She slowed her steps. "No. I must have been mistaken. He was looking at something else."

She didn't believe that, he thought.

"Mind if I walk you to your car?" he asked.

She shrugged. "Suit yourself."

Seconds later, they arrived at a dusty blue Subaru. She stopped and turned to him. Before she could say anything, he took a step back. "I'm not trying to be a creep or harass you," he said. "If you don't want to go out with me, that's your call. But I saw that guy on the trail Saturday and how you reacted to his attention. If you need help or you just want to talk to someone, I'm here. That's all I want you to know."

Some of the stiffness went out of her posture, and she looked at him with less suspicion. "Thanks," she said. "But it's not really anything you need to worry about." She clicked her key fob. The car beeped and flashed its lights, and she opened the rear driver's-side door. "In you go, Harley."

The dog started to jump into the car, then stopped and backed out, something in his mouth. "What has he got?" Rand leaned in for a closer look.

Chris took the object from the dog, and all the color left her face. She collapsed against the side of the car, eyes wide.

Rand took the item from her. It was a bird—a hummingbird, made of folded emerald green paper. "Is this origami?" he asked.

She nodded, the look on her face frantic now.

Still holding the paper bird, he reached for her. "Chris," he said.

But she turned away, clutching her stomach, and vomited on the gravel beside the car.

He pulled her close, half-afraid she would collapse. She leaned heavily against him, shudders running through her. "Tell me why you're so upset," he said.

"I can't."

Seventeen Years Ago

TEN-YEAR-OLD CHRIS was seated at a folding table in a cold, drafty room, a stack of colored paper in front of her—pink, blue, red, orange, purple, green. Pretty colors, but looking at them didn't make Chris happy. No one called her Chris then. They knew her as Elita. She willed away tears as she painstakingly folded and smoothed the paper to make a hummingbird like the model in front of her. "You need five thousand of them," the woman across from her—Helen— said. "You will make some every day. And when you are done, it will be time."

Tears slipped past her tight-closed lids and made a hot path down her cheeks. She tried to wipe them away, hoping Helen hadn't seen. "What if I can't make five thousand of them?" she asked. It seemed an impossibly large number.

"You will. You have a couple of years. It will take that long until you're ready for the duties ahead of you."

Chris shuddered. She didn't want to think about those "duties." Not that she had a terribly clear idea what those might include, but she had heard whispers...

She made a wrong fold, and the paper creased, the hummingbird crumpling in her hand. Helen took the mangled paper from her. "Start with a fresh sheet. Pay attention, and take your time."

"Maybe I can't do it because I'm not the right person," Chris said. "Maybe I'm not worthy."

Helen smiled. "You are the right person. You have been chosen."

Choose someone else! Chris wanted to shout. But she only bit her lip as another tear betrayed her.

Helen frowned. "You should be happy you have been singled out for such an honor. You shouldn't be so ungrateful."

"I'm… I'm not," she lied, and bit the inside of her cheek. Anything to stem the tears. She couldn't let Helen see what her true feelings were. Even at her young age, she knew that was dangerous.

"Chris." Rand snapped his fingers in front of her face. "What's going on? Why are you so afraid?"

"I have to go." She pushed him aside and slid into the car. Harley bolted in after her, climbing over Chris and settling in the passenger seat. Rand was talking to her, but she couldn't hear him over the buzzing panic in her head. She drove away, gripping the steering wheel so tightly her fingers ached. She checked her mirrors every few seconds, but no one appeared to be following her.

When she was in her parking space in the alley behind the gallery, she made sure the doors of her car were locked, then laid her head on the steering wheel and closed her eyes, her whole body trembling. She never had made the five thousand hummingbirds. She had believed getting away had ended her ordeal.

But someone had pushed that bird through the gap in her car window. When she had parked at search and rescue headquarters, she thought the lot was safe enough for her to leave the rear windows down just a few inches to keep the interior cool. Jedediah, or someone else, had taken advantage of that, letting her know she could never truly escape. They were telling her it was time to fulfill what they thought was her destiny. The one thing she was determined never to do.

Chapter Four

Early Saturday morning, Rand drove home from Junction. He had been called in after midnight to tend to a young man who had suffered multiple injuries as a result of wrapping his car around a tree along a curvy road—fractured sternum, broken ribs and collarbone, a fractured arm, and multiple bruises and cuts. Rand had spent hours wiring the man's bones back together. Weariness set in when he was halfway home, so he did what he always did to try to stay awake: he opened a window to let in fresh air and thought about something other than himself and his fatigue.

He had stayed away from Chris since Thursday night, even though the desire to know what was going on with her gnawed at him, a low-level ache. If she wanted his help, she would ask. To keep pressing himself on her could be seen as harassment. He wanted to be her friend, not someone else she was afraid of.

He thought of the origami hummingbird. Not exactly a threatening item, yet Chris had been physically ill at the sight of it. He had a bad feeling about that moment, but maybe he was putting too much of himself and his own history into it. Maybe the hummingbird had been a kind of sick joke that only had meaning to her, not a real threat.

But could anyone be so upset by a joke that they would throw up?

His phone vibrated, and seconds later the video screen on his dash showed he had an incoming text. He pressed the button to hear the message, and the car's mechanical female voice recited, "Wildfire on national forest land south end of County Road 3. All search and rescue volunteers needed to evacuate campers in the area."

Rand increased his speed and headed toward search and rescue headquarters. He parked and joined the crowd of volunteers just inside. He spotted Chris right away, her blue hair standing out in the sea of blondes and brunettes. "Hello," she said when he approached. No animosity. No particular warmth either.

"What should I do to help?" he asked.

She shoved a lidded plastic bin into his hands. "Put these first aid supplies in the Beast." She indicated a boxy orange Jeep with oversize tires and a red cross on the back door. "And do whatever Danny or whoever he appoints as incident commander tells you."

He joined a line of volunteers passing gear to the vehicles, then followed Ryan and Caleb to a Toyota truck. He, Caleb and Carrie Andrews squeezed into the back seat. Ryan drove, and Eldon took the passenger seat. They followed the Beast to the highway, then turned onto a county road that grew progressively narrower and bumpier as they climbed in elevation.

"Check out the smoke," Eldon said, and pointed at the windshield to a black plume rising in the distance.

"People who don't live here don't understand how dangerous these dry conditions are," Ryan said. "One spark from a campfire or a discarded cigarette can set a blaze that destroys hundreds of thousands of acres."

Ahead of them, the orange Jeep slowed, then pulled over to the side and stopped. Ryan pulled his truck in behind it and rolled down the window. The headlights of a vehicle moved toward them. Tony stepped out from the driver's side of the Jeep and flagged down the vehicle. Rand leaned his head out the open back window to hear the conversation. A second car idled behind the first. The driver of the first—a man perhaps in his fifties, his brown hair heavily streaked with white—spoke clearly enough for Rand to hear.

"Are you with the campers who are back here?" Danny asked.

"I don't know about that," the man said.

"Were you camped in the national forest?" Danny tried again.

"Yes. We saw the smoke getting heavier and decided to leave."

"How many are with you?" Danny glanced toward the other vehicle.

"There are six of us here."

"Only six?" Danny asked.

"More'll be along soon," the man said. "They're packing up camp."

"How many people?" Danny's tone signaled that he was quickly losing patience with the man's casual attitude.

"Maybe a dozen."

"Men? Women? Children?"

"What business is that of yours?" the driver asked.

"Whoever is back there needs to get out now," Danny said. "They don't have time to pack. The winds are pushing the fire this way. We're here to help with the evacuation."

"They're just a few miles back," the man said. "You won't have any trouble finding them." He shifted the car into gear and lurched forward, the other vehicle close on his bumper.

As they passed, Rand got a glimpse through tinted glass of two adults in the first vehicle and four in the second. All men, he thought.

Tony climbed back into the Beast, and the caravan of volunteers set out again, driving a little faster now, their sense of urgency heightened by the thickening smoke. "Do we know anything about these campers?" Rand asked after a moment. "Who they are or where they're from?"

"Danny said he got a call from the sheriff that one of the spotters in a plane flying over the fire saw a group of tents in a clearing and called it in," Caleb said. "Cell phone coverage is spotty to nonexistent back in here, so they might not have realized the fire had even started."

"No missing all this smoke," Eldon said. "Anyone with any sense would know to get out of Dodge by now."

The Jeep stopped again, this time in the middle of the road. Ryan halted the truck, too, and everyone piled out. Smoke stung Rand's eyes, and the scent of burning wood hung heavy in the air. "There's active flames ahead," Tony said. "We can't go any further or we risk getting trapped. We need to turn around."

"What about the other campers?" Carrie asked. "The driver of the car said there were others."

Danny glanced over his shoulder. Smoke obscured the road ahead, though occasional orange flares illuminated burning trees. "We don't know who or how many are in there," he said. "We can't put our own lives at risk. That doesn't help anyone."

Rand wanted to volunteer to go ahead on foot to scout the situation. But then what? He could end up injured or trapped, and the other volunteers might feel obligated to go in after him. But he hated this feeling of helplessness and defeat.

"Hello? Help! Oh, please help!"

They turned toward the sound as a woman stumbled down the road toward them. She was almost bent double beneath what Rand thought at first was a large pack but turned out to be a child wrapped in a sleeping bag, clinging to her back. As they rushed toward her, other figures emerged from the smoke—more women, half a dozen children and a single man, all carrying supplies and bundles of clothing, bedding, and who knew what else.

The lone man brought up the rear of the group. He had a blanket roll on his back and a large wooden box in his arms. "The truck broke down, and we had to walk," he said, his words cut short by a fit of coughing.

Rand stared at the collection of women and children—some with soot on their faces, holes from sparks burned in their clothing—and thought of the men in the two cars. They had left women and children to *walk* out of a fire?

He flinched at a crack like a gunshot, then realized it was a tree not thirty yards away, bursting into flame. "We have to get out of here," Danny said. He took the nearest woman's arm. "Into the vehicles. Drop whatever you're carrying and get in. You'll have to sit on laps, on the floorboards—wherever you can fit."

Another woman spoke up. "That isn't necessary." She seemed a little taller than the others, but maybe it was only that she stood straighter and looked them in the eye when she spoke. "We will carry our possessions and walk out."

"You can't walk fast enough to stay ahead of the fire," Danny said.

"We have divine protection."

The words snapped Rand's patience. "Get in the trucks now!" he shouted. He picked up the closest child and shoved them into the back seat of the truck.

Caleb and Ryan reached for other children. Eldon picked up a woman and deposited her in the front passenger seat. Others began relieving the stranded campers of their burdens and leading them to the vehicles. They seemed to come out of their trance then. The man and several of the women and older children crowded into the back of the truck.

"What about our things?" one of the women wailed.

"We don't have room for them," Tony said.

She began to cry. Others were already weeping, children screaming.

"Is there anyone else?" Danny asked. He had to raise his voice above the din . "Any stragglers we should wait for?"

"No." The man shook his head. "No one."

Rand hoped the man was telling the truth. The flames were near enough he could feel the heat now, smoke so heavy he could no longer make out the road, the roar of the fire so loud they had to shout to be heard. A hot wind swirled around them, sparks stinging bare skin and smoldering on clothing. They didn't have time to search for anyone who might have been left behind.

Somehow, they managed to turn the vehicles and head back down the road, forced by poor visibility to creep along yet driving as fast as they dared in order to escape the flames. Everyone was coughing now, everyone's eyes streaming tears.

They slowed to steer around a burning tree that had fallen on the side of the road, and the weight in the back of the truck shifted. The wailing rose in pitch, and Rand looked back to see that the man had jumped from the truck and was running down the road, back in the direction they had come. He had his hand on the door, about to open it, when Caleb gripped his arm. "Let him go. We have to save the rest."

Rand forced his body to relax and nodded. Even if he

had wanted, he couldn't have exited the vehicle. He was held down by a child on each thigh, a boy and a girl, who were about nine or ten. They sat stiffly and wouldn't meet his gaze, hands clenched in front of them, eyes downcast. Obviously, they were terrified. Traumatized. Maybe that explained why they weren't acting like any children he had ever met.

After what felt like the longest ride of his life but was probably only half an hour, they arrived at the staging area on the picnic grounds at the turnoff for the county road. Paramedics, the sheriff and his deputies, and other volunteers surrounded the Beast and the truck, someone taking charge of each of the campers as they emerged. "We found them trying to walk out of the fire," Danny explained to the sheriff.

Sheriff Travis Walker was a tall man in his midthirties, with dark hair and eyes, a sharply pressed khaki uniform, and a grim expression on his face. "Any idea what a bunch of women and children were doing camping back in there with no transportation?" he asked.

"There was a man with them," Ryan said. "He bailed out of the truck and ran back in the direction of the camp not long after we set out."

"There were six other men, in two vehicles," Tony said. "We passed them on the way out. They told us they had left the others—" he nodded at the women and children "—to pack up the camp and follow."

The sheriff's frown deepened. "We'll question them later, find out what's going on."

"I think they might belong to some kind of cult," Rand said.

Everyone turned to stare at him. "What makes you say that?" Travis asked.

"One of the women told us they weren't worried about the fire because they were under 'divine protection.' That, and the fact that a group of able-bodied men, probably the leaders, left a bunch of women and children to fend for themselves, and the women aren't questioning—at least not out loud—their right to do so. Blind obedience that goes against all common sense is one hallmark of a cult."

Thankfully, the sheriff didn't ask how Rand knew this. "We'll question them and find out as much as we can," he said.

"How do you know that? About cults?"

Rand tensed at the familiar voice and turned to look at Chris.

"My sister was in a cult," he said. "I learned a lot about them when we were trying to persuade her to leave."

"Did she leave?" Chris stared at him, lips parted, leaning toward him as if something important depended on his answer.

He shook his head. "No. She never did."

Her expression softened, and she put her hand on his arm. A familiar tightness rose in his throat, but he forced himself not to turn away. He didn't see pity in Chris's eyes, but some other emotion, one he couldn't quite read.

And then she whirled away from him, propelled by a hand on her shoulder. The driver of the car they had met in the burning forest stood with two other men, all crowded around Chris.

Rand moved in behind her, but the men ignored him. All three were middle-aged, from the fortysomething blond Rand had seen on the trail a week ago to the slightly older driver of the car, to a shorter, red-faced man with a round, boyish face but iron gray hair who stood between them. "Hello, Elita," the driver said.

"My name isn't Elita," Chris said. But her voice trembled.

"Your time has come," the blond said.

"I don't know what you're talking about." She tried to turn away, but the blond grabbed her.

Rand took the man's wrist and squeezed, hard, his thumb digging in between the fine bones in a way that was guaranteed to hurt. The man released her but turned on Rand. "This is no business of yours," he said.

"Don't touch her again," Rand said. He kept his voice low, but anyone would know he meant business. He was dimly aware that a crowd had gathered, among them the sheriff and one of his deputies.

The blond turned back to Chris. "You can't deny your destiny," he said. He glanced at those around them and raised his voice so that it carried to everyone. "We will start the wedding preparations today."

Chapter Five

Sheriff Walker stepped forward. "What is your name?" he asked the driver.

The blond spoke first. "This doesn't concern you, Sheriff," he said.

Travis's expression didn't change. "The three of you need to come to the sheriff's department and provide statements about the fire and how it started."

"We don't know how it started," the round-faced man said. "That has nothing to do with us."

"I also want to know why the three of you left a group of women and children to make their way out of the area on foot," Travis said.

The blond man moved closer. He was taller than the others, not large, but imposing. "We left a man in charge of the women and children," he said. "Joshua was bringing them in the truck." He looked around. "Where is Joshua?"

"The man who was with the women and children ran back into the woods," Rand said.

The blond shifted his attention to Rand. "Who are you?" It wasn't a question as much as a demand.

"I'm one of the volunteers who helped save those women and children you abandoned," Rand said.

The man glared at him but addressed the sheriff. "You need to talk to Joshua. I can't help you." He turned away, and the others started to follow him.

"Before you leave, I need your names and contact information," the sheriff said.

The blond man nodded to the round-faced man. He pulled a small case from his pocket and handed the sheriff a business card. "That's the name of our attorney," he said. "You can contact him."

The three walked away. Travis pocketed the card and glanced over as his brother, Sergeant Gage Walker, joined the group. "The car is registered to something called the Vine, LLC," he said.

Travis turned to Chris. She had remained silent since the men had approached, pale and still. "What do you know about this?" he asked.

She swallowed hard. "The blond man is named Jedediah," she said. "I don't know his last name. He works for a man named Edmund Harrison, though most people know him as the Exalted. He leads the Vine. I don't know the other two, but they're probably part of the Exalted's inner circle—the ones charged with keeping order within the group."

"What is the Vine?" Gage asked. "Some kind of vine-yard or something?"

Chris shook her head. "The Vine is, well, I guess you'd say it's a cult. A kind of religion, but not exactly. Edmund Harrison is the leader, the Exalted."

"What's your connection to the group?" Travis asked.

She stared at the ground. "My mother and father were members—a long time ago. My father died, and after that..." She paused. Rand could sense her struggling to control her emotions. Her shoulders drew inward, and she clenched her hands tightly. But after a long moment, she lifted her head. "My mother broke with the group when I was twelve. I haven't seen or heard from them since."

She was lying. Rand was sure of it. She had seen Jedediah on the trail last Saturday and had recognized him. And he had recognized her.

"What was all that about a wedding?" Ryan asked. "And why did he call you by that other name—Lisa or something?"

"Elita." She blew out a breath. "It's a long story."

"I'd like you to come to my office and tell me about it," Travis said. "If it turns out they were responsible for that fire, or the death of anyone in it, I need to know as much about them as possible."

"I'll come with you," Rand said.

Chris turned to him, and he braced himself for her to tell him to back off, that this was none of his business. "You don't have to do this alone," he said softly. Whatever was behind this, the encounter had clearly shaken her. He wanted to be there to lend her strength. To take away a little of her fear.

She nodded. "All right."

"We can go now," Travis said. "I want to get your statement before Jedidiah and the others have a chance to get too far away."

"They won't go far," Chris said. "Not until they have me. I'm the reason they're here."

Eighteen years ago

"WE'VE COME TODAY to reveal that Elita has been selected for an amazing honor."

Elita had been trying to teach herself to knit by following the illustrations in a library book when the two women and one man had knocked on the door of the travel trailer where she and her mother and father lived, on the edge of an apple grove owned by the Vine. The trailer was old—hot in the summer and cold in the winter, and when it rained, the roof over Elita's bunk bed leaked—but they had lived here since Elita was five years old, and she was nine now.

She hadn't been called *Elita* when they'd first moved here. She had been Christine Elizabeth back then. But one day, not long after they had arrived, her father had announced they were all taking new names. Her new name was Elita. "It means 'the chosen one,'" he told her. "The Exalted himself named you. It's a very special honor."

She thought it was strange to suddenly have a new name, but she knew better than to argue, and over time, she got used to being Elita instead of Christine.

The woman who spoke, Helen, was older than Elita's mom. She had long brown hair almost to her waist, the strands glinting with silver, and pale blue eyes. She oversaw the Sunday school Elita attended, and whenever she smiled at Elita, the little girl felt warm and happy.

The other woman, Sarai, was older and sour-faced. She taught the younger children and carried a switch when she walked between the rows of students, and didn't hesitate to pop them on the back of the hand if they gave a wrong answer to her questions. Elita didn't like her, and she avoided looking at her now.

But the man—Jedediah—was the one who really frightened her. The way he watched everyone, especially the girls, made her feel sick to her stomach. He was supposed to be one of the holiest among them, serving as the Exalted's right hand. But to her, he seemed evil.

Elita's mother—whom everyone called Lana now, though she had been born Amy—came and stood behind Elita, resting both hands on her shoulders. "This is a surprise," she said. "Why would Elita be singled out for an honor?"

"She has found favor with the Exalted," Helen said. She smiled at Elita, but this time the little girl didn't feel warm or happy. She felt cold and scared. Like Jedediah, the Exalted frightened her. Not because he was mean or creepy, but because everyone acted afraid of him, and there were a lot of rules about how to behave around him. Not just anyone could speak to the Exalted. And her mother had told her once that the best way to behave around the Exalted was to pretend to be invisible. Elita hadn't understood what she meant. People couldn't be invisible.

Mom's hands tightened on her shoulders. "What is this great honor?" she asked.

"The Exalted has chosen Elita to be his bride." Helen said the words with a breathless awe, her cheeks flushed and eyes alight.

Elita's mother gasped. "She's only nine years old."

"It isn't to happen right away," Helen said. "There will be years for her to prepare. But when she has reached maturity, there will be a grand wedding."

Her father moved in to stand beside them. He patted Elita's shoulder and smiled when she looked up at him. "This is indeed an honor," he said. "Thank the Exalted for us."

"But the Exalted is already married," Elita said. She had seen his wife, Miracle, seated beside him at the ceremonies. And they had children—four of them, all blond like Miracle.

"Yes." Helen turned to Elita, no longer smiling. "The Exalted has chosen you as his second wife."

Her mother's fingers were digging into Elita's shoulders now. "That is indeed a great honor," she said carefully. "But Elita is so young. Surely there are other, more suitable women…"

"He has chosen Elita," Jedediah said, his voice overly loud in the small space. Harsh. "How dare you question his choice."

"I meant no disrespect," Mom said, and bowed her head. But Elita could feel her trembling.

"Of course she doesn't," her father said. "And it's good that Elita has been chosen now. She will have years to learn all she will need to know for such an honored position."

"Of course," Helen said. She smiled at Elita once more. "We have much to do to prepare you for your future role."

"What does she need to do?" Mom asked.

"I will instruct her myself," Helen said. "I will teach her all she needs to know to be a fitting bride for our Exalted leader." She took a step back. "I'm sure you are both in awe. I will leave you to ponder your good fortune."

She and Sarai turned and left, but Jedediah stayed behind. He fixed them with a hard gaze. "Don't think you're going to get out of this," he said. "Remember what happened to Elim."

As soon as the door closed behind him, Elita's mother sank to her knees. Elita sat beside her. "Mom, what's wrong?" she asked.

Her mother pulled her close and stroked her hair. "I won't let anyone hurt you," she whispered.

"They're not going to hurt her," her father said. "This is a great honor."

"She's a child," her mother said, her expression fierce. "And if she does decide to marry one day, she should be free to make her own choice. The idea of her being married off to some old man who already has one wife—it's positively medieval."

"The Old Testament kings all had many wives," her father said.

"The Exalted is not an Old Testament king. And I can't believe you're going along with this."

Her father's expression sagged, and he looked away. "I don't see that we have any choice," he said. "No one goes against the Exalted's decrees."

"When we came here, it was because the Vine offered a better way of life—one full of cooperation and peace and contributing positive things to the world. No one ever said anything about marrying off children."

"She's not going to marry him right away," her father said. "The wedding will be years away, and anything could happen before then."

"We could leave," her mother said.

"We can't leave." He leaned closer and lowered his voice, as if Elita wasn't sitting right there between them. "You heard what Jedediah said—about Elim."

"Who's Elim?" Elita asked.

"Just…someone who used to belong to the Vine," her mother said.

"What happened to him?" Elita asked.

"He went away," her father said. "But we aren't going anywhere." He sounded almost angry. Elita leaned against her mom, trying to make herself smaller.

"We're going to take care of Elita," her mother said. "We're going to do whatever it takes to look after her." Her mother sounded angry, too, and Elita felt like crying. Whatever was going on was Jedediah's fault. And maybe the Exalted's fault too. Though she would never say that out loud. Everyone—even kids like her—knew that you didn't say anything bad about the Exalted. She didn't know what would happen to her if she did, but she was pretty sure it would be terrible.

"MY PARENTS JOINED the Vine when I was five." Chris was calmer now, seated next to Rand in an interview room at the sheriff's department, several hours after the confrontation in the woods. Travis and Gage Walker sat across from them—looking as relaxed as two uniformed lawmen could, she thought. She ran a hand through her bright blue hair. "They met some members at the ice-cream shop they owned in town and liked what they had to say and ended up selling everything and moving into a mobile home on some land the Vine owned. Or maybe the group was squatting on the land. I don't really know. Anyway, things were fine until the year I turned nine."

When she didn't continue, Travis prodded her. "What happened when you were nine?"

"One of the women who was close to the Exalted, came to my parents and told them that the Exalted had decided that I would be his second wife."

"When you were *nine*?" Rand didn't try to hide his shock.

She nodded. "The wedding wasn't going to take place until I was older. My dad told me it wouldn't happen until I was all grown up, and by then I would be looking forward to it. He went along with the idea that I'd been chosen for a great honor, but my mom didn't feel that way. I remember they argued about it."

The old sadness returned as she remembered the tense atmosphere in her family in the days after the announcement. "I had to take classes from a woman named Helen. Things like etiquette, and I had to memorize a lot of the Exalted's sayings. They were like proverbs, I guess. And I had to learn to sew and cook and read poetry. I was just a kid, and I thought a lot of it was dumb and boring, yet it didn't really feel dangerous or anything. But my mom really didn't like me taking the classes. My dad thought they wouldn't hurt anything, so they fought about that too." She sighed. "Things went along like that until I turned twelve. Then Jedediah and Helen showed up one evening and announced that the wedding would take place in a couple of weeks."

"When you were twelve," Rand clarified.

"Yes." She swallowed, recalling the details of that day. Details these people didn't need to hear. No one spoke, waiting. She could feel their eyes on her, especially Rand's. It was as if everyone in the room was holding their breath in anticipation of her next words. "My father died the day after that announcement was made. My mother said he tried to convince the Exalted that I was too young. The official story was that Dad died from eating poisonous mushrooms, but my mom and I always believed he was killed for getting in the way of something the Exalted wanted."

She studied her hands on the table, fingers laced together, reliving those awful days.

"You think someone in the group murdered your father?" Travis asked.

"Yes. But we don't have any proof, and my mom was too afraid to say anything. A few days later, she and I ran away."

"No one came after you?" Gage asked.

"They came looking for us," Chris said. "We knew they would. For years, we kept bags packed, and we would move every time we saw anyone we recognized from the Vine. Then, for a long time, we didn't see anyone. I thought we had gotten away." She glanced at Rand. "Until I saw Jedediah on the trail that day. I knew he recognized me, and it would be only a matter of time."

"He can't force you to marry someone," Travis said.

"The law may say he can't, but the Vine makes their own laws," she said.

"Have you found out anything more about these people?" Rand asked the sheriff. "Do they have any kind of criminal record?"

"We contacted the lawyer on the business card we were given," Travis said. "He declined to identify any of the principals in the Vine, LLC. We'll run a check on Edmund Harrison."

"Can you charge them in connection with the fire?" Rand asked.

"The fire appears to have started from a lightning strike. We haven't located the man you and others saw running away, back toward camp. No one else was harmed. Right now they haven't broken any laws."

"No one within the group will give evidence against them," Chris said. "They're either true believers who can't imagine the Exalted would ever do anything wrong or they're too afraid to speak out. And Harrison and those closest to him are careful."

"Have they made any specific threats to you?" Travis asked.

She shook her head. "Nothing more than what you heard, and that was more of a statement than a threat."

"That they would begin the wedding preparations today," Rand said. "But they can't force you to marry someone against your will."

"They believe they can." She hugged her arms across the chest. "They might try to kidnap me or drug me or threaten me. I don't know. I don't want to find out."

"If they do threaten you or try to force you to come with them, contact me." Travis handed her a business card. "Until then, there's not a lot we can do."

"I understand." She shoved back her chair. "If that's all, I'd like to go home now."

WHEN SHE STOOD, Rand rose also and followed her out. On the sidewalk, she turned to face him. "Thanks for the moral support, but I'm fine," she said. "I've dealt with these people most of my life. I know how to take care of myself."

"What are you going to do?" he asked.

"That's none of your business." She turned and started walking away.

She was right, but he followed her anyway. "Don't let them frighten you away."

"You don't know anything about it," she said, and kept walking.

"I know that you were strong enough to get away from them once," he said. "They may not like it, but it gives you the upper hand. You could expose them for what they really are and maybe save others."

"I just want them to leave me alone."

"I want that too. But I want more. I want to stop them from ruining other lives."

She halted alongside her Subaru, keys in hand. He stopped, too, five feet away, giving her space but hoping she would listen. "Why do you even care?" she asked.

"Because I like you. And I don't want you to leave when we've just met."

She shook her head and opened the driver's-side door of the car. "Sorry to disappoint you," she said.

"And because I didn't do enough to help my sister."

She stilled, holding her position for a long, breathless moment, until at last she lifted her head and met his gaze. "You mean, you couldn't persuade her to leave," she said. "But that was her decision to make, if she was an adult."

"I should have dragged her away from them when I had the chance," he said. "I'll never get over that regret, but I can help others now."

"You can't make someone leave that lifestyle unless they want to," she said.

"I should have at least tried." His face was flushed, his breathing ragged. "We tried for two years to persuade her to leave, but she wouldn't. And then we found out she had committed suicide." He could say the words now without the stabbing pain they had once caused, but the hurt would never completely go away.

"I'm sorry," she said, her previous anger replaced by softness.

"So am I. And I'm sorry there was nothing we could do to stop that cult from ensnaring others. But I'll do anything I can to help you stop the Vine."

"What do you think we could do?"

"I don't know. But if they're really going to stay around here until you go with them, that gives us a little time to find out what else they've been up to. And if they do come after you, we'll stop them."

"I'm not sure they can be stopped," she said. "They have a lot of money, and that gives them power."

"Does that give them power over you?"

She didn't hesitate in her reply. "No."

"And they don't have any power over me." He moved closer until he was standing right in front of her. "Together, maybe we can find a way to stop them from hurting anyone else."

"All right." She slid into the car. "I need time to think. And to talk to my mom. She might know or remember something that can help us."

"Call me," he said.

She nodded and started the engine.

He stepped back and watched her leave, his stomach in

knots. It was easy to make bold declarations about stopping these people, but all the talk in the world hadn't saved his sister.

Chapter Six

Chris gripped her phone tightly and paced her small living room as she told her mother about that morning's encounter with the Exalted's followers. "They walked right up and said all that about planning a wedding—in front of my friends and the sheriff and everyone. Now I know they all think I'm a freak."

Harley sat up on his bed by the sofa and watched her, forehead wrinkled in what seemed to Chris to be an expression of worry.

"It doesn't matter what they think of you," April said. "You can't let the Vine get you in their clutches again."

"I know that, Mom. And I'm being careful."

"Now that they've found you, they won't give up until they have you back," April said. "You need to leave."

Leaving had been Chris's first thought too. But Rand's plea wasn't the only thing that had stopped her from packing up and fleeing. "I have a good life here," she said. "I'm tired of running."

"Then come stay with me for a while. Just until they give up and leave town."

"And risk leading them to you? No." Her mother had worked hard to get away from the Vine. She had changed

her name, her job, and her appearance, and kept a low profile in a small town in Ohio. Chris stopped at the window
that looked down into the alley below. Her car was parked
there, next to a large trash bin. Otherwise, the alley was
empty. "I talked to the local sheriff today," she said. "I told
him about Dad."

"He'll never find evidence that he was murdered," her
mother said. "The Vine would make sure of that."

"I know we buried Dad in the woods," Chris said. "But
I don't remember much about it."

"There was a funeral. The Exalted gave the eulogy, which
was supposed to be a great honor. I don't remember anything he said."

"That didn't strike you as odd—that no law enforcement
was called, or a local coroner, or anything?"

"No. We didn't involve outsiders. Our motto was that
we took care of our own. Now I can see how that allowed
the group to get away with horrible things, but at the time
it seemed perfectly normal."

"There's a doctor here. He works with search and rescue, and he was there when Jedediah and two other men
confronted me. Rand—the doctor—said if I stay, he'll help
me fight the Vine."

"He doesn't know anything about them. He's probably
just trying to impress you."

"He said his sister belonged to a cult. She committed suicide. He wants to keep them from hurting anyone else." She
could still feel the impact of Rand's confession. He hadn't
dismissed the idea that strangers would try to force her to
marry or that she might be in danger from a harmless-look-
ing back-to-nature group. He knew the power groups like
the Vine could wield.

"Do you trust him?" April asked.

Chris didn't trust anyone. It had never felt safe to do so. "I believe he's sincere," she said. That wasn't the same as trust, exactly, but it was more than she could say about many of the people she'd met.

"Then let him help you. But don't depend on him."

"I know, Mom. The only person I can depend on is myself." How often had she repeated those words over the years? But they didn't make her feel stronger—only more alone.

"And me," April said. "You know I'll help you any way I can."

Harley stood and whined. Chris glanced at the dog. "I need to go now, Mom. I'll keep you posted on what happens here."

"I'll meet you anywhere, anytime you need me," April said. "I love you."

"I love you, too, Mom." She ended the call. Harley paced, the hair on the back of his neck and along his spine standing up. He let out a low growl and trotted over to the door.

Chris was on her way to the door when she heard footsteps in the hallway. Heart pounding, she checked the peephole. Jedediah's grim features glared back at her. Then he pounded on the door.

"Go away!" she said.

"We need to talk."

"I have nothing to say to you."

"The Exalted wants to see you."

"I don't have anything to say to him either. Go away."

"I'm here to take you to him."

"I'm calling the sheriff right now," she said, and pulled her phone from her pocket. She hit the nine and the one, then watched as Jedediah turned and left.

She sank to her knees and wrapped her arms around Harley, who still trembled with agitation. When she felt a little calmer, she focused on her phone once more. She didn't call 911. Instead, she selected the number she had programmed into the phone only that afternoon.

"Chris? Is everything okay?" Rand sounded a little out of breath. She tried to picture him, perhaps in doctor's scrubs. Or would he be at home?

"Jedediah was just here," she said.

"Did you call the sheriff?"

"I told him I would, so he left. I just… I wanted someone to know." Someone who might understand.

"I'm at the hospital in Junction. Is there someone else you can call to stay with you?"

"No, I'm okay. I have Harley. He let me know Jedediah was here before he even got to the door."

"What happened?" Rand asked. "What did he say to you?"

"He told me the Exalted wants to see me. I told him I didn't have anything to say to him, and then I said I was going to call the sheriff. He left. It's almost funny, really, that he thought I would meekly come with him. As if I was still nine years old."

"If he comes back, don't waste time talking to him," Rand said. "Dial 911 right away."

"I will. I won't keep you any longer. I'll see you at the training tonight."

"I'll pick you up, and we can go together," he said.

She started to protest, then imagined parking in that alley in the dark. It would be so easy for Jedediah and others to grab her. "All right," she said. "Thanks."

She ended the call and stood. Harley followed her to the desk in the corner, where Chris opened her laptop. She would write down everything she knew about the Vine and do some research online to learn whatever she could. Some people said knowledge was power. She would need every advantage to defeat someone like the Exalted, who was so accustomed to getting his own way.

RAND CHANGED OUT of his scrubs and made a quick stop at his house before he drove to pick up Chris. He removed his Sig Sauer M17 from the safe, loaded it and slipped it into his pocket. He didn't trust the members of the Vine not to come after Chris again, and he wanted to be prepared.

He parked in the alley next to Chris's Subaru and waited a moment after he shut off the engine, searching the darkness outside the circle of light cast by the single bulb over the door leading to the stairs to Chris's apartment. Nothing moved within those shadows, so he pulled out his phone and texted Chris. On my way up.

She met him at the door, her dog by her side. Harley eyed him warily but made no sound as Rand said hello, then offered the back of his hand for a sniff. "Good dog," Chris praised, rubbing behind the ridgeback's ear. "I'm ready to go," she said, and picked up her keys.

He waited while she locked her door, then preceded her down the steps, pausing to check the alley before he stepped out in it. He was a little surprised at how easily he slipped back into this mode of being on patrol, as if he was back in Afghanistan, where something as simple as walking to the latrine could make you a target.

Chris said nothing as she stood close behind him, then hurried after him to his car, head down. Harley followed, and hopped into the back seat of Rand's SUV. "I couldn't leave him," she said of the dog. "I'm too afraid Jedediah or someone else might try to hurt him."

"No problem," Rand said. "I like dogs."

She remained silent all the way to search and rescue head-quarters. The brightness of the room and the hum of conversation was jarring after the tension in his car, but he felt her relax as she sank into the end of the sofa and took out a notebook and pen. He sat beside her and did the same but couldn't shed his wariness as easily.

"Hey, Chris, how are you doing?"

"Everything okay, Chris?"

"Hey, Chris. You good?"

One by one, the gathered volunteers made a point to stop by and say hello. Those who hadn't been at the call-out for the fire would have heard about Chris's encounter with the members of the Vine. None of them asked any questions, though Rand read the curiosity in their eyes.

Chris accepted the attention calmly. "I'm good, thanks," she told anyone who inquired.

An elfin young woman with a cloud of dark curls approached. "Hey, Chris, how are you doing?" she asked. "I've been meaning to tell you how much I love your hair. And your tattoos." She glanced at her own bare arms. "I've been thinking of getting a tattoo myself, but my mom would probably have a heart attack if I did, and my three brothers would lose their minds." She grinned, deep dimples forming on either side of her mouth. "Which is kind of why I want to do it."

"Bethany, this is Rand," Chris said.

"Hey, Rand." Bethany offered her hand. "I'm glad you joined the group. For one thing, it means I'm no longer the newest rookie." She bent and patted Harley. "I miss my dog," she said. "But when I moved here my parents wouldn't let me take Charlie with me. I think they thought if they said that, I wouldn't leave, but they were wrong about that."

"Where are you from?" Rand asked, as much to spare

Chris from the steady stream of chatter as out of genuine curiosity.

"Waterbury, Vermont. I'm one of four and the only girl. To say that my parents and brothers are overprotective is an understatement. I practically had an armed guard with me everywhere I went. Living here, by myself, is a whole new experience."

Sheri Stevens took her place at the front of the room. "I better get to my seat," Bethany said. "I just wanted to say hi. Maybe we can get together for coffee or a drink sometime."

Before Chris could answer, she was gone.

"She's certainly friendly," Rand said.

"She's a little overwhelming," Chris said.

"All right, everyone. Let's focus on this evening's topic of wilderness first aid," Sheri began. "This will be a review for some of you, but it's a requirement, and standard practices do get updated from time to time, so pay attention."

Rand figured he could have taught the class, given his experiences in a field hospital, though he hoped a local search and rescue group would never have to deal with treating people who had been hit by improvised explosives or sniper fire. His mind drifted to his fellow volunteers. He didn't know most of them very well, but he was impressed that they would give so much time and attention to helping others, most of whom were probably strangers passing through the area, on vacation or on their way to somewhere else.

After an hour, they took a break. Ryan and Caleb joined him and Chris at the refreshment table. "We think that group that escaped the fire is camping out at Davis Draw," Ryan said. He picked up a peanut butter cookie and bit into it.

"Where is Davis Draw?" Chris asked. She didn't look alarmed.

"It's off a forest service road at the end of County Road

14," Caleb said. "It's not as nice as the area where they were—less trees, mostly desert scrub. And they'll have to haul water."

"How did you find this out?" Chris asked. She stirred sugar into a cup of coffee.

"We drove out there and saw a bunch of trailers and big tents," Ryan said. "Some guys asked what we were doing, and we told them we were looking for a place to camp. They said they had the whole area. We asked what they were doing, and they said it was a religious retreat."

Chris nodded but said nothing.

"I guess it's good to know where they are," Rand said.

"There's a two-week limit on camping in the area," Caleb said.

"I don't know how well that's enforced," Ryan added.

Chris shrugged. "They can do whatever they like," she said. "I really don't care."

"Time to get back to work," Sheri called, and they moved back to their places.

Chris leaned toward Rand again. "There may be a two-week camping limit, but they aren't going to leave until they have me," she said.

"They will if we persuade them that they're wasting their time," he said.

She pressed her lips together and shook her head, but she said nothing else as the lights dimmed and Sheri resumed her lecture.

At evening's end, they stayed to rearrange chairs and clean up. Danny found Rand carting the coffee urn into the tiny galley. "Did I tell you that one of your jobs as medical adviser is to help update our treatment protocols?"

"Sure, I can do that." Rand set the urn on the counter. "Any particular protocols?"

Danny made a face. "It's been a while since any of them were reviewed. Could you meet one day next week to go over them?"

"I'm off on Tuesday. Would that work?"

"That would be great." He glanced over his shoulder, then turned back, his voice lower. "I saw you sticking pretty close to Chris. Is she okay?"

"I'm fine." She moved in behind them with a handful of paper plates. She shoved the plates into the trash and faced Danny. "If you want to know how I'm doing, ask me."

"Sorry." He held up both hands. "But if you need anything—anything at all—you can call on any member of the team. We're not just about saving tourists, you know."

Her expression softened. "Thanks. That means a lot."

They exited the building and started across the parking lot, only to be hailed by Bethany. "I work at Peak Jeep Tours," she said. "Stop by if you're ever in the neighborhood. I'd really like to know you better."

"Um, sure." Chris hurried away, and Rand sped up to keep pace with her.

"Why is she so interested in me?" Chris asked when he caught up with her.

"I think she's just friendly."

"I'm not used to other people focusing on me—or caring so much," Chris said when she and Rand were in his car, headed back toward her apartment. "It feels a little uncomfortable."

"*Uncomfortable* but not *bad*, right?"

"Yeah."

"Can I ask you a personal question?"

"You can ask. That doesn't mean I'll answer."

"Fair enough. The blue hair and the tattoos—is that a fashion choice or another way of disguising yourself?"

She didn't say anything for so long he thought he might have offended her. But he had learned early in his medical career about the value of giving people plenty of time to answer hard questions. "A little of both, I think," she said. "My mother dyed my hair the day we escaped the camp, and I kept changing it over the years so I would look unfamiliar to anyone who knew me before. As for the tattoos—" she held out her arm "—we were taught that religious offerings were supposed to be perfect. Unblemished. I think in the back of my head I thought the Exalted would view a tattoo as an imperfection. That's why I got the first one, but after that, I liked it. It was another artistic expression." She shifted in the seat. "Why do you ask?"

"Just curious. They seem to suit you."

He pulled up to the door at the back of her building this time and met her beneath the light, waiting while she unlocked the outside entrance. They mounted the stairs side by side. She glanced down at his hand tensed at his side, as if reaching for something. "Are you carrying a gun?" she asked.

"Yes." He pulled up his shirt enough to show a holstered pistol. "I was in the military for years. I got used to walking around armed."

She nodded and they continued to her door. Once there, she turned to face him. "Look, I appreciate your concern. I really do. But these people are unpredictable. They seem nice and normal, until they aren't."

"I know that already. Remember, I've dealt with a cult before. They reel people in by appearing perfectly sensible and smarter than everyone else."

"Right. It's just…if something goes wrong, don't blame yourself, okay? You're not responsible for me. I'm not your sister."

Her expression was so earnest, her dark eyes so full of concern. As if she was more worried about him than about herself. His gaze shifted to her lips, full and slightly parted. "I don't feel about you like I do my sister." The words emerged more gruffly than he had planned. Then he yielded to temptation and kissed her.

For a fraction of a breath, she became a statue once his lips were on hers, unmoving. Not breathing. Then she pressed one hand to his chest, fingers slightly curled, seeking purchase. She arched into him, returning the kiss. He cupped his hand to her cheek, her skin hot, as if blushing at his touch. With a breathy moan, her lips parted, and she pressed against him, fitted to him, supple and strong. He wrapped both arms around her, cradling her to him yet holding back, his feelings so intense he feared crushing her.

She broke the kiss and stared up at him, a dazed expression in her eyes. "You'd better go," she whispered.

He wanted to argue but didn't. Instead, he reluctantly released his hold and waited while she unlocked her door and disappeared inside. He heard the dead bolt engage, then turned and moved away, down the stairs and into the darkness. So much of him was still there on that landing, wrapped up in that unexpected kiss.

He didn't see the person who came up behind him, only felt his presence and started to turn; then something hard crashed into his head, driving him to his knees. "Chris!" he tried to shout, but the word came out as a murmur as darkness swallowed him.

Chapter Seven

Chris sank onto the sofa, head back, eyes closed. That kiss! She hadn't even realized she was interested in Rand that way—that climb-his-body, take-me-now, where-have-you-been-all-my-life, passion-turned-up-to-ten kind of way— and then she was. When had she ever been kissed like that? Never. She had *never* been kissed like that. She didn't let men get that close. But Rand had vaulted right over her defenses and ambushed her with that kiss.

And she had willingly surrendered. Except it hadn't felt like losing—it felt like winning a grand prize. The rush of victory was overwhelming. It had been all she could do to pull herself together enough to send him away. At least she had that much of a sense of self-preservation left. After years of caution, she wasn't going to leap off that cliff just yet.

Harley climbed up onto the sofa beside her and began licking her cheek. She opened her eyes and hugged the dog. "I'm okay," she said. "Everything's okay."

Whomp!

The sound jolted her upright. Harley barked loudly, the ridge of hair along his back at attention. Something heavy had hit her door. It came again, an impact that made the door rattle in its frame. Heart pounding painfully, she jumped up, scrambling to free her phone from her pocket. A third impact shook the door, and Harley's barking became more frantic.

She stabbed at the phone as she moved toward the back door. "Nine-one-one. What is your emergency?"

"Someone is breaking into my apartment." She reached the kitchen just as the glass in the door's small window shattered inward. "Please hurry!"

"What is your location, ma'am?"

Chris rattled off her address as she grabbed the chef's knife from the magnet by the stove. She looked around for anything else she could use as a weapon. The frying pan? A rolling pin? Then she spotted the fire extinguisher and pulled it from its bracket on the wall. "Come on, Harley," she called, and headed toward the bedroom. She heard the back door give way as she dove into the closet and shut the door behind her and the dog. They would find her soon enough, but she hoped she would be able to hold them off until help arrived.

RAND GROANED AND tried to sit, but a wave of dizziness dragged him down again. He was aware of noises—someone shouting, pounding footsteps. Then hands grabbed him roughly. He fought back, punching out, and tried to shout, but no words emerged. He tried to open his eyes yet saw nothing but blackness.

"Hey, it's okay. You're all right now. You're safe. Lie still." The voice was firm but reassuring. Strong hands urged him to lie back, and he surrendered to the pull of gravity. A bright light shone on his face, and he squinted against it. A man he didn't know peered down at him. "Who are you?" Rand managed to force out.

"I'm Lee. I'm a paramedic with Rayford County Emergency Services. Looks like you hit your head pretty hard. Can you tell me what happened?"

Rand closed his eyes again, trying to remember. "Someone jumped me," he said.

"Lie still, okay? You're still bleeding a little. Do you know who hit you?"

He was starting to think more clearly, and the memory of what had happened before he was hit came flooding back. "Chris!" He tried to sit up again, though the EMTs held him down. "Is Chris all right? I have to go to her."

"Is Chris the person who called for an ambulance?" Lee asked someone out of Rand's field of vision. He was still holding Rand down. Rand lay back, gathering strength for another attempt to rise.

"No. Someone named Susan, in the apartment across the alley," a female voice answered. "She said she heard a shout and looked out the window to see someone fall to the ground and someone else run away. She called 911, and they dispatched us." A woman with strawberry blond hair and freckles leaned over Rand. "A sheriff's deputy is on the way. I hear the siren now."

Rand heard it too—a high-pitched wailing that grew louder and louder. He sat up again. This time no one stopped him. The woman probed at the back of his head while Lee unwrapped a blood pressure cuff from around Rand's left arm.

"Your vitals are good," Lee said. "How are you feeling?"

The dizziness and nausea had subsided. His head throbbed, but he could live with that. "I'm better," he said. "I have to check on Chris. The person who hit me could have got to her."

Lee's forehead wrinkled. "This Chris person was with you when you were attacked?"

"No. She lives upstairs, over the art gallery. I was just leaving her apartment. Whoever hit me must have been waiting in the alley."

"If she's upstairs, she should be all—" A loud crash interrupted him. He turned to look toward the sound behind him, and Rand staggered to his feet.

"Sir, you need to be still—"

Rand ignored the words and started for the building. He was certain now that his attacker had been waiting to disable him so he could go after Chris. But he had taken only a few steps when a sheriff's department SUV turned into the alley. The wail of the siren bounced off the buildings, and Rand instinctively put his hands to his ears. "Freeze, with your hands where I can see them!" a voice from the SUV ordered.

Rand did as he was asked and squinted in the glare of the spotlight centered on him. Then the light cut off, and a man stepped out from the car. "Rand, what are you doing here?"

Jake Gwynn moved toward Rand, converging on him at the same time the two EMTs caught up with him. "You need to check on Chris," Rand said. "I had just left her apartment when someone attacked me, but I think their real target was her."

"Chris called 911 and said someone was breaking into her apartment." Jake looked at the outer door. "Gage is on his way."

"We don't have time to wait," Rand said. "I'll back you up."

Jake's gaze shifted to Rand's head. "You're bleeding."

"I'll be fine. We don't have time to loo—"

A woman's scream overhead launched him toward the door, with Jake right behind him. But the door was locked.

Jake pounded on it. "Open up! Sheriff's department!" he shouted.

But the only reply was scuffling noises overhead and another loud crash. "Is there a back way in?" Jake asked.

"I don't know," Rand said. He tried to remember anything about Chris's apartment, but he hadn't been paying attention, and he hadn't been past the living room. "Maybe a fire escape?"

"Stay here. I'm going around back."

As soon as Jake was gone, Rand turned his attention back to the door. It was a heavy metal door; he doubted he could bash it in. He couldn't pick the lock either. Could he ram it with his car?

A second siren's wail filled the air. "That must be Gage," Lee said.

Rand moved to the middle of the alley and stared up at what he thought was Chris's window. "Chris!" he shouted. But no answer came.

A second black-and-white SUV entered the alley, and Sergeant Gage Walker stepped out almost before it had come to a complete stop. "What's going on?" he asked.

"Chris is upstairs," Rand said. "She called 911, saying someone was breaking into her apartment. I had just left her, and someone must have been waiting for me. They attacked me and knocked me out. I came to when the paramedics arrived."

"Dispatch sent us over in response to a call from a neighbor about a man being attacked in the alley," Lee said.

Gage pulled out his phone. "I'll call the building owner and see if we can get a key."

Rand shook his head and started around the corner of the building. Jake met him at the corner. "Where are you going?" he asked, his hands on Rand's shoulders.

"I'm going up the fire escape," Rand said. "I'm not waiting for a key."

"The stairs aren't down," Jake said. "No one's been up there."

"Or they've been up there and pulled the stairs up after them," Rand said. He pushed past Jake and headed toward the fire escape. As Jake had said, the bottom of the stairs was ten feet overhead, out of his reach.

Rand pulled out his phone and dialed Chris's number. It rang five times before going to voicemail. "I can't take your call right now..." He ended the call and shoved the phone back into his pocket. By this time, Jake had caught up with him. "She's not answering," Rand said. "I know something's wrong."

Gage called to them from the corner of the building. "The landlord is on the way," he said. "She said she'll be here in five minutes."

Rand looked up at the fire escape again. If he parked his SUV beneath it, he could climb on top and maybe reach the bottom of the ladder from there. He pulled his keys from his pocket. "Where are you going?" Jake asked.

"To help Chris." Waiting was only buying more time for her to end up hurt. Or worse.

CHRIS HEARD THE SIREN, growing louder by the second until the wailing was directly below. Then the sound shut off. Help was almost here. She just had to hang on a little longer.

The intruder was in the house now, footsteps lumbering as they—because it sounded like more than one person—searched the apartment. Something heavy, a piece of furniture, fell to the floor with a crash. "We know you're in here, Elita!" a man—Jedediah?—called out.

Harley growled, a low and menacing rumble. Chris buried her fingers in the thick ruff at his neck. "Quiet!" she hissed. They needed to remain hidden until the deputies arrived. What was taking them so long?

The footsteps entered the bedroom. Chris's heart hammered. She let go of the dog and gripped the knife in her right hand, then thought better of that and slid it into her pocket. She hefted the fire extinguisher and looped her finger into the metal ring on the handle.

Crash! A scream escaped her as something hit the closet door, causing it to bow inward. Harley lunged at the door, barking furiously. Chris braced against the back wall of the closet and stood, shoving clothes aside and balancing the fire extinguisher on one thigh. Her pulse sounded so loud in her ear she could scarcely hear anything else, though the dog's barking echoed in the small space.

The door burst open, splinters flying. Chris pulled the ring from the handle of the fire extinguisher, aimed the hose and squeezed the trigger. She hit her intruder right in the face. When the second man shoved the first out of the way and lunged for her, she got him, too, white powder billowing up and coating his glasses and hair and filling his mouth when he opened it to shout.

When the extinguisher was empty, Chris swung it like a club. She hit the second man hard on the shoulder. When he staggered back, the first man rushed forward, and she thrust the bottom of the extinguisher into his forehead, connecting with a sickening *thwack*—like a hammer hitting a watermelon. The first man grabbed on to the door of the closet but remained standing, only to be driven farther back by Harley, who rushed forward, teeth bared.

"Freeze! Sheriff's department!" came a shout from the front room.

The first man turned; then the second grabbed his shoulder. "We better get out of here," he said. They raced from the room. Chris dropped the fire extinguisher and sank to her knees, arms wrapped around Harley, who was still barking and lunging.

That was how Jake Gwynn found her. She had to calm the dog before he could approach, but once she had convinced Harley that everything was okay, Jake helped her to the end of the bed, where she sat and contemplated the closet's shattered door and the carpeting coated with white powder.

"There were two men," she said. "They broke in, and I hid in the closet with Harley. They ran when they heard you coming."

"Gage went after them," Jake said. "Do you know who they are?"

"Oh, I'm sure they were members of the Vine," she said. "They're the only ones who would want to hurt me. One of them might have been Jedediah."

"Did you get a good look at them?" Jake asked. "Could you identify them?"

She shook her head. "By the time I saw them, they were covered in the powder from the fire extinguisher." She closed her eyes, replaying those few split seconds. "And I think their faces were covered. They wore ski masks or something like that. And gloves." She had the image of black-gloved hands reaching for her fixed in her mind.

"Chris!"

Rand's cry made her sit up straighter. "We're in the bedroom," Jake called. "Don't come in. You could contaminate evidence." He indicated the footprints in the powder on the carpet, which he had avoided when he entered the room. "Those are from your attackers. We might be able to match them to their shoes later."

Rand appeared in the doorway. "Chris, are you all right?" he asked.

"I'm fine." She passed a shaky hand through her hair. "They never laid a hand on me."

Rand surveyed the chaos around the closet. "What happened?"

"She let off a fire extinguisher at them," Jake said, a note of admiration in his voice.

"I hit them with it too," she said. "And there's a kitchen knife in my pocket. I would have used it on them if I had to. And I had Harley." She hugged the dog, as much out of affection as to keep him from bounding across the powdered carpet to Rand.

"You shouldn't be in here, Rand," Jake said. "Go back outside and wait. Let the ambulance crew finish looking you over."

"Ambulance?" Chris turned to Rand. "Are you hurt? What happened?"

He touched the back of his head and winced. "Whoever went after you was waiting for me. They knocked me out, but I'm fine. Just a bump on the head."

Gage moved in behind him. "They got away down the fire escape," he said. "I didn't even get a good look at them. Two men dressed in black, covered in flour or something."

"Most of the contents of a fire extinguisher," Jake said. "Chris let them have it when they came after her."

"Good thinking." Gage studied the footprints on the floor. "I'll call for a forensics team. Are you all right, Chris? Do you need the paramedics?"

"I'm okay," she said.

"We'll need to get your statement," Gage said. "Jake, bring her in the other room." He turned to Rand. "We'll need your statement too."

Jake directed her in picking her way around the path the intruders had taken when they fled the apartment. She guided Harley, who wasn't in a cooperative mood, out of the apartment and down the stairs, where she found two patrol vehicles, an ambulance, two paramedics, her landlord and half a dozen curious onlookers.

Rand moved in beside her. "Are you sure you're okay?" he asked, his gaze taking her in from the top of her head to her feet.

She nodded and hugged her arms across her chest, having released Harley to sniff around, knowing the dog wouldn't go far. "I was terrified for a few minutes. Now I'm just exhausted."

Her landlord, Jasmine, approached. With no makeup on and wearing a sweatshirt pulled over plaid pajama pants, she looked very different from the polished professional Chris was used to. "Honey, are you okay?" Jasmine asked.

"I'm fine. I'm sorry about the apartment doors." She looked at the doors, both bent inward.

"The cops did that," Jasmine said. "I guess they couldn't wait for me to get here with the key."

Chris shuddered. "They got to me just in time."

"Who cares about doors, as long as you're okay." Jasmine patted her arm. "Don't worry about it. I have insurance. But is there anything else you need?"

"No, thanks. I'm okay, really."

"Your friend here looks a little worse for wear." Jasmine flashed a smile. "Still very easy on the eyes, mind you."

Chris studied Rand. His face was paler than usual, the fine lines around his eyes tighter, as if he was in pain. And was that blood in his hair?

"Rand, you're hurt!" she exclaimed.

"I'm okay. The paramedics have seen me."

"Jake, get Rand's statement," Gage said as he joined them. "Chris, you come with me."

She ended up sitting in the front seat of Gage's patrol car, reciting all the events of the evening, leaving out the part about her and Rand kissing before he left her and returned to his car. "I'm sure those two men were from the Vine," she said. "The group has made it clear they want me back."

"To marry their leader—have I got that right?" Gage asked.

She nodded. "It sounds ridiculous. I'm a grown woman. I'm not a member of the group anymore. They can't force me to marry someone. Especially since he's already married to someone else. But logic doesn't really matter. They think they can make me do this. And they believe they're above the law."

"Did the two men who broke into your apartment say anything?" Gage asked.

"One of them called me Elita," she said. "That was the name I used when I was a member of the group—when I was a little girl. That's one more reason I'm sure they were from the Vine. No one else knows me by that name."

Gage made a note. "Anything else you remember about them?"

"I thought the voice sounded like Jedediah. He's the man who confronted me at the fire the other day. I had seen him on a hiking trail the day before that, when search and rescue responded to a man on the Anderson Falls Trail who had heart trouble."

"We'll have forensics go over the place," Gage said. "You won't be able to stay here for a while. The front and back doors to your apartment were forced open."

"How did they get in from street level?" she asked.

"Best guess is they blocked the door from closing all the way while you and Rand were upstairs. He came down, and they ambushed him at his car, then went in the door and locked it behind them to delay anyone's ability to get to them."

"And to slow me down if I managed to run from them," she said.

"We had to break open the outer door to get to you," Gage said. "I was going to wait for Jasmine to bring us the key, but Rand insisted. I guess it's a good thing he did."

She said nothing, feeling Gage's eyes on her. She wondered what he thought of the tattoos and dyed hair. Of her strange past with a cult that seemed kooky to most people. "Have they threatened you before?" he asked. "Since you left?"

"Mom and I were approached a couple of times by members who recognized us." She shivered, remembering. "No direct threats. I think they're too clever for that. But if you had lived with them the way we did, you'd know how things that sound innocent can come across as really menacing."

"Give me an example."

She shifted in her seat, then blew out a breath. Why was this so hard to talk about? "If someone approached you and said, 'The Exalted is worried it will be really bad for you if you don't fulfill your destiny,' that sounds innocent enough, right? A little out there, but harmless. But when I hear that, I'm not thinking they're concerned about my karma or my mental health or even the threat of eternal damnation—I'm hearing code for 'If you don't do what we want, you could end up dead.'"

"Did that happen to other people who disobeyed the Exalted?" Gage asked.

"Oh yeah. No one ever used the word *murder*. They got sick. They had an accident. One young woman drowned."

"Were any of these deaths investigated by law enforcement?"

She shook her head. "They weren't even reported, as far

as I know. The victims were buried in the woods, wherever we were staying. That was the way we did things. Everyone said, 'We take care of our own,' and it was considered a good thing. We didn't need outsiders interfering."

Gage closed his notebook. "I'll probably have more questions later. Do you have some place you can stay? Or I can find you a bed at a women's shelter."

"I'll find a place." She could always go to her mother's, though the idea left a sour taste in her mouth. Hadn't she said she was tired of running away? And what about bringing the danger with her?

At a tapping on the glass, she turned and saw Rand outside the SUV. Gage rolled down the window. "You can't stay here," Rand said. "Come back to my place. No one from the Vine knows where I live."

"Rand, you're hurt," she said. "You should have someone look at your head. You might need an X-ray or stitches."

"I'm fine. I have a headache, but no dizziness. The bleeding has stopped. I know enough to go to the hospital if any concerning symptoms pop up. In the meantime, these people don't know where I live, and I have a good security system. You'll be safe there."

"I told her I could find her a bed in a women's shelter," Gage said. "The local animal shelter would look after your dog for you."

She didn't want to go to a shelter, and she wasn't going to leave Harley. "Can Harley come to your place?" she asked Rand.

"Of course." He opened the door. The dog was standing next to him. "He's ready to go."

Chapter Eight

Gage fetched a list of items Chris needed from her apartment, and Rand loaded them into his SUV before they headed out. No one said much. He didn't try to reassure her that everything would be all right or offer advice for how she should act or feel. She was grateful for that. She laid her head back and closed her eyes, the dark silence and the rhythm of the vehicle's tires on the road almost lulling her to sleep.

But not quite. The fear was still there, coiled inside her, waiting to spring to life. That fear made her open her eyes again and repeatedly check the side mirror, looking out for headlights coming up behind them.

"No one is following us," Rand said. "I've been watching."

"I'm sorry I pulled you into this," she said. This was why she didn't get close to people. She didn't want anyone to see the mess of her life. It was like having an acquaintance rifle through the contents of your kitchen garbage can or your dirty-clothes hamper.

"I want to help." He glanced at her, then back at the road. "Just to be clear, this invitation to stay with me comes with no strings attached."

Was he thinking of that kiss? The memory pulled at her, here in the dark, so close to him. Yet everything that happened afterward was a barrier between them now. "Thanks," she said. "I like you. I guess that's pretty clear from that kiss. But... I have a lot to process right now. And I'm not used to trusting other people."

"Fair enough. Just know you can trust me."

She wanted to believe that, but she had had so little practice in depending on other people. She thought of all the rescue calls she had been on, when strangers trusted her and her fellow volunteers to save them. Those people, injured or stranded in the wilderness, didn't have much choice in the matter. Maybe she didn't have much choice either. She wasn't strong enough to fight the Vine on her own. She believed Rand was strong, and she believed he really did want to help her. That was more than anyone else had given her, which made it a good place to start.

RAND'S HOME HAD once been a summer camp. He had purchased the long-abandoned property, torn down the dilapidated camper cabins and turned the log structure that had served as a lodge into a home. The remote location—the only property at the end of a long gravel road—had added to the hassle of the remodel, but now he appreciated the privacy and the safety it would offer Chris.

"The guest room and bath are upstairs," he told her as she and Harley followed him into the great room that made up most of the ground floor. "The primary suite is down here, so you'll have plenty of privacy." He led the way up the stairs to the guest room. "I use the room across the hall as my home office. Kitchen and laundry are downstairs, and there's a detached garage in back. There's an alarm system and a sensor on the driveway that will alert me if anyone tries to drive in."

"Is there something you need to tell me, Doctor?" she asked. "Some reason for all this security?"

"Let's just say I'm a naturally cautious person."

Harley sat beside her and leaned on her leg. She rubbed the dog's ears and looked into the bedroom but didn't go in. "Thank you," she said. "I couldn't ask for a better setup."

"You're welcome to stay as long as you like. I work three or four ten-to twelve-hour shifts per week at the hospital, so you'll be alone during that time. I hope that's not a problem."

"No. I'm used to being by myself." She entered the room, trailed by the dog, then looked back at him. "Good night," she said, and closed the door.

She had spoken so matter-of-factly about being accustomed to being alone, but her words made him feel a little hollow. He would have answered the same way and protested that he liked his own company. But there had been times when he had wished for companionship to fill that emptiness. He hoped he could be that for her.

Five years ago

"SOMEONE FROM THE VINE was here tonight."

Chris's mom sounded calm on the phone, but her words sent an icy shard of fear through Chris. "They came to your house? You spoke to them?"

"It was a man and a woman. They were waiting on the front steps when I came in from work. They were in the shadows, so I didn't see them until I was almost to the door. They were dressed in suits and carrying a big Bible, like missionaries going door-to-door. But when I told them

I wasn't interested and tried to move past them, the man grabbed me."

Chris sucked in her breath. "Mom! Did they hurt you?"

"They only frightened me. But that was what they intended."

"What did they say? What did they do?"

"They forced their way into the house and kept asking me where you were. They said the Exalted was ready to marry you and it was time for you to fulfill your destiny."

"I thought they would have forgotten me by now," Chris said. "That the Exalted would have found someone else to marry." After all this time, she still thought of him by that title. His given name—Edmund Harrison—felt too strange on her tongue.

"I promise I didn't tell them where you are," her mother said. "But they said to tell you they weren't going to give up looking for you. And they said…they said…" Her voice broke.

Chris took a deep breath, trying to stop the shaking that had taken over her body but failing. "What did they say?"

"They said if you won't come back to them, you're dead to them. And they'll make sure you're dead to everyone else too."

"They're going to kill me just because I won't come back to their cult and marry a man who's old enough to be my father and already has at least one wife?" The idea was absurd, yet Chris didn't have it in her to laugh. She still remembered how seriously the members of the group took the Exalted's every pronouncement.

"They killed your father," her mother said. "And I'm sure they've killed other people. Eliminating anyone who gets out of line is one way the Exalted keeps order."

"You defied them by taking me away," Chris said. "Did they threaten you too?"

"They said...if you didn't obey, they would find a way to hurt me."

"No." A wave of nausea rocked Chris, but she pulled herself together, allowing anger to overcome the sickness. "That's not going to happen."

"I'm packing my things already. And I have my extra ID." Back when they had first left the group, her mother had paid for new birth certificates and Social Security cards for the two of them. Later, she had paid even more for a second set of identification. Chris kept hers in a lockbox under her bed, but she hadn't even looked at the papers for years.

"I'm coming to get you," Chris said. "I'll help you move."

"No! They're probably watching me, and they'll see you. I have a friend who will help me. He's a former cop. He knows a little of my story. I trust him. I'll be in touch with my new information when it's safe to do so."

"What about going to the police?" Chris asked. "If we tell them about these threats..."

"There's nothing they can do," her mother said. "The Exalted can produce witnesses all day long to attest to his sterling character. He has money and powerful friends to protect him. We don't have any proof they've threatened us."

"We know they've killed people," Chris said.

"But we can't prove it. Better to start over with a new name. I'm getting used to it now."

Gloom settled over Chris. "Do you think I should move and change my name too?"

"No, no! They don't know where you are. If they did, they wouldn't have wasted their time with me. There's no need for you to worry. I wouldn't even have bothered you with this, except I wanted you to know I'll be unreachable for a few days. Just until I get resettled."

"Of course I'm worried, Mom! What if they come after you again?"

"They won't. I've gotten very good at covering my tracks. I'm going to hang up now, sweetie. Love you. Talk to you soon. Oh, and next time we talk, remember—my new name is April."

Chris hung up the phone and slumped onto the sofa, stomach churning. Her mother hadn't sounded scared or even terribly upset. The two of them had moved five times between Chris's twelfth and eighteenth birthdays, and her mother had relocated twice more since Chris had left home. After all these years of running and hiding, Chris sometimes thought her mother enjoyed the challenge and the chance to start over and remake herself once again.

Whereas all Chris had ever wanted was to sink roots in one place, to be part of a community. She had found that here in Eagle Mountain. She had artist friends and her search and rescue friends and people whom she believed cared about her. Though she wasn't particularly close to any single person, she felt comfortable with them all. The thought of having to leave that behind was too heavy a burden to carry.

And all because one evil man was fixated on her. The Exalted had been getting his way for so long he couldn't bear the thought of anyone denying him—even a child, as she had been when she ran away from him. She wanted the running and hiding to stop, but she didn't know how to make it happen.

She still remembered her father, lying on the bed in their little trailer, writhing in agony. This was what the Exalted's punishment looked like. If the Vine ever caught up with her, they would make sure she obeyed, or they would mete out a similar fate. She was as sure of that as she had once been certain of the other teachings she had learned as a little girl. She had left those other false beliefs behind, but watching her father die had sealed this one certainty within her. She couldn't risk the Exalted catching up with her, so she had to keep running.

BEFORE CHRIS EVEN opened her eyes the next morning, she had the dreamlike sensation of being in an unfamiliar place. She opened her eyes to a shadowed bedroom, a thin comforter over the top of the bed, Harley stretched out along her side. No dream, then. She was in the guest room in Rand's home. For a few seconds the terror of those moments in the closet, hearing heavy footsteps approach her hiding place, threatened to overwhelm her. She rested a hand on the dog, feeling his side rise and fall, and grew calmer. She was safe. No one was going to hurt her.

She sat up and looked around the plain but comfortable guest room. Moving around so much, she was used to being in unfamiliar places, but almost always alone or with her mother. Not in a house belonging to a man she really liked but wasn't sure she should be with.

She got up and got ready for the day. Dressed in jeans and a T-shirt, she went downstairs to let Harley out. The rooms were empty, Rand's SUV no longer parked out front. While Harley patrolled the property, she hunted in the kitchen for coffee and started it brewing. Rand had left a note on the kitchen table with a set of car keys.

My shift is 6–4 today. The keys are to the Jeep in the garage. Feel free to use it. Help yourself to anything you like. Text if you need anything. Rand

Harley scratched at the door, and after making sure the noise really was from the dog, she let him in, then carried a cup of coffee upstairs and started the shower.

After she and the dog both had breakfast, she wandered the house. Rand had a few decent pieces of art on the walls—a mix of photos and original oils or watercolors, some from local artists she knew. His bookshelves housed medical texts, historical nonfiction and detective stories. One photo showed him standing with an older man and woman, the man an older version of Rand himself. *So these must be his parents.* No photo of his sister. Maybe that reminder would be too painful.

She avoided his bedroom. She was nosy, but she wasn't going to be that intrusive. House tour over, she returned to her room and made her bed but was unable to settle. She needed something to focus on besides the Vine. Usually, she could lose herself in her art, but she didn't have any supplies.

"Want to go for a ride, Harley?"

The dog wagged his tail and trotted ahead of her down the stairs. She collected the keys from the kitchen table and headed for the garage. Nice that Rand had a spare vehicle. One the Vine wouldn't recognize as hers.

At the last minute, she texted him. If he came home before she returned, she didn't want him to think the worst. Plus, her work with search and rescue had ingrained in her the advice that when setting out alone on a risky activity like a hike or skiing, it was smart to let someone know your plans. Running errands in town shouldn't be risky, but considering her situation, it might be.

Decided to run a few errands in town. Back soon.

He responded with a thumbs-up emoji. She smiled. Odd how that made her feel better. She headed toward her apartment, almost without thinking. But she didn't park in back.

Instead, she pulled the Jeep into a parking spot right in front of the gallery and sat for a few minutes, observing passers-by. No one looked like anyone from the Vine. Over the years she had gotten good at spotting them, with their slightly outdated fashion and simple hairstyles; the men always clean shaven, the women without makeup. Even more important, no one was paying particular attention to the building or to her.

Harley waited on the sidewalk while Chris went inside the gallery. The bell on the door sounded, and Jasmine bustled out of the workroom in the back. She stopped short when she recognized Chris. Today the frames of her glasses were red, matching the large red stones in her earrings. "Chris, how are you?" she asked, then hurried over to give her a hug.

Chris patted Jasmine awkwardly on the back and stepped out of her embrace. "I'm fine."

Jasmine nodded. "You look better. Not so pale. What happened last night was horrible. Do you have any idea who would do such a thing?"

"None," she lied. "I stopped by to pick up some supplies."

She had hoped to change the subject, but Jasmine didn't take the hint. "I've got someone coming tomorrow to see about replacing the doors on your apartment," she said. "But you're going to have a major mess to clean up. The sheriff's department left fingerprint dust, or whatever you call it, everywhere."

"Don't worry about that," Chris said. "I'll take care of it. And I'll reimburse you for the doors."

Jasmine shook her head. "I told you, my insurance will take care of that. But what happened? The sheriff's deputy didn't say much, just that someone tried to break in."

"I think they had me confused with someone else," she lied again. She didn't want to go into the whole backstory.

The circumstances would probably make Jasmine think twice about renting to her. "I just came in for a few things, then I'll be out of your way." In addition to the artwork for sale, Jasmine stocked a small selection of canvases, paints, pastels, sketchbooks and other supplies.

"Oh, honey, you're no trouble. You're the best tenant I ever had. Most of the time I wouldn't even know you're up there, you're so quiet." Jasmine followed her over to the corner devoted to supplies. "Deputy Gwynn said there were two guys who tried to break in, but they got away. He told me to keep an eye out for anyone hanging around the store, but I haven't seen anyone. Did you get a good look at them? Do you know who they are?"

"I only had a brief glimpse of them." Chris selected a sketchbook and pencils. "It was dark, and they were wearing ski masks."

"It's just the wildest thing. I mean, you don't think about something like that happening here. I hope they don't come back. They might think there's money in the gallery, though I make it a point not to leave much cash on hand, and I wouldn't think artwork was something they could readily sell."

"I'm sure the sheriff's deputies scared them off." Chris added an art gum eraser to her purchases. "I'll take these."

"Where are you staying?" Jasmine asked as she rang up Chris's selections.

"With a friend," she said. She didn't wait for Jasmine to probe for more details, instead collecting the art supplies and her change and starting for the door. "I have to run. See you soon."

She decided to walk over to the bank and get some cash. She hadn't gone very far when someone called her name. "Chris!"

She turned to see Bethany Ames hurrying toward her. As usual, Bethany was smiling. "I'm glad I ran into you," Bethany said. "I came into town to grab some lunch. We could eat together."

Chris had already taken a step back. "I don't really have time right now. Thanks anyway."

Bethany's smile faded. "If you don't want to hang out with me, you can be honest. It's because I made such a fool of myself with Vince, isn't it?" She covered her eyes with her hand. "I'm never going to live that down. But honest, I didn't know he was involved with someone else. I'm new here in town, right? I'm trying to make friends—to be more outgoing and positive. That's what you're supposed to do, isn't it? But I keep getting it wrong. I'm sorry to bother you." She turned away.

"Wait," Chris called. Bethany's raw honesty was shocking, and also appealing. And Chris knew a little about being the "new kid" and trying to find a way to fit in. "I'll have lunch with you. What's this about you and Vince?" Vince Shepherd was a fellow search and rescue volunteer who was living with *Eagle Mountain Examiner* reporter Tammy Patterson.

"Are you sure?" Bethany asked. "I don't want to impose if you're busy."

"I have time," Chris said. "And I want to hear your story."

Bethany's smile returned. "In that case, I'm happy to give you the whole sad tale of me making a fool of myself. I thought Vince was so good looking and I would sweep him off his feet with my awkward but endearing charm." She rolled her eyes. "Unfortunately—or maybe *fortunately*, since he already had a girlfriend—he was immune to my flirting. When I found out he was involved with someone else, I was mortified. I figured everyone in search and rescue knew about my crush on him."

"I didn't know," Chris said. "But then, I'm not usually clued in on local gossip." She wasn't close enough to other people for them to confide in her.

But Bethany was willing to tell all. She obviously needed someone to talk to, so why couldn't Chris be that person? The thought surprised her. Six months ago that wasn't something that would have occurred to her. She had always believed she didn't need close friends.

But Rand had refused to be put off by her reserve. Apparently, Bethany felt the same way. Chris smiled at her. "Let's go over to the Cake Walk and have lunch. You can tell me how you ended up in Eagle Mountain."

"It's a doozy of a story, I promise," Bethany said.

An hour later, Chris had shared a cheeseburger with Harley on the patio of the Cake Walk Café and learned all about Bethany, her three overprotective brothers and the fiancé who had jilted her. Despite what some would have labeled a tragedy, the young woman remained sunny and optimistic, and excited about starting life over alone in a new place, despite some bumps in the road along the way. Chris could never see herself being so upbeat, but spending time with her new friend had inspired her to do a better job of not dwelling on the hurts of her past. Bethany's approach to moving on struck her as healthier, though she suspected a lot of determination lay beneath the young woman's cheerful exterior.

She ended her afternoon in town at the local grocery, for a few items to add to Rand's supplies. She hesitated in front of a display of portobello mushrooms. She had a recipe for grilled mushrooms that Rand might like. She could make dinner for the two of them.

And then what? Would that be too much like a date? A chance to repeat that kiss and see if it had been a fluke or as sensational as she remembered?

She shook her head. "Don't get ahead of yourself," she mumbled, but she put the mushrooms in her cart anyway.

She saw no one suspicious in town, and no one followed her back to Rand's place. She texted to let him know she had returned safely, but got no reply. Maybe he was in surgery.

She settled into a chair on the back deck and began to sketch the scene before her—a patch of woods, with mountains in the distance. Soon she was lost in the work. This was what she needed, what had always made her feel better—to let her unsettling thoughts find their way out through her pencil, transformed from fears to fantasies of a hidden world that she controlled.

RAND WAS HALFWAY home after his shift when he remembered he was supposed to meet Danny to review the medical protocols for search and rescue. He was tempted to call and cancel, but he resisted the urge and drove to SAR headquarters. Once there, he texted Chris to let her know he would be a little late. Should be done by 6:30 he said, and hit send before he could talk himself out of it. Had he assumed too much? It wasn't as if they were in a relationship and needed to report their comings and goings to each other. But he also didn't want to worry her when she already had so much to deal with.

Danny was waiting for him inside the building. "These are all our protocols," he said, hefting a large notebook. "Some of them are on the computer, too, but not all of them. Maybe eventually that will happen, but for now, we're still doing things the old-fashioned way."

"No problem," Rand said. "Let's see how many we can get through this afternoon."

They moved to a couple of folding chairs set up at a table near the front of the room. "I guess you heard about the commotion at Chris's last night," Danny said.

"You know about that?" Rand tried not to show his surprise.

Danny shrugged. "It's all over town. I guess people saw the sheriff's deputies there this morning."

"I did hear about it," Rand said, unsure how much to reveal. Should he mention that Chris was staying with him? He decided against it. Not that he didn't trust Danny, but it seemed safer for as few people as possible to know her whereabouts.

"I wonder if it was a random break-in or if someone targeted Chris," Danny said.

The comment surprised him. "Why would you think someone would target her?"

Danny shrugged. "She's pretty striking looking. Maybe she caught the wrong guy's attention. And for all she's been part of the group for four years, I don't know much about her. She's not one to talk much about herself. Which I respect, but most people aren't quite as, well, secretive as she is. And now there's this weird thing with some stranger declaring he's going to marry her?" He shook his head. "I just wonder if it's all connected."

Rand was sure the attack and Chris's past were connected, but would the sheriff be able to prove it? "Maybe the sheriff will find who did it," he said, and opened the notebook. "Let's get started on these protocols."

The work went quickly. The notebook was arranged alphabetically, with one to two sheets of paper outlining the proper treatment for each condition, from asthma attacks to wound care. Rand recommended a few updates and places where they might review their training. "Have you dealt with all of these conditions in the field?" he asked after he had studied the page for transient ischemic attack.

"Most of them," Danny said. "I've seen everything from third-degree burns from a campfire to heat exhaustion and broken bones. We've dealt with heart attacks, seizures and head injuries—if it can happen to someone when they're away from home, we might be called upon to treat it in the field, or at least stabilize the person until we can transport them to an ambulance."

"It looks to me like you're up to date on everything." Rand shut the notebook. "I'm impressed."

"Thanks," Danny said. "We try to run a professional organization, but when you rely on one hundred percent volunteers, things can fall through the cracks." He shoved back his chair. "Thanks again for your help."

Rand was about to tell him he was glad to be involved when hard pounding on the door made him flinch. He and Danny exchanged looks, then hurried toward the entrance, where the pounding continued. Danny opened the door. "What's going on?" he asked.

A twentysomething man with disheveled dark hair to his shoulders and deep shadows beneath his eyes stood on the doorstep. He wore jeans faded to a soft shade of gray blue, an equally worn denim work shirt over a gray T-shirt and dirty straw sandals. "I need a doctor right away," he said.

"I'm a doctor." Rand stepped forward. "What's the problem?"

"It's not for me. It's for my sister." He clutched Rand's arm. "You have to come with me. Now."

"Let me call an ambulance." Danny pulled out his phone. "Where is your sister?"

"There isn't time for that," the man said. He struck out, sending Danny's phone flying.

"Hey!" Danny shouted.

"What's wrong with your sister?" Rand asked, trying to gain control of the situation.

"I think she's dying. You have to help her."

"An ambulance will help her more than I can," Rand said.

"No ambulance!" The man let go of Rand and stepped back. Rand thought he might leave, but instead, he pulled a pistol from beneath his shirt and pointed it at Rand. The end of the barrel was less than two feet from Rand's stomach. One twitch of the man's finger would inflict a wound Rand doubted he would survive. "Come with me now," the man ordered.

Chapter Nine

"Killing him won't save your sister," Danny said. Rand could see him out of the corner of his eye, his face as white as milk, the muscle beside his left eye twitching. But he kept his cool and spoke firmly.

"Don't think I won't shoot," the young man said. He shifted the pistol's aim to Danny. "You come too. You can help him."

"All right," Rand said. "We'll come with you." They'd look for an opportunity to overpower the young man. The odds were in their favor—two against one.

Still holding the gun, the man urged them toward a mostly powder blue sedan, which had been manufactured sometime in the 1980s, by Rand's best guess. As they approached, a second, larger man got out of the passenger seat and frowned at them. He was older than the first man but dressed similarly, his shirt a faded blue-and-white-checkered flannel; his shoes old house slippers, the suede worn shiny at the toes. He opened the back door, and Danny, with another wary glance at the gun, got in.

"You sit up front," the bigger man told Rand before joining Danny in the back seat. His voice was a reedy tenor, nasal and thin.

So much for two against one. Rand wondered if the second man was also armed, then decided he didn't want to find out. Instead, he focused on the driver, who shifted into gear with one hand, the other still holding the gun. "What's wrong with your sister?" he asked.

"She's having a baby," he said. "But something isn't right."

"What isn't right?"

"She's been in labor a long time, but nothing is happening."

"How long?"

The younger man hunched over the steering wheel, the barrel of the gun balanced on top. "Two days. A little longer."

"How advanced is her pregnancy?" Rand asked. "Has she lost much blood? How is the baby presented?"

"I don't know! Stop asking questions. You'll find out everything when you see her."

"Where are you taking us?" Danny asked.

"You'll find that out soon enough too."

Rand was aware of his phone in the back pocket of his jeans. Could he get his hand back there and dial 911? He shifted and slowly moved his hand back.

A meaty fist wrapped around his bicep. "I'll take the phone," the bigger man said.

When Rand didn't respond, the man squeezed harder, a jolt of pain traveling to the tips of Rand's fingers. Reluctantly, he surrendered the phone.

The car turned away from town and down a county road, which, after a couple of miles, narrowed and became an unpaved forest service road. Realization washed over Rand. "You're with the Vine, aren't you?" he asked.

"Who told you that?" the man from the back seat asked.

He had released his hold on Rand but sat forward, within easy striking distance.

"I heard you had moved your camp to the woods," Rand said. He studied the driver more closely. Were these two the ones who had attacked him and Chris last night? Nothing about them looked familiar, but Rand hadn't gotten a look at whoever had hit him in the darkness.

Another turn onto an even narrower dirt lane brought them to a cluster of trailers and tents parked among the trees—everything from a battered Airstream to a truck camper up on blocks, old canvas tents, new nylon structures and even a large tepee. The driver stopped the car, and his companion got out and took hold of Rand's arm. "This way," he said.

People emerged from the various dwellings to stare as the two men led Danny and Rand past—men and women, many young, none older than middle age. Rand counted eight children and a couple of teens among them.

The driver stopped at a set of wooden steps that led into the back of a box truck. A door had been cut into the back panel of the box. "My sister is in here," the driver said, and pulled open the door.

The first thing that struck Rand was the smell—body odor and urine, but above that, the slightly sour, metallic scent of blood. The aroma plunged him back to the battlefield, trying to tend to soldiers who were bleeding out. He blinked, letting his eyes adjust to the dimness. The only light in the windowless space emanated from an LED camping lantern suspended from the ceiling. The woman was lying on a pallet in the middle of the floor, dark hair spread out around a narrow face bleached as white as the pillowcase, the swell of her pregnant belly mounding the sheets. A girl knelt beside her, laying a damp cloth on the woman's forehead. The girl couldn't have been more than nine or ten, with long dark hair and eyes that looked up at Rand with desperate pleading.

Three other people—two women and a man—were gathered around the pallet. They studied Rand and Danny with suspicion. "Who are they?" the man—blond and stocky, with thinning hair—asked.

"He's a doctor." The driver nudged Rand. "Go on."

Rand knelt beside the pallet. The girl started to get up and move, but Rand motioned her to stay. "It's all right," he said. "I might need your help." He wouldn't ordinarily ask a child to assist him, but this girl seemed calmer and more willing than the others in the room.

The woman on the pallet was so still that he thought at first she might already be dead. He took her wrist and tried to find a pulse. It was there. Weak and irregular. He looked up at her brother. "I can examine her, but I can tell you already, she needs an ambulance."

"Examine her. There must be something you can do," the driver said.

Danny knelt on the other side of the pallet "Is the baby's father here?" he asked.

The others in the room exchanged a look Rand couldn't interpret. "He isn't here," the stocky man said after a tense moment.

"I'm going to examine her," Rand told Danny. "Help me get her into position."

The woman was almost completely unresponsive, only moaning slightly when Danny moved her legs. The girl took the young woman's hand and held it. Rand used the sheets to form a drape around her and examined the woman and her unborn child as best he could. The situation wasn't pretty. The woman had lost a lot of blood, and the child was wedged firmly in her narrow pelvis. Without a stethoscope, he couldn't tell if the child was even alive.

He covered the woman again and stood. "Whoever is responsible for leaving her in this state and not calling for help should be shot," he said. "I think the baby is dead, and she will be, too, soon, unless you call an ambulance."

"No ambulance," the stocky man said.

The door opened, bringing in a rush of fresh air. The others in the truck rose to their feet or, if already standing, stood up straighter. Rand turned to see Jedediah moving toward him, followed by several other men and women, some of whom Rand remembered from the day of the fire.

"Thank you for coming," the woman's brother said to Jedediah. He sounded close to tears.

"I've come as an emissary from the Exalted," Jedediah said. He looked down at the woman, who now moaned almost continuously and moved her head from side to side, eyes closed. "He is sorry to hear our sister is troubled."

"She's not troubled. She's going to die if you don't get her to a hospital right away," Rand said. She would probably still die, he thought. But at least in a medical facility, she had a chance.

"Silence!" Jedediah clamped down on Rand's shoulder, fingers digging in painfully. Rand shook him off. If the man touched him again, he would fight back.

Jedediah held up a palm, and everyone fell silent. He knelt and took the woman's hand in his own. "Sister, the Exalted sends his strength to you," he said. "Strength to deliver this child. You need not rely on your own frailties, but on his power."

The others in the room murmured some kind of affirmation. Rand looked on in disgust. Danny didn't look any happier than he did. Jedediah stood and turned to Rand. He smiled and stared into Rand's eyes with an expression Rand read as a threat. "I'm confident you can heal her," Jedediah said. "Tell us what you need, and we will bring it to you."

"She needs to be in the hospital."

"We don't need a hospital. We take care of our own. It's up to you to help her."

CHRIS TIMED DINNER to be ready at seven. When Rand still hadn't shown up, she turned off the heat under the mushrooms and told herself he had probably gotten involved in something at SAR headquarters. By seven thirty, she debated texting him, but she decided that would be out of line. He didn't owe her any explanations for how he spent his time. She fixed a plate for herself and set aside the leftovers to reheat when he came in.

By nine o'clock, she was truly worried. Rand hadn't struck her as the type to disappear without letting her know what was going on. She texted him Everything OK?

No reply. She stared at the phone screen. He had said he was meeting Danny, right? She sent a quick text to Danny. Is Rand with you?

No reply. A chill shuddered through her, even as she tried to tell herself there was a logical explanation for the failure of both men to reply. Maybe they had decided to go out after finishing up at headquarters, and time had gotten away from them. She hesitated, then looked up the number for Carrie Andrews, Danny's partner and fellow search and rescue volunteer.

"Chris? What's up?" Carrie answered right away as if she had been waiting for a call.

"Is Danny there?" Chris asked.

"No. He was meeting Rand at SAR headquarters and

was supposed to be back by seven or so. I've been trying to reach him, but he's not answering his phone."

Chris's stomach clenched. "I've been trying to reach Rand. He's not answering either."

"I was going to drive over to headquarters and see if their cars are in the parking lot," Carrie said. "But I can't get hold of my mom to watch the kids, and I don't want to upset them."

"I'll go over there," Chris said, already pocketing the Jeep keys.

"Let me know what you find."

Chris had never realized how isolated the search and rescue headquarters building was before. Almost as soon as she turned onto the road leading up to the building, she left behind the lights of houses. She gripped the steering wheel tightly and checked her mirrors every few seconds to see if she was being followed. Relief momentarily relaxed her when she turned into the parking lot and spotted Rand's and Danny's vehicles side by side near the door. They must have become so engrossed in their work they had lost track of time.

She parked and hurried to the door, Harley at her heels. The security light flickered on at their approach. She grasped the knob, but the door was locked. "Hey, open up in there!" she called, and pounded on the door. No answer. She tried phoning Rand again. No answer. Next, she punched in Danny's number. He wasn't answering, either, but she could hear a phone ringing somewhere just on the other side of the door.

The phone stopped ringing, and she heard the electronic message telling her she had been redirected to a voice mailbox.

She ended the call, and almost immediately, her phone

rang. Carrie's voice was thin with worry. "Are you there? Did you find them?"

"Their cars are here, but no one is answering my knock," Chris said.

"Something's happened to them," Carrie said. "I'm going to call the sheriff."

"Do that," Chris said. "Tell them I'll wait for them here." She ended the call. Maybe she and Carrie were overreacting, but she didn't think so. Something was wrong. The knowledge tightened her gut and made her cold all over.

She waited twenty minutes, she and Harley sitting in her car with the doors locked, phone in hand, willing Rand to call. When headlights illuminated the lot, she sat up straighter. The Rayford County Sheriff's Department SUV swung in behind her, and Deputy Ryker Vernon got out. Chris went to meet him. "Hello, Chris," he said. "What's going on?"

"Rand Martin and Danny Irwin were supposed to meet here this afternoon about five o'clock," she said. "Their vehicles are here, but the door is locked and no one is answering my knock or my calls."

"What makes you think they didn't just go off with friends for a drink or something?" Ryker asked.

"Carrie was expecting Danny home. The last time I spoke with Rand, he said he would be home about six thirty. He's not answering his phone. It's not like either of them to disappear like this."

Ryker nodded. "Do you have any reason to suspect someone harmed them?"

"Rand was attacked outside my apartment last night," she said. "Maybe that person—or *persons*—came after him here."

A second vehicle pulled into the lot. Ryker and Chris

watched as the black-and-white SUV parked next to Ryker's cruiser. Deputy Jake Gwynn got out. "I heard the call for assistance here at headquarters and came to assist," he said. "I have a key to the building."

"Let's go inside and see what we find," Ryker said. He turned to Chris. "You wait out here."

She wanted to protest but only nodded. While they unlocked the door and went inside, she hugged her arms across her chest and paced beside her car. How could Ryker and Jake be so calm? Sure, she was known to be cool during a search and rescue emergency, but those situations rarely involved anyone she knew. But Rand and Danny were friends, both fit, capable men who wouldn't be pushovers. If something had happened to them, she couldn't help thinking it would be bad.

The deputies emerged from the building and Jake relocked the door. "There's no one in there," Ryker said. "But we found Danny's phone on the floor near the door. He must have dropped it."

"Are you sure Rand didn't have to report back to the hospital?" Jake asked. "Or maybe he's visiting a friend?"

She shook her head. "He wouldn't go back to work without his car. You need to talk to the members of the Vine. Someone told me they're camped out past County Road 14."

"Do you think they had something to do with Rand and Danny?" Jake asked.

"I'm sure they were the ones who attacked Rand and then me last night," she said. "I can't prove it, but I'm sure of it. Maybe they came back for Rand tonight."

"Why would they do that?" Ryker asked.

"To get back at me?" She shook her head. "I don't know. But please, go talk to them. Rand and Danny might be with them now."

"It wouldn't hurt to go out there," Jake said. "But there's a good chance we're wasting time."

"Do you have a better idea of where to look?" Chris asked.

Ryker pocketed his notebook. "We'll drive out there and take a look," he said. "You go home. We'll be in touch."

"I'm staying at Rand's place," she admitted. "My apartment needs the doors and locks replaced."

"Go there, then," Jake said. "We'll let you know what we find."

They returned to their vehicles and she to hers. The deputies waited for her to drive away, then followed her back toward town. They turned off toward County Road 14 while she continued toward Rand's place. She didn't like the idea of returning to the unfamiliar house alone. At least Harley would be there with her.

And what if Ryker and Jake didn't find Rand and Danny with the Vine? What if someone else had taken them or they had left for some other reason? She might have wasted the deputies' time and put the two men in further danger.

"WE DON'T HAVE proper medical equipment or medications," Rand protested. "We can't help this woman without the right tools."

"We're very good at making do," Jedediah said. "Tell us what you need, and we'll supply a reasonable substitute."

Which was how Rand and Danny found themselves minutes later with a stack of clean towels, a selection of sharp knives, a sewing kit, a bar of soap, and a bottle of what looked and smelled like grain alcohol. "I'm not going to perform surgery without anesthesia," Rand said.

"If you don't operate, she's going to die anyway," Danny said softly. The two huddled over their patient, having sent everyone else to wait either outside or against the far wall. Jedediah had left, but the patient's brother stood nearby, the gun tucked into the front of his jeans, quickly accessible if he decided he needed to use it again.

The two men knelt beside the woman, and Rand once more assessed her condition, which he could only classify as poor. She was barely conscious and mostly unresponsive, her pulse faint. She needed an emergency C-section, and even then her chances of survival were slim. But he couldn't do nothing and watch her die. "I can try to turn the baby," Rand said. "Let's see if we can revive her enough to help us." He looked up at her brother. "What's her name?"

"Lana," the man said.

"Get down here and talk to her," Rand said.

The brother shook his head and backed away. Exasperated, Rand looked across at the girl, who hadn't spoken and had scarcely moved since he and Danny entered the truck. "What's your name?" he asked.

"Serena."

"Serena, is Lana a relative of yours?"

The girl shook her head.

"Then why are you here?" Danny asked.

"It's my job to help the healer."

Rand would have told whoever was in charge that this was no place for a child so young, but since Serena was already here, he asked if she would hold Lana's hand and talk to her while he and Danny worked. "She may be able to hear you, even if she doesn't respond," he explained.

Serena nodded. "All right."

Rand looked back at one of the older women against the wall. "I need some ammonia."

"Ammonia?" She looked puzzled.

"The cleaning fluid. You must have some somewhere."

"I'll see what I can find."

Lana's brother moved a little closer, though he didn't kneel beside the pallet. "What's your name?" Danny asked.

"Robert."

"Why did you wait so long to go for help?" Rand asked as he busied himself with cleaning his hands and drying them on one of the towels.

Robert shoved his fingers through his lank hair. "We don't believe in doctors," he said. "We're supposed to trust in the Exalted."

"Are you going to be in trouble for bringing us here?" Danny asked.

Robert shrugged. "Maybe. Probably. Can you help her?"

"We're going to try," Rand said. "But it may be too late."

"Here." The woman returned and thrust a plastic bottle filled with yellow liquid at Rand.

He twisted off the cap and sniffed, his eyes watering. It was ammonia, all right. He poured some on a cloth and held it under Lana's nose. She moaned and turned her head away. "Lana, wake up," he said. "Open your eyes and look at me, please."

Her eyes flickered open, and she stared up at him. Her eyes were dark brown, fringed with long dark lashes. She was probably beautiful when she was feeling better. "My name is Rand," he said. "I'm a doctor, and I'm going to try to help you. I need to try to turn the baby. When I tell you, you need to push."

She nodded. Rand looked at Serena. "Talk to her. Encourage her."

Serena leaned close and whispered to Lana. Rand couldn't hear what she said, and he didn't care. Her job was to try to calm and distract Lana, if that was even possible, given her condition. He nodded to Danny, and the two of them moved down to tackle the dilemma of somehow delivering this baby. Rand was searching for some way to lubricate his hands when the door to the trailer opened, a woman's strident protests breaking the tense silence. "You can't go in there—"

Rand turned to see what the commotion was about just as two Rayford County sheriff's deputies stepped in. "Rand?" one of the deputies asked.

As the officers moved closer, Rand recognized Jake Gwynn. "We need a medical helicopter," he said. "Right away."

"I'll make the call," the other deputy said, and stepped out of the trailer.

Jake took in the woman on the pallet and the people gathered around her. "Are you and Danny okay?" he asked.

"We're fine, but this woman needs emergency surgery."

"No surgery." The older woman who had fetched the ammonia stepped between Rand and Lana. "No hospital. The Exalted forbids it."

"Then if she dies, I'll be happy to testify in the Exalted's murder trial." Rand stood.

Robert stood also. There was no sign of the gun now, and he moved toward the door. Jake moved to intercept him. "You need to stay here," he said.

The other deputy returned. "This is Ryker Vernon," Jake said. "What happened?"

"Two men grabbed us outside search and rescue headquarters," Danny said. "They forced us to come here to help this woman."

The four men looked down at Lana, who lay still, her breathing slow and labored. "They should have called for help hours ago," Rand said.

"They forced you to come here?" Ryker asked.

"They had a gun," Danny said.

"The Exalted had nothing to do with that," the older woman said. "He forbids the use of violence."

"Apparently, he also forbids outside help, even for a medical emergency," Rand said.

"I think we need to talk to this Exalted person," Jake said. "Where can we find him?"

"I have no idea," Rand said. "I've only spoken to his representative, a man named Jedediah." He turned to Danny. "Let's get Lana ready for transport."

They were making Lana as comfortable as possible when an approaching siren signaled the arrival of the ambulance. Moments later, two paramedics pushed into the trailer, ignoring the orders to stop from some of the onlookers. The first paramedic to enter, a burly fortysomething with close-cropped gray hair, surveyed the room. "We need to get this crowd out of here so we can work."

"You heard the man," Jake said. "Everybody out."

When no one moved, Jake and Ryker began taking hold of people and escorting them out.

Rand introduced himself and Danny and provided what medical information he had been able to assess, then stepped back to allow the paramedics to take over. By the time he heard the distant throb of a helicopter over the camp, they had started an IV line and fitted Lana with an oxygen mask and various equipment to monitor her vitals. The deputies were still outside, presumably dealing with the other campers. Jedediah didn't make an appearance, and Robert and his fellow kidnapper had disappeared. Serena was gone, too, pulled away by one of the women as the paramedics started their work.

Rand and Danny followed the stretcher out of the trailer and watched as Lana was loaded into the ambulance. She

would be driven to the cleared area that had been designated as a landing spot for the helicopter, then rushed to
the hospital.

Jake joined Rand and Danny as the ambulance pulled
away. "Can you identify the men who kidnapped you?" he
asked.

"I can." The crowd of onlookers was mostly moving away
now, presumably to the trailers and tents scattered among
the trees, their faces indistinguishable in the darkness. "My
guess is you won't find them here tonight."

"Give us a description, and we'll conduct a search."

Danny and Rand each described what they knew about
the two men who had waylaid them and also provided what
they knew about Jedediah.

"How did you know where to find us?" Danny asked
when that was done.

"Chris went to SAR headquarters to look for you and
found the place locked up tight," Ryker said. "Both your
cars were there, and we found your phone on the ground.
Carrie called 911 and reported you missing. Chris said she
thought the persons who attacked the two of you last night
were from the Vine and that they might have gone after
you again tonight."

"These men didn't hurt us," Rand said.

"One of them was the woman's brother," Danny said. "I
don't think he would have harmed us. I think he was desperate to help his sister."

"Threatening someone with a gun and forcing them to go
somewhere against their will is still a crime," Ryker said.

"Let's get you out of here," Jake said.

Rand and Danny shared the back seat of Jake's SUV for
the ride to search and rescue headquarters. Neither spoke.
Rand was exhausted. The sight of Lana, struggling to stay

alive while he was helpless to do anything, would remain with him for a long time. If the Exalted and his followers were willing to sacrifice one of their own for the sake of their misguided beliefs, he could believe they wouldn't hesitate to break laws in order to obey their leader's command to bring a former member back into the fold.

Chapter Ten

Fifteen years ago

Chris, drowsing under the covers in her bunk bed in her family's trailer at the Vine's camp, woke to raised voices. She pulled back the curtain over the bunk and peered toward the glow of light from the other end of the small trailer. Her father sounded angry about something.

"I'm going to talk to him. This isn't right."

"He's made up his mind," her mother said. "You'll never get anywhere arguing with him."

"There must be some misunderstanding. Jedediah got the message wrong. The Exalted has children—daughters. Would he want one of them married off when she's only twelve? Not to mention he already has a wife his age. It's just sick."

"Lower your voice." Mom sounded afraid. "You don't want to let anyone hear you say that."

"It's not right, you know that."

"I know. But what are we going to do? He owns this trailer. He owns everything we have."

"You don't have to remind me," her father said. "I was the one foolish enough to turn everything over to him."

"You weren't foolish. You believed in the message. We're supposed to share with each other. No one has more than anyone else."

"I still believe that. But not if it means giving him my daughter. I'll talk to him. I'm sure I can make him understand."

"What if he won't listen to you?" her mother asked.

"He will. He has to."

More conversation, but too soft for Chris to hear. A few moments later, the door to the trailer opened and closed. Chris waited but heard nothing more. Finally, she slipped out of bed and padded on bare feet to the front of the trailer. Her mother sat on the edge of the sofa, head in her hands. Was she crying?

Chris hurried to her. "What's wrong?" she asked. "Where is Daddy?" She didn't call him *Daddy* much anymore. It sounded too babyish. But she was too scared to worry about that now.

Her mother pulled her close, arms squeezing her tight. "It's okay," she said, and wiped her eyes with her fingers.

"Where did Daddy go?" Chris asked.

Her mother sniffed. "He went to talk to the Exalted."

"About me?"

Her mother hesitated, then nodded. "Yes." She pulled Chris into her lap even though Chris was too big for that; her feet almost touched the floor when she sat on her mother's lap.

"Helen says there's going to be a wedding soon," Chris said. "That I'll be a bride and wear a white dress and have a big party just for me."

Her mother studied her, deep lines across her forehead. "Do you know what it means to be a bride?" she asked.

Chris thought for a moment. "Helen says I have to live

with the Exalted and do what he tells me." Then she said something she had never dared say before: "I don't want to live with him."

Her mother hugged her tightly again. "Maybe your father can talk him into waiting until you're a little older," she said.

Chris didn't think that when she was older she would want to marry the Exalted, either, but she didn't say anything. "You should go back to bed," her mother said. "It's not even six o'clock yet."

"I'm awake," Chris said. "And hungry. Can I have breakfast?"

Her mother made breakfast; then they both dressed and Chris helped her mother clean house, which didn't take long because the trailer was small and they didn't have much stuff. Mom tried to be extra cheerful, but she kept glancing out the window. "Shouldn't Dad be back by now?" Chris asked after a couple of hours.

"The Exalted probably sent him to do some work," Mom said. Everyone in the Vine was expected to pitch in. For the men, that often meant building things, cutting trees, or digging ditches, latrines or garden beds.

Chris did her lessons. Children in the Vine didn't go to school. Instead, the parents taught them. Some children didn't have to learn anything at all, but Chris's parents made her read and study math, reading, geography, history and science every day. She didn't mind so much. Most of the time the lessons were interesting, and she usually found them easy.

Her mother got out a quilt she was working on, but often, when Chris looked up from her schoolwork, she found her mother staring out the front window, her hands idle.

They ate lunch without Dad. By three o'clock, her mother could hardly sit still. She put away her quilting. "I'm going to look for your father," she said. "Lock the door behind me, and don't let anyone in unless it's me or your dad. Do you understand?"

Chris nodded. "What am I supposed to tell anyone who comes by?"

"Don't tell them anything," Mom said. "Stay quiet and let them think no one is home."

Chris wanted to ask what her mother was afraid of, but she didn't. Instead, she turned the lock after her mother was gone and sat on the sofa to wait.

She was back in half an hour. "Jedediah told me your father left the Exalted's home this morning with some other men. They went into the woods to pick mushrooms."

"Isn't it the wrong time of year for mushrooms?" Chris asked. Always before, they had looked for mushrooms in the spring and fall, when they would pop up after wet weather. Now it was midsummer, warm and dry.

"Maybe this was a different kind of mushroom," her mother said. "Or someone found some by a spring or something. Come, help me peel potatoes. We'll make a special dinner. Maybe we'll even make a cake."

Making the cake, and the potatoes and vegetables and meat loaf, took a while, but six o'clock—the hour they usually ate supper—passed with no sign of her father. Her mother filled a plate and told Chris to sit down at the table and eat it, but Chris only stared at the food, her stomach too queasy for her to even think of putting anything into her mouth.

A little before nine o'clock, they heard voices outside. Mom rushed to the door, then, with a cry, opened it to admit Jedediah and a man Chris didn't know. Between them, they carried her father, his face gray, his hair and clothes wet.

"He ate some of the mushrooms he found," Jedediah said. "I think they must have been poisonous."

They carried her father past Chris to her parents' bed at the back of the trailer. Mom hurried after them. Chris tried to follow, but Jedediah shut the door in her face.

A few minutes later, the door opened again and the two men emerged. "What's going on?" Chris asked.

"We're going to fetch the healing woman," the man she didn't know said. Jedediah only scowled at her.

When they were gone, Chris went to the bedroom door and knocked. "Mom?" she called.

"You can't come in," her mother called. "Go to your room and wait for me."

Chris didn't really have a room, just a bunk bed with a curtain to separate it from the rest of the trailer. Not knowing what else to do, she went there and sat. She switched on the light her father had fixed up for her and took her sketchbook from the lidded box at the end of the bed that he had made for her art supplies. She turned to a fresh page and began to draw. When she started, she had no idea what she would sketch, but after a few moments, the figure of a man took shape. The Exalted, but not the beautiful, caring figure people often praised. This was the Exalted with his mouth twisted in a sneer, his eyes glaring, deep lines marring his forehead and running alongside his mouth. Instead of an angel, this man was a demon.

After a while, Chris began to get sleepy. She drifted off and woke up much later to an old woman shaking her— Elizabeth, one of the healers. "Come and say goodbye to your father," she said.

"Where is he going?" Chris asked. She glanced over at the sketchbook and was relieved to see she had remembered to close it before she fell asleep.

"He is going to his reward," Elizabeth said. "He ate poison, and there is nothing I can do for him."

Chris began to cry, then to wail. Elizabeth shook her. "Quiet!" she ordered. "He's going to a better place. There's no reason for you to be sad."

Even at twelve, Chris knew that was one of the most ridiculous things anyone had ever said. He was her father. He belonged here with her. There was no better place.

But she fell silent and allowed Elizabeth to lead her into her parents' bedroom. Her mother held out her hand. Chris took it, and her mother pulled her close. She stared at her father, who lay with his eyes closed, his skin that awful gray, his face all hollows. He didn't even look like himself. "Give him a kiss," Elizabeth commanded.

Chris shook her head and buried her face in her mother's shoulder. "It's all right," her mother murmured. "You're safe here with me."

No one said anything else. Chris heard movement, and when she looked up again, she and her mother were alone with her father. "Where did they all go?" Chris whispered.

Her mother had to try a couple of times before she could speak. "They went to prepare for...for the funeral," she said.

Chris looked at her father. He didn't look any different to her. "Is he...dead?" she asked.

"Yes," her mother said. "He's gone." Then she started to cry. Chris cried, too, grateful there was no one to tell them it was wrong to do so.

Everything about the next few days was a blur. They buried her father in the woods the next morning, his body wrapped in a bedsheet and lowered into a deep hole, far away from camp. Everyone came and gathered around the little grave, and when they were all assembled, the Exalted arrived. The crowd parted to allow him to draw close. He was dressed all in white, his hair and face shining. He smiled as if this was a happy occasion, and he talked about what a good man her father was and how he had moved on to a better place than this.

When he finished speaking, men with shovels moved forward and began to fill in the grave. The scent of fresh earth filled Chris's nose, and she began to sob again.

A hand rested on her shoulder, heavy and warm. She looked up and stared into the Exalted's eyes. "Your father is gone," he said. "I will be your father now. I will be your brother and uncle. And your husband. Soon." He smiled, but Chris could only shiver.

Chris knew then that she didn't like the Exalted, no matter how wonderful people said he was. But she kept that knowledge to herself. She was pretty sure if she said something like that out loud, she would be struck by lightning or something worse. If she was the only one who thought someone was bad when everyone said he was good, there must be something wrong with her.

Her mother was much quieter after that. Sad.

Three days later, Helen came to their trailer. "It's time to measure Elita for her wedding dress," she said.

Her mother's face paled. "So soon?"

"Now that your husband is gone, the Exalted believes it's even more important that he take Elita under his wing." Helen pulled out a tape measure. "Fetch a chair for her to stand on."

Her mother brought a chair from the kitchen table. "Shouldn't there be a period of mourning?" she asked as she helped Chris to stand on the chair.

"Mourning won't bring back the dead." Helen wrapped the tape measure around Chris's chest, over the gentle swelling her mother had told her would one day be breasts. "Better to focus on the joy of this occasion."

Neither Chris nor her mother said anything after Helen left. What was there to say? No one disobeyed the Exalted. It would be like disobeying God. The next day, her mother worked at the farmers market stand the Vine operated at the fairgrounds. She came home later than usual. "Something terrible has happened," she said. "Someone stole the money from our booth. The cash box was there one moment, and then it was gone."

"Was there a lot of money in it?" Chris asked.

"Several hundred dollars. Jedediah is very upset." Jedediah was the treasurer for the Vine, in charge of all the money the group earned from selling crafts, produce, firewood and anything else. All the money went to Jedediah, who doled it out as needed.

Not long after Chris's mother had set supper on the table, someone pounded on the door, hard enough to make the trailer shake. Mom opened it, and Jedediah and a trio of men filled the small front room. "We need to search this place," Jedediah said.

"What for?" Mom asked.

"We're looking for the money that was stolen. We're searching the homes of everyone who worked that booth today."

Was he accusing her mother of being a thief? Chris expected her mother to be upset about this. Instead, she stepped back and bowed her head. "Of course," she said. "I have nothing to hide."

For the next hour, the four men searched every inch of the trailer. They emptied all the clothing from the dresser and dumped all Chris's art supplies on the bed. She thought of the picture of the Exalted—the devil picture—in her sketchbook. When they found it, would they punish her? But they only flipped through the book, paying no attention to the drawings. They took the food from the refrigerator and opened every jar and bottle as if they expected to find coins and bills instead of mayonnaise and ketchup.

All they found was five dollars and forty-two cents in change in an old pickle jar. Members of the Vine were allowed to keep this change when they sold cans they picked up on the side of the highway, so Jedediah reluctantly set the jar back on the dresser. "There's nothing here," he said at last, and the men left.

Mom sank into a chair. She looked very pale, but when she saw Chris watching her, she forced a smile. "That was upsetting, but it's over now," she said. "There's nothing for you to worry about. Why don't you get ready for bed?"

Chris started to point out that it was an hour before her bedtime but thought better of it. She washed her face and hands, then put on her pajamas and crawled under the covers. Her mother kissed her forehead and pulled the curtain over the bunk. Within minutes, Chris was asleep.

It was still dark when she woke again. Her mother sat on the edge of the bunk. "Get dressed," Mom said. "We're going to leave now." She handed Chris a pair of jeans and a T-shirt. "I packed a bag for us. I put in as many of your art supplies as I could, but we can't take everything."

"Where are we going?" Chris asked, pulling off her pajamas and sliding into the jeans.

"We're leaving the Vine," her mother said. "And we're never coming back."

Chapter Eleven

If Chris was upset about what had happened to Rand and Danny, she kept her feelings hidden. She was clearly relieved Rand was all right, but when he thanked her for alerting the sheriff's deputies to what must have happened to them, she dismissed his thanks. "It was a lucky guess," she said. "I'm glad it worked out."

"Why were they so set against calling in medical help for that woman?" he asked. "Is it because they don't believe in medicine? Or they think it's some kind of spiritual weakness to rely on doctors?"

"It's mostly because they don't want outsiders coming into the camp," she said. "We were always told we didn't need anyone but each other and the Exalted."

"Because outsiders might see something illegal they shouldn't see?" Rand asked.

She blew out a breath. "I don't know. I was taught—all the kids were—that outsiders were dangerous. That they would take us away from our families and sell us to people who would do bad things to us. For the first few months after Mom and I left the Vine, I was terrified to let her out of my sight or to talk to anyone."

"The woman I tried to help, Lana, looked younger than

you—maybe not even out of her teens. I wonder if you knew her."

"I've been away for a long time," she said. "I doubt I know any of the current members. I don't remember anyone called Lana."

"Jedediah is still there," Rand said. "There are probably others you knew who are still with the group."

"Maybe I would know their names," she said. "But I don't know them. I never did."

Her tone was defiant, her expression fierce. When she turned away, he didn't press her. He knew plenty of soldiers who refused to discuss things that had happened during their military service. Maybe it was the same for survivors of cults.

Three days after Rand returned home, Sheriff Travis Walker and Deputy Ryker Vernon came to Rand's house at four thirty, shortly after he arrived home after a shift at the hospital. "We wanted to bring you up to date on a few things," Travis said after Rand had welcomed the lawmen inside.

Chris came in from the kitchen and stopped short. "Oh, hello." She glanced at Rand. "Is something wrong?"

"We just have some updates," Travis said. "For both of you. Sit down, please."

They sat—Rand on the sofa and Chris in a chair facing him. "First of all, I'm sorry to tell you that Lana and her baby died," Travis said.

"Yes, I know," Rand said. "I had a colleague track her down for me."

Chris turned to him. "You didn't tell me."

"I didn't want to upset you," he said.

Chris studied her hands, knotted in her lap. "It's just such a sad story."

"We searched the camp for her brother and the other man you described," Ryker said. "We were told they had been banished."

"Did you look for any fresh graves in the woods?" Chris asked.

Rand felt the shock of her words. "You think they were murdered?" he asked.

She looked as if she regretted saying anything.

"Why graves?" Travis prompted.

She shifted in her chair. "I don't have any proof, but other people who did things the Exalted didn't like had a way of disappearing or meeting with accidents or sudden illness."

"Your father," Travis said.

"Yes. And there were others. Anyone who complained too much or spread what the Exalted deemed to be 'radical ideas,' and certainly anyone who opposed the Exalted, was soon gone, and everyone else was forbidden to even say their names."

"We'll continue searching for the two men," Travis said.

"What about this guy who calls himself the Exalted, Edmund Harrison?" Rand asked. "His refusal to allow anyone to summon outside help is the reason Lana died."

Travis's expression tightened. "Harrison denies having that policy, and no one would admit otherwise when we spoke with them," he said. "We researched his history, and he has no criminal record."

"The official story is that Lana herself refused help and that her brother went to fetch help against her wishes," Ryker said.

"The Exalted has brainwashed everyone to see outsiders as the enemy," Chris said. "If you bring anyone from outside into the group, you risk having families torn apart, horrible diseases inflicted on the group by way of things like vaccinations and medications, children forced to attend public schools, et cetera. If there's a bogeyman the Exalted and his enforcers can conjure to keep people obedient, he's happy to preach about it until fear is as much a part of them as breathing."

"He says they have no record of you ever being a member of his group, and he doesn't understand why you would be so fixated on them," Travis said.

Color flooded her face. "I'm not lying. My parents were members of the Vine, and we lived with them for seven years. And you were there the day Jedediah came up to me and said it was time for me to marry the Exalted."

"Edmund Harrison says you misunderstood," Travis said.

The lines around her mouth tightened. "There was no misunderstanding."

"Has he made any more threats against you?" Travis asked.

"He doesn't know where I am right now," she said. "But once he does, he'll send someone after me."

"Why is he so focused on you?" Ryker asked.

"No one defies him," she said. "My mother and I did. He's like a spoiled child that way. Deny him something and he's going to do everything he can to get it." She smoothed her hand down the tattoos on her left arm. "But he doesn't want me, really. He just wants to punish me. Maybe make an example of me."

"We interviewed him," Travis said. "By Zoom. He is supposedly in Texas right now—on business, he said. He denies knowing you. Denies having more than one wife. Denies keeping anyone in the group against their will."

"I'm sure he told you the group is all about peace, love and free will," she said.

"That's about it," Ryker agreed.

"Harrison told us the group planned to leave Colorado and move on to Oklahoma," Travis said. "When we returned to the camp yesterday, everyone was gone. They didn't leave one piece of trash or so much as a food scrap behind."

"Where did they go?" Rand asked.

"We don't know," Travis said. "They may have decided they were getting too much attention from law enforcement."

"They're probably putting as much distance between us and them as possible," Ryker added.

Chris said nothing, though Rand felt the tension radiating off her. "Is there anything else you think we need to know?" Travis asked.

"Don't believe it when they tell you they're just a close-knit community of nature lovers," Chris said. "And I don't think they've left the area."

"We'll keep our eyes and ears open," Travis said. "Let us know if you hear anything."

Ryker and Travis left. Chris stared out the front window after them, then began to pace. "The sheriff doesn't believe me," she said. "He thinks I'm making up a story to get attention or something."

"He didn't say that," Rand said. "I think he's trying to look at the case from every angle." He moved in beside her and put his hand on her shoulder. "I believe you."

She wouldn't look at him. She held herself rigid, jaw tight, as if fighting for control. "I feel like I'm waiting for something to happen," she said after a long silence. "Something bad."

"You believe they're still here," Rand said.

"They've been pursuing me for fifteen years," she said. "Why leave when they've gotten this close?"

He nodded. While some might dismiss Chris's protests,

his experience with the ruthlessness of his sister's cult made him inclined to believe her. He wanted to put his arm around her and try to comfort her, but he wasn't sure she would be receptive. "What can I do?" he asked instead.

She pressed her lips together, arms crossed, shoulders hunched. Then she raised her eyes to his. "Tell me about your sister," she said.

CHRIS SAT ON the sofa and patted the cushion next to her. She needed a distraction to pull her out of the worry cycle she was in. "I want to hear about her, if you don't mind talking about it," she said.

Rand sat, the cushion compressing under his weight, shifting her toward him. He leaned forward, hands clasped, elbows on knees. "I haven't talked about Teri in a long time," he said. "But I'd like to tell you."

Chris let out a breath, some of the tension easing. She had been afraid he would shut her down—as she herself might have done in his shoes. "She was younger than you?"

"Yes. Nineteen. I was completing my first tour in Afghanistan when she met this group of people. At a local coffee shop, she said. They approached her table and asked if they could sit down. The place was crowded, so she said yes. They fell into conversation and apparently talked for hours. They introduced themselves as volunteers, working on a project to help the poor in the area. Teri always had a soft heart and wanted to help people. They picked up on that right away and used her sympathy to reel her in."

"The Vine taught the same technique," Chris said. "Identify what you have in common with the person, what they are concerned about or appear to need, and play up that connection."

"There was a guy in the group—Mark or Mike or Mitch,

I never did learn his real name. In the group, he was known as Starfire. They all had names like that—Rainbow and Cloud, Surfer and Starfire. The next thing I heard, Teri was calling herself Aurora. She quit school and moved out of the dorm and into a camper van with Starfire, and then the group left town. My parents were frantic when they contacted me, hoping I had heard from her. But I hadn't heard a thing."

"What did you do?"

"There was nothing I could do. I was in a field hospital in a war zone. I couldn't leave. My parents contacted the police but were told if Teri left of her own free will, there wasn't anything they could do. Mom and Dad had a couple of phone calls from her saying she was fine and they didn't need to worry, and that was it."

"We had people join the Vine who left families behind," Chris said. "I never thought much about the anguish those parents must have felt. And their brothers and sisters."

"One day Teri was with us, then she was gone, with a group of people we didn't know anything about. On one hand, I understood what the police were telling us. An adult has the right to make her own decisions. But putting together what I learned when I researched online and what I heard from my parents, the group felt wrong to me."

"What did you find out online?" she asked.

"Mostly there were postings on various websites from relatives who were desperate to get in touch with their missing children or siblings. A few complaints from businesses in areas where the group had stayed, alleging that members had stolen items or harassed customers."

"What was the name of the group?"

"They called themselves Atlantis or the Seekers."

Chris shook her head. "I haven't heard of them, but most

people have never heard of the Vine either. These groups try to keep a low profile."

"I was able to piece together some of their story after I was discharged from the army. By then, she had been with the group for almost two years. They made a living by recruiting members, who were obligated to turn over all their money to the group. They also begged and, I think, stole, though they always left town before anyone reported them to the local law enforcement."

Chris nodded. "The Vine did that, too—made new members turn over all their assets. They were told they were contributing to the group, but I think most of the money went to the Exalted. While we lived in tents and trailers, he had a fancy motorhome and, supposedly, owned houses in several states. He traveled a lot, managing his various properties, and often delivered his messages to us via videotaped lectures. The rare times he did come to our camp were big occasions. Everyone turned out for a glimpse of him."

"From the research I did, a lot of these groups operate the same way," Rand said.

"What happened to your sister?" Chris asked. He had said she'd committed suicide, but how? When?

"It took me a long time to find her," he said. "By the time I located her, she had been with the group over two years and was fully brainwashed, and refused my pleas to leave the group."

"You spoke to her?"

"Yes. I tracked the group down to a little town in Eastern Oregon. Teri was there. She looked terrible. She had lost weight and wore this shapeless sack of a dress, her hair uncombed in these kind of dreadlocks. She had lost a front tooth—she wouldn't say how. And when I tried to talk to her, she said she wasn't allowed to talk to outsiders and ran away."

"Oh, Rand." Chris laid a hand on his arm.

"I went after her. I told her I was her brother and she owed me more than she owed her so-called friends. I was furious. I told her all those people had done was take her away from her home and family, take her money, and give her nothing in return. She told me I didn't understand, that the inner peace the Seekers had given her was worth all the money in the world. She said they were her family now and she didn't need anyone else. Then she left."

Chris felt sick. "All of that sounds familiar," she said. "It's the kind of thing we were all drilled on saying. I never saw it, but my mother said a couple of times families had tracked down their loved ones to one of our camps. The Exalted had people who were trained in how to deal with them to get them to leave."

"What did they say?"

"What your sister said—that we were that person's family now and they didn't need anyone else."

"I wanted to grab Teri and drag her out of there, but I figured that would only get me arrested for kidnapping. One of the Seekers said if I laid a hand on Aurora that he would call the police. So I let her be. But I kept track of the group as best I could."

"Not easy to do," Chris said. "The Vine was expert at packing up in the middle of the night and showing up across the country a week later. Mom was able to find a few people who have family who are members. They sometimes let her know where the group is living at the moment, but even they can't always keep up."

"I had a buddy from the military who was a private detective, and he took an interest in the group and did what he could to track them," Rand said. "He kept me up to date. About six months later I had a meeting in California, not far from the latest Seeker gathering. They weren't camping this time but were renting, or maybe squatting, in an old hotel. The place was a dump, with a leaking roof, water damage to the walls and no electricity. I couldn't see that they had done any work on it, except to erect a large brightly painted sign announcing that it was the Atlantis Center for Enlightenment."

He fell silent. Chris waited, and found herself matching her breathing to his own. When the silence stretched to minutes, she asked, "Your sister was there?"

"She was. I played it cool this time. I gave a fake name at the door and said I was interested in learning about Atlantis. I was taken to a room, and three disciples entered. They were dressed in jeans and T-shirts and looked very normal. They asked me a lot of questions about how I had found out about them, what I was seeking, et cetera. I gave vague answers, and they seemed pretty suspicious at first, but after I said I had inherited a lot of money from my grandfather and was looking for a worthy group that would benefit from the cash, their demeanor changed. They invited me to have dinner with them that evening.

"Teri was there. She was one of the women who were serving the food. I guess they probably cooked it too. She didn't look any better than the last time I had seen her, and when she saw me, she dropped a platter of vegetables and ran from the room. I almost turned over a chair going after her. I cornered her in an upstairs bedroom and begged her to leave with me. She just cried and shook her head and said she couldn't.

"I told her I wasn't leaving without her. One of the men threatened to call the police, and I told him to do it—that

I had plenty of proof there were people there being held against their will. That was a bluff, but it worked. They backed off."

Chris could see it all in her mind, from his frightened sister to the threatening Seekers—and Rand caught in the middle but determined to win. "What happened?" she asked.

"I took Teri by the hand and led her out of there. She came with me, still crying. I drove four hours away, checked us into a hotel under a fake name, paid cash for the room and ordered pizza. She started crying again when she saw the pizza. She said she hadn't had any since she had left with the group. I asked her what she had been eating, and she said they had a special diet of only natural foods and they had to fast three days a week. She said that was healthier, and it took everything in me not to point out that she didn't look healthy.

"After we ate, she fell asleep. She looked exhausted, and I know I was."

Ominous silence followed. Silence with weight. Chris had trouble breathing. For a long time Rand didn't say anything, his jaw tight, hands clenched.

"When I woke the next morning, she was gone," he said finally. "She had run away in the middle of the night. I went back to the abandoned hotel looking for her, but everyone there said they hadn't seen her. The police couldn't help me. I lost it at them, and they ended up threatening to arrest me. I stayed in town for a while, watching the group, but I never saw Teri again."

"But you believe she had returned to the group?" Chris asked.

"I know she did. Three months later, my parents received a phone call from someone with the group, telling them Teri's body was at the morgue in Bend, Oregon, and they could claim her body if they wanted. They said Teri had killed herself. The coroner said she had slit her wrists. She left a note—a lot of incoherent nonsense about destiny and enlightenment and final bliss."

Tears stung her eyes—tears for him and for his poor, hurting sister. "It wasn't your fault," she said.

"I could have handled it better. I could have forced her to come with me and taken her to a deprogrammer or something."

"That could have failed too." She rubbed his arm. "It wasn't your fault."

He let out a shaky breath. "The police in Bend investigated, but they couldn't find anything suspicious. The group left town and dropped off the radar. The last I heard, they were in South America."

"I'm so sorry about your sister," she said. The words seemed so paltry compared to what he had suffered, but she had nothing else to give.

"I haven't talked about this with anyone for a long time." He looked at her, his eyes damp but his expression calm. "You're a good listener."

She leaned closer, drawn to him, pulled in by the sadness in his eyes and a sense of shared grief. She hadn't lost a sister but a father, and the chance to grow up without the fear that had dogged her all her life. Her gaze shifted to his lips. She recalled the connection they had shared before, and she wanted that again.

She meant to kiss him gently, but the strength of her longing drove her harder than she had intended. He gripped her shoulders and responded with a gentling pressure of his own. He wanted this, too, his body seemed to say, but he wanted to savor the moment, to linger over the sensation of the two of them together.

She leaned into him, letting him take her weight, his arm wrapped around her. She could definitely get used to this...

She opened her eyes to find him looking at her as if he could see everything. The idea was unnerving, and she pulled away. "Something wrong?" he asked.

"No. Of course not." She sat up straighter, putting a little distance between them. "I really like you. A lot. But I'm not ready to take things any further."

"I respect that," he said. "No pressure. I want you to feel safe here."

"I can't feel safe anywhere as long as I know the Vine is so close by." She laid her head on his shoulder. "But being here is better than being alone."

"It is." He squeezed her shoulder. "Better for me too."

Chapter Twelve

The next morning Rand awoke early—a habit from so many dawn hospital shifts. He dressed and moved to the kitchen, hearing no indication Chris was awake. Good. She had looked exhausted when she had retired to her room last night. He had felt drained, too, but not in a bad way. Revisiting the events surrounding Teri's death had been wrenching, but cleansing too.

He had coffee brewing and was chopping vegetables for omelets when Chris came into the kitchen. "I thought you would have left for work," she said as she headed for the coffeepot.

"I have a couple of days off." He began cracking eggs into a bowl. "Do you want to do something today to get out of the house? Maybe a hike or a drive in the mountains?"

She sipped the coffee and closed her eyes, a look of satisfaction tugging up the corners of her mouth. He almost chuckled. He had experienced those first-sip nirvana moments himself. Then the smile faded, and she opened her eyes again. "I should probably check in with Jasmine and see if my doors have been repaired. Now that the Vine has moved on, I should go home."

"Do you really think they've moved away?" Rand asked. He began sautéing the peppers, onions and mushrooms.

"Maybe they've just relocated to a new campsite the sheriff doesn't know about."

She cradled her mug in both hands. "Honestly, I would be surprised if they gave up on me so easily," she said. "They've been pursuing me for years. This is the first time they've gotten close enough to confront me face-to-face. That must feel like a victory to them."

"I agree," he said. "Groups like this count on people underestimating them." The way he had underestimated the Seekers. "I think they're probably lying low and waiting for another opportunity."

She nodded.

"I think you should stay here until we're sure there's not a threat." He turned back to the stove and added the eggs to the pan. "So, what about taking a drive into the mountains today? Maybe find a trail to hike?"

"Sure. That's a great idea." She straightened. "Is there anything I can do to help with breakfast?"

"Get two plates out of that cabinet there, will you?" He added cheese to the omelet, then folded it over.

She brought out the plates, and he divided the omelet between them; then they carried the meal to the table. "You've lived here longer than I have," he said. "Where would be a good place for us to check out this morning?"

They discussed options. Chris's mood seemed to lift as they talked. Rand hoped the prospect of a day spent with him—not just the momentary distraction from her concerns about the Vine—was at least partially responsible for her change in mood.

THEY WERE CLEARING the dishes when Chris's phone rang. She didn't recognize the number. "Hello?" she asked, expecting a junk call.

"I'm panicking and I need someone to talk me down off a ledge." Bethany sounded breathless.

Chris laughed. "What's going on?" She moved into the living room.

"I'm serious. Something terrible has happened. I need help."

"What's wrong?" Chris gripped the phone more tightly. "What can I do?"

"I'm thinking we could blow up the stretch of highway leading into Eagle Mountain, but my family probably wouldn't let an obstacle like that stop them. Plus, there's the jail time to think of, not to mention I'm afraid of explosives."

"What are you talking about? You're not making sense."

"Sorry. But I'm so freaked out. My family has decided if I won't come back to Vermont to them, they will come here."

"Your family is coming to visit you? That doesn't sound so bad." Leave it to Bethany—who clearly liked drama—to make something like this into a big deal.

"No, they're moving here. All of them. My mom and dad and all three of my brothers."

"Oh, wow. What brought this on?"

"They're not just moving here—they're buying the Jeep-rental business I work for. And not just the business but the building it's in. Where my apartment is located. So now they're going to be my bosses and my landlords as well as my parents."

"Yikes. You weren't kidding when you said they're overprotective."

"I knew the business was for sale, but I never imagined my parents would buy it. Mom and Dad said they're ready to try something new, and they're super excited we're all going to be together again."

"And your brothers are coming too. How old are they?"

"Aaron is twenty-seven. The twins, Carter and Dalton, are twenty-four. The twins are going to work for Mom and Dad. Which means they'll be my coworkers." She groaned. "The oldest, Aaron, has a job in town, too, though he wouldn't tell me what it was. Which is just like him. He's the devious one among us."

"I'm sorry," Chris said. "But obviously, they love you very much."

Bethany sighed. "They do. And I love them. But they still treat me like a child. And my brothers—it's like being surrounded by a bunch of spies. Once, when I was fourteen, some girlfriends and I toilet-papered another girl's house, and I wasn't back home before Mom and Dad knew about it. They made me get out of bed at six in the morning to clean up the mess I made. And forget dating. Until I was eighteen, I had to double-date with one of my brothers and his girlfriend. Even after that, bringing someone home to meet the family was a huge ordeal. I can't tell you how many guys I never heard from again after they got the third degree from the Ames men."

Chris laughed. "I know it's not funny to you, but it's so different from how I grew up. It was just my mom and me. I used to think it would be great to be part of a big, loving family." A real family. Not one like the Vine.

"You're right. Most of the time it is fun. I do love them, and I know they love me. But this is too much."

"Maybe you can find another apartment. That might help some."

"Maybe. But this apartment is one of the perks of the job. It's part of my compensation package. I could look for a new job, but I really like this. It's a perfect fit for me. What am I going to do?"

"I'm not sure I'm the right person to give advice to anyone," Chris said.

"Of course you are. You have your own apartment. You're an artist. A full-time artist. That's an incredible accomplishment. And I hear you've been seeing a certain very good-looking doctor."

Chris made a face, even though Bethany couldn't see her. "Where did you hear that?"

"Oh, you know. Someone saw you two together and told someone else, and the next thing you know, the two of you are practically engaged. You're not, are you? Engaged, I mean?"

"No." Chris's stomach quivered at the thought. "Rand and I are just friends."

"Okay, so you have a hot friend. Anyway, I bet you never did anything in your life you didn't want to do, no matter what your friends and family said. So tell me what to do about this."

"I don't think there's a lot you can do. If they've bought this business and are determined to move to Eagle Mountain, you can't stop them. Maybe practice smiling and thanking them for whatever advice they feel compelled to hand out—then do whatever you want without feeling guilty. Maybe that will help them to see you in a new light."

"You make it sound easy, but you haven't met my family. They can be very persuasive."

Now Chris felt queasy as she recalled some of the methods of "persuasion" the Vine had used. "They're not, well, abusive, are they?"

"What? No! Of course not!"

"I'm sorry. I had to make sure."

"I forget you haven't met them yet. You know the phrase 'killing them with kindness'? My parents are masters of that

technique. I don't think it's possible to really love someone to death, but if it were, my parents could do it. And my
brothers are all so good looking and charming they have
every female, and half the men, in our hometown conned
into believing they're perfect angels. It's infuriating, really."

"I can't wait to meet these people," Chris said, suppress-
ing a laugh.

"Oh, you'll meet them. They'll know everyone in town
inside of two weeks. They're that kind of friendly. And
they'll ask you all kinds of nosy questions. Feel free to ignore them, but I probably don't have to tell you that. Please
teach me how to fight my natural tendency to want people
to like me. It's painful and embarrassing, I tell you."

"No, it's sweet." Chris was laughing now; she couldn't
help it. But not at Bethany. The young woman was really
starting to grow on her.

"No, you're sweet to say so." She sighed. "Anyway, I feel
better having gotten all that off my chest. What are you up
to today?"

"I'm going hiking."

"By yourself? Be careful. I don't want to get a call later
that we have to go rescue you. Not to mention—how embarrassing would that be?"

"No, I'm going with…" She started to say *a friend* but decided to share a little bit more with Bethany. "With Rand."

"Oooh. Have fun. Not that you wouldn't. He really has
that hot-older-guy thing going on. I want to hear all about
it later. Or not. I'm nosy, but feel free to tell me to mind my
own. One good thing about having three overbearing brothers is that I have a very thick skin."

Chris laughed again. "Have a good day, Bethany. And
I'm sure things will work out with your parents."

"If it doesn't, I'll be living with them when I'm forty, after they've scared away every single man within a hundred-mile radius. But it won't be so terrible. My mom's a great cook, and my dad never beats me at cards."

Chris ended the call and returned to the kitchen, where Rand was finishing the dishes. "How old are you?" she asked.

"I'm forty-one. Why?"

"No reason. You just seem...younger." She knew he was a little older than she was, but fourteen years older? Then again, there were plenty of times when she felt decades older than someone like Bethany, who was probably much closer to Chris's age than Rand.

"Having second thoughts about hanging out with an old man?" he asked.

"No. I appreciate maturity."

"Ouch!"

She turned away, smiling to herself. Bethany was right. Rand was definitely a hot older guy. There were worse ways to spend a summer afternoon than with him.

RAND DROVE HIS SUV as far as he could into the high country above town, until they reached the roads only a Jeep or similar vehicle could navigate. They chose a trail that promised a hike to a high mountain lake and set out, Harley trotting ahead. The trail climbed gradually, and they passed areas where wildflowers grew hip-deep in an extravagance of pink, purple, yellow and white. Bees and hummingbird moths wove erratic paths between blossoms, heavy with pollen, and the air was as perfumed as a boudoir. Harley stalked through the grass, then burst out ahead of them, shaking a shower of flower petals from his coat and grinning in that way dogs have, an expression of ecstasy.

"Have you been married before?" Chris asked when they had been hiking a while.

"Where did that question come from?"

She shrugged. "If you're forty-one, I figured there was a chance you'd been married before."

"I haven't."

"Why not?"

His first instinct was to say *because I haven't*, but Chris deserved something less flippant. "Let's see—six years of medical school and residency, terrible hours and no money, three years in a surgical unit in a war zone… Not conducive to long-term relationships."

"That only takes you up to, what, thirty?"

"Three more years in a military hospital stateside. I had girlfriends but nothing ever lasted." He shrugged. "Marriage is a big decision. One I don't want to make unless I'm sure."

"Fair enough."

"Does it bother you that I'm so much older than you?"

"I didn't even think about it until Bethany said something."

"What did Bethany say?"

Chris smiled. "I'm not going to tell you. It will go to your head. But she referred to you as an older guy."

"I like to think I've got a lot of good years left. For what it's worth, when we first met, I thought you were older. Not because of your looks but because of your attitude."

"Guess I'm just an old soul. And today I'm just enjoying being in a beautiful place." She sent him a look that held a little sizzle. "With you."

All right, then. He suddenly felt a foot taller—but also like it was time to dial back the tension. "Race you to the top of the next ridge."

Rand beat her to the top, but just barely. They stood side

by side, looking out across the mountain peaks and rolling valleys. "What is that down there?" She indicated a cluster of colored shapes in the shadow of a jagged pinnacle.

Rand dug his binoculars from his pack and focused on the spot. As he adjusted the focus, a dozen or more colorful tents came into view. "It's a bunch of tents and people," he said. "Didn't Danny announce something about a scout group up here?"

"That's next month." She held out her hand. "Let me see."

She studied the encampment for a long moment, her body tense. Then she returned the binoculars to him. When she didn't say anything, he asked, "Do you think it's the Vine?"

She nodded. "I can't prove it. And I'm afraid if I report this to the sheriff, he'll think I'm either paranoid or vying for more attention."

He scanned the area again. He counted at least fifteen smaller tents and several large ones. Lots of people—men, women and children—milled about. "It could be them," he said. He lowered the binoculars again. "I'll call the sheriff when we get back to my place. He can't accuse me of seeking attention. He needs to know about this—he's still looking for those involved in Lana's death."

"He can't prove a crime. A grown woman has a right to refuse medical care. And she probably did refuse at first. Members of the Vine are taught that relying on outside care is a sign of weak faith. No one wants to be accused of that."

She turned and began walking back down the way they had come. This glimpse of the Vine—or what she thought was the Vine—had changed the mood of the day. Chris now walked with her head down and shoulders bowed, unspeaking.

He wanted to tell her to cheer up. She wasn't part of the group anymore, and they had no hold on her. But he dismissed the impulse as soon as it surfaced. Some of the members of that group had knocked him out and broken into her home. They had threatened her verbally and physically. She had every right to be afraid and to wonder if she would ever be rid of them.

So he settled for moving up beside her on the trail. "It may not feel like it, but you've got a lot of friends in this town," he said. "Every member of search and rescue would help you if you asked. Jasmine thinks of you like a daughter. Bethany thinks you're a superhero—and she wouldn't be wrong. And of course, there's me."

She glanced up at him. "And what are you?"

"I'm just someone who likes being with you," he said. "I'm the one who'll break the trail ahead or stand by your side or watch your back. Whatever you need."

She didn't answer right away. He started to ask if he had overwhelmed her with bad-romance dialogue when she said, "I've never had anyone to do those things before. I'm usually charting my own path."

"I'm not stopping you," he said. "I just want you to know I'm here. If you need me."

She straightened. "And what's in it for you, Doctor?"

He flashed his most insolent grin. "I get to hang out with a hot younger woman. It does wonders for my image, I tell you."

As he had hoped, she burst out laughing, then punched his shoulder. He laughed too. "For that, I think you owe me dinner," she said.

It's a date, he thought. But no, he wouldn't use the D word. He didn't want to scare her off. "That's a great idea." He hooked his thumbs beneath the straps of his pack. "First one down gets to pick the restaurant." Then he set off, long strides eating up the distance.

"That's not fair. You have longer legs than me," she called.

"What was that? I'm an old man, remember? I'm probably losing my hearing."

He was still enjoying her laughter when she blew past him, shoes raising puffs of dust as she raced down the trail.

Nineteen years ago

"Mom! Mom! Peace and Victory and I were playing by the creek, and we saw the biggest fish!" Elita skidded to a stop in the middle of the trailer's main room and stared at the boxes stacked around the room. "What's going on?"

Her mother looked up from one of the boxes. "We're moving. Come on. You can help me wrap these dishes." She indicated the stack of plates on the coffee table beside her.

"Why do we have to move?" Elita stamped her foot. "I like it here." There were the woods to play in and the little creek, and the secret playhouse she and her friends had made with sticks and vines in a spot no one knew about but them.

"The Exalted says it's time to move, so we're moving." Mom didn't look any happier about the relocation than Elita.

"We're moving to an even better location." Her father came into the room, carrying the stack of old blankets they used to cushion fragile items for the move.

"How do you know that?" her mother asked. "This was supposed to be a better location, too, but we've only been here six months, and already we have to move."

"The Exalted said it's not fertile ground," her father said.

"Is he planting a garden?" Elita asked. Some of their neighbors had little gardens planted around their tents or trailers. Elita and her friends sometimes dug in the dirt and "planted" flowers and twigs and things. She liked playing in the cool dirt.

"He means there aren't many people around here who want to learn the Exalted's teachings." Her dad patted her head.

"Or maybe the locals have complained about us squatting here," her mother said.

Her father's expression darkened. "Don't let anyone hear you say that," he said. "If people really understood the gift the Exalted could give them, they would welcome us with open arms and beg us to stay as long as possible so they could hear his teachings."

Her mother bent over the dishes again, shaking her head. "There are some old newspapers in the kitchen, Elita," she said. "Would you get them for me?"

She had just picked up the stack of papers when someone knocked on the back door. She walked over and opened it, and stared, open mouthed, at the man who stood there. The man—tall and broad shouldered, with a mop of blond hair and piercing blue eyes—stared back at her. He reminded Elita of a picture of Jack in the copy of *Jack and the Beanstalk* her mother had read to her. "Hello, Elita," the man said. "Is your father here?"

"How did you know my name?" she asked.

"I know all about you," the man said. "The Exalted has asked me to keep an eye on you. You're a lucky girl to be so fated."

"Jedediah! What can I do for you?" Her father hurried to greet the man.

"You need to be ready to head out by one o'clock," Jedediah said. "Cephus will be here then to tow your trailer. You and your family will travel in the bus."

"I don't want to move," Elita said.

Both men turned to her. "Elita, hush!" her father ordered. "It's not your place to question the Exalted."

"Your father is right," Jedediah said. "Your job is to obey. The sooner you master that job, the better for you and for the group. No supper for you tonight, to teach you to master your impulses."

He exited the trailer, and Elita began to cry. Her mother came into the room. "What's going on? Elita, why are you crying?"

"Jedediah was here," her father said. "Elita told him she didn't want to move. He said for questioning the Exalted, she was forbidden to have supper tonight."

"Who is he to tell us how to discipline our daughter?" Her mother put an arm around Elita. "And she's only eight."

Her father looked troubled. "We can't disobey Jedediah," he said. "He's the Exalted's right-hand man."

"I'm not going to starve my child."

"She won't starve. She's gone longer than one night without food during the ritual fasts."

"And you know I don't agree with those either. Not for children."

Her father glanced out the window. "Lower your voice. Someone will hear you. And get back to packing. They're coming for the trailer at one." The family didn't own a truck, so they relied on one of the other members of the Vine to tow their travel trailer to the next camp. They would ride with other families in a converted school bus the group owned.

Chris's mother frowned at her husband, then marched to the cabinet and took out bread and peanut butter. "What are you doing?" her father asked.

"I'm making a sandwich."

"You can't give it to Elita."

"The sandwich is for me." She spread peanut butter between two slices of bread, then wrapped it in wax paper and tucked it in her pocket. As she exited the room, she caught Elita's eye and winked. Elita immediately felt better. Later on, when no one was looking, she knew her mother would give her the sandwich. Her father might believe in strict obedience to the Exalted, but her mother had different priorities, and Elita was one of them.

Chapter Thirteen

Rand was off work the next day and spent the morning doing yard work around the cabin while Chris worked on a new painting on the screened-in porch she had appropriated as a temporary studio. Every time he passed by, he looked up to see her poised before an easel, sometimes working with a brush or pencil, other times standing back and considering the work so far.

He could get used to her presence in his life, though he wanted more. An intimacy she wasn't ready to give and a trust he didn't know if he could ever earn.

He had just fetched a can of wasp spray from the garage to deal with a yellow jacket nest under the back deck when his phone emitted an alert. He checked the screen and found a message from the 911 dispatcher: Missing hikers, Guthrie Mill area. All available volunteers needed for search.

He went inside, still carrying the spray. He set the can on the counter and went in search of Chris. She had laid aside her paintbrush and was staring at her phone also. "Where is Guthrie Mill?" he asked.

She pocketed her phone. "It's an old stamp mill for processing gold ore in the mountains, about ten thousand feet in elevation," she said. "It's south of Gallagher's Basin."

"That's not far from where we were hiking yesterday."

"Not far as the crow flies," she said. "A lot longer if you travel by road. It's a beautiful area but a terrible place to be lost. Lots of hazards."

Rand thought of the first search and rescue training class he had attended, about the psychology of searches. "Let's hope we can find these people before they get into trouble," he said.

"I'll get my gear," she said, and left the room.

They met up at the front door a few moments later and rode together to search and rescue headquarters, where a crowd had gathered of both SAR volunteers and others who had gotten word of the need for searchers. "The 911 call came in at ten this morning," Danny said when the SAR team gathered around him. "Two adults—a husband and wife in their forties, and their fifteen-year-old son. They set out two days ago to explore the area around Guthrie Mill. The neighbors noticed this morning they hadn't returned and became concerned and made the call."

"Are we sure they're really missing?" Ryan asked. "Maybe they took off somewhere else and didn't bother informing their neighbor of the change of plans."

"The caller was insistent that something was wrong," Danny said. "He said none of the family members were answering their phones and the husband was supposed to report for work this morning and didn't. He also said the boy is a diabetic and needs regular insulin."

"Do we know their names?" Sheri asked.

"The caller referred to the man as Mike and the son as AJ," Danny said. "The woman is Ruth. No last names. And the caller lost the connection before giving his own information. The 911 operator said the connection was poor, and the caller spoke with a thick accent she had trouble understanding. She thinks his name was Morris or Maurice, but the call dropped before she was able to get more information. She thought maybe he had driven into the mountains to look for the family. His phone didn't register with the 911 system."

"That's a little suspicious," Chris said.

"Maybe," Danny said. "But bad phone service is pretty common in these mountains and canyons. We can't risk ignoring this in case it is legitimate. That area around the mill is particularly hazardous. There are open pits, collapsing structures and rusting equipment."

"That kid could be in trouble if he needs insulin," Hannah said.

"The sheriff's department is looking for vehicles at trailheads in the area that might belong to this family," Danny continued. "They've asked us to begin our search at the mill and move outward. We'll work in teams of four."

Rand and Chris teamed up with Carrie Andrews and Caleb Garrison. "We're supposed to focus from the area south of the mill to Raccoon Creek." Caleb looked up from the map the group had been given. "Are any of you familiar with the area?"

"I am," Carrie and Chris replied at the same time.

"I've been to the mill a couple of times but not recently," Caleb said.

"I've never been there," Rand admitted.

"Just follow us." Carrie stashed the map in her pack. "Let's go, and hope we can find this lost family."

ONLY THE SHELL of the Guthrie Mill remained—the weathered wooden walls, three stories high, topped by a metal roof streaked with orange rust. Light streamed through gaps in the boards, and the whole structure leaned a foot to the left, the victim of almost a century of punishing winds and deep winter snows. The ground around the structure was a junkyard of splintered boards and rusting metal, the husk of a boiler, snarls of thick cable, discarded tin cans, and the remnants of the iron rails that had once been a path for ore cars bringing raw materials for the mill to process.

Chris was drawn to places like this, and she had painted many similar scenes. Wildflowers grew among the debris, bending in a stiff breeze, and fluffy clouds scudded by in a delft-blue sky. It was the perfect setting for a summer outing—and a terrible place to be lost. The ground sloped away on all sides into deep ravines and rock-filled gullies, rock uplifts, and the remnants of other buildings that had supported the mill's operation, making it impossible to see clearly for more than a few dozen yards in any direction. "When was the last time you were up here?" Rand asked as the four searchers picked their way over the rough ground.

"Harley and I were up here last summer," Chris said. "I had an idea for a new painting and spent a couple of hours poking around and making sketches. We were the only ones here that afternoon."

"Did you complete the painting?" he asked.

"I did. It sold right away. To a woman from Cincinnati, I think." She scanned the surroundings for any clue that someone else had passed by here recently—a torn bit of clothing, a food wrapper, debris that appeared disturbed—but saw nothing.

"What are we supposed to be looking for?" Rand asked. "Besides the obvious, a person or persons?"

"Look for anything that could have attracted someone off the trail," Chris said.

"They might have followed the old tramway" Carrie said. She indicated the remains of the towers evenly spaced across the mountain. "There's a lot of old cable and tram cars beneath the towers that interest people. And a lot of rough terrain where someone could fall or get hurt."

"Then let's follow the tramline," Caleb said.

They set out along the tramline, but Chris had trouble focusing on the search. She couldn't shake the sense that something wasn't right. Why had the 911 caller provided so many specific details—the family's destination and the fact that the boy had diabetes—but failed to lead with important information, such as the family's name or his own contact info? And if the family had really been gone for two days, why hadn't a relative or coworker reported them missing?

She reminded herself that it wasn't her job to raise suspicions about the call. She was here to search for people who might be in trouble and to help them if they were found. If they were all wasting their time, there were worse ways to spend a summer afternoon than in this beautiful spot.

A delicate melody, like someone playing a flute, drifted to her. Was that music or a trick of the wind? She stopped.

Ahead of her, Rand stopped also. "What is it?" he asked.

She shook her head. "I thought I heard music."

"I don't hear anything," Caleb said.

"Which direction was it coming from?" Rand asked.

"I don't know. Let's keep going." She was freaking herself out, hearing things that weren't there. Better to focus on the search.

They hadn't gone much farther when Caleb halted. "I thought I saw movement over there." He pointed to a copse of stunted pinions.

"Yes." Chris leaned forward. "A flash of blue—like a shirt or something." She had just glimpsed the motion through the trees, the brightness of the blue out of place amid the greens and browns of the landscape.

"Is it another searcher?" Rand asked.

"No one else is assigned to this sector." Carrie started forward.

They all followed. Chris was at the back of the line, and kept looking toward the trees. *There!* She had seen the flash of color again.

Then she heard the music once more. A high-pitched melody. She stopped, but the others kept going, intent on reaching the trees. She tried to figure out where the music was coming from. Back the way they had come and to the left. She just needed to get close enough to verify there was really someone there.

She took a few steps off the trail, keeping the others in sight. She would check this out, then catch back up with them to report. Abruptly, the music stopped, replaced by a voice: "Help!" The sound was faint and high pitched. A woman, or maybe a child.

Heart pounding, she broke into a trot, moving toward the sound. "Hello?" she called. "Is someone there?"

Something landed on her head, covering her face. She clawed at the rough cloth, but someone grabbed her hands. She tried to cry out, but her voice was barely audible. And then there was nothing but darkness.

CARRIE STOPPED AGAIN and stared intently ahead of them. Rand stood beside her. "There's definitely someone up there," he said.

"I see them." Carrie took off again at a jog. "Hey!" she shouted. "We're with search and rescue!"

"Why are they running away?" Caleb asked. He caught up with Rand and Carrie. The person they had been pursuing had disappeared behind a grouping of boulders.

"Stop!" Carrie called. "We need to talk to you."

"Where did they go?" Caleb asked. "I don't see them."

Rand looked back over his shoulder, expecting to see Chris hurrying to catch up with them. Instead, there was no one there. "Where's Chris?" he asked.

Carrie stopped. "She was right behind us."

"Chris!" Rand listened for a response but heard nothing. He cupped his hands around his mouth and shouted again: "Chris!"

"Caleb, wait!" Carrie called. "We can't find Chris."

Caleb jogged back to them. "I can't find whoever we saw up there either." He removed his cap and wiped the sweat from his forehead. "What happened to Chris?"

"I don't know." Rand started back the way they had come. "Chris!" he shouted. Fear constricted his chest, making it hard to breathe. He searched the ground for any sign of a scuffle, but the hard surface showed no footprints or indications of a disturbance.

Carrie took out her radio. "The sheriff's department is supposed to have a drone up to help with the search," she said. "I'll ask them to head this way, see if they can spot Chris."

"How could she have just disappeared?" Caleb asked. "And where did that guy we were chasing vanish to?"

"I think he lured us away on purpose," Rand said.

Caleb frowned. "Why would he do that?"

"So that someone else could grab Chris." He scanned the empty landscape, seeing nothing but mining ruins, rocks and a distant bank of dark clouds in the distance. Rain was coming, though it wasn't here yet. "The Vine didn't leave the county after all. Yesterday Chris and I hiked the Blue Sky Trail, and we spotted some campers across the valley that we thought might be them. I meant to report the sighting to the sheriff but never got the chance. The story about the missing family may have been a ruse to get us up here to the mill so they could snatch her." A cold knot in the pit of his stomach told him he was right.

Carrie ended her call. "Danny wants us to report back to the trailhead. They're calling off the search."

"Why are they calling it off?" Caleb asked.

Carrie shrugged. "Not sure. He just said to meet at the trailhead."

"Did you let him know Chris is missing?" Rand asked.

"I did. He says we need to talk to the sheriff. They need coordinates to pinpoint the search." She clapped Rand on the back. "Let's go. The sooner we tell them what we know, the sooner they can find her."

"You two go on to the trailhead," Rand said. "I'll stay here."

"No way," Caleb said. "First rule of working in the wilderness is you don't split up."

"Something must have distracted Chris, or she would have remembered that," Carrie said.

Rand wanted to know what that something was. He thought about arguing with the others, but that was delaying the search. He took out his phone and called up a mapping app to pinpoint their location. He would come back here—with or without the others. He wasn't going to abandon Chris.

"WE'VE CALLED OFF the search because we've determined the call was a hoax," Sheriff Travis Walker addressed the crowd of searchers gathered at the Guthrie Mill trailhead. "We haven't identified anyone who fits the description the caller gave, the phone itself was a temporary 'burner' phone purchased at the local gas station by someone the clerk could only describe as 'an average-looking, middle-aged white male.' We haven't located any vehicles left overnight at any of the trailheads, not just in the area of the mill but anywhere in the county. We have issued a plea for any information from anyone who might know the family described or the person who called in the report, but at this time we feel there's too great a risk that someone else will be hurt while searching for someone we can't be satisfied even exists."

"What about Chris Mercer's disappearance?" Rand asked. "What are you doing about that?"

"We're sending up a drone to survey the area where she went missing, and we're enlisting search and rescue to assist in a targeted search for her." Travis scanned the faces of those around him. "I know you're concerned that one of your own is missing," he said. "I promise, we're doing everything in our power to locate her. She is our number one priority."

"Search and rescue has a search dog, right?" Rand remembered meeting the woman who had trained the dog— Anna something.

"Anna and Jacquie are away for the week doing a course for an additional certification," Danny said. "By the time we got another dog and handler here, the rain would have degraded any scent trail."

At his words, Rand and several others looked up at the dark clouds moving toward them. "Can you think of anything else that would help us find her?" Travis asked.

"Chris and I hiked the Blue Sky Trail yesterday," Rand said. "We spotted some campers across the valley. We thought it might be some of the members of the Vine. I meant to call and tell you about it this morning, but I forgot." He had been too distracted by his new closeness with Chris to want to think about the Vine.

"Do you have coordinates for this camp?" Travis asked.

"We were standing at the top of the ridge at the end of the trail, looking south."

Deputy Dwight Prentice approached. "Sheriff, if I could speak to you for a moment."

Travis moved away with Dwight. Rand followed, listening in on their conversation while trying to appear uninterested. "Wes has located a group of campers with the drone," Dwight said. "They have a couple of tents set up in the next basin over from the mill. There's no sign of Chris Mercer or of anyone fitting the description of the supposed missing family."

Travis looked back at Rand. "How many people were in this camp you and Chris saw from the Blue Sky Trail?" he asked.

"There were over a dozen small tents and several large ones," he said. "Easily a couple of dozen people of all ages."

"The drone reported only a couple of tents and five or six people," Dwight said.

"And where are they, exactly?" Travis asked.

Dwight consulted his notebook. "A basin to the west of Guthrie Mill, next to a big outcropping of rock."

"That's a different area than the one Chris and I were looking into," Rand said.

"Let's talk to these people anyway," Travis said. "Maybe they've seen or heard something." He keyed his radio microphone and told Wes to keep searching with the drone. "Dwight, come with me to talk to these campers."

Rand moved forward. "I want to come too."

"No," Travis said.

"I've spent more time in the Vine's camp than anyone else here except Danny," Rand said. "I'll recognize if these campers are part of the group."

"Why do you think the Vine is involved?" Travis asked.

"Because Chris is missing. The group has been hunting her for fifteen years, and they've already tried to take her once recently. I'm sure they had something to do with her disappearance."

Travis and Dwight exchanged a look Rand interpreted as skeptical. "You can't come with us," Travis said.

"Then I'll follow you up there."

"I could have you detained for interfering with an investigation."

"What would that do but create more paperwork and hassle for you?" Rand did his best to look calm and non-threatening even though inside, this waste of time chafed. "I promise I'll stay out of the way. But you'll have a third set of eyes on hand to watch these people while you question them."

Travis fixed him with a hard stare, but Rand didn't relent. The sheriff was the first to blink. "You can come with us," he said. "But you'll stay back, follow orders and keep quiet."

"Yes, sir."

Travis and Dwight collected packs from their cruiser and set out up the trail to the mill, Rand following behind. None of them spoke for the first mile; then Travis glanced back at Rand. "How long have you known Chris?" he asked.

"A few weeks."

"And you believe what she's told you about this group, the Vine?"

"Yes. You heard that man on the trail the day Chris and I met—the one who told her to get ready for her wedding."

"People with mistaken beliefs or delusions aren't necessarily threatening," Travis said.

"She said the Vine killed her father when he opposed their leader."

"She was a child. Maybe he really did eat poisonous mushrooms."

"I believe Chris. And she didn't make up the two men who attacked me and broke into her apartment. What I saw when Danny and I went to the camp fit with her description of the group."

Travis nodded. "Tell me again what happened when she disappeared this morning."

Rand repeated the story of seeing someone moving ahead and going to investigate. "Chris was bringing up the rear of the group. I was focused on whoever was ahead of us and didn't notice she had fallen farther behind. When I did look back, she was gone."

"What do you think happened?" Travis asked.

"I think you're right about the missing persons call being a hoax. I think whoever called in that story did so to lure search and rescue into the area around the mill. They knew Chris was likely to respond to the call."

"They couldn't be sure she would volunteer to be part of the search," Dwight said.

"If she didn't, they didn't lose anything," Rand said.

"They took a big chance," Travis said. "The area around the mill was crawling with searchers."

"It's a big area," Rand said. "Even with so many people searching, we were spread out. And there's a lot of cover up there—rocks, clumps of trees, old mine buildings and the changing terrain itself."

"Maybe she fell and was injured," Dwight said.

That was a possibility Rand had considered. "Why didn't we hear her cry out?"

"Maybe you were too far away," Dwight said. "Or she lost consciousness."

"Maybe." Rand didn't like to think Chris had been hurt, but if the injury wasn't serious, wouldn't that be better than being back in the clutches of the Vine? "Is the drone still looking for her?" he asked.

"It is," the sheriff said. "And I spoke with Danny. There's a new team of searchers headed up right behind us."

After three miles and an hour of steady hiking, they reached the mill. Dwight checked the coordinates he had received from the drone. "Looks like we head this way," he said, and pointed toward the same copse of trees where Rand and his group of searchers had seen someone running away from them.

They passed through the trees and hiked for another forty-five minutes before they spotted two tents—one orange and one lime green—set in a broad bowl on the side of the mountain. As they drew nearer, Rand counted five people, all adults, moving among the tents. Backpacks and other camping gear had been arranged near a fire ring.

Two young couples made up the group. A slender man in his twenties, with straight dark hair and glasses, moved forward. He focused on Dwight's and Travis's uniforms. "Is something wrong?" he asked.

"We're looking for a missing woman," Travis said. "Midtwenties, five foot six, medium build, shoulder-length blue hair."

The man shook his head. "We haven't seen anyone like that." The second man and the two women, who had gathered around him, shook their heads also.

Travis looked around at the tents and other gear. The tents were small—not the place to hide someone. "How long have you been camping here?" Travis asked.

"We set up last night. It's okay to be camped here, isn't it?"

"It's not illegal to camp here," Travis said.

Something rustled in the trees, and Rand glanced over in time to see a dark-haired girl step into the clearing. At the sight of Travis and the others, she started and moved back into the cover of the leaves. "Who was that?" Travis asked.

"That's my niece," the second man, a broad-shouldered blond, said. "She's very shy."

Rand stared after the girl. "Ask her to come back," he said. "I want to talk to her."

"Who are you?" the first man asked.

Travis sent Rand a quelling look. "Can your niece answer a few questions for us?" the sheriff asked.

"You won't get anything useful from her," the second man said. "She's got the mental capacity of a three-year-old. A sad situation, really."

"I'd still like to talk to her," Travis said.

The two men looked at each other. "I'm going to have to refuse," the blond said. "No disrespect, Sheriff, but I don't see any need to upset her. She couldn't tell you anything useful."

Silence stretched as Travis and the blond faced each other; then the sheriff took a step back. "We'll be back if we have more questions," he said.

Rand waited until they were a quarter mile from camp before he burst out. "I know that girl," he said. "She was in the Vine's camp the night Danny and I tried to help that pregnant woman, Lana. They called her Serena. And she seemed as smart as any ten-or eleven-year-old."

"If they've got Chris, she isn't in that camp," Dwight said. "I got a good look at the tents. They're so small I don't think they could hide anyone in them."

"She's probably in the woods," Rand said. "Wherever

the girl was coming from. That's why they didn't want us talking to her."

"Or they might not want strangers interviewing a child," Dwight said.

"We'll get searchers up here," Travis said. "It's public land. They can't stop us from searching."

"And while we're waiting, they'll move Chris," Rand said. He turned back toward the camp. "I'm going back there to look for Chris myself."

"Don't do it," Travis said.

Rand made a move to turn away, but Dwight took hold of his arm. "Don't do anything rash," Dwight said. "You're not going to face off by yourself against four of them, and who knows how many more? If they do have Chris, they probably have her guarded. Smarter to let us check out the situation with a drone and get back up there with the numbers to deal with whatever kind of offense they try to present."

Rand glanced at Travis. "We may not have a lot of time," he said. "Groups like this are used to moving around a lot, avoiding any attention from police."

"We're wasting time right now," Travis said. "Don't delay us any longer."

Rand glanced back over his shoulder. He wanted to go back and look for Chris, but he could see the foolishness of trying to take on the group by himself, unarmed. "All right," he said. "I'll wait." But he wouldn't wait long.

Chapter Fourteen

Chris woke up with a pounding head, the pain worse than any tension headache or hangover she had ever experienced. She forced open her eyes and was met with a wave of nausea, and she broke into a cold sweat. "Drink this. It will help." A gentle, cool hand briefly rested on her forehead, and the hand's owner, a dark-haired girl, helped Chris sit up against some rough surface. She pressed a mug into Chris's hands. "Don't worry. It's just ginger tea. It will help, I promise."

Chris sipped the drink, which indeed tasted of ginger and smelled of lemons and honey. She realized suddenly how parched she was and ended up draining the cup. The girl smiled and took the cup from her. "That's good. You should feel better soon."

The only light in the dim space was from an old-fashioned camping lantern, which gave off an erratic yellow glow and the faint odor of gas. Chris shoved herself up into a sitting position, fighting a new wave of dizziness and nausea. She had been lying—and was now sitting—on what appeared to be an old sleeping bag laid out on the floor of a chamber hewed out of rock. The entrance wasn't visible from where she sat, but a draft of fresh air to her left probably came from that opening. "Where am I?" she asked.

"We're in a cave, I think. Or maybe something to do with one of the mines around here." The girl set the empty cup aside and picked up a basin filled with water. "Let me look at the back of your head. I want to make sure the bleeding has stopped."

Most of her fogginess had cleared, and the memory of what had happened on the trail returned, sharp and enraging. Chris leaned away from the girl. "Who are you? Why am I here?"

"My name is Serena." The girl's expression was guarded. Unsmiling. Nevertheless, she was strikingly beautiful. She had the kind of arresting beauty that might grace magazine covers or classical paintings. "And we are both here because the Exalted wills it."

Of course. Chris hadn't really had to ask the question. The Exalted was the only person who would want to kidnap her. "You're a member of the Vine," she clarified.

Serena dipped a cloth into the water and wrung it out. "I was born into the Vine."

"How old are you?"

"I'm ten."

"Who else is here?" Chris looked around the cave. Anything more than a few feet from the lantern's flame was pitch black, but it didn't feel as if anyone else was nearby.

"There is a guard outside the entrance. Probably several guards. Please, let me look at your injury."

Chris hesitated, then turned her back to the girl. Serena was so slight that even in her injured state, Chris felt sure she could defend herself against the child if necessary.

"I'm going to clean away some of the dried blood in your hair," Serena said.

Chris winced as the cool water—or maybe the soap in it—stung the gash on her head. "That was a nasty fall you took," Serena said as she dabbed at the wound. "You must have hit a big rock."

"I didn't fall," Chris said. "Someone hit me, though maybe they used a rock."

"Who would do that?" Serena asked.

Chris didn't answer. How could she explain anything to this child?

Heavy bootheels striking rock echoed around them. Serena's hand stilled, and Chris turned to see Jedediah. The lantern's flickering flame cast macabre shadows over his face, deepening every crag and crevice, turning his eyes to dark smudges and highlighting his large yellowing teeth. "Good, you're awake," he said.

"She said she didn't fall," Serena said. "Someone hit her in the head."

Jedediah didn't look at the girl. "She's confused. She fell."

"I didn't fall until someone hit me." Chris wanted to stand up to face him, but she was afraid if she did so, she might faint. She had to settle for glaring up at him. "You can't keep me here. People will be looking for me."

"They won't find you."

"Where am I?" She didn't remember any caves in the area around Guthrie Mill, but there were plenty of old mines.

"It doesn't matter," he said. "We're not going to stay here long. We're moving you to a new hiding place right away. By tomorrow you'll be halfway across the country." He turned to Serena. "Get her dressed in those clothes I left. And don't forget the wig."

He left, his footsteps echoing behind him. Serena moved to Chris's side, a bundle of fabric in one hand, a curly blond wig in the other. "You need to put these on," she said. "I can help you if you're still feeling dizzy."

Chris eyed the long-sleeved dress, with its high neckline and long skirt, and the blond wig. "Why do I have to wear those things?" she asked, even though she thought she knew the answer. Once she put on that outfit, no one would be able to see her tattoos or blue hair—the very things anyone searching for her would be looking for.

"I don't know." Serena thrust them at her again. "The Exalted wills it."

This was the reasoning given for any number of actions within the Vine, from a designated fasting day to a dictate of what clothing people would wear, to the decision to move to a new location. Chris eyed the dress—a particularly drab shade of faded gray. "I won't wear any of that," she said.

Serena bit her lower lip. "If you don't put them on, they'll punish you," she said.

"I'm not afraid of their punishment." Not entirely true, but right now she was too angry to pay much attention to the fear lurking at the back of her throat.

"They'll punish me too." The words came out as a whisper, but they stung like a scream. The child had been hurt before.

"Where are your parents?" Chris asked.

"My parents have gone on to glory," she answered, blurting the statement like a child reciting the multiplication tables.

The familiar phrase sent another chill through Chris. "Do you mean they're dead?" she asked. "Both of them?"

Serena nodded. "Please put the clothing on," she said.

"All right."

Serena—who was strong despite her slight frame—helped Chris stand. "Do you need help undressing?" she asked.

"I'll just put this on over my old clothes." Before the girl could protest, Chris slipped the dress over her head. Burlap sacks had more shape than this piece of clothing, Chris decided. "Do you know where we're going?" she asked.

Serena fussed with the tie at the back of the dress. Chris thought she wasn't going to answer, but after a moment she spoke very softly. "I wasn't supposed to hear, but Jedediah said something earlier about a helicopter flying in to take you and the Exalted to a safe place."

"A helicopter?"

"Yes. The Exalted flies in one sometimes."

This was certainly a step up from Edmund Harrison's mode of transportation back when Chris and her mother were part of his followers. Then again, he had been collecting money from his acolytes for a long time. Enough, apparently, to pay for a private helicopter. If he took Chris away in that, her friends would have a very difficult time locating her.

Before she could prod the girl for more details, Jedediah returned with three other men. "We need to go now." He took Chris's arm. One of the other three took hold of Serena. "Don't try to fight," Jedediah said. "If you do, we'll hurt the girl."

The look in his eyes made her believe he would enjoy doing so. She bowed her head and meekly went with him. But inside, she was seething, her mind furiously searching for some way out of the mess.

She was startled to find it was almost dark out, the sun only a lavender afterglow above the mountains, the air cool despite her layers of clothing. It would be full dark soon, an inky blackness without the benefit of light from buildings or cars or streetlights. The kind of darkness in which a person could step off a cliff and never know it until they were falling.

The guard's headlamps lit the way up the trail. The group climbed higher, up into the mountains. Were they taking her to a place where the helicopter could land and pick her up? It seemed very late in the day for that. If walking in the mountains after dark was dangerous, flying then presented a host of other hazards. The rescue helicopters they sometimes used needed daylight for their maneuvers.

They stopped before what was clearly a mine entrance, complete with a massive iron gate designed to keep out treasure hunters who might end up falling down a shaft or crushed by collapsing rock or drowned in flooded tunnels. Jedediah pulled open the gate and shoved hard at Chris's back so that she stumbled forward. Serena was pushed in after her, and the gate clanged shut. Jedediah fitted a heavy chain and a brass lock to the entrance. "You can't break the lock," he said. "Don't waste time trying. And we won't be far away."

They left, and Serena began to sob. Chris put her arms around the girl and tried to comfort her even as she fought her own fear. "It's going to be okay," she whispered. "I have a lot of friends looking for me."

"Are the police your friends?" Serena asked.

"Yes." At least, Chris was sure law enforcement would be part of the search. The sheriff and the deputies she knew were friendly and good at their job, even if she wasn't close to them. She wasn't really close to anyone other than her mother.

And Rand. She was beginning to feel close to him. Surely he would be looking for her.

"I saw two men in uniform with guns," Serena said. "I came to the camp where Jedediah had sent a few of us. I wanted to get water for you, and the ginger tea. The two uniformed men and a third man with them saw me. That made the others angry at me. They told me it wasn't smart of me to let the lawmen see me."

"You are smart," Chris said. "I had only known you a few minutes before I figured that out. And it's good that the officers saw you." And the third man—had that been Rand? "That means they were close. They'll keep looking for us."

"How will they find us now that we've moved?"

They had probably been moved in order to get farther away from the searchers. "Search and rescue has a dog that can follow people's scents and find them," Chris said. She had marveled at how adept fellow SAR volunteer Anna Trent's standard poodle, Jacquie, was at locating lost and missing people.

"A dog?" Serena sounded skeptical.

"It doesn't matter how they find us," Chris said. "I know they won't give up until they do." And Chris wouldn't give up either. She would find a way to fight back. She would follow her mother's example and do whatever it took to break free of the Vine once again.

DESPITE RAND'S DETERMINATION to search for Chris all night if necessary, he was sent home as darkness fell. Danny had cornered him as he prepared to set out with a new group of volunteers who planned to focus around the area where he and Travis and Dwight had interviewed the campers. "Go home," Danny said. "You're dead on your feet, and you're going to end up hurt and we'll have to rescue you too." Before Rand could protest, he added, "I haven't announced it yet, but we're pulling in all the searchers. It's not safe to have people up on the mountains after dark. Try to get some rest, and we'll start up in the morning."

Rand wanted to protest that he could keep going. He'd be careful, stick to known trails and use his headlamp. But he saw the wisdom in Danny's words. The chances of finding Chris in the dark were minuscule, and the odds of himself or someone with him getting hurt increased with the loss of daylight.

When he unlocked his door, he was greeted by Harley, who howled and sniffed him all over, then gave him what seemed to Rand a reproachful look. "I'm sorry, but she's not with me," he said, rubbing the dog's ears. "I promise we're going to find her soon." He hoped that was a promise he could keep.

He fed the dog and forced himself to eat a ham sandwich. He should take a shower and go to bed, but he was too agitated. He riffled through his collection of hiking maps and found one for the area around Guthrie Mill and spread it on the table. While Harley watched from his dog bed in the corner, Rand studied the map. He circled the spot where he thought the campers he had visited today had been with a yellow highlighter, then chose a blue marker to inscribe a circle around this spot. At least half the circle was occupied by a rocky couloir falling away from a 13,000-foot peak that was unnamed on the map. Hard to get to for searchers, but also for anyone trying to hide Chris.

That left the rest of the area encompassed by the circle—a network of abandoned mines, lesser peaks and high mountain meadows. Chris could be anywhere in this area. There were no roads up there, so the only way to get her away from the trail near the mill where they had taken her was to walk. And they would be able to walk only so far in the approximately six hours since they had kidnapped her. Darkness would halt their progress, just as it had the progress of searchers. Or at least, it would slow them down, if they were foolish enough to try to traverse the terrain by starlight. So the odds were high that she was still in the area within that blue circle.

Harley followed Rand into his bedroom, where he filled his pack with extra clothing and first aid supplies. Then the two of them went into the kitchen, where Rand packed food and water. He glanced at the dog, then stuck in packets of canine food and biscuits. Harley wasn't a trained tracker, but he was devoted to Chris. Rand counted on the dog to home in on any scent of her.

Lastly, he returned to the bedroom and unlocked the safe where he kept the sidearm he had owned since his days in the service. He had no doubt the members of the Vine were armed, and he wanted to be prepared.

Only then did he take a shower and go to bed. He set his alarm for an hour before sunrise. At first light, he and Harley would be back at the spot where he had seen the girl, Serena, emerging from the woods. The girl was part of the Vine. Following her should lead him to the group and—he hoped—to Chris.

CHRIS COULDN'T SLEEP. Her head pounded and her stomach churned. Everywhere she tried to sit or lie was uncomfortable. Her stomach growled, and she realized she hadn't eaten since breakfast. And what about the girl? "Are they not going to feed us?" she asked.

"I guess not." Serena sat nearby, close enough that Chris could hear her breathing. "The Exalted says fasting is good for purifying one's thoughts."

It was another one of those things members of the Vine said, parroting their leader. Chris had said those things, too, when she was a child, trying to please the adults around her and not stand out from the group. She couldn't say if she had actually believed those things, having become part of the group when she was five. But Serena had been taught these lessons since birth. That was the only reality she knew—a frightening thought itself.

"Come sit beside me," she said, and patted the ground next to her.

Serena slid over, and Chris put an arm around her. "I lived with the Vine when I was your age," she said. "My father died. They said it was from eating poisonous mushrooms. After that, my mother decided she and I should leave the group."

She waited for Serena to express the usual horror that anyone would leave the Exalted and his teachings. How could someone give up the chance for new life on a higher plane? How could they sacrifice the opportunity for true enlightenment and rejoin an evil and dangerous world?

"I never knew anyone who left," Serena said. She cuddled closer to Chris's side. "I mean, I've heard people whisper about ones who left, but they were just…gone. No one ever heard from them again."

"I never knew anyone who left either," Chris admitted. She knew there were others who had escaped, and her mother remembered some of the names. But they never met any former members out in the "real" world. Had some of them, like her father, been eliminated at the Exalted's orders? Was it possible she and her mother were the only ones who got away, and that was part of the reason for the Exalted's dogged pursuit? "What happened to your parents?" she asked.

"Something was wrong with the heater in our trailer, and they went to sleep and never woke up," Serena said.

"Do you mean carbon monoxide poisoning?"

"Yes, I think so."

"Where were you when this happened?"

"I was spending the night with Helen. I was eight, and it was supposed to be a special treat."

So Helen was still with the group. "Is Helen your friend?" she asked.

"More of a teacher, I guess."

"Had you spent the night with Helen before?" Chris asked.

"No. This was the first time. We made pizza and played Chinese checkers."

A treat, or a means of getting the little girl out of the way while her parents were gotten rid of? "Where do you live now?"

"With Helen. We have our own trailer, next to the Exalted. I have my own room. Sometimes he comes to visit me. When I'm older, I'm going to marry him. But you're going to marry him first."

A shudder went through Chris. The life Serena was living would have been Chris's life if she and her mother had stayed with the Vine. Chris squeezed the girl's shoulders. She was furious but trying not to show it. Someone had to stop this man, who preyed on innocent children in the name of religion. "I'm not going to marry the Exalted," she said. "I'm going to get away."

"You can't do that. You'll suffer for all eternity."

"Not as much as I'd suffer if I married the Exalted. I'm going to get away."

Serena didn't say anything for so long that Chris thought the child might have fallen asleep. Then she stretched up, her mouth very close to Chris's ear. "When you go, will you take me with you?" she whispered.

Chapter Fifteen

Seven years ago

Chris sat at a coffee shop near the campus of the Rhode Island School of Design, her mocha latte growing cold as she struggled with a sketch of the older woman seated across the room. The deep lines and weathered skin of the woman fascinated Chris, but she was having a hard time conveying the depth and texture to the drawing on the page.

"Do you mind if I sit here? All the other tables are full."

She looked up to see a smiling young man with a mop of sandy curls. She glanced around the room and saw that business had picked up since she had sat down an hour ago, and all the tables were occupied. "Uh, sure." She moved a stack of books over to make more room.

"Thanks." He sat and dropped his backpack on the floor beside his chair. "Are you a student at RIS-D?"

"Yes. Are you?"

He shook his head as he sipped his coffee. "I guess you could say I'm studying philosophy."

"Where are you studying?"

"I'm part of a group led by a fantastic teacher. It's an incredible program. And totally tuition free. I'm learning so much, and it's such a great group of people."

Goose bumps rose along Chris's arms. She closed the sketchbook and slid it into her backpack. "Where is this program?" she asked.

"It's wherever we want it to be. That's the best part. I'm getting this incredible education, for free, and I get to see incredible places like this while I do so."

Providence, Rhode Island, was a nice place, but Chris didn't think it qualified as *incredible.* She reached for the textbooks on the table.

Her table companion put his hand on hers to stop her. "I'll bet you would really like the program I'm in," he said. "Being an artist, you're used to looking at the world with more intention than the average person, am I right? My teacher could show you so much more. It would really enhance your art and your life."

Chris pulled her hand away and picked up the books. The young man's spiel was too familiar, but she needed to find out a little more before she ran away. She needed to know exactly what she was up against. So she forced herself to relax. "What's your teacher's name?" she asked.

"Have you ever heard of a group called the Vine?"

The name sent ice through her, but she somehow managed to remain seated at the table, a pleasant expression on her face. "I don't think so. Is it some kind of winery or something?"

The young man laughed. "Not exactly. It's a group of like-minded people working toward a better world. Our teacher is a tremendous thinker and leader."

"What's his name?" she asked.

The young man sipped his coffee again. "We call him the

Exalted. He's just so enlightened. And really caring. I'd like to take you to meet him. You'll be blown away, I promise."

Chris shoved the books into her backpack and stood, almost knocking over her chair in the process. "I just remembered," she said, "I'm late for a class."

She hurried out of the coffee shop and broke into a jog when she reached the sidewalk. The Vine was here, in the smallest state in the union, at a small art school where she happened to be enrolled.

She didn't believe in coincidence. Walking across campus, she pulled out her cell phone and dialed her mother's number.

"Is something wrong?" her mother asked. "You never call me in the middle of the day."

"The Vine is here, in Providence. I just talked to a young man who tried to recruit me."

"Did he know who you are?"

"No. He was just trolling the local coffee shop."

"You need to come home. Now. Before they see you."

"I'll leave this afternoon. As soon as I can pack a few things."

"What will you tell the school?"

"The usual—a family emergency." It wasn't the first time she had left a school or a job suddenly. It was an inconvenience and unfair. But it was better than letting the Vine get her in its clutches again.

THE FIRST RAYS of the sun were burning off the gray of dawn as Rand crouched behind a boulder, looking down on the campsite he and the sheriff and deputy had visited yesterday. He and Harley had been sitting here, cold seeping in, for forty-five minutes, the camp so still he might have thought it abandoned if not for the faint growl of snoring from the closest tent.

He shifted, fighting a cramp in his left thigh, and Harley let out a low whine. Rand froze as two people moved out of the trees, toward the orange tent. He raised his binoculars and recognized Jedediah and an older woman. After a moment, the door to the tent parted, and the younger man with glasses emerged. The three conferred for a moment, then looked up at the sky. Rand followed their gaze and saw a bank of dark clouds moving toward them. A storm would make travel up here more difficult and dangerous, but maybe it would give him and Chris an advantage when it came time to flee. After a moment, Jedediah, the woman and the man from the camp turned and walked back the way they had come.

Rand stowed the binoculars and stood. He picked up the pack, and Harley rose also. "Let's follow them," Rand said.

The dog led the way but stayed close. He had alerted to Rand's wary attitude and followed suit, picking his way carefully over the terrain and keeping silent. Without being told, he set a course that would intersect the route taken by the three they had been watching. When they were near enough to catch a flash of movement in the trees ahead, Rand stopped, and the dog stopped too.

They waited until the trio had passed, then moved forward cautiously, halting every few steps to listen. Rand froze and moved behind a tree when someone—he thought it was Jedediah—spoke, close enough that Rand could understand every word: "Wake up. The helicopter will be here soon, and you need to be ready to go."

Rand didn't hear the answer, but Jedediah and the woman left, leaving the dark-haired man behind, apparently to stand guard.

Harley whined. The hair along the dog's back rose in a ridge, and he stood stiff-legged, tail and ears alert. "That's where they're holding Chris, isn't it?" Rand said quietly.

He waited until he was sure Jedediah and the woman were gone, then crept closer. He needed to find a way to get rid of the guard without raising an alarm. He watched as the man took a seat on a rock near the mine entrance. He looked disgruntled, pulled from his sleeping bag by Jedediah's early arrival, marched to stand guard without even a cup of coffee.

How to get rid of the man so that Rand could free Chris? He thought back to his military service. He had been a surgeon, not a soldier, but he had heard hundreds of stories from the men and women he cared for, and had seen the results of their efforts on both themselves and the people they fought. The classic approach for dealing with a lone sentry was to sneak up and overpower the guard. Even if the man was only half-awake, Rand didn't see how he could possibly get close enough to do any damage before the guard shouted for help.

A sniper could take him out, but bullets made noise, and Rand wasn't a good enough shot to be sure of hitting the man with a pistol shot from any distance. And the idea of killing someone who had done nothing to harm him repelled him.

He took out his binoculars and scanned the man carefully. If he was armed, the weapon was well hidden. Rand was taller and heavier, so in hand-to-hand combat, he had a good chance of overcoming the guy. He just had to get close enough to launch a surprise attack.

Rustling in the bushes to his right startled him. He turned, one hand on the weapon at his side, in time to see Harley disappearing into the underbrush. He resisted the temptation to call the dog back. What was he doing? This wasn't the time to take off after a rabbit.

"Who's there?"

The guard was staring toward the underbrush where the dog had disappeared. He must have heard the rustling too. The man moved toward the sound. A few more paces and he would be practically on top of Rand. Rand took a careful step back. He started to replace the pistol in its holster, then thought better of it and moved into the underbrush after the dog, both the guard's and the dog's movements helping to drown out any noise he made.

"Who's there?" the guard demanded again. "Come out with your hands up, or I'll shoot."

He's bluffing, Rand thought. The man didn't have a gun. Unless he had drawn one just now. From Rand's position in the clump of scrubby pinion trees, he could see only the side of the man's head. He froze and waited, holding his breath, as the man pushed past him. Then Rand raised his pistol and hit the guard on the back of the head.

The man's legs folded under him, and he toppled with a groan. Rand caught him before he was flat on the ground and dragged him backward, behind a shelf of rock and mostly hidden by a pile of weathered logs that was probably once a miner's cabin. He felt for the man's pulse—strong and steady—then used a bandanna from his pack as a gag and tied him up with rope he also took from his pack.

Harley returned and sniffed at the unconscious man. When the guard was safely silenced and trussed, Rand patted the dog. "I don't know if you meant to distract him and make him walk over, but it worked." He straightened. "Come on. We don't have time to waste. Let's find your mom."

Harley raced ahead to the gate across the opening to the

mine and barked. "Chris!" Rand called, keeping his voice low. "Chris, are you in there?"

"Rand? Harley?" Then Chris was standing there—or at least, a woman who sounded like Chris but was dressed in a shapeless gray dress that came almost to her ankles and a blond wig that sat crookedly on her head. "Rand, what are you doing here? Where's the guard?"

"The guard is tied up behind some rocks. And I'm here to get you out."

"There's a lock on the door." This, from a girl who appeared beside Chris—the same girl Rand had seen emerging from the woods on his visit to the camp with the sheriff and his deputy. Serena.

"This is Serena." Chris put a hand on the girl's shoulder.

"We've met before," he said.

"You're the man who tried to help Lana," Serena said. "How are you going to get us out of here? The gate is locked."

Rand moved over to examine the chain and heavy padlock. Then he turned his attention back to Chris. "I'm going to have to shoot the lock off." He drew the pistol once more.

Chris looked alarmed. "Someone will hear you."

"They probably will," he said. "So you have to be prepared to run as soon as I get the gate open."

Chris pulled the wig from her head and tossed it to the ground, then shucked the dress off over her head, revealing the jeans and top she had been wearing yesterday. "I'm ready." She took the girl's hand. "And Serena is coming with us."

Serena pulled free of Chris's grasp. "I'm too slow. I'll hold you back."

"No. I promised I wouldn't leave you. You're coming with us."

"You're coming with us," Rand agreed. He hefted the pistol. "Stand back, then get ready to run."

CHRIS COULD HARDLY believe Rand had found her, but she had no illusions that getting away from Jedediah and the others would be easy. They would have to have luck on their side.

Serena huddled against her. Chris clasped one of the girl's hands tightly and pulled her closer. The child was trembling. "It's going to be okay," Chris whispered.

A deafening blast of gunfire shook the air. Chris flinched and wrapped both arms around Serena. "Come on!" Rand shouted as he dragged open the gate. "Hurry!"

They scrambled out of the cave and up the steep slope to the left, loose rock sliding beneath their feet. Harley bounded ahead of them, leaping from rock to rock like a mountain goat. Chris grabbed hold of clumps of grass to pull herself up, while Serena scrambled on hands and knees ahead of her. "This way," Rand urged.

As they topped the rise, shouts rose behind them. "They're coming!" Serena cried.

"Run!" Rand urged.

They ran, the dog bounding along beside them. Serena cried out and she stumbled and fell. Rand doubled back and scooped her up. He boosted her onto his back, and she clung there, gripping his shoulders, her legs wrapped around his torso. Chris looked forward again and ran.

Though she was in good shape from training for search and rescue, she wasn't a runner. The rocky, uneven ground made it impossible to achieve any kind of regular pace. Every few feet, she stumbled or planted a foot wrong, and the thin air at this altitude soon had her gasping for breath. She could hear Rand laboring behind her.

She slowed, panting, and looked back the way they had come. "I don't see anyone coming after us," she said.

"Keep moving," he said. "We need to put as much distance between us and them as possible." He led the way, cutting across the top of the ridge, then plunging down a long barren slope. Thunder shook the sky, and fat raindrops began to fall. Chris's feet slid out from under her and she fell, but she scrambled up again, ignoring the pain in her left ankle, and staggered after Rand.

At the bottom of the slope was an area of scrubby trees. They plunged into this cover as the rain began to fall harder, staying closer together. "You can put me down now," Serena said.

Rand lowered her to the ground and straightened. "This way!" He pointed to their right, and they set off at a fast walk.

"Where are we going?" Chris asked.

"Back toward the mill," he said. "There will be searchers and probably law enforcement there."

"Will they help us?" Serena asked.

"Yes," Rand said. "They will help us."

"I'm scared," Serena said.

"I am too," Chris said. "But it's going to be okay."

The trees where they had sought cover thinned, and they emerged on open ground once more.

"Stop right there." Jedediah and two men armed with rifles stepped out to surround them.

SERENA HUDDLED BESIDE CHRIS, her shoulders shaking as she silently wept. Chris rubbed her shoulder. "It's going to be okay," she murmured. Was that the right thing to say or only one more lie to a child who had been raised on lies?

Jedediah moved toward them. Harley put himself between Chris and the men with guns, barking furiously.

Jedediah aimed the rifle at the dog. "No!" Chris shouted, and lunged for the dog's collar. "Harley, no!"

The dog quieted. Chris continued to hold him and glared at Jedediah. "You will have to learn obedience," he said. "The Exalted will make sure you do."

Serena began to weep more loudly. "I didn't want to go with them!" she said. "They made me." She sank to her knees at Jedediah's feet. "Please forgive me! I would never betray the Exalted! He is everything!"

Rand stood a few feet away, a guard on either side of him. They had taken his pistol and his pack. He caught Chris's eye, his expression questioning. She shook her head. Serena had certainly come with them willingly, but now she was terrified, saying what she had to in order to survive.

"Get up," Jedediah ordered.

When Serena didn't move, the fourth man pulled her upright and marched her away. Jedediah moved in beside Chris. She stood. Harley remained between her and Jedediah but kept quiet. "Move," Jedediah said.

They trudged for almost an hour in silence, only the occasional crunch of gravel beneath their feet or labored breathing on a steep slope punctuating their steady pace. A steady downpour soaked their clothing and left them shivering. Thunder rumbled, and jagged lightning forked across the sky. Chris flinched with each mighty crack and wondered at the chances of being struck by one of the bolts.

They descended into a narrow valley and finally stopped beside a metal shipping container set against a large boulder. Jedediah nudged Chris in the ribs with the barrel of the rifle. "Get in," he ordered. "You'll wait here for the helicopter."

Fighting rising panic, Chris moved into the container—

a long metal box without windows. Her footsteps rang hollowly, a dull sound beneath the staccato beat of rain on the metal top and sides of the container. Harley trotted in beside her, the tick of his toenails signaling his path across the floor. Rand stumbled in last. As the door swung shut behind them, Chris caught a glimpse of Serena's tear-streaked face as she stared after them.

The door closed, plunging them into darkness. Chris reached out a hand and Rand clasped it, a reassuring anchor in this sea of fear. The sound of a bar being fit over the door, followed by the drag of chains, signaled their imprisonment. She put her free hand over her chest, as if to keep her painfully beating heart from bursting from her skin.

They stood there for a long moment, saying nothing. Gradually, her eyes adjusted and she realized they weren't in total darkness. Light showed around the door and broke through pinpoint holes in the container's metal sides. The container was empty except for a metal pail in the corner, which she assumed was meant to serve as their toilet. Rand released her hand and walked over to the door. He ran his fingers along the gaps around it, then shook his head. "I don't see any way to pry it open."

"I doubt if we'll be here long," Chris said.

Rand returned to your side. "What was that about a helicopter?"

"The Exalted apparently has a helicopter now. He's sending it to pick me up."

"A helicopter won't fly in this storm," Rand said.

"It sounds like the rain is slowing," Chris said. The drops were more intermittent now, and she only had to raise her voice slightly to be heard over their patter.

"What will happen to Serena?" Rand asked.

"I don't know." She clasped Rand's hand again. His warm

grasp calmed her. "You know she only said those things because she was frightened," she said. "She was born to the group. She's been told all her life that if she ever leaves them, she'll be condemned for eternity. She's just a child."

"I'm not blaming her," he said. He squeezed her hand. "Was it like that for you? Were you afraid to leave?"

"No. But I wasn't born in the group. And while my father was a true believer—at least for a while—my mother never really was. She went along to be with my father. She said at first it wasn't so bad. She liked the idea of living off the land with a like-minded group of people. But the more time passed, and the more she saw how the Exalted brainwashed people into obedience, the more resistant she was to remaining in the group. I remember she and my dad argued about it." She fell silent, trying to judge if the rain was really slowing. "I won't get on that helicopter with him," she said. "I won't."

He put his arm around her shoulder. "I'll do everything I can to stop him," he said. "For now, all we can do is wait." He sat and she lowered herself to sit beside him. Harley settled on her other side. The metal floor and sides of the container were cold, and she shivered in her damp clothing, her wet hair plastered around her head. She laid her head on Rand's shoulder and closed her eyes. She was still afraid, worried about what Jedediah and the others might do to her, about what would happen if she was taken away with the Exalted, and about where Serena might be right now.

The rain and Rand's warmth must have lulled her to sleep. She started awake at the scrape of the bar over the metal door being lifted and Harley's loud barking. "Harley, hush!" she commanded, and the dog fell silent once more. The door of the container opened wider, enough for someone to be shoved inside, then it clanged shut once more.

Rand was already kneeling beside the crumpled figure on the floor. "Serena, are you okay?" he asked.

Chris joined him, then gasped as Rand gently shifted the girl toward the light. One side of her face was swollen and bruised, and a thin trickle of blood trailed from the corner of her lip. "Did Jedediah do this?" Chris demanded.

Serena nodded and continued to sob.

Chris pulled her close. "It's okay," she murmured. "They had no right to hurt you."

Serena sobbed harder. "I didn't mean it," he said. "Those things I said about you making me go with you. I was scared of Jedediah. I didn't want him to hurt me."

"I know." Chris stroked the girl's back.

"Bad things happen to people who disobey the Exalted," Serena said. "That's why my parents died."

"I told you my mother and I left the Vine when I was about your age," Chris said. "I was scared, like you. But things worked out for us. I make my living as an artist. I have friends and I volunteer to help others. I never could have done any of those things if I had stayed with the Vine."

Serena sniffed and wiped her eyes with her fingers. "But they caught you. They made you come back."

"They won't keep me," Chris said. "And they won't keep you either."

"How are we going to get away?" Serena asked. "There are more guards this time."

"We'll find a way," Chris said. She couldn't afford not to believe that. There was so much more at stake than her own safety. Serena's and Rand's lives were also at stake—two people who were becoming more and more important to her.

Chapter Sixteen

Rand left Chris to deal with Serena and paced the shipping container, his steps ringing on the floor. In the dim light, he examined the sides of the container. "I'm trying to find some weakness we can use to our advantage," he said. After a full circuit of the box, he ended up beside Chris and Serena once more. Serena had stopped crying and was sitting with her arm around Harley, stroking his side.

"Search and rescue and the sheriff's department will still be searching for us," he said. He spoke just loud enough to be heard over the rain but not loud enough for the guards to make out his words.

"Maybe not in this rain," Chris said. "The safety of the searchers always comes first."

"I could try to overpower the guards," he said.

"There are three of them, plus Jedediah," Serena said.

"And they have guns," Chris said. "I think our best opportunity is going to be when they try to move us. Maybe we can create some kind of distraction. I could pretend to faint?" Even to her ears, the plan sounded dubious.

"When they come to get us, they're going to have all three guards and maybe some reinforcements from the camp or the helicopter," Rand said. "That's also likely to be when they decide to deal with me—either right before or right after you leave."

An icy shiver raced through her. "What do you mean, 'deal' with you?" she asked.

"They don't have any intention of sending me with you and Serena in that helicopter," he said. "They'll get me out of the way as soon as possible."

Chris stared. She wanted to protest, but she saw the truth in his words. Jedediah wouldn't want to deal with Harley either. If they were all going to get out of this alive, they had to figure out a way to escape before the helicopter arrived.

"We need to eliminate the guards one at a time," Rand said. He looked toward the door. "It would help if we could see who was out there. I'm guessing the guards take shifts, with only one or two at a time here at the container."

"There's a gap around the door," Serena said. She moved over to the door and pressed her eye to the gap. "From down here I can see out." Pause. "I see two guys. One is sitting on a rock, huddled under a tarp. The other is pacing back and forth. He's wearing a poncho. They both look pretty wet and miserable."

Rand moved closer to Chris. One hand resting on her shoulder, he leaned over and spoke in her ear. "If you can create some kind of distraction, maybe we can get the guards inside and overpower them."

"That will only work if they both come in here," she said.

"They might welcome the chance to get out of the rain. Or, if you can create a big enough ruckus, they might believe they'll need to work together to subdue you."

She nodded. "I'm willing to try."

He looked around. "I wish I had something I could use to hit them over the head. Even a big rock would do."

There were no rocks in the shipping container, and the

guards had taken their packs. "There's the slop bucket," she said. "But it's empty."

"It has sand or cat litter in it," he said. "If we throw that in their faces, it will momentarily blind them. Maybe enough for me to get hold of one of their guns."

"That's a lot of *if*s," she said. "But I can't think of a better idea."

RAND WASN'T CONVINCED his plan would work, but he couldn't see a viable alternative. "Serena," he called. "We need your help."

She joined them, and Rand explained their plan. "We need you to stay to one side and keep hold of Harley," Rand said. "As soon as I give the word, you take off running, out of the container and away from the area. Chris and I will be right behind you."

She nodded. "All right." She took hold of the dog's collar and coaxed him to the front corner of the container, just to the right of the door.

Rand looked at Chris. "Are you ready?"

She blew out a breath. "Ready."

He moved to the left of the door and she faced it, then threw back her head and let out a shriek. Rand started. "Oh no, oh no, oh no!" she shouted. "Help! Someone please help!" The hair on the back of his neck rose. If he hadn't known she was faking, he would have been totally convinced.

Someone pounded on the door. "Quiet down in there!" a man yelled.

Chris shrieked even louder. "No! No! Please help! Help!"

"What's going on?" a second male voice demanded.

More shrieks and wails from Chris. Serena joined in. "Oh no! It's horrible. Help! Help!"

The chain rattled, followed by the scrape of the bar. The door creaked open, and one man stuck his head inside. "What's going on in here?"

Chris sank to the floor and thrashed around, moaning and groaning. The first guard moved inside. Chris thrashed harder and shrieked more. "You have to help her!" Serena pleaded.

Harley began barking, adding to the deafening echo within the container. The first guard knelt beside Chris and grabbed her arm. She rolled away from him, thrashing harder.

"You need to hold her down, or she'll hurt herself," Serena cried.

"Joel, get in here!" the first guard cried. "I need your help!"

The second guard stepped inside. "What's going on?"

"Help me with her," the first guard said.

Joel moved in and stood beside the first man.

Rand rushed forward. He hurled the contents of the pail into the face of first one man and then the other. They staggered, and he punched the first man, breaking his nose. Then he wrenched the rifle from the guard's hands and used it as a club to hit the second man. He went down, and Harley immediately bit him.

"Get him off me!" the first man screamed.

"Harley, release!" Chris shouted. She was on her feet now. She picked up the second man's rifle and hit him over the head. Both men were on the ground now—one unconscious, the other groaning.

"Let's go!" Rand grabbed her hand.

"Serena!" Chris called.

"I'm right here. Harley, follow me." She raced out the door, and the others followed.

The rain hit them in an icy downpour. Rand scanned the area but saw no other guards. Maybe the storm had muffled the sounds of their struggle enough that Jedediah and the third guard hadn't heard. "Which way do we go?" Chris asked.

Rand had no idea, but he reasoned Jedediah and the other guard were probably somewhere facing the door of the container. "This way!" He pointed to the rear of their former prison.

They ran, slipping on mud and slick rock but getting up and going again. Serena stayed with them, the dog at her side. Their course gradually took them downhill. Rand tried to picture the topo map of the area he had studied last night, but he couldn't relate this soggy landscape to what had been printed there. All they could do was continue to put distance between themselves and their captors.

After what felt like an hour but was probably only a fraction of that, they entered a drainage, clumps of grass and wildflowers replacing bare rock, a thin trickle of water cutting a path ahead of them. The rain slowed, then stopped, and the sky began to clear. Rand stopped beneath a rock ledge and they rested, waiting for their breathing to return to normal before anyone spoke. "Where are we going?" Serena asked.

"I don't know," Rand admitted. "But a drainage like this should lead to a stream or a road or something." He hoped. He wasn't certain that was true.

Chris looked up the way they had just come. "I don't hear anyone following us," she said.

"Maybe they're gathering reinforcements." He straightened. "Let's keep going."

They walked now, instead of running, but they kept a steady pace. No one complained, though he knew they were all hungry and tired. He fell into step beside Serena. "How are you doing?" he asked. "Are you in pain?"

She shrugged. "My face hurts. But I'll be okay."

The drainage they had been following did end—not at a stream or road but in a box canyon. They spent the next two hours picking their way up the canyon walls, grappling with mud and loose rock before finally emerging at the top as the sun was sinking. "We need to find a place to spend the night," Rand said.

They studied the landscape. Rand wished he had his pack and binoculars. "That looks like a building over there." Chris pointed to the west. "Maybe an old mine ruin."

They trudged in the fading light toward the structure, which proved to be the remains of a cabin, the roof mostly gone and one wall collapsing. But they cleared out a dry spot at the back. With the darkness, the temperature had dropped, and they were all shivering, with no way to make a fire.

"Let's huddle together," Chris said. "We'll keep each other warm."

They put Serena between them, with Harley at her feet. Soon, she was breathing evenly, asleep. Chris stroked her hair. "I'm still so angry that they beat her," she said softly. "She's just a child."

"She's safe with us now," Rand said. But for how much longer? The Exalted and his followers had proved they were relentless in their pursuit.

"Why does he want me so badly?" she asked. "Why go to so much trouble to have me?"

"Maybe it's because you defied him and got away," Rand said. "He wants revenge, or to make an example of you for his followers. Or maybe he's obsessed. He's decided he has to have you, and that's what drives him." He wrapped his arm around her. "But I'm not going to let him have you." He didn't know how he could stop them, but he would do everything in his power to keep her with him.

She tilted her head back and looked up, blinking rapidly. He wondered if she was holding back tears.

"THE WORLD LOOKS so big from here," Rand said.

She nodded. Her world inside the Vine had been so small. Everything revolved around the Exalted and life in the camps. Their whole focus was obeying the Exalted, serving him and, thus, somehow, perfecting themselves. Even though she had told Rand she wasn't as fully indoctrinated as Serena, it had taken her a long time after she and her mother had left to accept that no one and no situation was perfect.

Rand leaned in closer, and she turned toward him. She shifted until she was pressed against him, then kissed him. The kiss was a surrender—not to him as much as to the part of her that wanted to rest, to feel safe in his arms. And it was a release of the tension she had been holding in too long. She had fought against trusting anyone else for so many years that it had become second nature, but Rand made her want to trust him, with her secrets, her fears and her very life. The feeling both frightened and thrilled her, and she did her best to translate those sensations into that kiss.

He brought his hand up to caress the side of her neck, and she leaned into his touch. She wanted to be closer to him, but the child between them prevented that. She had to be content with drinking in the taste of him, the soft pressure of his lips, the firm caress of his hand. She wished she could see more of his face in the darkness, but maybe that only heightened the experience of that kiss. It warmed her through and fed a growing desire within her. "I wish we were alone, somewhere more comfortable," she whispered.

"If I have to be here," he said, "I'm glad it's with you."

She laughed, more nerves than mirth. "You have a strange idea of romance."

He kissed her again. Okay, not strange at all. If he could make her feel this way with a kiss, imagine what he could do with more time and room.

Serena moaned and stirred between them, and they pulled apart a little. Their situation was truly awful—stranded and lost, pursued by people who probably wanted to kill Rand and Harley and make Serena's and Chris's lives miserable. But Chris was no longer afraid. Was this what it was like to be in love?

RAND WOKE BEFORE DAWN, cold and stiff and hungry. He tried to extricate himself from the tangle they had slept in without disturbing the others, but Chris woke up. "Is something wrong?" she asked.

"I'm just getting up to stretch my legs." He stood, wincing as he straightened his aching limbs. "I'm going to see if I can find us some water."

Outside, the damp chill of early morning stung his skin. The sky had lightened from black to sooty gray. Rand picked his way across a stretch of gravel into a clump of willows. Just beyond the willows, a spring seeped from the ground into a moss-rimmed pool. He knelt and scooped water into his hand. It was clear and sweet smelling. He drank deeply, scooping water into his mouth over and over. They would all probably have to be treated for the giardia bacteria that was endemic in mountain waterways, but that was a small price to pay for freedom.

A buzzing startled him and he leaped to his feet, searching for the source of the sound. It came from the sky. He looked up and saw a drone hovering overhead. He immediately crouched and burrowed farther into the cover of the willows. Had the drone seen him? The sheriff's department had a drone they were using to search for Chris. Was this it? Or did it belong to the Vine?

He waited until the drone was out of sight, the sound of its buzzing fading, and hurried back to the miner's shack. Chris and Serena were both up now, and Chris was braiding Serena's long dark hair. "I found a spring," Rand said. "The water is cool and sweet."

"I'm so thirsty," Serena said. She rubbed her stomach. "Hungry too."

"I know." Rand patted her shoulder. "I'm hoping we'll be safe and eating a good dinner by tonight."

"Did you see anything to indicate which way we should go?" Chris asked. She finished the braid and wrapped the end with a strip of what looked like torn T-shirt. Dark shadows beneath her eyes and her pale complexion betrayed her weariness. But she was still the most beautiful woman he knew. The memory of the kisses they had shared last night sent heat through him. He believed she was starting to trust him, and he hoped that would lead to a future together.

She was looking at him curiously, and he realized he hadn't answered her question. "I didn't look around much." He hesitated, then added, "I spotted a drone. I don't know if it saw me or not."

"What's a drone?" Serena asked.

"It's like a miniature helicopter with a camera attached," Rand said. "It can fly around and take pictures of anything on the ground. Do you know if the Vine has anything like that?"

She shook her head. "I never saw anything like that."

Rand glanced at Chris. "The sheriff said he would be using a drone to search for you. I'm hoping this one belongs to them, but I wasn't sure, so I stayed out of the open."

Chris dusted off her hands. "Let's get a drink and see if we can figure out where to head next."

Rand led the way to the little spring, and they took turns drinking the water. Chris walked along the stream for a short distance, then returned. "I can't tell if it goes anywhere or not."

"Let's climb up a little higher and see if we can find a spot with a better view of the countryside."

They moved slowly up a steep hill behind the ruins of the cabin. Even Serena was moving with little energy today. If they didn't find help soon, they were going to be in real trouble. No food, little water and little sleep were starting to take their toll. At the top, Rand studied the land spread out before them—a cream-and-brown-and-gold expanse of rock, like taffy spilling from the pot. Clumps of trees and falling-down mine ruins and rusted equipment dotted the landscape as if scattered by a child's hand. He fixed his gaze on a narrow band of white cutting across a slope below.

"Is that a road?" Chris asked.

He nodded. "I think so." Probably a backcountry Jeep road, but if they could reach it and head downhill, they would eventually come to a more major road, with traffic and people and the help they needed.

They set off, grateful for the easier downhill travel but at the same time aware of how exposed they were on the treeless slope. He kept glancing overhead, wondering if the drone would return.

As if responding to his thoughts, a distant buzzing reached them. "What's that noise?" Serena asked.

Rand scanned the sky. The drone was flying straight toward them. There was nowhere to hide. He dropped into a squat. "Get down," he said. "If we can blend into the rock, it might not see us." It was a trick used by prey animals— freeze and hope the predator doesn't notice.

They huddled together on the ground as the drone passed over them. It didn't hover or circle back. Was it possible they had avoided detection again?

They hurried on. Rand was anxious to reach the cover of the trees. They were almost there when a much louder sound cut the air—a deep throbbing he felt in his chest. "It's a helicopter!" Serena shouted.

"Run for the trees!" Rand yelled.

Chapter Seventeen

They ran, but the helicopter was gaining fast. They were still a hundred yards from the tree line when the first bullet struck a rock near Rand's feet, sending chips of granite flying. "Spread out!" he shouted. The farther apart they were, the harder it would be for whoever was firing to get them all.

Chris headed off in a sharp diagonal. Serena took off after her. Rand headed in the opposite direction. Another bullet hit a boulder near him. A fragment of rock hit the side of his face. He wiped at it, and his fingers came away bloody. He put his head down and kept running.

He was almost to cover when gunfire ripped from the trees. Yet the bullets weren't aimed at him—but at the helicopter. The chopper rose sharply and veered away. A man in black tactical gear stepped out of the trees, a rifle cradled in his arms. Rand froze.

"Are you all right, Rand?" The man lifted the visor of his helmet, and Rand recognized Deputy Ryker Vernon.

Chris and Serena caught up with them. Serena clung to Chris and stared at Ryker. "We're good now that we're with you," Rand said.

Ryker looked up at the sky. "Do you know who that was, shooting at you?"

"The helicopter belongs to the Vine," Chris said. "Their leader, Edmund Harrison, was probably in there with some of his followers."

"They kidnapped Chris and Serena and were going to take them away from here in a helicopter," Rand said. "The storm yesterday delayed them, and we managed to get away."

"I'm still nervous, out in the open like this," Chris said. "Can we please leave?"

"There's a group coming up to help us," Ryker said.

Rand heard voices approaching. Soon, two deputies and half a dozen search and rescue members joined them. "Is everybody okay?" Danny asked.

"We're good," Chris said.

"Rand, you're bleeding." Hannah studied his face.

Rand swiped at his cheek. "A rock chip hit me. I'll be okay. You can clean it up later. Right now I just want to leave."

"Who is this?" Danny addressed Chris, but he was looking at Serena.

"This is Serena." Chris kept her hand on the girl's shoulder.

"What's your last name, Serena?" Bethany asked.

"It's Rogers." Serena looked up at Chris. "I'd almost forgotten that."

Chris nodded. "Members of the Vine don't use last names," she explained to the others.

"Chris!"

She looked up to see Bethany hurrying toward her. The younger woman threw her arms around Chris and hugged her, hard. After a second's hesitation, Chris returned the hug. It felt good. "I'm so glad to see you!" Bethany said. "I've been so worried." Her voice broke.

"Hey, it's okay." Chris patted her shoulder. "I'm good."

Bethany released her hold and wiped her eyes. "I'm glad to hear it. I'd hate to think I'd lost a new friend."

"Yeah. I'd hate that too," Chris said. She meant it. "Let's get together for lunch again soon."

"Let's. I can fill you in on my family's latest plan for taking over my life." Bethany laughed and turned away.

"We have some vehicles waiting at the road to take you back to Eagle Mountain," Jake said.

"Do you have any food?" Serena asked. "We're starving."

This prompted the rescuers to dig into their packs and produce an assortment of nuts, dried fruit, protein bars, chocolate and gummy candy. Chris, Serena and Rand gratefully accepted this bounty. Danny examined Serena's bruises and treated her busted lip. They ate as they walked, a new vigor in their step. Rand glanced ahead toward Chris, who was chatting with Bethany. They were safe, for now. But could he continue to protect her from the Vine, as long as they were still free?

"WHAT WILL HAPPEN to Edmund Harrison and the rest of his followers?" Chris addressed this question to Sheriff Walker as soon as he entered the interview room at the sheriff's department, where she and Rand were seated, only a few hours after their rescue.

"We have a BOLO out for his arrest," Travis said. "And we're continuing to search for the rest of the group."

"Where is Serena?" Chris asked. "You can't let her go back to those people. You saw the bruises on her, right?"

"She's with Deputy Jamie Douglas right now," Travis said. "We've summoned a child-welfare advocate. They're working on finding an emergency placement for her."

"She can stay with me," Chris said. She leaned forward,

hands clenched in her lap. "She trusts me, and I understand some of what she's been through."

"You'll have to take that up with the child-welfare person," Travis said. He settled into the chair across from them. "What I need from you is everything you know about the people who kidnapped you."

The last thing Chris wanted was to sit there and give them all the details about the Vine. But she pushed aside her annoyance and told Travis what she knew, about the group's history, its habits and the people involved in the group now. She and Rand described the various guards and the woman they had seen with Jedediah. "Jedediah is the one you really need to find," she said. "He's the Exalted's right-hand man."

"The Exalted is what they call Edmund Harrison?" Travis verified.

"Yes. And he's got most of them so brainwashed they'll do anything he says."

"And you indicated they're armed?"

"I saw at least three rifles," Rand said. "And one of them took my pistol."

"I never saw firearms when I was with the group," Chris said. "But that was fifteen years ago. And they never shied away from violence against their own members, though they called it 'punishment.'"

"We'll talk to Serena once the child advocate is with her," Travis said. "She may be able to tell us more, including where the group might be now."

"They're very skilled at packing up and vanishing in the middle of the night," Chris said. "They did it often when I was living with them. They talked about moving on to enlighten a new audience of people who could benefit from their message, but later I decided they probably left to avoid too much attention from local law enforcement."

Travis nodded, then stood. "You two are free to go. We'll be in touch."

"I think Chris—and maybe Serena too—are still in danger," Rand said. "The Exalted has gone to a lot of trouble to pursue them. I'm not sure he'll give up so easily."

"Do you want us to find a shelter for you to stay in?" Travis asked.

"No." She looked at Rand but said nothing. If the Vine tracked her to his place, she would be endangering him also. "But maybe I should go somewhere like that."

"You can stay with me." Rand took her hand. "But it wouldn't hurt to have a deputy cruise by occasionally."

"We're spread thin as it is, searching for all these people," Travis said. "But I'll do what I can."

Harley was waiting for them in the lobby. Someone had fed and watered the dog, and he looked none the worse for the ordeal of the last forty-eight hours. Chris wished she could say the same. She was exhausted, as well as worried about Serena and about the Exalted. Those moments when that helicopter had hovered over them, bullets ricocheting off the rocks, had been among the most terrifying of her life.

Back at Rand's house, he insisted on checking everything before she and Harley went in. She spent several anxious moments on his front porch, waiting until he returned. "Nothing's disturbed," he said. "You can come in now."

They filed inside. The house was quiet, nothing out of place. She told herself she could relax, but tension still pulled at her shoulders. "You can have the shower first," he told her.

"Can I have a bath?" she asked. "I'd really like to soak in a tub."

"Sure. There's a tub in the primary bath. Let me get my things, and I'll shower in the guest room while you soak."

"Thanks," she said, too weary to make even a polite token protest about him giving up his bathroom for her.

She went to the guest room and dug out clean clothes and her toiletries. Rand still hadn't appeared by the time she returned to the hall outside his room. She heard running water. Had he decided to take a shower first after all?

She was about to knock and check on him when he finally came out of his bedroom. "I was just getting everything ready for you," he said.

She followed him back into the primary bedroom, past the king-size bed with its blue duvet neatly pulled over the pillows. He opened the bathroom door to a fog of steam and gestured toward a garden tub, already filled, froths of bubbles floating on the top. He had arranged candles along the far edge of the tub and lit them, and the scents of lavender and vanilla made a soothing cloud around them.

Tears stung her eyes. "You didn't have to go to so much trouble."

"You're worth any amount of effort," he said, and took her in his arms.

They kissed, a heady caress that left her dizzy and breathless. Rand slid his hand beneath her shirt and rested it at her waist. "I should let you bathe in peace," he said.

She moved in even closer. "I think that tub is big enough for two."

He didn't protest, but pushed her shirt up farther. She helped him guide it over her head, then reached back to unsnap her bra. His hands were hot on her breasts, his fingers gentle but deft as he stroked and teased her. She stripped off the rest of her clothing with shaking hands, clinging to him for balance but also because she wanted to be closer to him.

He was naked in no time, and her breath caught at the sight of him. It had been a long time since she had been this excited about a man, and she was both eager and anxious. When he stepped into the tub, she followed, the silky, warm bubbles closing over them. She let out a sigh as she sank beneath the water, then lay back, her head on a folded towel, and closed her eyes.

The water sloshed as Rand shifted, and then something soft and slightly ticklish glided over her body. She started to open her eyes and sit up. "Relax," he said. "Keep your eyes closed. Enjoy your bath."

She decided the soft and ticklish thing was a soapy sponge he was using to caress first her shoulders, then her breasts. The sponge coasted across her stomach and stroked her thighs, then traveled down her legs to her foot and her toes. She suppressed a giggle as Rand soaped each digit, then slid his hand up the back of her leg, gently massaging. He did the same to the other leg. His touch was gentle but firm, enjoyable but not exactly relaxing.

She wasn't sure when he replaced the sponge with his hands, but she realized it had happened when he began stroking between her thighs, caressing her sex, stoking the passion that began to build.

A moan escaped her, and she opened her eyes and stared at him. His eyes locked on hers, the heat in his expression scorching. "Do you want me to stop?" he asked.

"No." Her answer came out barely audible. She cleared her throat. "No." But even as he continued to tease her, she straightened and wrapped her hand around his erection.

His reaction was immediate and gratifying—a widening of his eyes and a renewed alertness. His hand stilled as she began to stroke him. "Do you want me to stop?" she teased.

"No." But his hand moved from between her legs to her shoulders. He pulled her forward until she was resting on top of them, water sloshing over the edge of the tub as she moved.

"The floor's getting wet," she said.

"That's not the only thing," he said as he slid two fingers inside her.

There she went, giggling again. Definitely not like her. But being with Rand did that—made her feel like someone else. Someone freer and happier than she had ever been.

They kissed again, hands exploring, caressing, teasing as their lips tasted and nipped and murmured appreciation. "That feels so good."

"You're so beautiful."

"Whatever you do, don't stop."

A second tidal wave of water sloshed over when she moved to crouch over him. "Maybe it's time to take this to the bed," she said.

"Good idea."

They helped each other out of the tub; then he insisted on toweling her off, the plush but slightly rough surface of the towel gliding over sensitive nerve endings, ramping up her arousal. He paused to suck first one nipple, then another, a delicious torture that had her squirming.

At last he raised his head, grinning. She realized he had taken the time to shave, the stubble that had grown in the past two days erased, replaced by smooth skin. "Let me get a condom," he said, and opened a drawer beside the sink.

His bedroom was dark and cool, the bed soft, the scent of lavender and vanilla drifting out with the steam from the bathroom. But she only noted these details in passing. Her focus was on him as he lay beside her and pulled her into his arms. They stared into each other's eyes. She didn't let herself look away, as she might have done before. Whatever there was to see in her, she wanted him to see it.

"Why did you come looking for me?" she asked. "By yourself, I mean, instead of part of the official search."

"I thought I knew where to find you, and I didn't want to wait on the others."

"But why look at all?" she asked. "I'm not your responsibility."

"Because I love you," he said.

She flinched at the words. She tried to hide her reaction, but he couldn't miss it. "Does that scare you, when I say it out loud?" he asked.

"A little," she admitted.

"You're strong enough to face your fear," he said.

"Yes, I am." But the wonderful thing about being with Rand was that she didn't have to be strong. She didn't have to fight or resist or do anything. She could relax and surrender without giving up anything.

So she did. She smiled and closed her eyes. She allowed him to touch her in all the ways that felt good, and she did the same for him, until they came together with urgency and need. She gave herself up to the building passion and the incredible release that followed.

Afterward, she lay curled in his arms, tears sliding down her cheeks. "Why are you crying?" he asked.

"I don't know," she admitted. "But it feels good." She hadn't allowed herself many tears over the years, afraid they made her look weak. Rand had taught her to see things differently. Feeling wasn't a weakness, and being vulnerable wasn't wrong. She would have to practice to fully believe those things, but she was willing to make the effort.

THEY HAD BEEN asleep for a while when Rand woke to Harley's frantic barking. "What is it?" Chris asked.

"I don't know." He got out of bed and put on his pants and shoved his feet into his shoes. "I'll check."

Harley ran ahead of him down the hall and began barking again—angry, staccato barks like shouts. "No!" someone commanded.

Rand switched on the living room light and found Harley cowering submissively at a man's feet. The man was fit and trim, with stylishly cut silver hair and a tan. He wore a light gray suit with a white shirt and no tie, like a well-off businessman relaxing after work. The man looked from the dog to Rand. "Even dogs know to obey me," he said.

"Who are you?" Rand demanded.

"I'm the Exalted." He smiled a smug grin.

"Edmund Harrison," Rand said.

"That person hasn't existed for years," he said. "I'm the Exalted. And I'm here for Elita. Or, as you know her, Chris. Hand her over and there won't be any trouble."

Rand pressed his back to the wall and surveyed the room.

"Oh, don't worry," Harrison said. "I came alone. The sheriff arrested Jedediah and the rest of my inner circle this afternoon. But I don't need them. All I need is Elita. With her, I'll start a new band of followers."

"How did you find us?" Rand asked.

"Did you forget we have your phone? There's a lot of information on a person's cell phone. I had your address within minutes of my people handing it over to me."

The hallway floor creaked. Rand forced himself not to look back, his eyes fixed on Harrison. The man was walking around the room, studying the books on a shelf. He didn't register that he had heard the noise, though Harley had turned his head that way.

"Harley, come here." Rand snapped his fingers at the dog, who obediently trotted over.

Harrison stopped and looked at Rand. "I'm waiting," he said. "Bring Elita to me, and I'll leave you alone."

"I'm not going to hand Chris over to you," Rand said.

"Then you leave me no choice." Harrison withdrew a pistol from the jacket of his suit. Rand recognized his own gun—the one Jedediah had taken from him. Harrison raised the weapon and aimed it at Rand. "You don't have to worry," he said. "I'm a very good shot. You'll die quickly."

"No!" Chris burst into the room, something in her outstretched hand. When she aimed the item at Harrison, Rand realized it was the wasp spray he had left on the kitchen counter. She squeezed the trigger, and the spray arced across the room, striking Harrison in the face.

Harrison screamed, and the pistol fired twice, striking the floor and the wall. He bent double, clawing at his eyes and coughing. Then Rand was on top of him, wrestling the gun free. Chris dropped the can of insect killer and began kicking at the man who writhed on the floor. Then Harley moved in and began tearing at his arm.

"Stop!" Harrison cried. "He's going to kill me."

"Harley, release!" Chris shouted.

The dog let go, and Rand grabbed the man's bleeding arm and brought it behind his back. "Get me something to tie him with," he said.

Chris left and returned seconds later, tearing at a pillowcase. She handed a strip of fabric to Rand and he used it to bind first Harrison's hands, then his feet. Meanwhile, Chris called 911.

By the time the sheriff arrived, Rand had retrieved his first aid kit and bandaged Harrison's arm. The man hadn't shut up the whole time. He had variously cursed Rand, condemned him to perdition, prophesied a disastrous future for him and railed against the injustice of someone like him being treated this way. "You have no right," Harrison yelled. "This man attacked me without provocation. I want to talk to my lawyer."

"You'll be given a chance to contact your attorney," Travis said. "Meanwhile, anything you say may be used against you in a court of law." He recited the rest of the Miranda rights, even as Harrison continued to rant.

"This is unforgivable," he said. "Why are you arresting me?"

"We'll start with kidnapping, child molestation, theft and murder."

"Murder?" Chris asked.

"We found the bodies of the two young men who brought Danny and Rand into the camp," Travis said.

"I'm innocent," Harrison protested. "This is an outrage."

He was still ranting as Dwight and Ryker led him away.

Travis turned to Chris and Rand. "We'll need your statement as soon as you can come to the station," he said.

"He said something about Jedediah being arrested?" Rand asked.

"Yes. We have him and several others in custody. We'll need you to identify the people involved in your kidnapping."

"What about the others?" Chris asked. "The rank and file members of the Vine?"

"We believe we've identified most of them. We're running background checks on all of them, which will take some time. The state is involved, seeing to the welfare of the children in the group. A few people have already been cleared and released. Social services will work to find shelter and assistance for those who might need them."

"Where is Serena?" Chris asked. "When can I see her?"

Travis slipped a card from his pocket. "Here's the number for her caseworker. I told her to expect a call from you."

He said goodbye and left. Chris sank onto the sofa. Rand sat beside her. "I guess it's over," she said.

"We still need to give our statements, and we might have to testify at a trial."

"I meant the Vine. Without the Exalted and his cronies, the group is dead."

Rand took her hand. "How do you feel about that?"

"Relieved," she said. "And...sad. I mean, it could have been something good, but it was just a waste." She looked at him. "I want to do something to help them. Some of those families gave everything they had to the group. Now they'll have nothing."

"We'll see if there are ways we can help them," Rand agreed.

"And I want..." She hesitated, then blurted out, "I want to adopt Serena. I'll contact the state and see what's involved, but I really want to do it."

"You'll make a great mom," he said. He had difficulty getting the words past the sudden lump in his throat.

"Will you help me?" she asked.

"Of course." He squeezed her hand. "I love you."

"I... I love you too," she said.

He kissed her—a gentle caress to seal those words of love. "We're going to figure this out," he said.

"What exactly do you mean?"

"We're going to figure out how to love each other and make it work. How to build a life where you don't have to be afraid of the Vine coming to get you. And we're going to help Serena. Did I leave anything out?"

"I don't think so." They kissed again, and then she rested her head on his shoulder. "You make me believe in things that used to seem impossible. And I mean that in a good way."

"I believe in you. And in us. That's the only thing that matters."

"It is, isn't it?"

Epilogue

Party this way! Posterboard signs directed guests to a gazebo in the town park, which was festooned with helium balloons and crepe paper streamers. Chris stood on the top step of the gazebo and waved to Danny Irwin, Carrie Andrews, and Jake and Hannah Gwynn as they arrived, Carrie's son and daughter in tow. They joined the crowd, which included most of their fellow search and rescue members and all the friends who had made the day possible.

Chris's mom, April, came to stand beside her. "I've got the cake safely stowed in the cooler in the ballfield concession stand," she said. "I'll get a couple of guys to help me bring it over here when it's time."

"Thanks, Mom." April wore a sundress in a pink-rose print, another rose tucked into her pinned-up hair. Her eyes were shining, and she looked younger than her fifty years. "It's so good having you here with us," Chris said.

"It's good to be here."

Danny and Carrie mounted the steps, a large wrapped gift in Danny's hand. Serena skipped up the steps behind them. "Is that present for me?" she asked. In the months since she had come to live with first Chris, then Chris and Rand, she had blossomed into a smart, sensitive child with a deep affection for animals and a love of learning. She had also experienced a growth spurt, necessitating a whole new wardrobe, including the tie-dyed sundress "with the twirly skirt" that she was wearing now. The three of them were in counseling to deal with the trauma she had endured. Chris was surprised by how much the regular meetings with a therapist had helped her deal with her own struggles with her past.

"That depends," Danny said. "Who is this party for?"

"It's for me!" Serena threw her hands into the air.

Danny laughed. "Of course. How could I forget!" He handed over the gift. "Then this is for you."

"Don't mind him." Carrie nudged him. "Happy birthday, Serena."

"Happy birthday!" those around them chorused.

"Do you want to open your gifts before or after the cake?" Chris asked.

"After." She grinned. "It makes it more exciting to wait." She added the package to the pile of gifts on a table in the center of the gazebo, then came over to wrap one arm around Chris and lean against her. "I already got my favorite present."

"You mean, the bicycle?" Rand joined them.

"No. I mean you and Mom."

Chris's heart still struck an extra beat at that word—Mom. It had been a long process through the foster care system to get to this day, but the struggle had been worth it for this precious girl—her daughter.

"And I thought that was the best present *we* ever received," Rand said. He kissed Serena's cheek. She grinned, then caught sight of someone across the yard. "Amber!" she shouted, and ran to catch up with Carrie's daughter.

"Is the adoption final already?" Hannah asked.

"We have a few more months to wait," Chris said. "But there haven't been any setbacks so far." She held up crossed fingers.

"And no more noise from Edmund Harrison and his followers?" Danny asked.

"Harrison is facing more than a dozen charges," Jake said. "He'll go to prison for a long time."

Bethany bounded up the steps to join them. She had made an attempt to confine her brown curls in a bun, but they were already escaping to form a halo around her face. "My dad wants to know when to fire up the grill," she said.

"Tell him any time he's ready," Chris said.

"I'll go tell him," Danny said. "See if he wants some help."

"He's already put my brothers to work," Bethany said. She turned to April. "How are you enjoying your visit to Eagle Mountain, Mrs. Mercer?" she asked.

"Please, call me April. And I'm enjoying it very much. So much I'm thinking of staying. With the Vine uprooted and the Exalted behind bars, it's safe for me to live near my daughter without fear of drawing the wrong sort of attention to her. And I want to get to know my new granddaughter better." She looked over to where Serena stood, surrounded by a trio of girls her age.

"We have something else to celebrate today," Bethany said. She nudged Chris.

Smiling, Chris held out her left hand, sun glinting on the sapphire on the third finger. "We do."

"Congratulations!" Carrie and Hannah chorused, then leaned in for a closer look at the ring.

"Rand, you finally worked up the nerve to propose?" Jake said.

"I asked her months ago," Rand said. "It just took her a while to decide to have me."

Chris blushed. "I wanted to be sure."

He pulled her close. "You were worth waiting for."

Bethany sighed. "If I didn't like you two so much, I'd be jealous. Well, okay, I am a little jealous. But I'm thrilled for you too."

Chris looked down at the ring on her hand. "Everything okay?" Rand whispered.

She nodded. "It's just…overwhelming at times. I have so much—friends, my mom, and you and Serena. All things I thought were out of reach for me."

"I thought they were out of reach for me too," he said. "I used to think the fine details were what made a difference in life. Those were the things that were small enough for me to control. Now I can appreciate the big things—it doesn't get much bigger than having a family and raising a child."

Her eyes met his. The thrill of seeing her love reflected back to her never faded. "We're going to do this," she said. "We are." They kissed, and she was only dimly aware of the cheering around her.

* * * * *

SPECIAL FORCES
K-9

JULIE MILLER

For service, therapy, emotional support animals and pets. (Yes, there is a difference in both training and legal designation.) Thank you for all the ways you make our lives better.

Always be sure to ask before petting a dog. (Even if the dog is a pet, this is essential to prevent bites.) Service dogs should not be petted, fed or otherwise given attention while at work. Please be respectful and allow these dogs to do their jobs. They make a major difference in the lives of people with disabilities.

Chapter One

This was a bad idea.

"Mr. Hunter?"

Ben Hunter dragged his attention away from the inde-finable noises that were reverberating inside his head and focused on the fiftyish woman who ran the dog-training business where he was interviewing for a job. If he thought about it, he could identify the noises—children playing, dogs barking, a man talking on the phone, someone rapping along with a song in the barn behind him. Not the footsteps of an enemy sneaking up behind him, nor the babble of a foreign language threatening him with words he barely un-derstood. Not the click of a land mine being triggered, nor the screaming agony of his teammates dying in a barrage of gunfire. Sometimes, too much of any kind of noise was a headache-inducing time bomb that could flash him back to the nightmare he could never truly wake up from.

He probably wasn't making a good impression on his po-tential new boss with his distracted thoughts. "I'm sorry, ma'am. Could you say that again?"

Jessie Caldwell offered him a friendly smile as if this wasn't the first time she'd had to repeat a question to a pro-spective employee. Or a man. Or a stitched-together soldier like him, trying to make a new life for himself now that the Army couldn't use him. Not with his PTSD or his scars or...his missing hand. "I asked if you had any experience milking a goat."

"Goats? Uh, yeah." Ben shook his head and tried to smile. But *friendly* wasn't a look he was much good at pulling off these days. "When I was a kid, we'd visit my aunt and uncle on their farm in the Ozarks, down near Carthage. We'd help with chores, including moving hay, feeding the animals, mucking stalls, driving the tractor and milking their cow and goat." He instinctively looked down at the prosthesis sticking out from the end of his left sleeve. "I suppose I could still manage it with one hand."

She hugged her arms over the insulated vest she wore on top of her flannel shirt and studied his labored attempts to engage in casual conversation. "Sounds like a fun experience for a kid growing up."

"Yep." *Oh, so eloquent, Hunter*, he silently chided himself.

The idea of getting a job where he had to interact with people like this nice lady was about as bad as breaching that rebel encampment in the middle of a Central American jungle when every instinct inside Ben's head had told him he and his team were heading into a trap, that their intel was flawed, that their mission to rescue a kidnapped diplomat and his family was about to go sideways. Even his K-9 partner, Smitty, had barked furiously, warning them to stand down—that he sensed a danger they could not see.

But Ben had been a soldier who followed orders. When the captain had ordered his team to go in hot, they had. Then all hell broke loose, and Sergeant Ben Hunter's life had changed forever.

Ben curled his right fist against his thigh, tapping it several times in an effort to slow his breathing and keep himself in the moment. To pay attention to what the woman beside him was saying. "We've recently expanded and are almost to capacity with our kennels and barn stalls," Mrs. Caldwell explained. "I have a teenager who comes in part-time to help. But my husband and I have recently adopted our two children, and motherhood happily demands more of my time. I'm looking for someone to live on the property and work full-time, to take over some of the appointments and duties I've done on my own for a few years now. I'm assuming the salary and furnished apartment I mentioned sound like fair compensation?"

Easing the grip of his fingers, Ben nodded his understanding, even though he hadn't heard the first few words she'd said. Maybe it was the noisy dog in the last kennel at the end of the run, barking his fool head off, that was mentally sending him back to that botched mission. Smitty had raised a ruckus just like that on that fateful morning.

But there were no guns here, no enemy combatants. He wasn't even in uniform anymore, save for the long camo Army jacket he wore to ward off the cool autumn breeze and to hide the prosthetic hook strapped onto his left elbow and shoulder. His jeans, work boots and beard that was neatly trimmed, but several inches past the length he'd worn on missions, should have helped him feel like a civilian. He was just a man looking for a job, walking through a neat, sophisticated setup of barn, kennels and outbuildings with a polite, but uncomfortably perceptive, businesswoman who was interviewing him for a position at K-9 Ranch—a rescue and training center for dogs just outside of Kansas City, Missouri.

His counselor said he was ready for this. Sure, he could live on his Army pension. But he needed to find a reason to get up every morning—a purpose he could focus on that would distract him from the memories of his best friends and a call to duty that morphed into nightmares or angry outbursts of frustration. Plus, it wouldn't hurt his psyche to get out of that plain, functional hotel room where he'd been living for the past year and to breathe in fresh country air and enjoy the golds, reds and oranges of the changing deciduous trees and harvested fields of Jackson County.

This was a different kind of apprehensive feeling.

His brownish-blond hair, still cut military short, stood at attention on the back of his neck. It was too noisy here. There was too much chaotic activity. He had thought the rural setting would help him relax, that living outside the city limits would offer the peace his mind craved.

But there was no peace here.

Kids played in the backyard. Puppies trailed after a skinny poodle mix who was heavy with milk. They yipped at the surly looking teenager who'd gone inside the barn with them. A big galoot of a black Lab insisted on pushing his cold nose into Ben's good hand and making friends with him as they walked through the working part of the property. Plus, there was that dog down in the last kennel on the left barking loudly and viciously enough to alert the neighboring farms on either side of K-9 Ranch, if not the entire county.

Damn, if that didn't sound like a warning. One he should acknowledge and react to. But this was a job interview, not a Delta Force mission. And that noisy, angry dog who needed to learn a few manners wasn't Smitty.

Mrs. Caldwell must have read the tension in his posture, or maybe she heard his steadying huff of breath. "I don't suppose you have any experience in dealing with devil dogs?" the older woman asked. Jessie Caldwell tossed her long blond braid behind her back and shooed the friendly Lab out of the kennel area. "Toby." She held up one finger and the dog automatically sat. This woman was a skilled trainer. No wonder her ranch was gaining a reputation as the place to adopt and train rescue dogs for a variety of skills— from a family pet to a detection dog for seizures and other chronic medical or psychological issues to a guard dog. "Find Nate. Go." Obeying her hand signal and verbal command, the dog got up, gathered speed and ran off to tackle the shaggy-haired boy playing in the backyard.

"Tobes!" the boy shouted.

Mrs. Caldwell shook her head as boy and dog wrestled in the dirt and grass together. "Toby is one of the smartest dogs I have. But he's too friendly to be much of a guard dog."

Ben nodded, understanding that she was trying to put him at ease. Part of this interview, he supposed, was seeing if he could interact with people as well as the nearly twenty dogs and three goats on the property. "Bet he'd protect your kids, though."

Jessie smiled and waved to the little girl who seemed to be having a tea party with the Australian shepherd that was stretched out on a blanket beside her. "He would. He has. Toby is devoted to my son, and the feeling is mutual. Abby Caldwell!" The little girl with a matching blond braid down her back whipped her face around to her adoptive mother. "Don't feed Charlie any of those cookies! Dog treats only."

"Yes, Mama." The little girl popped the entire cookie into her mouth and pulled a more appropriate snack from her pocket to feed to the dog beside her.

Feeling uncomfortable with the sudden urge to grin at the sweet girl's antics, Ben tugged on the sleeve of his desert camo jacket, making sure the titanium hook at the end of his arm was covered before he tucked his good hand into the front pocket of his jeans. He didn't want to scare Mrs. Caldwell's daughter if she happened to see his robotic-looking appendage. He'd been up-front about his injury when he'd applied for the position and had assured his potential new employer that he was otherwise a fit, healthy man and that he'd been going through extensive physical and occupational therapy to adapt to the prosthetic device—from using the hook at the end like a set of pliers to grab things to maintaining the strength in his upper arm so that he could safely drive his truck, manhandle a dog, lift a hay bale or manage the physical tasks necessary to train the dogs and handle their care.

Ben beat back another urge to smile that inevitably came when he thought of his time at veterans' clinic where he'd come a long way from an angry, self-pitying man with a stump below his elbow to the functioning member of society he was now. At least he was able to take care of himself. After making a slight modification to the steering wheel, he could drive his own truck; he could dress himself and even tie his own boots. He'd made some friends at the PT/OT center who seemed to understand the particular challenges of working with a veteran.

And then there was Sweetcheeks. Aka Maeve Phillips, the shy, sometimes skittish, occupational therapist who rarely looked him in the eye when she spoke to him, but who, with her curly dark hair, plump, naturally rosy cheeks and unique eyes, had filled more than a few of his daydreams. He had an ongoing silent research project to determine exactly what color her eyes were. Hazel was the generic term, he supposed. But he'd seen gold centers rimmed with a grayish-green, green flecked with gold-and-silver specks, and a beautifully cool shade of smoky gray in her gaze, depending on the color of scrubs or sweater she wore.

It also depended on her mood. The cooler colors dominated when she was her usual, serene self. But when her temper flared—often at him because her soft words and shy looks and gentle touches seemed to get under his skin—he'd react to the discomfort with some crass, brash, belligerent comment to deflect his attraction to her and remind himself that she looked on him as a patient, not a man. Then the gold in her pretty eyes flashed a warning signal that he was being a dumbass, and that she rightly wasn't going to put up with his attitude. He'd want to apologize or skip the rest of their session so that he wouldn't offend her with his surly attitude or worse, frighten her.

Ben's smile faded, and he got back to the business at hand. He had no business thinking about Maeve or any other woman. Piecing his life back together after losing so much was a long, painful process. Getting involved with a woman was a long way down the recovery road—if building a relationship with someone should even be on his to-do list at all. Certainly not until he got his PTSD under control and found something meaningful to do with his life now that his career in Special Forces had been taken from him.

"You mentioned devil dogs? I assume you're talking about the loudmouth at the end and not a Marine?"

Mrs. Caldwell chuckled, although he hadn't meant it as a joke. "That would be Rocky. He used to be a Marine, in fact. He's a hard-luck case who has only been here a couple of days. Sad story. His partner was killed in a training accident, and he didn't take to being reassigned to another Marine very well. They can't muster him out to a family because he's…unpredictable. And I hate the idea of having to put him down after he's already served his country."

Yeah. That was the joke he'd told himself that first morning in the hospital, knowing his hand had been shot away and he was being medically discharged from the job he'd loved. The doctors should have just put him down. What else was he good for besides being a soldier?

The dog snarled, and he got a glimpse of a coal black snout pushing through the chain link gate at the front of his kennel.

Counseling was keeping Ben sane, and months of physical and occupational therapy were making him a human being again. But what did the military do for a dog who could no longer serve? A dog who wasn't fit for civilian life any more than he was?

"Miss Jessie?" The teenager who'd trudged into the barn trudged back out. He wore a Kansas City Chiefs ball cap backward on top of his long, reddish-brown hair. He spoke a little loudly because he still had his earbuds in and had the music turned up loud enough for Ben to hear the thumping bass notes. "I got 'em all fed. Except for him." He pointed his thumb toward the black shepherd. "Do I have to feed Killer?"

The moment the teen's thumb got too close to the gate, Rocky lunged at him. The boy pulled his hand to his chest and jumped back.

"Stand down," Ben snapped. He met the dog's dark eyes before the ranch owner could intervene. He held his hand up in a fist the same way he would have ordered his platoon to halt.

Rocky sank back onto his haunches and sat, recognizing the command. Maybe responding to the camo uniform or the authority in his tone. Or maybe the muscular black shepherd sensed a fellow veteran dealing with emotional issues and was smart enough to be cautious around him.

"Good boy." Ben praised the dog and opened his hand, silently telling the dog he was off duty. The black dog walked forward and lay down. His red tongue lolled out of the side of his muzzle, and he panted heavily, as though relieved to understand he was off duty.

"Whoa, dude." The teenager pulled the buds from his ears and gaped at Ben. "He's never done that for me before. How'd you do that?"

"We'll take care of feeding him, Soren." The blonde woman put her hand on the sleeve of the teen's denim jacket. "This is Ben Hunter. Soren Hauck. His family lives on the farm next to my place. He works a few afternoons a week and Saturday mornings for me. His grandfather used to work for me. But Hugo suffered a stroke and needs to take it easy for a while." She gave the young man a sharp look, urging him to hold out his hand.

Ben extended his good hand to shake the boy's. "Good to meet you."

"Yeah."

"Yeah?" Mrs. Caldwell tapped the teen lightly on the shoulder, urging him to come up with a more polite response. "Ben is going to be your supervisor now that your grandfather is out of commission."

"He is?"

"I am?" Ben answered at the same time, both of them looking at her in surprise.

But she was cool as a cucumber with that soft smile that reminded him too much of Maeve. "Grab my keys and go to the storage room. A delivery of new supplies came this morning. I need you to open the boxes and put everything away on the shelves."

"Yes, ma'am." When the boy gaped at the hook on Ben's left arm, Ben pulled it farther into the sleeve of his jacket. But then the teen was pulling out his cell phone and jogging back to the barn, probably texting his buddies about the gimp he'd just met. Or maybe he was pulling his music back up and tuning out the adults.

"You're hiring me?" Ben didn't know whether to be put off by her presumptuous statement or relieved that some-body wanted him for a job. "I'd have to work with the kid?"

She laughed, nodding toward the barn where Soren had gone. "Typical moody teenager. Doesn't always make the best choices, but I think he's a good kid at heart. His grand-father had taken him under his wing. I think he misses his guidance."

"Look, ma'am, dogs I can handle." He had to be honest with her. "But I'm not great with people."

"We don't get crowds here," she assured him. "And you just impressed Soren, which is hard to do. We get some veterans and former police officers here, looking for dogs. I bet you could get along with them, that you'd speak the same language."

He nodded. "Probably."

She glanced back at the man in a sheriff's department uniform standing at the railing on the back deck, talking on his cell phone, and gave him a thumbs-up. Without inter-rupting his phone call, the man responded with an answer-ing thumbs-up and smiled.

Ben had been briefly introduced to Jessie Caldwell's hus-band, Garrett, when he'd first arrived for this afternoon's interview. Now the man was keeping an eye on the children and Ben, while his wife walked him around the property. Ben approved of that kind of vigilance. Not that he was any kind of threat to the Caldwell family or their animals. But the Army had trained him to be a threat to the enemy, to have his teammates' backs and to be alert to any poten-tial threat that might come at them. Deputy Sheriff Garrett Caldwell didn't make him feel ill at ease. Quite the opposite. It felt good—normal—to have another warrior on the premises since Ben had neither his teammates, a weapon nor his service dog to rely on for protection anymore.

But Jessica Caldwell wasn't asking for her husband's permission with her hiring decision. "Look, as far as I'm concerned, you just worked a miracle getting Rocky to mind you." She pointed to the athletically built black shepherd, and he growled in response. Ben snapped his fingers and pointed to the dog, who instantly fell silent and tilted his nearly black eyes up to Ben. Mrs. Caldwell was smiling when Ben faced her again. "One of your jobs will be to train Rocky so we can hopefully get him well-behaved and predictable enough that it'll be safe to adopt him out."

"He lost his partner?" Ben asked, trying not to think of dragging Smitty's broken body back to the evac chopper that had rescued the survivors that day in the jungle.

"Yes." She shrugged. "I'm sure he's grieving and lost without the job and surroundings he's familiar with. But as you know, Ben, he's a weaponized dog. He's too dangerous to be uncontrollable. K-9 Ranch is his last stop before it's determined he can't be rehabilitated and has to be put down."

"You're not putting him down!" Ben growled, perhaps a little too harshly for a man looking for a job here. Apparently, Rocky was as much of a head case as he was. But if Sergeant Ben Hunter could acclimate to civilian life, then he'd bet money that, with the right support and emotional healing, Rocky could find a new, meaningful role to play outside of Army life, too. "I'm sorry, ma'am. I'd like him to have a decent chance at a normal life."

"He won't be put down," Mrs. Caldwell reassured him, her voice calm. "Not if you do as good a job training him as I think you can."

"You've got that much faith in me?"

"I have good instincts about dogs." He could see the woman believed what she was saying, and he had to respect that. "I'm pretty good at matching the right dog to the person he or she needs. I think you and Rocky speak the same language. I don't trust him around my children yet. Clearly, Soren's afraid of him. And he and my Anatolian got into it the first day he was here, trying to decide who was top dog on my ranch."

"Your dog okay?" he asked, hoping Rocky hadn't seriously injured the big dog.

Her smile widened. "Rex isn't a very social dog. But he guards this place like the champion he is. He made it clear to Mr. Grumpy Butt there that *he* was the big boss."

Ben's beard almost shifted with a smile. "Rocky needs boundaries. He needs a mission. Once he understands who the enemy is, who's an ally and what his purpose is, he'll mind his manners."

"Unfortunately, he seems to see enemies everywhere."

Didn't that sound familiar? Hell, he and that dog had too much in common.

"Until me."

"Until you." She extended her hand. "Want the job?"

Saving Rocky? Training dogs? Doing a little ranch work? Was that enough reason for him to get up in the morning? He reached out his hand to shake hers. "Yes."

She held his hand a moment longer, challenging him to be sure about his decision. "I haven't even shown you the apartment above the barn yet."

"I don't need much, and I travel light," he assured her. "You said the bed is new and the appliances all work?"

"It's nothing fancy, but it's a new addition we had built over the barn these past few months, so yes, everything's new."

Ben nodded, then looked back at the black shepherd who was still watching him through the gate, as if waiting for his next command. "Then I'm your man."

Chapter Two

"He's not your man. Not anymore. You had good reason to kick him to the curb."

"Give it a rest, Maevie. I know what I'm doing." The tall blonde smacked her full lips, as if making sure the deep red color she'd just applied was still there. "I plan to at least hear Austin out. Even if he doesn't want to get back together, I at least need his help at work, to keep my boss, Mr. Summerfield, from hitting on me."

Yes, a boss with groping hands who hinted at a promotion in exchange for sexual favors was bad news. But surely, anyone associated with this place was something worse.

"Austin's going to make excuses and say all the things you want to hear. Bertram Summerfield is a senior partner in your firm. Do you really think Austin is going to stand up to the man who signs his paycheck? You deserve better than him." Maeve Phillips followed her roommate, Stephanie Ward, out of the gross excuse for a women's bathroom into the back hallway of Shotz's bar. Conditions out here weren't much better, but at least she could take a deep breath.

But she regretted it as soon as she did.

Her nose crinkled at the pungent odor of weed seeping in through the back door and blending with the stale beer smell that seemed to permeate every floorboard in the place. Shotz's wasn't a bar she would have picked for a girls' night out to boost Steph's ego after a particularly painful breakup with her now ex-boyfriend. Kansas City had many wonderful bars—historic reclamations that served yummy food and unique drinks, dance bars, sports bars, karaoke bars and more.

Maeve nervously moved her hands up and down the long strap of the small cross-body purse she wore. Oh, how she wished they were at one of those places. Shotz's was none of those things, and she couldn't wait to be gone. She wasn't even sure the place qualified as a pick-up bar, although there were certainly plenty of men and women here looking to do just that. No, she'd say the foul-smelling, dimly lit, music-blasting bar was more of a place to buy drugs, pick up a hooker or plan a bank heist than to sip a fruity drink and flirt with some cute guys in an effort to help her friend forget how her relationship had ended.

Too late, she'd realized that Steph's desire to hit so many bars wasn't about drowning her pain or meeting someone new, but about tracking down her ex and patching things up with him. Although, she still couldn't be sure if Steph's desperation was prompted by love or career goals or some combination of both. At Shotz's, they'd finally run into a man who claimed to be a buddy of Austin Bukowski's and who'd made a phone call, and now Austin was on his way here to meet them.

"Joker is bad news." Maeve eyed the muscle-bound man with the stringy black hair and some seriously offensive tattoos waiting for them at the end of the hallway. The way everyone either said hi to him or ducked their heads and walked a wide berth around him told her he was a regular here. Customers and waitstaff knew him, and they either wanted to be part of his entourage of hangers-on, or they wanted to avoid him. Maeve was definitely in the latter camp. She had no idea how he'd gotten that silly nickname he'd introduced himself by, but she doubted it had anything to do with being a comedian. Not with those muscles, those disturbingly dark eyes and those tattoos that made her believe he didn't allow anyone—especially a woman—to say no to him. "How does Austin even know a guy like that, anyway? He wasn't going to help us until you slipped him that twenty-dollar bill. I don't think we should trust him."

Steph held up her hands in an apologetic concession. "Maybe Joker is a little creepy, but Austin's not."

"Austin's not here," Maeve reminded her friend.

"But he will be," Steph argued. "He was concerned that I was here, too. Let him ride to my rescue. Everything will be just fine."

As her watch crept past midnight, Maeve worried about her own rescue. She didn't have a boyfriend, brother or reliable male friend she could call to see her safely home. She had an ex she refused to call. And the only family she had was a mother who probably wouldn't pick up the phone if she *did* call. Maeve had agreed to be the designated driver tonight, so her car was parked a block down the street. Even if Austin did show up to sweep Steph off her feet, how was *she* going to safely get to her car? Asking Joker or the bouncer at the front door who shared some of the same crude tattoos wasn't an option. She didn't see any other likely heroes she'd trust in here.

Maeve felt a little queasy when a pair of men bumped past them on their way out the back door. She hadn't missed their hesitation to enter the back hallway. Or Joker's subtle nod that seemed to give them permission to exit into the alley behind the bar. Wait. Was Joker blocking the end of the hallway to keep people out? Or to keep her and Stephanie trapped back here. "Steph...?"

"Five minutes, okay?" her roommate grumbled. "We'll give Austin five minutes to show. Maybe ten. If he's not here by then, I promise we'll blow this pop stand."

It wasn't much of a promise, but Maeve thought it was the best she was going to get from her tipsy, heartsick friend tonight. "Five minutes," she agreed, checking her watch before crossing her arms over the front of the gray cardigan sweater she wore, mentally counting down the time.

When her housemate and friend since high school, Stephanie Ward, had asked her to be her wingwoman to troll a few bars to rebuild her ego after a big fight and breakup with her ex, she didn't realize they'd be barhopping until midnight. Or that tonight wasn't about reminding Steph she was a beautiful, sexy, accomplished catch—it was about hunting down her ex-boyfriend and attempting to patch things up with him because *alone* wasn't a condition Steph was used to.

As far as Maeve was concerned, *alone* was a far better alternative to being stuck with the wrong man, as she'd been for two years before walking away from a dangerous, soul-sucking relationship, finishing college and moving to Kansas City, where she was not only earning her master's degree in occupational therapy, but she was also working full-time using her undergrad training in physical therapy. Back in tiny Grangeport, Missouri, where they'd graduated high school, Maeve had allowed herself to be sucked in by the social norm of being identified by the man she was with. Ray Maddox might be the son of Grangeport's former mayor, but his handsome, outward appearance hid an ego the size of the entire state and a mean streak she'd been eager to leave behind. Steph had already moved to Kansas

City to earn her paralegal degree and get a job. Meanwhile, small-town drama in the form of her ex followed Maeve to college in Columbia, Missouri, and she'd been forced to transfer schools to finish at the University of Central Missouri in Warrensburg with a degree in Kinesiology. Maeve had had to work for a couple of years to save money for graduate school. When Steph had invited Maeve to move in with her and split the cost of a house in a nice neighborhood, Maeve had jumped at the chance. Not only could she pursue her master's at Saint Luke's College of Nursing and Health Sciences through Rockhurst University, but she'd have a friend and a home to start her new journey with, instead of being completely on her own.

Oh, she had a mother back in Grangeport or wherever Claudia Phillips's latest boyfriend was living now. But since Maeve had been more of a parent to Claudia than the other way around, and her dad had abandoned them before she was born and had never been part of her life, Maeve had seen life at home as an anchor on a sinking ship, rather than the safety net for any new adventure.

But Steph had changed since high school. Or maybe Maeve was the one who had changed.

Tonight's search for Mr. Right seemed to have a desperate edge to it, as if Steph believed the same lies Maeve's mother had about needing a man in her life to be happy, to pay bills, to feel complete. Meanwhile, Steph's outgoing personality, sexy shape and bright red lips made Maeve feel like a prudish stick-in-the-mud, by comparison.

"He's still my boyfriend. We needed a little time apart so that he could miss me and realize how much I mean to him." Steph unbuttoned the top button of her blouse, showing off a little more cleavage as she watched the bar's entrance, waiting for Austin to show. "Do you think this is too much?"

In Maeve's opinion, she was showing way too much skin with the suspect sanitary regulations being met in a place like Shotz's. And yeah, Maeve wasn't comfortable with all the stray gazes being drawn to her busty friend. "It shouldn't matter what you're wearing if he really cares about you. A good guy doesn't talk to you like he did. Trust me, I know."

"Not every guy is a jerk like your ex."

That was a low blow. "Yes, but some of the signs with Austin are the same—"

"Austin is not Ray Maddox."

"I know, but—"

Steph raised her voice to be heard above the music and conversations around them. "Since you can't seem to pick up a guy, with that turtleneck up to your chin and all your paranoia, I'm not going to go with your advice on men."

"I'm not trying to pick up anyone—"

"Enough, Maevie. I'm sorry you were hurt so badly that you can't be happy for me. But Austin is a junior partner in our law firm. He's going places, and I'm going with him. He's into me. He said he wants me back. I believe him. Now go home."

Maeve felt dark eyes burning through the sensible clothes she wore, making her feel extremely uncomfortable. When she tilted her gaze to Joker and watched him stroke his tongue around his lips, the queasiness returned, and she quickly looked away. There was no way Joker was an attorney, like Austin. She worried about how the two men knew each other. She pushed aside those worries and kept her voice even in one last attempt to reason with her roommate. "I don't think we should wait here a minute longer. You asked me to be your designated driver. I'm trying to look out for you."

"I'm not that drunk. Can't you just be happy for me?"

"I don't think you're making the best decision here. He said terrible things to you. He stole money from you. He stole from me, too."

"I paid you back. He hit some hard times. Obviously, he's doing better now."

"*He* should have paid me back," Maeve pointed out, not for the first time wondering what a junior partner in a law firm had needed the hundreds of dollars he'd taken for. "Meet him another time when you're stone-cold sober, in a place less creepy than Shotz's. If he's serious about getting back together with you, he'll do it."

"Thanks for looking out for me, sweetie, but I'll be okay. I need to do this. I love him." Steph leaned in and wrapped Maeve up in a surprisingly tight hug. As she pulled away, her hand got caught in the strap of Maeve's purse. By the time they disentangled themselves Steph was smiling down at her. She patted the big catchall bag she'd borrowed from Maeve. "Besides, I've taken precautions this time. I've got the upper hand," she whispered. "He's not going to hurt me again."

Maeve was happy to return the hug, but she frowned at the cryptic comment. "What do you mean by precautions? What are you talking about?"

"There's my woman." Suddenly, there were two men at the end of the hallway. Steph spun around a little too quickly, gripping Maeve's shoulder to steady herself, and beamed Austin Bukowski a gorgeous smile. She gave Maeve a reassuring wink and crossed to the man wearing a gray suit and crisp white shirt without a tie. He wrapped Steph up in a hug and kissed her temple. "Joker, I'm glad you called me."

"It's what bros do for bros." Joker elbowed Austin in the arm, hard enough that the move jostled Steph. The nudge seemed a little too hard to be playful, but the two men laughed.

Maeve gave rescuing her friend from this dubious re-union one more shot. "Steph, please."

"Go. Home." Steph wound her arms around Austin's waist and nestled against his side. "I'm good now."

"Yeah, you are." Austin draped a heavy arm around Steph's shoulders and pressed a kiss to her blond hair. "Missed you, babe." He raised his blue eyes that seemed bloodshot with fatigue and grinned at Maeve. "Your friend staying for a threesome?"

Maeve bristled. "What? No!"

"Too bad. Good to see you again, Maevie." Austin and Joker both laughed. She assumed he was teasing but didn't appreciate the joke. "Why don't you double up with my buddy, Joker." He nodded toward the dark-haired man standing behind his shoulder. "He's here stag tonight. He could teach you a thing or two about losing that turtleneck and lightening up."

"No, thank you," she articulated, sounding every bit like the uptight prude Steph had accused her of being.

Joker laughed and clapped his hand over Austin's shoulder. "Ooh, so proper. I bet she doesn't even know how to party. No thanks, bro. I don't want to work that hard. She's a buzzkill."

"Guys, go easy on her. She's shy." While she was glad to hear Steph defending her against the insulting innuendoes, she was less pleased to see Joker guiding the couple out of the hallway. "Besides, I'm enough woman for you, baby."

"Don't I know it." The blond attorney dipped his head to capture her lips in a big smooch. "Missed you."

"Not as much as I missed you."

The conversation continued as they walked away. "You gonna give me what I want?" Austin asked.

"Talk first. I'm giving you a second chance. But I want

to make sure this time around that we both understand the ground rules of this relationship."

"Rules, huh?" Austin didn't seem too pleased with that statement. "Then we get to the good stuff?"

"Maybe."

Maeve pushed through the patrons at the end of the hallway. "Steph—"

"Buzzkill." Joker stepped in front of Maeve, stopping her in her tracks. He clamped his heavy hand over her shoulder and dragged it down her arm, tightening his grip when she tried to jerk away. His eyes raked her from head to toe and he laughed. "Too much work." Then he abruptly released her and followed Steph and Austin through the crowd.

There were no goodbyes. No more arguments to be made. Stephanie and Austin stumbled toward a booth across the bar, with Joker following and sliding into the bench seat across from them. Maeve and her worries were long forgotten. Maybe with her history, Maeve *was* a little paranoid when it came to men, and she couldn't trust what her gut was screaming at her. Maybe Ray had done such a number on her that she'd never be able to tell a good guy from a threat again. It wasn't as if her mother had taught her what a good relationship looked like. She'd learned plenty of hard lessons from Claudia Phillips about using men, how to hurt and be hurt and how to ignore your heart, forget your child and swallow your pride to go after the next guy who might just be the one—only to see the whole, hopeless cycle start all over again.

She hadn't been able to save her mother from humiliation and heartbreak. And, apparently, Maeve couldn't help Steph, either. "Might as well go home."

"Don't go yet, sweetheart."

She put up her hand, deterring the sketchy man, reeking

of alcohol, who pulled out the stool next to him at the bar and offered to buy her a drink.

"No, thanks." She ventured outside, took note of the traffic and the people around her before clutching her purse to her chest and setting out at a good pace to get to her car.

Only when she was safely locked inside and the engine was running, did she pause to send her roommate a text, knowing Steph probably wouldn't see it until the next morning. But at least her own conscience would be clear.

Fingers crossed that this is the HEA you're hoping for. If you decide you need a ride, after all, call or text me. Anytime. Day or night, I'll be there. Be safe. See you at home. Love ya.-M

Then she tucked her phone into the cup holder in the center console and pulled out into the sporadic flow of traffic moving through the western edge of Kansas City. The drive home would be quicker if she cut through the streets downtown and headed straight east. But after that unsettling visit to Shotz's, she decided to skirt around the city on the highways. She was on her own and the hour was late, and she didn't want to risk stopping at a traffic light, much less breaking down somewhere along the way.

But when she pulled out onto I-35, a black sports car zipped around a semitruck and pulled in right behind her. She pressed a little harder on the gas pedal to put some distance between them and was relieved to see another car pull into the gap between them.

She might have forgotten about the black car, except it merged onto I-70 behind her. Even that shouldn't have alarmed her. I-70 was the main east-west highway through the city, forming the main line through a nexus of intersect-

ing highways and city streets. When she slowed to take some
tight S-curves around the exit ramps and overpasses where
several roads crossed and merged, she expected the speeding car to pass her. Instead, the car between them pulled
out to pass, and the sports car closed the distance between
them, creeping right up to her bumper, its lights blinding
her in the rearview mirror. "What the hell, buddy?"

Glancing away, she gripped the wheel tighter and shivered. She wasn't sure it was safe on this serpentine stretch
of road, with vehicles merging and exiting in front of and
beside her like a choreographed dance, to remove one hand
from the wheel to crank the heat inside her car. But this guy
was a menace, and after her time at Shotz's and her worry
about Steph, this whole night was giving her the chills.

He flashed his bright lights at her, and she jerked. Was
there something wrong with her car? Was he trying to help?
Or was he being the consummate jerk, warning her to kick
it into a higher speed so that he could get to his destination
faster? "Pass me, already," she urged.

But no such luck. If anything, the lights in her mirrors
grew brighter. He was so close, she feared his car would
smash into her trunk if she slowed down even a fraction.

Since she was already driving above the speed limit, and
she wasn't about to pull off onto the shoulder in this high
traffic area, she switched on her turn signal and exited the
interstate, turning back toward the downtown area she'd
been trying to avoid. She glanced back in her rearview mirror. "Oh, hell."

The sports car exited right along with her.

"Are you following me?" Who was that guy? Or was
this a simple coincidence made creepy by losing her argument with Steph and her unsettling encounter with Joker
and the patrons at Shotz's? Maeve quickly ran through her

options. Keep turning to see if she finally lost him? Slow
her speed so much that he'd be forced to drive around her
or risk an accident?

A yellow stoplight loomed in front of her, and she
stomped on the accelerator to fly through the intersection.

Double hell. He ran the red light and stayed right on her
backside.

Could she read the license plate? Identify the driver? She
hadn't seen anyone leaving the bar after she did, but she'd
been distracted with her phone, worried about Steph.

Her fingers ached with their tight grip on the steering
wheel, and she was almost panting with nervous energy
when she thought of another option. A smarter option. A
piece of advice she'd learned from a campus police officer
one of the times she'd called them about Ray stalking her.

This could be nothing more than a jerk driver or someone heading to the same part of the city. But if someone
had followed her from Shotz's—and there wasn't anyone
there besides Steph whom she wanted to see again—then
she was going to drive to a place where she'd have backup.
Maybe not a friend or brother or boyfriend.

But a cop.

Chapter Three

Traffic and stoplights at nearly every corner forced Maeve to slow down. But the black sports car was still riding her tail. Squinting into her mirrors as she turned a corner, she could finally see the make of the car. Dodge Charger. Everything about it was black, from its shiny paint color and the trim on the hubcaps to the tinted windows that kept her from identifying the driver.

Ray, her ex-nightmare, had told her a Charger was a man's car, built with power and style. And for a split second, she had a weird, panicked flashback to Ray following her around Columbia as she walked home from campus one night. But Ray's Charger had been a bright cherry red, meant to be noticed, not blend into the shadows like the car behind her now. Besides, Ray had moved on to his next woman, one who was beautiful enough to make him look like a stud and meek enough so that she wouldn't rebel against him the way Maeve finally had. She doubted Ray cared enough to leave central Missouri and track her to KC.

She turned and drove down the hill of Locust Street toward KCPD headquarters.

The black car was right behind her again, its lights blinding her.

She hoped that driving straight to a police station would deter anyone who made her feel threatened. She wasn't sure if the downtown headquarters housed a patrol office, but a cop was a cop, right? Even if the administrative offices were closed for the night, there should be someone with a gun and a badge around 24/7, right? She'd pull up in front of the building and wait for an officer to come out and help her. If it turned out this idiot behind her wasn't a threat, she'd be embarrassed. But she wouldn't be scared anymore, and she wouldn't be leading a stranger to her home where she'd be alone against him if he did mean her harm.

"Great." No place to park near the building. The driver had to know her intention by now as she slowed down in front of the tall limestone building. There were several black-and-white KCPD vehicles in the employees-only parking lot off to her left. But that lot was blocked off with security gates. Then she spotted two uniformed officers heading down the sidewalk toward the parking garage across the street.

Giving her car a little more gas, she whipped around into the garage entrance, forcing the two officers to jerk back out of her path. She heard them yelling at her as she hit the brakes and screeched to a rocking halt in front of them.

Both officers had their hands on the butt of their weapons at their waist as the female officer came to her passenger side door, and the male officer circled around the car. The faceless shadow of the driver following her had the audacity to honk his horn and wave as he hurried on past. Maeve lowered her window and held up her hands.

"Sorry. I'm sorry." Her fingers shook, from nerves or finally releasing her death grip on the steering wheel or both. She nodded toward the black car now zipping away down the street. "That car has been following me for several miles. On the interstate, through town. I didn't notice it until after I left Shotz's bar."

"Shotz's? What were you doing there, ma'am?" The male officer stayed at her window while the woman hurried out to the edge of the sidewalk.

"Trying to help a friend who didn't want to be helped."

"That's a dangerous place."

"I know. That's why I came here. I didn't want him to know where I lived."

"That was smart." The police officer gently urged her to lower her hands. "Do you want to pull into the garage and park for a few minutes? Catch your breath and get your heart rate down a little bit?"

"I... I'm fine."

"No, ma'am, you're not. You're about to hyperventilate." He pointed into the garage. "Just pull around the security booth and put your car in Park. You can sit for a few minutes. Call someone if you need to."

"Thank you." Maeve tucked her dark shoulder-length curls behind her ears and held on to either side of her head for a few seconds, acknowledging the pulse racing in the side of her neck. She thought she'd been handling the situation. She'd made the smart move to come to the police, right? But she suddenly realized she was on the verge of a panic attack as her adrenaline level crashed and the fear she'd pushed aside surged to the surface. She nodded and moved her shaking hands back to the steering wheel. She pulled into the garage where the officer had indicated and cut the engine.

"You're safe now, ma'am," he assured her, coming to her window again to introduce himself as Officer Lane and his partner as Officer Mendez. "And you are?"

"Maeve Phillips. D-do you need to see my license?"

"If it's handy." The officer wrote down the pertinent information before returning her license. "Do you know that guy, Ms. Phillips? Do you want to file a report?"

Maeve shook her head. "I never saw the driver. I don't know who that was. But I got so scared. Am I being paranoid?"

Officer Mendez tucked her radio back onto her shoulder strap as she stepped up beside her partner. "I couldn't get any numbers off the license plate. He had it covered in a dark film. Ought to be ticketed for that. But I put out a BOLO for a black—"

"Dodge Charger," Maeve finished, then glanced up to see both officers looking at her with indulgent curiosity. She shrugged. "I had a boyfriend who was into cars."

Officer Mendez picked up on that detail. "Do you think that was him?"

"No." Maeve forced herself to breathe in deeply, flaring her nostrils before exhaling. "He's an *ex*," she emphasized, "and he doesn't live in Kansas City."

"Where *does* he live?" The female officer pulled a notepad and pen from her pocket.

"Grangeport. A little town on the river in central Missouri. At least, he did the last time I knew."

"Your ex have a name?" the officer asked.

"Ray Maddox." She watched the other woman writing down the details. "But that wasn't him."

"You said you couldn't see the driver," Officer Lane pointed out.

"But it's been two years since we've even talked. And I made it clear that I didn't want to see him ever again." She shrugged, feeling that sense of being a helpless pawn in the games Ray had enjoyed playing with her. She wasn't going down that road again. "I changed schools and jobs to get away from him."

Officer Mendez tapped her pen against the end of her notepad, her eyes narrowed with a suspicious understanding. "Did Mr. Maddox ever hurt you?"

After a moment, Maeve nodded. Her cheeks heated with embarrassment that she'd stayed with Ray for as long as she had. But he hadn't been her Mr. Right any more than any of her mother's boyfriends had been right for her. "It couldn't be Ray. It'd be too much work for him to come after me now. He's moved on to make some other woman miserable. He hasn't been any part of my life for a while now. I can't deal with it being him after everything else that happened tonight."

"What happened at Shotz's?" the man asked.

Maeve explained the whole evening with Steph hunting down Austin, and how she'd been creeped out by Joker and nearly everything else at the seedy bar.

Officer Lane turned to his partner. "Let's expand that BOLO to that area of downtown. Find out what Joker's real name is. Could be Ms. Phillips picked up an unwanted friend down at the bar." While Officer Mendez picked up her radio again, Officer Lane asked another question. "Do you have a husband or boyfriend here in Kansas City?"

"No." She answered so quickly that he raised his eyebrows. "There's been no one since Ray. I don't have a boyfriend. I don't have anyone in my life." Wow. That sounded pitiful. She hastened to explain herself. "Except for my roommate and some friends at the physical and occupational therapy clinic where I work with veterans and their families. I'm either working or going to school for my master's degree."

Only one man had turned her head since she'd moved

to Kansas City. Sergeant Ben Hunter. Broad-shouldered. Bearded. Tattooed across both shoulders and partway down both arms. Beautiful, meaningful artwork from his time in the military, from what she could see, certainly nothing as frightening or demeaning as the black ink she'd seen on Joker. He was a stubborn man of few words with incredible sadness in his deep blue eyes. But the veteran who'd lost his hand fighting a war in some distant land was surly and unpredictable and seemed to have made it one of his goals in life to get under her skin by teasing her one minute and snapping in frustration in the next.

She'd probably been initially drawn to him because he was completely unlike her polished suit-and-tie of an ex. She wondered if Ben Hunter even owned a tie. She'd never seen him in anything but jeans and sweats or his Army fatigues. He'd given her a silly nickname that somehow made her feel special because he hadn't christened anyone else at the clinic with a nickname.

Sweetcheeks.

She felt her face warming at the memory of him calling her by that name. Then the moment she thought he might say something sweet to her, he'd be cursing at himself because he'd knocked over three chess pieces in his attempt to pick up one with his prosthetic hand. Then he'd stormed away to run for ten minutes on the treadmill until he had his temper under control and could come back to practice the occupational procedure all over again.

Ultimately, though, she was too shy, too cautious, to even flirt with a man like that, much less ask him out or strike up more of a friendship. His mood swings were too reminiscent of Ray. And though Ben had never slapped her, cursed her, or blamed her or threatened her mother or monitored her every coming and going, Maeve knew she needed someone quieter, tamer, safer to give her heart to—if indeed she ever felt like she could trust her heart to another man again.

"I don't really socialize." Nope. Still sounded pitiful. "I'm not a nun or anything. I'm just…busy."

She thought she heard a chuckle in Officer Lane's throat. "That's okay, ma'am. You don't have to explain your social life to me." After he and Mendez exchanged a few bits of information, the female officer tucked her notebook back into her pocket. The man rested his arm on the roof of her car and leaned in. "We've got all the information we need. We're just glad you're safe. Take a few minutes to let that guy get well on his way to wherever he's going. Then you can head home. We'll wait with you until you leave."

"But you're off duty now, aren't you? You were walking to your cars to leave, right?"

"We'll wait," he assured her, stepping away to continue a conversation with his partner about a school activity his son was taking part in.

"Thank you." Maeve took a few deep breaths, calming her frayed nerves and wondering what all that had been about.

Without knowing who the driver was, she couldn't pinpoint why he'd targeted her. Had she captured someone's interest at Shotz's? She hadn't talked to anyone except for the drunk at the bar. And Joker and Austin. But they'd been cozying up in that corner booth with Steph when she'd left. Maybe terrorizing her was some teenager's idea of a joke. But what teen could afford that modified muscle car? And Ray? No, it absolutely could not be Ray. He lived two hours away. There was no way he'd suddenly track her down in a dangerous part of the city where she'd never been before tonight, just to follow her home.

She could use a friend right now. Someone who could

give her a hug and tell her she was getting herself worked up about a random event that probably didn't have anything to do with her at all.

Maeve startled when her phone beeped in the center console, but she gasped with relief when she read Steph's name on the screen. She quickly snatched it up and unlocked her screen to read through her friend's incoming text.

Love ya back. Sorry we had a difference of opinion. Austin is being really sweet with me tonight. I'm stopping by the house in a bit to pick up my car and work clothes. Thanks for letting me borrow your purse to put my overnight things in, but I think I'm going to need a little more. ;) I'll go ahead and pack my travel bag and leave your purse at the house. Then we're going over to his place. And yes, Mom, I'm staying a few nights before I leave on my business trip on Monday. Hopefully, you won't see me until after my trip. ;)

Maeve shook her head. Did that mean Steph and Austin were back together again? Maeve wondered how long their tempestuous relationship would last this time. She thanked Officers Lane and Mendez and drove away, this time without a black car following her. She wanted to get home, to see with her own eyes that her friend was safe and happy and that Austin was treating her like gold.

Only, when Maeve finally got home, there was no Steph. She checked her roommate's bedroom and saw the dent in her mattress where she must have set her overnight bag. It did look as though she'd rifled through her dresser drawers and closet to pull out some clean clothes. Maeve found her big purse on her own bed with a sticky note and a scribbled *Thank you!* along with a big drawing of a heart. Steph and

Austin must have stopped in while Maeve had been at the police station parking garage.

Maeve sent her friend a quick text.

Sorry I missed you at home. Have fun. Be safe. See you soon.

Steph's reply had been a simple thumbs-up, followed by a kiss-blowing emoji.

Although she hadn't really expected it, she was disappointed when there was no sign of Steph the next day. Hopefully, the reunion was everything Steph wanted it to be, and she'd be giving Maeve a detailed account about how wonderful true love could be over dinner once she got back from her trip. Blaming that nagging feeling of something being wrong on growing up surrounded by her mother's bad choices in men, and then her own resounding failure to fall for a man she could trust, Maeve pulled on her scrubs and a sweater and headed for work.

When Maeve got home for the weekend, there was still no car in the driveway. She pulled out her phone to double-check her messages in case she'd missed one while she'd been working with a patient. Not one word from Steph. Not even an accounting about how hot her night with Austin had been and how she'd proved Maeve wrong about her concerns. Or, conversely, how he'd taken her money again, accused her of being too demanding and shoved her out the door the way he had when they'd broken up.

Maeve dialed her best friend's number. The call went straight to voicemail. "Hey, Steph. It's Maeve. Just checking in. Call when you get this."

There was no word the next morning or the next evening. She tried calling Steph's father, but he hadn't heard from her since they'd had dinner two weeks earlier. No more clothes or toiletries had been touched, either. Maeve checked her friend's closet. There were still a lot of work clothes hanging there. If she had an overnight business trip to St. Louis coming up, she'd surely need to come by the house to do laundry and pack.

On the fourth morning without any word from Stephanie, or any sign that she'd returned home at some point, Maeve punched in Austin Bukowski's number. It rang six times before it went to voicemail. She ignored the queasy sense of unease in her stomach. Had she been wrong to let this slide for three days? What if they'd been in a car accident, and both Steph and Austin were laid up in the hospital? Or something worse?

Before that thought could grab hold, she punched in Austin's number again. She'd leave a message with him this time.

But after three rings, the call was picked up and a groggy man's voice answered. "This better the hell be an emergency, or I'm hanging up and turning off my phone."

"Don't hang up," Maeve answered quickly before Austin did what he promised. "It *is* an emergency. At least, it could be."

Austin grumbled a curse. "Is this Maeve? You've got a hell of a lot of nerve, Buzzkill."

Maeve ignored that he'd picked up the demeaning nickname Joker had given her. They'd probably had a good laugh about her after she'd left Shotz's, but Maeve didn't care about hurt feelings or arguing misconceptions right now. "I haven't seen or heard from Steph since that night at Shotz's. That's three days and four nights. Have you seen her?"

"I don't know."

He didn't know? Or was he too sleepy or hungover to think right now? "Austin, please. Steph's as social as I am shy. It's not like her to not see or talk to or text me for that long. She's been with you, right?"

His scratchy tone became more articulate as he started to wake up. "She left for work the morning after you ducked out on us."

Ducked out? That was more like she'd served her purpose and had been abruptly dismissed. She wasn't wanted or needed. What else was she supposed to do besides leave? "Didn't she stay the weekend with you?"

"Part of it. Summerfield called her in on Saturday to prep for their trip."

Steph's boss. The older man who made Steph dance through hoops and dodge his hands to earn a pay raise and a promotion. "But you saw her that night?"

"I went out with friends Saturday night."

"Without Steph?"

"She's a big girl. She doesn't need your permission to spend the weekend with me. I don't appreciate you trying to talk her out of getting back together with me."

"Then you two are together? You *have* seen her?" Maeve held on to a little piece of hope. She'd be hurt that her friend hadn't answered any of her messages, but if Steph was all right, she could easily forgive that.

"Yeah. We had a long talk and figured some things out. She has a better understanding of what I need." Maeve bit her tongue at the egocentrism of that statement and let him continue. "She's not here now. She's probably already at the airport on her way to St. Louis with Summerfield for those depositions."

That made sense. Steph took pride in her work as a paralegal in his firm's office, and when her boss had asked her to accompany him on the trip, she'd been understandably cautious about spending time alone with the man. But she'd been equally excited about how the opportunity would look on her next promotion evaluation. But still... "She never came home to pack a bag and her lucky suit."

"Lucky suit?"

"She always wears it when she travels."

Austin muttered a curse. "Look, I'm not her babysitter. I was blitzed Saturday night, so I stayed at my friend's house." She hoped that friend wasn't Joker. "I was in the office myself yesterday, prepping for a case of my own. She wasn't here when I got home last night, and she's not here now."

"She hasn't contacted her dad, either. I'm worried about her. Aren't you?"

Austin's heavy sigh made her think he just might be worried about Steph, too. "Let me see if I can get ahold of her." Maeve waited a few minutes for Austin to call back. When he did, the news wasn't good. "She doesn't answer for me. Goes straight to voicemail. I called the office, and they said Summerfield is gone, but she missed the flight. He had to call for a last-minute replacement."

Maeve checked her watch, seeing that she'd be late for work this morning. "That doesn't concern you? What if she's been in an accident?"

"Of course, it concerns me," he insisted. "Let me grab a shower and some coffee, then I'll drive around and check out some of her usual haunts."

He ended the call without even a thanks for alerting him to her worries about Steph, or giving her a chance to tell him that she'd already contacted some of Steph's friends and driven past her favorite coffee shop and other hangouts to see if she could spot Steph's car.

Maeve ran her fingers through her hair and tucked the curls behind her ear. When she'd needed help with Ray, there'd been no one for her to call. The few friends she'd had back in Grangeport had sided with Ray, wanting to stay on the Maddox family's good side. And asking her mom for any kind of help was a nonstarter. Maeve had been frightened and alone. Her only option had been to run away and start a new life on her own.

She owed Steph. Even if they'd gone down different paths after high school, Maeve wasn't going to let her friend be alone if she was in some kind of trouble. She intended to be there for Steph, even if her smooth-talking jerk of a boyfriend—or anyone else—refused to help.

Was her next step to start calling hospitals around Kansas City to see if Steph had been admitted after a car accident or some other kind of medical emergency?

Two nights without anyone seeing her. Three days without contacting the people closest to her.

Maeve walked around her silent, empty house, ending up in Steph's bedroom, staring at that lucky suit.

She picked up her cell phone one more time and punched in a number. When the woman on the other end answered, Maeve didn't hesitate, "I need to report a missing person."

Chapter Four

Thursday afternoon...

Ben Hunter stomped out the last few minutes of his warm-up run on the treadmill at the physical and occupational therapy center where he should have started his dexterity session ten minutes ago.

Sweetcheeks was late.

That irritated him. Although he couldn't honestly say he was upset by Maeve Phillips's uncharacteristic lack of punctuality. What irritated him was that he'd been looking forward to seeing her again. She was a breath of fresh air and sunshine in his dark life. She was a smile he didn't deserve. She was fifty minutes of his trying to be a better man, or maybe the man he'd once been, just to see her sweet face and soak in a little of her goodness.

Why couldn't he have the hots for some sassy bad girl who was into his beard and tats and antisocial behavior? Maybe someone who had an obsession with amputees? No, he had to have a thing for soft-spoken innocence and buttoned-up sensuality that made his hormones itch to get under Maeve's skin and find out if the glimpses of temper he'd seen meant there was passion there too.

Never gonna happen, Hunter.

Maybe his guilt-riddled subconscious had put the pretty occupational therapist in his life just so he would want something he could never have. So yeah, he was irritated.

It always took him a little while to get into the right head-space whenever Maeve Phillips was around. Hence the running. Whenever his emotions threatened to get the better of him, he turned to either his weekly group therapy session at St. Luke's Hospital, or he did something physical until his energy was spent and he sweated out the memories and feelings. And his emotions were all over the place when it came to Maeve.

He'd purposely moved his biweekly therapy appointments to the end of the day so that he could put in a full day of work at K-9 Ranch before driving into the city. The clean air and physical labor of ranch life seemed to be helping him with his PTSD. It hadn't taken him long to settle into a routine. He got up early, just like he had for years in the Army. He fed, watered and exercised the dogs, put in a hard training session with Rocky and the other dogs he was in charge of and helped out with some of the farm chores. Then he either worked out or came into the city for a therapy session and to run errands. At night, he'd hole up in his new barn apartment with Rocky and a good book or a football game on TV.

He hadn't yet volunteered to work with any of the people who came to the ranch for training sessions, and Mrs. Caldwell hadn't pushed him to do so. He supposed the toughest part of his new job was dealing with Soren Hauck. The teenager was about as closed-off and antisocial as Ben was, so drawing him into a conversation, teaching him more about dog training and supposedly mentoring the young man was proving to be harder than gathering intel and planning a clandestine mission into some war-torn area of the world.

As Ben slowed the treadmill to a cooldown walk, he wondered if he could just skip the humiliating repetition of stacking blocks or playing chess or whatever cutesy game Maeve had planned for him. As if that could mask the fact that he had no left hand and that the sterile titanium hook he wore was closer to a club than a tool for any kind of fine motor skills.

Maybe he could duck out of here with the excuse that he needed to check on Rocky. He'd left the black dog in the back seat of his truck. It wouldn't be a complete lie. Rocky was a smart, athletic, driven dog who had a tendency to chew up things when he got bored or antsy, and he suspected the upholstery in his truck would be fair game. Ben had put up a cage to keep the dog out of the front seat, but he'd yet to install a complete pen, or cover the back seat with a wood panel and some carpet to protect the upholstery in the back of his extended cab pickup. It wasn't like he was that good with his hands anymore. Tinkering with his truck took longer than it ever had in the past. And there were just some things a man with one hand couldn't do on his own.

But even after only a week of treating Rocky like the military K-9s he'd once worked with, the dog was already showing an improvement in his temperament. Ben supposed a shredded truck seat was a small price to pay to keep Rocky from being euthanized. Ben was slowly building the dog's trust and keeping him from his dangerous tendencies by keeping him focused on specific jobs rather than allowing the dog to determine for himself what might be a threat. He was no longer starting fights with other dogs, and he'd stopped barking his fool head off once Mrs. Caldwell had given Ben the okay to move the dog into the apartment with him and had taken over 100 percent of his acclimation to civilian life.

Yeah. That's what he'd do. He could avoid pretty Miss Maeve by excusing himself from his occupational therapy altogether and checking on the dog who actually needed him.

No lusty thoughts to tamp down. No embarrassment. No regrets that he was struggling to remember how to even talk to a woman he was interested in anymore.

The treadmill timer beeped, and the machine stopped. Ben grabbed the towel off the handle and swiped it over his face and hair to mop up the sweat from his short but fast run. Then he pulled his prosthetic arm over the protective sleeve of his stump. He looped the straps of the harness around his good arm and over the back of his head, adjusting the fitting over the top of his faded Army T-shirt. His balance was typically better without the weight of the prosthesis when he ran. Plus, it was important to air out the stump, so nothing chafed beneath his prosthesis or developed any kind of skin infection.

He stepped off the treadmill and spun toward the patient lockers, plowing into the woman he'd been hoping to avoid. She dropped the box of blocks and computer pad she'd been carrying, and wooden cubes of various sizes scattered across the floor. His instinct to grab Maeve's arm to steady her quickly died when she grimaced and flinched away from his touch. "Ow."

"Sorry." Ben quickly released her and stepped back. "You okay?"

How the hell had she snuck up on him without him noticing her? Some soldier he was. Were his situational awareness skills getting that rusty? Or had he been so deep in thought about how he was going to avoid Maeve that he'd missed the soft tread of her footsteps and that sweet vanilla scent that subtly radiated from her shampoo or skin lotion? He fisted his right hand at his side and tapped his thigh, willing the tension roiling in him to ratchet itself down a notch.

"You're getting much more adept at getting your prosthesis on by yourself. That's excellent progress." Her gaze dropped to his fist, as if she knew he was trying to calm himself, and he instantly stopped the habitual movement. She picked up her computer pad where she monitored each patient's progress and set it on the nearest table, then she knelt on the carpet and started gathering blocks, ignoring his apology, his question and the visual evidence of his post-traumatic stress and dove right into training mode. "Are you warmed up now? In the right headspace and ready to go to work?"

Ben realized he wasn't the only one struggling to keep things *normal*. Something was way wrong with Maeve. He spotted bruises on the left side of her face, the slight swelling at the left corner of her mouth, and the strawberries of scraped skin that grazed her jaw and cheekbone, despite the makeup she'd caked around her pale hazel eyes.

He went down on his knees in front of her and picked up blocks with his right hand and tossed them into her box. But his focus remained on her downturned gaze. "What the hell happened to you?"

"Charming as ever, Mr. Hunter." She nodded toward the prosthetic arm hanging at his side. "You should pick up blocks with that hand, too."

"It's not a hand," he pointed out needlessly. His concern ratcheted up at her avoidance of his question, no matter how bluntly he'd asked it. "How did you get hurt? Is your arm bruised, too? Did I make it worse?"

Her shoulders lifted as she took a deep breath. But in-

stead of explaining the injuries that made Ben think she'd
been in a fight or a horrible accident, she shook her head,
as if dismissing the impulse to share. "Sorry I'm running
late. I just got off the phone with the police again. It's been
a long day. A long week."

There was so much wrong with what she'd just said. *Police. Again? Long week?* What was going on with her? And
why did he think it was any of his business? It wasn't. Ben
immediately felt contrite. "No. I should apologize. I tend
to speak before thinking the words through." No kidding.
Tact hadn't been his best skill even when he'd been on active duty. Probably one reason why his so-called relationships—even before his body and career had been shot to
hell—hadn't lasted beyond a handful of dates. "It's none of
my business." But Maeve Phillips had been part of his world
twice a week for months now, and she felt like his business,
so he wasn't moving away. He hooked his prosthesis over
the edge of the box and held it on the floor to keep her from
standing. "Just answer one question. Are you all right?"

"I'm okay." Her gaze focused on the faded block letters
that read ARMY across his chest. "You didn't make anything worse."

"Look me in the eye when you say that, Sweetcheeks.
Otherwise, I'm going to think you're not telling me the
truth."

Her gaze finally darted up to meet his, giving him a clear
glimpse of the shadows under her eyes, too. Shadows that
bespoke fatigue and stress, in addition to her injuries. But
the instinct to gently touch her bruised face and pull her into
the shelter of his arms to shield her from whatever hell she'd
gone through went unacknowledged as the raw emotion in
her eyes quickly shuttered. Maeve pushed to her feet and
carried the box to the nearby worktable.

"I'm not lying," she insisted, setting out the blocks in a pattern *he* was supposed to be mastering.

Ben rested his good hand over hers to still her frantic movements. "Maybe not. But I can't be certain unless I can see those pretty eyes."

She tilted her face up to his again, this time holding his gaze. "Most of the time, you're the biggest grouch on the planet—the moodiest man I've ever met. And then you give me a compliment like that, and it kind of freaks me out."

He pulled his hand away. "I'm not trying to be nice."

"You're succeeding."

He didn't deserve that hint of a teasing smile she gave him. "Clearly, you've been injured. I'm trying to make sure you're okay."

"I appreciate that." She pulled the navy-blue cardigan she wore together over her pink scrubs and hugged her arms beneath her chest. "I feel like I've been asked that a hundred times over the last twenty-four hours. I don't honestly know how to answer that question anymore."

"I'm not helping any by pushing, am I. I'm used to identifying a problem and solving it. That's probably the reason I'm so impatient with my therapy. Needing a new hand isn't a problem I can solve. I'm sorry. I..." He scrubbed his fingers and palm over his jaw and beard, needing to clear his thoughts. He wasn't a cop, or even a soldier, anymore. This wasn't a problem he could solve. Maeve Phillips getting hurt wasn't his problem, period. He'd be doing her a kindness to simply walk away and not add any more stress to her life. "You'd better assign someone else to work with me today. Or better yet, I'll just head on home."

He'd taken two steps toward the patient lockers when her soft voice stopped him. "I was mugged last night."

Ben slowly turned to face her again and found those gray-tinted eyes focused squarely on him. *That* was the truth. The fear stamped on her expression snuck right past his good intentions of walking away. Knowing someone had targeted and intentionally hurt this sweet, shy woman brought out his protective instincts and a surprisingly vindictive need to punish the unknown perp. But Maeve didn't need his anger. He had a feeling she just needed someone to listen. He might not be the best candidate for patience and empathy, but he was...here. "That's rough. Did you get your injuries checked out by a doctor? You reported it to the police?"

She nodded. Then her gaze drifted to the middle of his chest again and the words spewed forth. "First, some guy is following me around town. I lose my roommate, and then these two guys come out of nowhere and knock me to the ground, shove my face into the concrete and shout at me. I didn't know what they were talking about. They dumped out my purse and rifled through my pockets, you know, touching me—but I'm not even sure they took anything. Maybe it was just a case of mistaken identity. I don't understand why any of this is happening to me."

"Whoa. Go back. Someone is following you? Do you know who attacked you?"

Her eyes met his again. "No."

"You lost your roommate? What does that mean? Did she leave? Are you not able to pay the rent or something?"

"She's a missing person. I filed a report." Maeve turned her attention back to the table where she'd set up the manipulatives for him. She picked up a block that she rolled between her hands. "We went out last Thursday, and she never came home. At least, not while I was there. Her boyfriend thought she was out of town on Monday, but she never got on the plane. I haven't seen her in a week. No one has. No one at the law firm where she works. Not her boyfriend. Not me."

Ben rejoined her at the table. He wasn't the best at engaging in meaningful conversation, but she had already spoken more words to him than any other time over the past several months they'd worked together, and he was anxious to learn more about her. Even if the details she was sharing were a little confusing and a lot unsettling. "You were fine when we met Tuesday." Was she really that good at hiding her feelings? Or had he just been too preoccupied with his own troubles to notice? If it hadn't been for the bruises, he might not have noticed today, either. "This has all happened in the past few days?"

"This week has certainly gone downhill." Her lips parted with the saddest laugh he'd ever heard. "If it weren't for bad luck, I'd have no luck at all."

Her attempt at humor to blow off his concern irritated him. "Don't do cutesy with me. That's not who we are."

That hint of a smile vanished as she lifted her gaze up to his once more. "Who *we* are? There's a *we*?"

Where had that statement come from? Those errant fantasies he'd had over the past few months about taking her out or kissing her or stripping off those shapeless scrubs and sweaters to discover the curves she hid underneath didn't need to be part of the conversation. She didn't need his out-of-whack hormones dumped on top of all she'd been through this week. Ben scrubbed his palm over the top of his short hair and massaged the tension at the back of his neck. "We're acquaintances. Sort of...friends. We've known each other a while now. I'm the patient. You're the therapist. We do serious stuff. You're the know-it-all lady who pushes me when I don't want to be pushed. Then I get mouthy, you call me on it, and I regret the words as soon as I say them."

"You regret when you're rude to me?"

"Yeah. I'm not a monster. Although some days you probably think I am. I'm tired and frustrated and I miss the Army and my damn hand, but I shouldn't take it out on you." He shifted on his feet, as uncomfortable with this turn in the conversation as he was when asked to share something personal during his weekly group therapy session for veterans and others who suffered from PTSD. But still he forged on because *he* wasn't the one who'd been attacked and injured this time. "Especially when you're hurting like this. I don't know why you put up with me."

Maeve continued to stare at him, and he was briefly distracted by the spatters of green warming her cool eyes. Then her lips curved with a hint of a serene smile that seemed more genuine than that last smile she'd tried to appease him with. "You're not a monster, Ben. You're a man who's been given some heavy stuff to deal with. I've put up with you for almost a year. And I'm still here. I can handle your grumpiness."

Putting up with his surly attitude was a little different than him badgering her about how someone had shoved her, hit her, terrorized her, all for what—a credit card and some spare change? It wasn't as if he was a cop who could help her. He was a washed-up veteran. A dog trainer. He was hardly the Delta Force soldier who'd charged in to save the day he'd once been. "I'm sorry you got hurt."

"I know you are. Thanks."

Her delicate nostrils flared with a deep breath, and then she was pulling out the two stools on either side of the table. She didn't speak for several seconds while she pulled a flash drive from the pocket of her scrubs and inserted it into her computer tablet. He thought the conversation was over and she was ready to start assessing the lists of tasks she had scheduled for him today.

But she surprised him by explaining her grumpiness comment. "What you see as brusqueness, I see as honesty. There's no filter on you. I've been lied to a lot in the past. It's nice to know I can count on you to tell me the truth." Who lied to her? What kind of lies? Was she still talking about getting mugged or a missing roommate? Or something else from her past? "I'm tired of people telling me everything is going to be okay and not to worry. That I'm imagining something is wrong when I know I'm not." She gestured to the stool nearest the wall, where she knew he preferred to sit, rather than having his back to the entire room that was busy with patients and therapists. He dutifully circled around the table and waited for her to sit before he straddled his own stool. "If I promise to be brave enough to look you in the eye, will you promise to always be the Ben Hunter-brand of honest with me?"

Grumpy? Brusque? Unfiltered? Didn't sound like a fair trade to him, but if that was what she wanted... "Sure. I can do that."

"Then that's who *we* are. 'Sort-of friends' who are honest with each other." She was smiling again. Smiling with that bruised face and making him regret every harsh word and foul temper she'd witnessed with him. "Shall we?"

Ben reached for the largest block and opened his hook to grasp it, slowly building a pyramid of blocks from largest to smallest. He hated that she had to see his hook. Hated more that he was still sometimes as awkward with it as a toddler learning to walk. He wished he was a whole man, that she could see the man he used to be. That man would have hunted down the loser who'd attacked her and taught him in no uncertain terms that Maeve Phillips was off-limits to any sort of violence or terror campaign. That man might have asked her out. He most certainly would have flirted with her, just to get past that shyness and get a rise out of her, to hear her giving him a little well-deserved sass before offering that sweet smile that lit up her eyes and warmed him inside.

That man was long gone, buried in a pile of rubble in an unnamed jungle along with three of his teammates, his K-9 partner and his Army career. But the man he was now—healing both inside and out—could at least suck up his temper and embarrassment and do what the lady asked. He might not be able to make anything right for her, but he silently vowed to, at the very least, not to make anything worse.

Chapter Five

Maeve's knuckles turned white as she gripped the handle on the door leading out of the clinic into the chilly night. She gauged the distance between the light above the door and the streetlight on the opposite sidewalk. The circle of illumination from one light to the next left a shadowy strip in the middle of the street out front. A car drove past, its headlights momentarily erasing the darkness before it moved on down the street, and the shadow reappeared. Maeve hated shadows. She lifted her gaze to the rectangles of darkness between thick concrete posts in the parking garage across the street and felt her stomach clench with dread.

She'd parked in that garage and crossed this street every day and night she'd worked at the clinic for almost a year now. She'd braved rain and snow and sweltering heat. Last night, she'd appreciated the crisp autumn air and how it raised goose bumps on her skin, reviving her spirit after a tiring day. She'd thought about how she needed to pull a heavier jacket out of her closet because the sweaters she loved weren't warm enough by themselves anymore. She'd thought about the last few hours of clinic fieldwork she had left before earning her master's degree and just how close she was to finally attaining that goal. And she'd thought of

Steph. How the two of them had braved the autumn chill that night they'd ended up at Shotz's, and how she hoped her friend had a jacket or coat to keep her warm wherever she might be right now.

But tonight, Maeve couldn't seem to make herself push open the door.

She dreaded what was out there in the shadows as much as she'd dreaded opening her bedroom door when her mother had brought a gentleman friend home to the trailer where she'd grown up. Maeve's job had been to remain silent and locked away while her mother entertained whatever man she'd picked up for the night. If Maeve hadn't fed herself beforehand, she knew there'd be no dinner for her that night. She'd really wanted to leave her room, to get a drink of water, scrounge up a snack or enjoy some fresh air. But it was dangerous outside her room. Her mother might slap her for interrupting her *date*. She'd certainly yell. Maybe the man would say something crude about mother and daughter, not unlike Austin and Joker's taunting comments that night at Shotz's bar. And if finding out Claudia Phillips had a daughter made her boyfriend du jour go away, then there'd most certainly be a verbal haranguing waiting for Maeve.

So, Maeve never opened that door. And that same fear, that survivor's need to avoid pain and heartbreak and whatever danger waited for her on the other side of that door, kept her rooted in place tonight.

But she was no longer a little girl, and she hadn't thought of herself as a coward since the day she'd stood up to Ray Maddox and her mother, packed up her little car and left Mizzou, Grangeport and central Missouri for good. Grown-up, independent Maeve knew she couldn't very well spend the night here in the lobby. Her car was just across the street and up a flight of stairs. It would take her all of five minutes to get there.

But those damn shadows, where someone had watched and waited for her...or the tinted windows of a car hiding the threat following her—

"Maeve?" She jumped at the man's deep voice behind her, smacking her knuckles against the glass. "Easy, Sweetcheeks. Sorry. I didn't mean to startle you. You okay?"

She tilted her chin up as Ben Hunter moved into her peripheral vision. Her patient was a shade over six feet tall, she knew from his medical chart, and she was of average height. But with those broad, muscular shoulders pushing at the seams of his Army-issue camo jacket, he seemed to tower over her, surround her, especially when he stood this close. She rubbed her bruised hand and sidled away half a step before she tilted her head to face him. "I thought you'd already left."

"I hung around to talk to Grayson."

Her friend and coworker Allie Malone's new husband. She could tell from conversations the two men had shared that they were friends. "I see."

"He agreed to speak to my PTSD group. We were working out some scheduling details." Right. Because Grayson Malone was a veteran Marine and a double leg amputee, and the two men had become friends to help protect Allie when she'd become the obsession of a dangerous stalker. Although Grayson was no longer a patient here, Maeve did still see him at the clinic occasionally when he stopped by to share a ride home with his wife or to surprise her with lunch. "Maeve? I really need you to answer my question. Are you okay?"

Her focus had turned back to the shadows and potential for danger waiting for her outside. *Just say yes. He'll move on and leave you alone.* Her reflection in the glass showed her mouth opening, but the word wouldn't come. She'd felt alone all week. Except for those unseen eyes that always seemed to be watching her. She'd been alone most of her adult life. She was so damn tired of being alone.

Protect. A single word from her train of thought a moment ago lit a dim candle of hope in the overwhelming fog of fear that had kept her from opening that door.

Ben had helped Grayson *protect* Allie.

Would he? Could he?

"Ah, hell." Ben faced the door and followed her gaze to the street outside. "Were you mugged outside the clinic after work? In the parking garage?"

Maeve nodded. Would the surly patient with PTSD issues do her a favor if she asked? He'd already listened to her spew out all the frightening, soul-numbing details she'd been dealing with this week. Then he'd curbed his temper and done every task she'd challenged him to accomplish to make their time together an easy session for her. Maybe she could be brave enough to ask him to be nice for a little while longer.

"Would you walk me to my car?" She tilted her gaze up to his, boldly making eye contact so he would know she was sincere. "You said you were good at solving problems. And, I seem to have one. Namely, an inability to go outside after dark."

"You afraid of the dark?"

"I am now. I was on my own, walking to my car like I always do, and then they were there. Now I can't stop thinking what else might be lying in wait for me in the shadows."

"I can do that." He nodded toward the therapy center behind them, indicating the staff who were still on the premises. "Don't you want to ask one of your friends, though? You'd feel more comfortable with them."

"I don't care about comfort. I want to feel safe. No one is going to mess with a man like you."

He rocked back on the heels of his work boots, as if her explanation made him wary of her request. "Like me?"

The tats? The beard? The muscles? The haunted look in his eyes? He didn't need the long camo jacket for anyone to realize that he was a soldier and a protector. The way he talked and carried himself and zeroed in on every aspect of his surroundings would make even someone as cocky and tough as Joker think twice about messing with Ben Hunter. "Like someone who has seen too much and doesn't care what he has to do in order to get a job done."

"And that job would be making you feel safe?" His blue eyes challenged her for a moment. But something about her looking straight up into those eyes seemed to convince him. "Where are you parked?"

"Second floor. South side. At the far end. It was as close as I could get this morning."

He nodded once, just a curt dip of his chin, before he reached around her and pushed the door open for her to precede him. His instinct to put his hand at the small of her back was thwarted when she fell into step at his left side— the side with his prosthetic hand—and that arm fell back to the space between them.

No way. If she could be brave enough to look him in the eye and share her fears, then he could be brave enough to let her touch him. Maeve reached out and curled her fingers around the crook of his elbow. She could feel where the hard plastic of his prosthesis met warm skin beneath the sleeve of his jacket, and she clung to the promise of warmth and strength there. After a brief second when she thought he'd pull away, she felt his bicep flex as he curled his arm in front of him to support her grasp as they stepped off the curb into the street.

Maeve felt her pulse rate kick up as they walked beneath the archway into the garage. Maybe it was a trick of her imagination, but the air chilled a few degrees as they crossed into the shadows created by the streetlight outside. Instinctively, she leaned closer to the heat she could feel emanating from Ben.

"Do you mind if we stop by my truck first?" He pointed to a spot around the corner from the entrance of the garage. "My dog will be an even bigger deterrent than I am if someone's out to hurt you again."

"You have a dog?" she asked, switching directions with him. Although she was genuinely curious to learn this loner wasn't completely alone, she wondered if he sensed her fear and had started a new conversation to distract her from it. Didn't matter. She was willing to stick close to his side and go wherever he wanted right now.

"He's a new acquisition. He's a military K-9 that I'm training to acclimate to a new role in civilian life."

"You took the job at K-9 Ranch. You mentioned you had an interview last week."

"Yeah. It's about all that I'm fit for these days."

In a moment of clarity, Maeve realized that maybe Ben was the one who needed the conversation to distract him from how uneasy he had become in granting her this favor. She squeezed his arm in a silent thank-you and reassurance. "Don't say that. Rescuing and training dogs is a wonderful calling, I think. You've adopted one of your students already?"

"For the time being. No one else would have him right now. He's a hard case, and he needs some extra training to learn how to get along with other folks." Maeve bit down on the smile that threatened to form. It sounded like there was more similarity between dog and master than Ben realized. "If he was my partner and we were both still on active duty, we'd be together almost 24/7. It's what he's used to."

"You're not going to adopt him permanently?" That made her a little sad. She liked the idea of Ben having a partner.

"He's a service dog, Maeve. He needs to work, not be a family pet."

"Have you ever thought about getting a service dog?"

"You mean like to turn on the lights or fetch me a beer out of the fridge?"

She ignored the sarcasm in his tone as they approached a dusty silver pickup truck. "I mean to be your companion. To help you when you get into moods, or you have PTSD episodes." She felt him stiffen at the reminder of what he sometimes struggled with as a veteran. "You know, if you register him as your service dog, he could come to PT and OT sessions with you. Instead of running a hundred miles to work off that antsy energy when it gets the better of you, you could pet the dog. Or he could put his head on your lap or lick your face or be trained to do whatever you find comforting."

He made a scoffing noise. "Because the world needs to see me as a weaker man than I already am."

"I don't see you as weak."

"Right. I'm the scary dude no one wants to mess with."

This time she did smile. "Exactly."

A brief laugh rumbled in his throat, and he shook his head. "But I don't scare *you*?"

"A lot of things scare me, Ben. But not you. It took me a while to figure it out, but I've learned that you're all bark and no bite. With me, at least."

"That isn't always the case," he warned her.

"And that's why I asked you to walk me to my car." She hugged herself more closely around his arm and discovered a uniquely masculine scent of musk from his run and something lightly spicy emanating from his beard and skin. His shower gel or shampoo, perhaps. "What's your dog's name?" she asked, stopping herself from inhaling a deep breath of his delicious scent. Plus, she was genuinely curious about what kind of dog this man would choose.

"Rocky."

"I always wanted a pet growing up, but our lives and income were never stable enough to— Oh!" She jerked back a step when she heard a thunderous barking, intermixed with a menacing growl and saw a furry black beast lunge at the window cracked open in the back seat of his truck. "Is he an attack dog?"

"Rocky!" Ben raised his right hand in a fist. "Stand down."

Maeve slipped partway behind Ben, her fingers curling into the canvas at the back of his jacket. She'd been startled, but she wasn't afraid, not when she heard Ben's firm tone and saw the dog settle back onto his haunches in the back seat of the truck. Instead, she was a little in awe of the control he had over the dog. Rocky's dark eyes were nearly the same color as his sleek black coat, and they were focused squarely on Ben. "Is he safe?"

"He will be. Stay put. Give me a second."

He attached a thick, leather leash to the top of the harness Rocky wore, then urged him down out of the truck. Maeve dutifully stood still while Ben went down on one knee and wrestled with the dog for a moment, praising the black shepherd with silly, deep-pitched phrases that seemed to excite the dog. Then he straightened and ordered the dog to sit. The beast immediately complied. His eyes once again focused on Ben. "Good boy."

"He really listens to you."

"I want him to listen to you, too." Needing his right hand to control the dog's leash, Ben reached back to her with his left arm. "Sorry. You're going to have to hold on to the hook. Come up here beside me." Maeve had been working with him for months. That prosthetic hand was part of who he was, not some abomination she was afraid to touch. She wrapped her fingers around the cold titanium and did as he instructed. Then he was talking to the dog again, as if Rocky understood every word he said. "This is Maeve. She's with me. So, you mind your manners." Ben spoke to her over the jut of his shoulder. "Talk to him. Normal tone. He needs to be familiar with your voice."

She had a feeling it wasn't the tone of her voice so much as Ben's steely control over the K-9 that would keep him from biting her face off. But since Ben was the expert here, and she wanted to stay by his side until she was safely inside her car, she started talking.

"Hey, Rocky. I'm Maeve. Did anyone ever tell you that you remind them of Ben?"

"What?" When Ben glanced her way, the dog did too.

"You're both veterans. Both tough guys. He's got that whole loner thing going, and it works for him, whereas you are totally rockin' that sleek black Goth look. And let me tell you, you both have a bark that can be pretty darn intimidating. I could have used you last night to scare the bad guys." The dog's gaze darted toward her as she talked, acknowledging her presence. But mostly he kept checking with Ben to make sure he was earning his approval by behaving the way he wanted him to. It wasn't until Rocky settled down into a sphinxlike position on the concrete that Maeve felt it was safe to stop rattling on and breathe a sigh of relief. She looked up to find Ben staring at her. "Did I do okay?"

Ben nodded once before turning to the dog again. "Good boy," Ben praised him. "Rocky, up. Fall in." The dog pushed to his feet and stood at Ben's right thigh. "I think we can trust him to walk with us now. I'm the commanding officer, and you're a teammate I vouched for, so you're part of our unit in his canine brain. Heel."

When Ben and Rocky stepped out, Maeve quickly moved her hand up to the crook of Ben's elbow to keep them connected. "Are you training him to be a guard dog?"

"He's got that instinct in him already. Right now, he thinks pretty much anybody is a bad guy, but he has to be able to control it. He needs to understand who he's protecting and who the enemy is. Based on the relationship I'm building with him and him learning to respond to my commands, he'll get there."

"Why isn't he in the military anymore?"

"His partner died in an accident. Rocky didn't bond with any other handlers, so he was mustered out. K-9 Ranch is his last chance to adapt to civilian life before the only safe option for society is to euthanize him."

Gasping at the tragedy of putting down this beautiful animal, Maeve hugged herself a little more tightly around Ben's arm. "Maybe he has survivor's guilt. Feels like he should have saved his partner."

"Like me?" he grumbled between tightly clenched teeth. "I lost three men and my K-9 that day. We never should have stormed that compound."

Maeve had suspected that was one of the triggers Ben was dealing with as he reintegrated into civilian life. "Maybe he just doesn't know how to express the grief and guilt he's feeling, so he lashes out."

"Again. Like me?"

If Ben was expecting her to suddenly to see him as less than a good man or a hero who'd served his country, she wasn't taking the bait. "Maybe he just needs to find a new purpose in life. He needs to surround himself with people he can rely on, at least one or two good friends, so that he can relax his guard and learn to believe in himself again. I can't tell you how many times in my life I wish I had someone I could trust like that."

They took several more steps before Ben spoke again. "This is the most words you've ever said to me. All that you said to Rocky and then this little mini-therapy session."

She shrugged. "You're easy to talk to."

He snorted at that. "No, I'm not."

"I know I don't say much beyond work because I'm shy. I'm cautious around people I don't know or I'm not comfortable with. But shy people have ideas and wishes and opinions, like everybody else. A lot of us have a sense of humor. If we feel safe with someone who listens to us, then all those pent-up thoughts and emotions come spewing out. I may be boring you to tears with my prattle, and I'll probably replay everything we've said at some point and regret something I said, or wish I'd said something else because overthinking is a big part of what shy people—"

"You're not boring me. I'm learning about you."

She smiled at that nice comment. "See? You listen."

"I'm a grump," he argued, refusing the compliment. "The more you talk, the less I have to."

"You're a grump who listens." He snorted. "You're a grump who saw that I was struggling to face my fear, and you offered to help." He shook his head. "You're a grump who's working to save this dog's life and who hasn't told me to shut up yet, even though you're probably regretting offering to walk me to my car by now because I'm nervous and rambling on like an idiot."

Ben stopped in his tracks, forcing both her and Rocky to stop. "Who told you to shut up?"

The lines creasing beside his narrowed blue eyes and the irritation in his tone might have frightened her if his reaction had been taken out of context. But she could tell he was angry on her behalf, not angry with her. And Maeve had had enough experience with Ray Maddox and her mother to know the difference.

She squeezed his arm above his prosthesis, wanting to calm him. "It's okay. It was in a relationship I was finally smart enough to walk away from."

The lines beside his eyes softened, although the hard set of his mouth remained. "You're sure?"

She had an odd urge to reach up and touch his mouth, to gentle the unyielding line it cut through his beard. And then she wondered if the wheat-and whiskey-colored strands of his dark blond beard around that firm mouth would be prickly and ticklish or silky and soft if she touched it.

Maeve curled her fingers into her palm and pulled away, surprised by the jolt of attraction she felt. Her gaze dropped to the letters on his T-shirt peeking out between the open ends of his jacket. "I'm okay," she assured him. "I had a boyfriend who didn't like it when I got nervous and started rambling like this. And my mother pretty much wanted me to be seen and not heard. Sometimes I forgot."

"Eyes, Sweetcheeks." Her eyes snapped up to his. When he had her attention, he held out his bent elbow to her. "Nobody gets to say that to you. If they do, you let me know, and they won't say it again."

Even when he didn't realize it, this man was a protector. "I'm beginning to think I like grumpy men."

When he snorted at the compliment this time, she laughed. She curled her fingers into the crook of his arm, and he tucked it against his side before moving toward the entrance again. "Did you take the elevator or the steps last night?"

"Elevator. I didn't see the two men when I stepped off. They were wearing dark clothes and ski masks. They came out from between my car and the one parked next to it and…" She remembered the fist flying at her head and her body hitting the concrete, hard. Her steps faltered as she remembered one man shoving her face into the oil-stained concrete while the other rifled through her pockets and ripped her bag off her shoulder.

"Stay with me, Sweetcheeks." She tumbled against his side as Ben turned them toward the stairs. "I'm not a big fan of tight spaces, anyway." As they reached the concrete steps, he gave the muscular black dog a command and let out the length of his leash a tad. "Rocky. Patrol."

"What does that mean?"

She watched the dog's ears perk up and swivel to catch every sound. His head dipped closer to the ground when they reached the second floor. She could tell by Rocky's hyper-alertness what Ben's answer was going to be.

"I ordered him to be on the lookout for anyone suspicious or anything that seems out of place. He'll hear or smell a would-be assailant long before you or I see anything." Considering how Ben's gaze was continually scanning their surroundings for any sign of trouble, that was saying something.

"Those men wouldn't have attacked me last night if Rocky was here. He would have known they were there. I could have gotten away."

"Maybe you should come out to K-9 Ranch, and we can match you up with that dog you always wanted."

He *had* listened to everything she'd said. "You think I need a guard dog?"

"Usually, just having a dog who raises a ruckus when there's cause for alarm is enough to deter someone who wants to rob you or hurt you." He paused to look down at her. "But if you don't feel safe walking alone at night, then a guard dog like Rocky could be the answer."

Or she could ask Ben to walk her to her car each night.

But that would be even more of an imposition than tonight's request for help. And as much as she was enjoying being held at Ben's side and sharing conversation with him, this wasn't a moonlit stroll, and they weren't on a date. In fact, it was probably the last time he'd agree to do her such a personal favor outside of their OT sessions. She needed to let go any thoughts of attraction and the security she craved, or she'd be setting herself up for disappointment and potential heartbreak.

"This is me." She pointed to her blue Chevy Impala that was a decade old and had high mileage. But it had been what she could afford, and she took good care of it. "Thank you."

She dropped her gaze to speak to the dog as well, but Rocky was sniffing her back left tire and all around the wheel well. He stretched his nose out to follow the curve of her bumper around to the back of her car. When he reached the spot below the trunk latch, he inhaled deeply, then sneezed as though something there had tickled his nose.

"What's he doing?"

"I'm not sure," Ben answered, pulling Rocky back to his side before checking it out. "Did you find something, boy?"

She leaned in beside Ben and spied the small black circle on the top of her bumper. "That's new."

Ben touched it with his finger, then rubbed it against his thumb before smelling them. "It's a burn mark. You don't smoke, do you?"

"No."

He brushed his fingers off on his pant leg and shook his head. "Looks to me like somebody put out their cigarette on your bumper."

Maeve's grip tightened around his arm. "The man who hit me smelled like smoke. I wonder how long they were waiting at my car for me to come out?"

"Hey." He faced her and tapped the bottom of her chin with his cold hook, urging her to look up at him. "Those men aren't here now. Rocky would be going ballistic if he sensed a threat. It was just a lingering scent that caught that big nose's attention."

"I know. It's just a reminder of everything that's happened."

"You should be able to polish that mark off there. You might need to touch it up with some silver paint." Perhaps he misunderstood why the mark was so unsettling. Or maybe he just didn't want to delve into any more feelings with her tonight.

"I'll look into it." She moved away from his touch and smiled down at Rocky. "Thank you both." Still unwilling to lose this reprieve from the stress she'd been under since leaving Shotz's bar last week, she tilted her gaze up to Ben. "Would he let me pet him?"

"Maybe. Just a sec." He held his hand up in a fist. "Rocky. Sit." The dog quickly obeyed, and Ben dropped the leash to the ground and stepped on it before reaching out to her. "Give me your hand." She was more than curious about what he was doing when he placed her hand on the flat of his stomach and covered it with his own. "Is this okay?"

Feeling the warm skin beneath the soft cotton of his faded Army T-shirt? Acknowledging the quiver of muscle beneath her touch and trail of goose bumps running up her arm at the intimate contact? Um, when was the last time she'd touched a man's body outside of work? And when had she ever experienced the zing of electricity she felt with her hand trapped between Ben's fingers and body? He rubbed her hand over his stomach, and Maeve raised her eyebrows in curiosity. "What are you doing?"

"Getting my scent on you. He's used to me and my smell. He associates me as his commanding officer and friend. Now he'll hopefully associate you as part of me, not a stranger." He pulled her hand from the warmth of his body. "Now make a fist to protect your fingers. Hold it to his nose and let him sniff you."

When the dog ran his cold nose against her skin, she giggled. "That tickles." She glanced back up at Ben. "Do I meet with his approval?"

"He's still relaxed, so I think you're good." Ben's warm hand engulfed hers. He unfolded her fingers and pressed them to the top of Rocky's head. "Go ahead. He likes to be scratched around his ears and under his collar."

"Should I talk to him, too?"

Ben nodded.

Maeve moved her fingers over the top of Rocky's coarse, warm fur, testing the velvety softness of his ears before working her way over the top of his head and scratching his neck. "Hey, good boy. You've done such a good job making me feel safe tonight. I work with Sergeant Hunter. I'm his *sort-of* friend. You can trust me, too."

Ben kept his hand on top of hers the whole time, protecting her in case the dog decided he didn't like her touch or smell, and generating a mesmerizing awareness of heat and muscle. She slipped her fingers beneath the dog's collar and dug her short fingernails into his fur to scratch him there. Rocky's jaw opened and his tongue lolled out of the side of his mouth. She was surprised that she felt no sense of panic at the sight of all those sharp white teeth. She felt safe with Ben at her side, his wary eyes watching the dog and his warm hand on hers.

Maeve smiled as the big shepherd pushed his head into her hand and demanded she give him the harder scratch around his ears again. "Does he like this? Or is he just tolerating me because you told him it was okay?"

"He likes it." Ben's hand left hers to rub against the dog's chest and pat his flanks. "You think you're a ladies' man now, huh?"

She giggled at his indulgent tone and wondered if he ever talked to a woman with that same deep, teasing pitch. Maeve made an unsettling discovery right then and there. Ben Hunter wasn't just a patient or *sort-of friend*—he was an attractive man. She supposed the long beard and short hair and tattoos she'd seen peeking from the edges of his sleeves and neckline would be a turn-off for some women. But they intrigued her, made her curious to know more about the man behind the facade. The prosthetic hand would certainly make some people wary of him, as would the grouchy attitude he wore like armor some days.

But Maeve knew he exuded body heat and strength, and that he was honest to a fault. She knew that he was kind enough to listen to a frightened, exhausted woman—and that he'd protected her from shadows and dogs and the fearful imaginings that tried to make her feel helpless tonight.

Sergeant Hunter was wounded and wary, but he was a good man. He outclassed the likes of Austin Bukowski and Joker, and certainly Ray Maddox. And she liked him. A lot.

Surprised by the visceral admission, Maeve quickly drew her hand away and straightened. "Thank you. For walking me to my car and for sharing Rocky with me."

She pulled her keys from her purse and clicked open the door.

"You okay?" Ben asked, picking up Rocky's leash and pulling him back to his side so she could open her door.

"Sure I am. Why do you ask?"

"Because you're talking to my chest again."

Well, it was a very nice chest. But she understood what he meant. He didn't seem to believe a thing she said unless she looked him in the eye. Fixing a smile on her lips, she tilted her face up to his handsome blue eyes. "I really am grateful. I'll try to be braver tomorrow when I get off work. And maybe I will think about a dog. I'll probably wait until my degree is finished in December and I have more time…"

Her phone rang in her pocket, and she pulled it out to see who'd be calling. Honestly, outside of work, Steph and an occasional call from her mother, it wasn't like her phone rang all that often. Expecting to read Potential Spam, she hesitated when she saw the local area code and prefix.

"Maeve?" She was aware of Ben moving closer, leaning over her shoulder to read the screen on her phone. "Is it your roommate?" She shook her head. "You worried whoever mugged you would try to harass you now? Could they have gotten your number last night?"

"I don't know. I keep it locked. But… I don't know."

"Answer it and put it on speaker. If it's somebody threatening you, I'll take care of it."

She nodded and did as he asked, holding the phone up in her palm between them. "Hello?"

A man's voice, deeply pitched and articulate, answered. "Is this Maeve Phillips?"

Ben answered for her. "This is Ms. Phillips's phone. Who's calling?"

"I'm Detective Atticus Kincaid from KCPD. I'd like to speak to Ms. Phillips if she's available."

"I'm here." A tight fist of dread squeezed her stomach. "Is this about Steph? My friend, Stephanie Ward?"

The detective took a deep breath. "You filed the missing person report?"

"Yes. Have you found her? Is she okay? Is she hurt?"

"I'm sorry, ma'am, but I need you to come down to the Jackson County Medical Examiner's Office on East Twenty-first Street. We've found someone who matches your friend's description."

Maeve wasn't sure when she'd reached for Ben, but her fingers dug into his bicep. "Why do I need to go to the ME's office?" she asked, already dreading the answer.

"To identify the body. I'm sorry if this is your friend. I don't know any easy way to say this, ma'am. I'm a homicide detective. And I could use your help. Whoever this Jane Doe is, she's been murdered."

Maeve's vision shrank to the middle of Ben's chest. The faded letters there blurred as tears filled her eyes. "Murdered?"

The blurry letters moved as Ben leaned in to ask, "Does it have to be done tonight?"

"The sooner we ID this victim, the sooner we can find her killer."

Easing her death grip on Ben's arm, Maeve swiped away the tears that spilled over onto her cheeks. "I can do that. I'll head there now."

"Thank you, Ms. Phillips. My partner and I will meet you there."

After the call disconnected, she tucked her phone back into her pocket. She used the sleeve of her sweater to blot the dampness on her cheeks and tried to remain hopeful. "I don't even know if it's her yet, and I'm already crying."

"Change in plans."

"What?"

"Lock your car. You're coming with me." Curling his damaged arm around the small of her back, Ben pulled her away from the vehicle.

Maeve turned and slipped out of his grasp. "I have to go to the ME's office."

"No, *we* have to go there."

"You don't need to do that. I'm grateful that you and Rocky got me to my car without incident. I'll take care of that mark later. I'll be safe once I'm inside and the doors are locked."

"I'm not letting you go to the morgue to identify a body by yourself," he snapped.

"I've already taken up too much of your time. Don't you have plans? Someplace you need to be?"

His blue eyes drilled into hers. "I need to be at the morgue tonight."

She puffed up a little bit, standing her ground. "You know, for a man who usually doesn't say more than two words to me unless it's to growl or cuss, you're being awfully bossy right now."

"If you want my help, you'd better get used to it, Sweetcheeks."

"I can do this on my own if I have to."

"I have no doubt. But you *don't* have to." She studied him for a moment before he muttered one of those curses and drifted back a step. "Give me a break. I'm using up all my social graces this evening. We'd better do this before they run out entirely. I'm not letting you go by yourself, and I don't want to embarrass you when we get there."

That apologetic, almost frantic, tone got to her. She stepped into his space and rested her hand against his chest. She looked up into the turbulence darkening his eyes to midnight blue. "Even in your worst mood, you could never embarrass me, Ben. You might be a pain in my backside at times, but you and Rocky have made me feel safe tonight. Safer than I've felt in a long time. You helped me get out of my head and brave the shadows." His labored breathing began to calm beneath her hand, and his gaze never wavered from hers. "I was trying to let you off the hook. I'm not your responsibility. But I would be grateful if you would go with me. I probably wouldn't be in any shape to drive home afterward, anyway, if it does turn out to be Steph. And if it's not her, then I'll be feeling more helpless and frustrated, and worried about that poor woman I have to look at, and I shouldn't be behind the wheel in that condition, either."

He reached up, as if he wanted to cover her hand where it rested against his heart. But he was using his good hand to hold Rocky's leash, and when he saw how close he was to touching her with his prosthetic hand, he dropped his arm and backed away from her touch.

"All right. Lock up. Let's go." His clipped tone didn't offend her. This was the man who saw a problem and did what was necessary to solve it. She wondered what it would be like if he did touch her in some gentle way. Although, she had a feeling any sign of tenderness right now would trigger more tears. She needed his strength, his toughness, to help her keep her emotions in check.

Because as much as she wanted to know the truth about her friend's disappearance, she really didn't want that body at the morgue to be the answer.

Chapter Six

Ben found the medical examiner's office easily enough with his phone. Located between a sea of parking garages and university medical buildings just east of downtown Kansas City, it was an unassuming beige cinder-block building with garage bays for ambulances and coroners' vans and a single gray metal door for the public to enter. He wasn't surprised to find only a handful of vehicles in the parking lot after typical work hours. Most people were home with their families or out with their friends, living normal lives.

But there was nothing *normal* about Maeve being asked to identify a murdered woman's body. He'd been through enough briefings with superior officers and after-action reports in his time serving with Delta Force to know the questions about a dead friend would be clinical and to the point, and that Maeve would be asked to confirm for the police that it was her friend's body. Then they'd want to ask her more questions, possibly the same questions over and over again, until the facts, as she knew them, were laid out in black and white for the superior officer or detective, in this case. When she finally had time to stop and think, she'd either be hit with the grief and anger that came with mourning the loss of a friend—or she'd be stuck back in the fear and worry of the unknown that had been plaguing her all week.

He wasn't surprised that she had reverted to the quiet woman he worked with at the physical and occupational therapy clinic. For the last few miles, the only sound in the truck had been Rocky pacing and huffing in the back seat, the click of the turn signal as they drove through the city and an occasional sigh from Maeve's side of the truck. After he pulled into a parking space and turned off the engine, he glanced over to see her staring straight ahead, maybe seeing nothing as she imagined every worst-case scenario waiting inside for her. Several strands of her dark curly hair had come loose from the short ponytail she wore. His fingers itched with the need to brush her hair back from the ugly contusion on her cheekbone and tuck it gently behind her ear. He wanted to offer her his understanding and whatever comfort he could.

But she needed him to be tough and strong for her right now. Walking her to her car tonight, she'd hinted at the verbal, mental and possibly physical abuse she'd endured in her past. Yet here she was, an accomplished professional about to earn a master's degree, continuing the search for her missing friend right up until what could prove to be a tragic end. Ben believed the woman sitting across from him was stronger than she knew. Hell, she'd put up with him as a patient for long enough. That took a certain kind of grit most people had in short supply. Tonight, she'd admitted to him that she was afraid and had asked for what she needed to help her conquer that fear. Asking for help was sometimes harder than suffering the original trauma. There were vets in his PTSD group who demonstrated that same kind of courage every damn day. He *knew* she was strong.

But he wondered if she believed it.

So, he'd offer his strength until she figured that out for herself. He just wasn't sure he was in a place where he could offer her anything more.

Not that she'd asked for anything more than the scary dude no one wanted to mess with. But damn if he couldn't stop thinking about having her patience and kindness in his life for a lot longer than one night.

He gave himself a minute to park those thoughts in the never-gonna-happen file before he asked, "Ready?"

"No." She finally turned and looked at him with a weary smile and a look of utter fatigue. "But let's get this done."

Stronger than she even knew.

He ordered Rocky to stay and guard the truck before climbing out. When Maeve met him on the sidewalk in front of the truck, he extended his elbow to her, leaving his good hand free for locking the truck, grabbing door handles and making a fist, in case he needed to defend her from anything in the shadows.

Once inside, they were greeted in the brightly lit lobby by Detectives Kincaid and Grove. They pointed to the row of chairs opposite the unattended counter and asked her to take a seat for a few minutes. When he saw her sitting ramrod straight on the edge of the chair, as if she was an AWOL who'd been summoned to appear before a commanding officer, Ben went and stood beside her, lending his silent support.

Kincaid and Grove were both suit-and-tie guys with five-o'clock shadows and wrinkled shirt collars that made Ben think they were putting in overtime on the case they were working. Beyond that, the two men had little in common. Atticus Kincaid was tall and slender, reserved, keen-eyed and precise with his words and movements, giving Ben the impression that he was probably the smartest guy in the room. Kevin Grove was harder to read. His build was over-sized in every dimension, like one of the Chiefs' defensive linemen. He might have played football or boxed at some point because he'd taken a few hard hits that had misshapen his nose. He opened a notebook and tapped information into a computer tablet while his partner did most of the talking. He glanced over at Ben and Maeve, and then he'd type some more. What notes was that guy taking, anyway? Ben didn't want to get on the wrong side of either guy. But he would if either one upset Maeve on top of everything she was already dealing with tonight.

"Thank you again for coming in so quickly, Ms. Phillips. I know this is hard for you, but we appreciate your coopera-tion." Detective Kincaid lightly pressed her hand in greet-ing. Then he turned to Ben, no doubt assessing his scruffy appearance and edgy demeanor. "And you are?"

"Sergeant Ben Hunter, Special Forces. US Army, re-tired." He recited the information, not liking the unspo-ken suspicion in the detective's eyes, or the way Detective Grove suddenly bent his head and typed again. *Yeah. Look me up, buddy.* Because of his time in Delta Force, running off-the-books missions the rest of the world knew nothing about, he knew he wouldn't find much. "You want my se-rial number, too?"

"I don't think that will be necessary." Unfazed by his curt response, Detective Kincaid dropped his gaze to his pros-thetic hand, read the name stamped onto his Army jacket, then briefly swung his gaze over to the bruises and scrapes on Maeve's pale face before looking Ben straight in the eye. Hell. He thought *he'd* hurt Maeve? "Who are you to Ms. Phillips, Sergeant?"

How did he answer that? Patient? Sort-of friend? Bodyguard? He sure as hell wasn't the guy who'd put his hands on her.

But before he uttered his defensive response, Maeve shot to her feet and linked her hand into the crook of his elbow in a way that was beginning to feel far too familiar and incredibly right. "Ben is my friend. He didn't hurt me. I resent you even thinking that he would." She'd intuited the detective's subtle accusation and quickly negated any doubts about his presence here with her. "I was mugged last night after work. Understandably, I was skittish about something like that happening again. Ben and his dog have been helping me."

"What kind of dog?" Kincaid asked.

"Military working K-9," Ben answered, still snapping as if he was responding to a superior officer. "We're both learning to adapt to civilian life. I train dogs at K-9 Ranch."

"That place has a good reputation." Kevin Grove looked up from his tablet. His eyes went from Ben to Maeve and back again. "You two keeping an eye on her?"

"Yes, sir."

The big man nodded. "I think that's smart. At least until we can figure out what's going on." He skimmed the information on his screen. "You've made three reports to KCPD in the past seven days, Ms. Phillips. You reported a car following you, you filed the missing person report on your roommate, and now you've been mugged. I don't see any listing of what was stolen."

Maeve shrugged. "I don't think anything was. I only have one credit card and my debit card. Those and a handful of cash are all accounted for. I don't have any expensive jewelry. I wouldn't wear it to work, anyway, if I did." She glanced from one detective to the other. "Shouldn't you be asking me questions about Steph?"

"The events surrounding you could have been a case of

mistaken identity," Grove suggested. "You and Ms. Ward do share a residence."

Maeve shook her head. "We share a house, but we lead separate lives most of the time. We work in different professions, have vastly different personalities and social lives. She's busty and outgoing and gorgeous. I'm—"

"Gorgeous." The word slipped out of Ben's mouth without thinking. If she was about to say she was the opposite of her friend, he intended to set her straight. "You're gorgeous, too."

She patted his upper arm, maybe thanking him for the compliment or warning him to keep control of his temper. "I'm an introvert. Because of her big personality alone, guys are going to notice her before they notice me. Currently, I'm gone a lot because I'm working my practicum for my master's degree and finishing up a class, but usually I'm a homebody. Last Thursday was the first time we'd gone out together socially in ages."

"Maybe it was a random mugging." Atticus Kincaid leaned against the tall front counter. His relaxed posture was deceptive as he continued to push Maeve for answers. "Was the attack interrupted before they got what they were after?"

"I don't know. It happened fast, and then they ran away. I don't know if they heard someone coming or—"

"Or they realized you weren't the person they were looking for. Did they attempt to sexually assault you? Tear or cut through any of your clothing?" the detective asked.

"No."

"Back off, Detective," Ben warned. When had a mugging turned into attempted rape? "It's already difficult enough for her to be here."

"It's okay, Ben. If I can help, I want to."

He didn't like how quiet her voice sounded, or the way her gaze had settled on the knot of the detective's tie, but Detective Kincaid took her response as permission to continue the interrogation. "Did they say anything to you? Maybe they called you by a different name—mistook you for someone else."

"The only thing they said to me was, 'Where is it?' And I heard one guy telling the other that the boss was going to be pissed at them." Her fingers trembled against Ben's arm, and he covered them with his good hand. "I didn't know what they were talking about."

"Did they mention your friend?"

Her head came up. "I don't think so. You think what happened to me is related to Steph going missing?"

"Maybe they were looking for her. Are you sure they didn't ask, 'Where is *she*?' Could she be hiding from someone for any reason? A bad relationship? Someone she owes money to?"

What were these guys getting at? Maybe it was a cop thing, but they kept talking in the present tense, as if they suspected the body they wanted Maeve to identify wasn't her housemate, that Stephanie Ward was still a missing person. If so, why put Maeve through all this? "There's nothing wrong with Maeve's recall," Ben insisted. "If they'd asked about her friend, she would have said so."

"They never said anything about Steph. The whole thing confuses me. It just seemed like the one guy was really mad at me, like I'd insulted him somehow or stolen from him, if that makes any sense. He was the one who hit me." Ben had to release her and step away before his grip tightened painfully over hers. "It felt as if it was personal to him, or maybe he just likes hurting women."

Ben bit down on the temper that was rising inside him

again. He moved his fist to his thigh and started tapping, silently counting out a cadence that was supposed to get him out of his head when his emotions flared. She hadn't told him that part about the mugging. It made him wish he still had his K-9 partner, Smitty, and they could track down the bastards who'd put their hands on her. Maybe he should see what kind of tracking skills Rocky had.

But there wasn't time for retribution or any more probing questions.

Another man, wearing dark-framed glasses and a white lab coat, pushed through a swinging door down the hallway and strode toward them with a purpose. His coat and the ID badge hanging around his neck identified him as the medical examiner.

Detective Kincaid straightened and made the introductions. "Ms. Phillips, this is Dr. Niall Watson from the crime lab. He's the medical examiner on duty this evening. Niall, Maeve Phillips and her friend, Ben Hunter. She's the roommate who reported the missing person. You ready for us?"

The ME nodded, then pushed his glasses up over the bridge of his nose as he turned to Maeve. "I'm ready for the identification whenever you are."

"Do you want to wait out here, Sergeant?" Detective Kincaid asked, taking note of how he'd distanced himself from Maeve.

"I'm with her." This conversation was triggering all the ways he'd let his teammates down—not trusting his gut about the flawed intel, not heeding the warning his dog gave soon enough. Nobody else was going to die—or suffer—on his watch. Maybe he was overdoing his bodyguard routine, but it felt like Maeve needed backup. His gaze bore down into hers. "Unless she tells me differently."

She linked her hand through his arm again, and they all had their answer.

Dr. Watson led them down the long hallway, listing off protocols they had to follow—no touching the body, putting on one of the disposable masks when they entered the examination room. He warned them of the cooler temperature in the morgue and explained that he'd be pulling the body out of what looked like a refrigerator, but that the victim would be respectfully covered.

Once they were all in position, the medical examiner opened the middle door in a wall of stainless-steel doors and pulled out the tray with a still figure draped in a white sheet lying on it. While the two detectives stood on the opposite side, Maeve stepped up beside the doctor.

She tugged the cuffs of her sweater down past her wrists and hugged her arms around her waist, shivering as they waited. Ben shrugged out of his jacket and draped the insulated canvas around her shoulders. It was cold as winter in the sterile air, but he also worried that a week's worth of stress and emotional exhaustion were taking their toll on her. Relieved to see her tug the jacket together beneath her chin, Ben moved in behind her to watch over her shoulder.

"You ready, Ms. Phillips?" the ME asked.

She bravely nodded.

"Have you done anything like this before?"

"Dr. Watson, I've worked as a physical therapist and occupational therapist. I've seen my fair share of gruesome injuries and post-surgical wounds."

"On a friend?"

Ben was keenly aware that his prosthetic hand and the bracing that held it in place across his shoulders were on display for all to see. But she made no indication that his stump and scars and artificial appendage were included on that gruesome wounds list.

Instead, she raised her chin up another brave notch and looked the dark-haired man in the eye. "Please. I just need to know if this is Stephanie or not."

Without further discussion, Dr. Watson pulled back the sheet and arranged it modestly across the dead woman's chest.

Maeve's sharp, little cry seemed like answer enough. She pressed her hand to the mask covering her lips and re-treated half a step. When she bumped into Ben and started to move away, he wrapped his arm around her waist and kept her snugged against him, sharing his warmth and sup-port. With both hands clutching his forearm, she nodded. "That's her. That's Stephanie Ward." She sniffed once. "I guess she's been found."

Dr. Watson swiped his finger across the screen of his tab-let. "Do you know a next of kin I can notify?"

"Her father. Russell Ward. He and her stepmother live in Grangeport." Ben recognized the tiny river town in cen-tral Missouri. "Her mother died when she was in the fifth grade. Steph and her dad didn't always get along—she was a bit of a rebel in high school. But they were working on patching things up. She was going home for Thanksgiving next month."

"Thank you." Dr. Watson jotted the information on his computer pad, while Grove and Kincaid made notes, as well.

Her fingers dug into the muscles of Ben's arm around her waist. "He'll be devastated. How am I going to tell him?"

"We'll handle the notification, Ms. Phillips," the doctor explained.

"Could the same men who attacked me...?" Instead of exiting the room now that she'd done what the other men had asked of her, Maeve pointed to the wide band of discoloration around her friend's pale neck. "Those bruises and the petechiae around her eyes... Do they mean...?"

"She was strangled. I haven't conducted the full autopsy yet, but my preliminary cause of death is asphyxiation." The ME's plain recitation of facts seemed to calm her emotions more than his cautious words and considerate warnings had. "I won't show you the other marks on her body. She fought hard against her assailant, but she was overpowered."

"Was she raped?" Maeve glanced across the body to the two detectives. "Is that why you asked if I was sexually assaulted?"

When Maeve's fingers drifted up to the marks of violence on her own face, Ben grabbed her hand and pulled her to his side. "Is that all you need from her, Doctor?"

Dr. Watson nodded. "I'll take good care of your friend. Get her safely into her father's care once I gather all the evidence I need." He pulled the sheet back over Stephanie Ward's face. "I imagine the detectives will have more questions for you."

Ben faced the two detectives over the dead body. "Can we at least take this back out front, so she doesn't have to stay here and continue to see her friend like this?"

When the ME nodded, Ben tugged on Maeve's hand and led her back into the hallway. They were all peeling off their masks and chucking them in the trash when Maeve turned to the detectives. "Do you know what happened to her? Where was she found? She's been missing for a week. How long has she been...dead?"

Detective Kincaid answered. "We were hoping you could fill us in on a few details. She was found in the landfill south of the city. Her body had been covered in lime to delay decomp. Dr. Watson estimates her time of death was some-time last weekend."

"After her boyfriend last saw her, and before I was at-tacked." Ben wasn't sure if Maeve was playing detective herself, or if she needed answers to help keep her grief at bay. "She was tossed there like a bag of trash?"

The two detectives exchanged a look before Detective Kincaid asked, "Where did you last see your friend?"

"Shotz's bar. Last Thursday. We went there so she could reconnect with her boyfriend. I didn't stay once he showed up. I just wanted to get out of that place."

"Smart," Detective Grove mumbled under his breath.

"What's the boyfriend's name?" Kincaid asked.

"Austin Bukowski."

That answer seemed to surprise the detective. "The at-torney?"

She nodded. "Do you know him?"

"Of him. He's an up-and-comer. He and his firm handle a lot of big-name clients. Not always ones KCPD approves of."

Ben simmered at the idea of yet another man in Maeve's life who could be a threat to her. "You mean he defends the bad guys in court?"

Kincaid nodded. "A few of them."

Ben wasn't surprised when Maeve jumped to her friend's defense. "Steph worked at the same firm. As a paralegal. She always said that criminals require a fair defense so that their cases can't be overturned—if they're guilty. Of course, if they're innocent, the accused needs someone fighting for them as hard as they can." Oh, this was just getting better and better. Ben felt the antsy need to punch something or run out into the night. What the hell had Maeve gotten her-self in the middle of? Even if she was an innocent bystander to something her roommate was involved with, Sweetcheeks was in this up to her eyeballs. He had a feeling the detectives were beginning to think the same thing—whether she was aware of it or not, Maeve was the key to breaking this case open and solving her friend's murder. "She was supposed to travel to St. Louis on Monday with her boss on their current case but missed the flight. She must have already been…" She refused to say the word *dead*. "Who would want to kill her? Why?"

Grove pulled out his tablet again and spoke to his partner. "You think this is job-related?"

"It's an angle we need to check out," Kincaid agreed. He pulled a notebook from inside his jacket and wrote something on a list. "Let's pull a list of clients Ms. Ward would have had contact with. What's her boss's name?"

"Bertram Summerfield," Maeve answered before the big detective found the information on his screen. "He's a founding partner at the same law firm. Sometimes he was inappropriate with her. But she said she'd put up with worse. He paid her well, so she never reported any sexual harassment."

Detective Grove nodded. "I'm running Summerfield now. I'm guessing a guy like that has a history of inappropriate behavior."

Now that she had their attention again, Maeve inhaled a steadying breath and added, "I don't know if this is important, but there was another man with Steph and Austin at Shotz's. He's the one who called Austin to meet us there. Said they were friends. I don't know his real name. He called himself Joker. He gave me the creeps."

Ben could tell by their reactions that the detectives were familiar with Joker. "You know this guy. Who is he?"

"Judd Lasko," Detective Kincaid confirmed. "Street name Joker. If there's money to be made, this guy's into it.

Loan-sharking. Dealing drugs. Human trafficking. Usually, he's the hired muscle. But word is that he's working for some big names now, moving up in rank. I wonder what his relationship to Bukowski is."

"Maybe Bukowski defended him?" Grove suggested. "He's been arrested often enough. He couldn't afford a firm like Summerfield's, though. And he's probably too far below their pay grade to take him on pro bono."

Ben wasn't worried about the details; he just didn't want this creep or anyone else coming after this gentle, special woman again. "Could Joker be one of the two men who attacked Maeve? Maybe he was hired to go after both her and Steph."

"But why?" Maeve's voice sounded about as brittle as he was feeling. "I'm nobody. And Steph might have been a little ambitious, but mostly, she just wanted to be with the man she loved."

Detective Kincaid answered them both. "Right now, we're trying to get all the information we can. Then we'll sort through what's relevant and what's not." He circled the name *Joker* on his notepad. "Did either of your attackers look or sound familiar to you?"

"You mean did either one of them remind me of Joker?" She shook her head. "I never saw their faces. They were both big—like you are, Detective Grove. The man who held me down never spoke. He smelled like cigarette smoke if that helps. I can't tell you if that means it was him because everything in that bar smelled like smoke when we were there."

Hell. This purposeful assault that she'd tried to dismiss as a *mugging* was sounding more personal and violent with every detail that came out of her mouth. Ben planted his hand at the small of Maeve's back and urged her toward the door. "We're out of here."

"But the detectives—"

"Now, Maeve." He wasn't sure how much longer he could ignore the fiery need to break the necks of those two goons without scaring Maeve with an outburst that might also put him back on Grove and Kincaid's radar as a person of interest.

Either recognizing the fist at his thigh for the pressure valve it was, or sensing just how tightly he was holding his anger in check, Maeve tilted her gaze up to his. "We should be going. I could use some fresh air."

He nodded sharply and she nudged him toward the door.

They had almost reached the exit when the door swung open and two men in tailored suits with pricey shoes and watches burst into the lobby. A blond man about Ben's age and an older, white-haired gentleman with the paunch of wealth bore down on Maeve.

"Maevie? Is it true? Is Steph dead?"

When the younger man reached for Maeve, Ben stepped between them. "Back off."

The detectives circled around Maeve to block him from getting any closer, too.

The blond hotshot pulled back. Ben couldn't tell if the man had been crying or if he was slightly drunk. But his eyes were bloodshot, and he smelled of alcohol and smoke, as if he'd just come from a club. He jabbed a finger at Ben's chest. "Who are you?"

Atticus Kincaid's cool voice intervened. "We're KCPD. Who are you?"

Maeve's fingers were curled into the back of Ben's belt. "That's Steph's boyfriend, Austin Bukowski. And her boss, Bertram Summerfield."

Bertram Summerfield's tone was as cool and composed

as Kincaid's had been. "Ms. Ward was a valued member of our firm. I hate that the rumor is true."

"How did you know to come here?" the detective asked.

The white-haired man nodded. "I have connections. Word gets around. I called Austin as soon as I heard. I know the two of them were…an item," he finished as if he found the idea of an interoffice romance distasteful.

The detectives exchanged a look. "Gentlemen, we have some questions for you."

"It *is* Steph," Austin wailed. "I want to see her."

Dr. Watson had replaced his lab coat with a sports jacket and joined the group at the front door. "Not tonight, you're not. Not unless you're family."

"But I dated—"

"That's not family."

As a terse argument between cops and attorneys over their desire to see Stephanie Ward's body with their own eyes ensued, Ben pointed Maeve toward the door. "You ready to go home?"

"Please."

"Better get her out of here," Detective Kincaid said to Ben under his breath, as he pulled out a business card and handed it to Maeve. "We'll stall these two as long as we can. If we have more questions, we'll contact you later. Or if you think of anything else, call. Again, we're sorry for your loss."

Ben was pushing the door open when Maeve was yanked from his grasp.

He whirled around to find Austin Bukowski's hand clamped around her wrist. "Maevie, what am I going to do? I loved her."

"Don't touch her." Ben was done with being patient and polite. He grabbed the other man's wrist, hit a pressure point and popped his grip open before shoving him out of her space.

"What the hell?" Austin cursed and massaged his wrist. "I'm suing you for assault."

"She'll sue you first."

"Stop!" Even as exhausted as she must be, meek and mild Maeve Phillips had a temper. "You should have treated Steph like gold, Austin—she loved you that much. But she was just a roll in the hay and an extra ATM to you, wasn't she? I told you something was wrong, but you wouldn't listen. Nobody listened to me. And now it's too late."

She turned and pushed Ben out the door, letting it slam shut behind them. The cold night air should have chilled his skin, but he didn't feel it as she led him on a fast march to his truck. She didn't even flinch at Rocky barking through the crack in the rear window at their approach. Whether he was sounding an alarm or welcoming them, his bark was a vicious thing.

Just as Ben raised his fist to order the dog to cool it, Maeve simply stopped and turned her face into his shoulder, finally succumbing to her tears.

His arms automatically went around her as her fingers clawed for a grip at either side of his waist. Ben wasn't sure what to do except stand silently by and let her cry. He hadn't been this close to a woman since…hell, since before he went on that fateful mission. Talk about being out of practice. Maybe Rocky was responding to her breathy sobs the same way he was. The dog seemed to sense that something was wrong and quieted as Maeve worked her way through her grief.

She shook. Or maybe that was him shaking as his roiling temper cooled and his injured psyche accepted that he wasn't the person in the most pain here. She sniffed, and he knew the woman was going to need a tissue, but he didn't mind a mess. The front of his T-shirt dampened through to his skin as her tears fell, unchecked.

Ben loved feeling her clutched against him, but hated the reason she was there. The pillowing of her small, round breasts against his hard chest felt as foreign as her strong, nimble fingers digging into his flanks. Yet, as unfamiliar as her touch might be, he found it calmed something in him to have her close like this. Sure, his male body responded to the obvious femaleness of hers—her curves, her scent, her softness. But the connection he felt even more than physical attraction was the emotional acceptance, the trust she gifted him with. In this moment, with this woman, Ben Hunter was a whole man again. She needed someone tonight, and with every grasp, every word, every action, she made him believe that he was enough. He wasn't going to fail her. Whatever strength he had was hers.

He moved to cradle the back of her head and pull her more fully into his embrace. But his hook tangled into the ponytail at the back of her head, and the polished titanium reflected the garish light from the streetlight overhead, making the fake hand stand out like an anathema against her sable curls, jarring him from the calming, healing moment. But when he started to pull it away, her arms slid to the back of his waist, and she hugged herself more tightly against him. Ben wasn't sure what words he could say that wouldn't be platitudes that she'd said she didn't want to hear from him. So, he just stood there quietly, held her close and let her cry.

It turned out he didn't need words as she rubbed her cheek against his beard and tucked her head beneath his chin a few minutes later. "I don't know how I would have gotten through tonight without you." Her voice was husky with tears. "I am so talked out. My emotions are all used up. I wish I could hole up at home for a couple of days and recharge my batteries. No phone, no TV news, no questions, no well-meaning friends, nothing." He wished he had a handkerchief to offer her, but she pulled a tissue from the pocket of her sweater and leaned back just enough to wipe her nose and dab her eyes. "But that's not going to be my reality for a while, is it."

"Probably not." He plucked the soiled tissue from her fingers and stuffed it into the pocket of his jeans.

"You don't have to...thank you." She caught her bottom lip between her teeth and summoned an apologetic smile as she met his downturned gaze. "Sorry about your shirt."

"It washes."

"Oh." A realization occurred to her, and she started to shrug his jacket off her shoulders. "It's chilly out here. You must be freezing."

"Leave it." Ben gathered it together at the neck and Velcroed it together. Then he encouraged her to slide her arms into the sleeves. "You may be in a little bit of shock. I don't want you to get cold on top of that. I'll crank the heat once we're in the truck."

She snugged the collar up around her chin and dipped her nose inside. "It smells good. Like you." Right. Because a man who spent the day with dogs and worked out must smell like a daisy by this time of night. But if inhaling his scent gave her some kind of comfort, he wasn't going to argue. Besides, he was half hoping her sweet vanilla scent would cling to the material of his jacket, giving him a reminder of just how close they'd gotten to each other tonight. "I didn't realize how much I'd be demanding of you when I asked you to walk me to my car. I could feel the tension radiating off you in there, and I know you need a physical outlet when you get fired up like this. FYI, I'm not a runner like you. But I am willing to go for a walk if that would help. I wouldn't mind breathing some air that doesn't smell like chemicals and clearing my head."

He snorted and gave in to the urge to brush a stray lock of hair away from her sticky cheeks. He marveled at how the wave curled around his fingers as if she was still clinging to him. "Don't you be taking care of me, Sweetcheeks. You're the one going through hell tonight."

"We'd be helping each other, I think."

Ben tucked the curl behind her ear and grinned when it sprang back out of place. It was getting harder to refuse this woman anything she asked of him. "Okay. Let me get Rocky. He can do his business while we're walking."

Yep. He'd do just about anything to see that shy smile. "And help protect me from what's lurking in the shadows?"

"You know us so well."

He unlocked the truck door and hooked Rocky up to his leash. Most of the lingering tension in him settled when he felt her fingers sliding around his elbow near his prosthesis.

They walked around the perimeter of the parking lot, staying near the lights while letting Rocky's nose lead the way. By the time they got back to the truck, Maeve's color seemed a little better, and her eyes weren't quite so red and puffy. And she'd been right, either the exercise or the night air or feeling her hand clinging to him had eased the stress he'd been dealing with, too. He could still feel that need to strike out against the men who'd hurt her—but that mission-focused anger was beneath the surface now, where he could control it.

He opened the passenger door for Maeve to climb in, but the ME office door swung open and Rocky spun around, growling, barking and lunging at Austin Bukowski as he jogged toward them. "Maevie! Thank goodness I caught you."

Bertram Summerfield was close on his heels, followed by the detectives and Dr. Watson.

"What is that thing?" The young attorney stopped moving, jerking back a step when Rocky bared his teeth and growled.

Summerfield pulled his junior partner back another step yet managed to keep Austin between him and the growling dog. "He's a menace. He ought to be reported for threatening innocent people."

"Not threatening. Protecting," Maeve insisted. Ben mentally swore when she added her hand to the taut leash, sending her surprisingly calm energy down the line to the dangerous dog. Rocky could have just as easily felt the unfamiliar handler and turned on her. Maybe after combining their scents and teaching her the proper way to approach an unfamiliar dog, Rocky had accepted her as another teammate. She went on to define the relationship he hadn't put a name to yet. "Rocky is Ben's K-9 partner. He's doing his job. I wouldn't sneak up behind us again if I were you."

Austin had to shout to be heard over the barking dog. "Shut him up!" He scowled at Ben, but he was all charming smiles for Maeve. "I just want to talk. We understand each other's grief. Can we go someplace private? Maybe get a drink?"

"Rocky. Stand down." Maeve uttered the command in a sharp tone and raised her fist the way she'd seen him do.

By damn, the dog obeyed her. His out-of-control warrior dog *could* be trained. "Good boy, Rocky." He praised the dog, then stepped up beside Maeve to give her the same level of protection his partner had. "Maeve said she's all talked out. You need to respect that."

"But—"

"This is too many people for my office this late at night." Dr. Watson locked the door and walked up to the detectives, joining the conversation. "I'm locking things up and heading to the crime lab with the evidence I've taken off the body."

The senior attorney turned to the ME. "If there were any papers on her—"

The medical examiner shifted his evidence kit to the other hand and headed to the Jeep parked closest to the door. "If there were any papers on her, they're in evidence now."

But Summerfield blocked his path. "They could have been on a thumb drive or tablet or laptop. Did she have her bag with her?"

"Still my jurisdiction." Dr. Watson stepped around the older man and hit the key fob to start his vehicle. "You all need to leave the premises. I'd like to get home to see my wife and children sometime tonight."

"I hear that." Kevin Grove came up behind the white-haired man. "Call me tomorrow, Mr. Summerfield, and I'll see if there's anything of yours or your firm's we need to secure in the lab."

"That's not satisfactory. There's sensitive information in those files. What about attorney-client privilege?"

The big man didn't budge. "It's not open for discussion."

Austin pulled Bertram away and headed toward a white BMW across the parking lot. "Come on, Bert." He glanced at Detective Grove as they hurried past. "We'll be calling in the morning."

"Look forward to it." Kevin Grove's monotone was complete sarcasm.

With Rocky subdued, and the latest irritations peeling out of their parking space and leaving the parking lot, Ben eyed the two detectives. "You need Maeve to stay any longer? She's running on fumes."

"Thank you for your assistance tonight." Kincaid did the talking, but Grove was nodding beside him. "We probably will have more questions, but I understand you need some time to grieve."

"Thank you," Maeve whispered, her shoulders sagging as if standing up to Bukowski had drained the last of her energy out of her. "Just find out who killed my friend. I'll help any way I can."

"I don't like those two showing up tonight. Summerfield is looking for something, but I don't know what it is yet. I definitely don't like Joker being anywhere in your orbit, and I really don't like knowing there are men in my city who would victimize brave women like you and your friend." Detective Kincaid extended his hand to shake Ben's. "Thank you for your service, Sergeant. To our country—and to Ms. Phillips. She's going to need a champion like you if tonight's any indication. I apologize if I made you uncomfortable earlier. I'm afraid that suspicion goes along with the badge. I trust you'll see her safely home?"

"Yes, sir."

And that's what he did.

Chapter Seven

"You could have dropped me off at my car," Maeve offered for the third time as Ben pulled his truck into the driveway of the ranch-style house she shared with Steph. Make that, *had* shared. The automatic lights coming on over the garage and front porch welcomed her, as always. The teal door and grayish-blue trim she'd painted herself still sang to the creative side of her brain. But somehow the place didn't feel much like home tonight. "Now I'll have to call a car service to get to work in the morning."

"You were in no shape to drive." Ben set the brake but left the engine running so that the heater would keep the interior warm. "What time do you need to be there?"

"Oh, no." She mustered what felt like a smile. "You've already done more than I asked of you, and I will be forever grateful. You got me through a rough patch tonight, Ben. But you don't have to babysit me. I've gotten pretty good at being on my own."

He rested his elbow above the knob on his steering wheel where he held on with his prosthesis to drive, just like she'd taught him in occupational therapy. His eyes were shadowed with only the dashboard lights on in the truck cab, and his beard hid the expression on his mouth, so she couldn't tell if he was teasing or serious when he asked, "If I drive off and leave you now, what will you do?"

She shrugged and gave him an honest answer. "I'm exhausted. I'm going to go to bed."

"Without dinner?"

"I'll probably eat a bowl of cereal."

He made that soft snort that she'd learned could mean disbelief, derision or amusement. "You're in the medical profession. You have heard about nutrition and the five food groups?"

"Cereal is comfort food," she argued, feeling she'd earned the right to eat whatever she wanted tonight. "And it's easy."

He hunched down enough to bring his intense blue eyes into the dim light. "Will you sleep?" Maeve couldn't deal with *intense* right now and dropped her gaze to the faded patch of nearly white denim on the jeans that hugged his muscular thighs. "Will you stay up all night crying? Lie awake listening to every creak in the house? Every brush of wind through the tree branches? Every car door closing or horn honking in the night?" She wanted to say something funny and dismiss him, but she had a feeling he was right. "Eyes, Sweetcheeks."

She looked up at him. "You're being mean. Coming up with all the things that could scare me tonight. I haven't even gotten through the door yet."

"I'm being honest. It's what you asked for. I'm more than happy to spend the night out here in my truck if it'll help you feel safe enough to rest."

"In my driveway?" Maeve glanced around and checked the side-view mirror. She'd always thought she lived in a safe part of the city, here in middle-class suburbia. But now all she could see were the shadows between the houses and beneath the cars parked in driveways. There was even a shadow on her own front porch underneath the bench she and Steph had put there.

Misreading her hesitation to accept his offer, he turned back to the steering wheel and tapped it with his titanium hook. "Unless you think the neighbors will talk."

Maeve reached for that faded spot on his thigh. She tried to ignore the quiver of corded muscles beneath her hand and the suffusion of heat that warmed her fingers and seeped into her blood. "I don't care what the neighbors say. You're not leaving?"

His gaze locked on to hers. "Not tonight. Not until we get some answers from Grove and Kincaid and have a better idea of what's going on around you."

"And if I say I'll be perfectly fine without the US Army babysitting me tonight, you'll go home and get a good night's sleep yourself?"

She waited through one, two, three beats of unblinking silence before she pulled her hand away.

"I take it that's a no?" Maeve turned in her seat to look through the cage into the back seat where Rocky had sat up once they'd stopped. "What about you? Do you have enough sense to go home and get a good night's sleep?"

The dog huffed a response that could mean he was with her on sending the boys home, or that he supported Ben, no matter what his human partner decided. Or...judging by the way he circled and plopped down facing away from her, he was just put out that she had included him in their conversation when he wanted to nap.

She skipped Ben's gaze as she faced the dashboard again and sank back into the insulated jacket that he'd put around her tonight. She needed to take it off and give it back to him. Even with his camo jacket back on, it was too cold to be sitting outside all night, and if he ran the engine, he'd be wasting gas and risk breathing in too many carbon monoxide fumes. He'd need to take off his prosthesis and rest his arm for a while. Wouldn't that leave him vulnerable if something should happen? Besides, her driveway would be too far away if someone broke through a window on the back side of the house where her bedroom was located. Or if they busted down the back door. She'd feel guilty about leaving Ben and Rocky out here, plus, she'd still be afraid.

"What are you overthinking in that pretty head of yours?" His deep, gravelly voice skittered across her eardrums, warming her like the jacket and the heat of his body. His indulgent tone, and the fact that he was still with her after everything that had happened since leaving work, made it easy to risk speaking her mind again.

Maybe she was pushing her luck and taxing his patience, but she met his gaze and asked for what she wanted, and perhaps what he needed, once more. "How are you at sleeping on couches?"

The grin that split his beard triggered a hopeful smile of her own. "Honey, I've slept in mud and bugs in the jungle, and with sand and scorpions in the desert. Your couch sounds pretty comfy right about now."

"I'll feed you breakfast. And something tonight, too, if you want," she offered. "Not cereal. I may not have any appetite, but you have muscles to fuel. I have a leftover hamburger, or I can scrounge up something else for Rocky to eat, too."

"You don't have to bribe me to stick close to you. Are you okay having Rocky in the house?" he asked, his tone more serious. "He has a penchant for chewing on things when he gets upset or frustrated. I've got a knotted rope in the back he can play with, but he might find a shoe if you're not careful."

"A shoe is a small price to pay for his protection."

"Not everybody feels that way."

Maeve shrugged. "Well, I've never really run with the popular crowd. I'm okay with having you both in the house."

"I'll have to get up around sunrise to exercise him and get to the ranch for morning chores. If you don't mind going to the clinic early, I'd be happy to drop you off on my way home."

She looked him straight in the eye, so he'd know she was sincere. "Still okay."

He turned off the engine and pulled out his keys. "Then let's get inside. You're shivering again, and I'm hungry for a bowl of cereal."

Laughter felt a hell of a lot better than all the crying she'd done tonight. While Ben and Rocky checked her front yard and fenced-in backyard, and Ben secured every window and door in the house, Maeve heated up soup and fixed a chicken sandwich for Ben and shredded another poached chicken breast for Rocky. Then she gathered blankets and a pillow for man and dog, and got them settled in the living room. She scrounged up a new toothbrush for Ben, took a quick hot shower and put on a pair of comfy flannel pajamas to combat the emotional chill she was still feeling, and they said their good-nights.

But Maeve still couldn't sleep.

Maybe it was the memory of Steph's bruised neck and face and the loss of that vibrant, generous spirit in the world that kept her mind racing. Or maybe it was the bruises on her own face staring back at her from the bathroom mirror that reminded her of how easily *she* could have been the woman lying under that sheet that made her determined to figure out why her life had imploded so quickly since that night at Shotz's.

Not everything about the past few days was a puzzle or downer. Who knew how protective and caring her grumpy Gus of a patient, Ben Hunter, would turn out to be? Yes, he had PTSD and physical recovery issues he was dealing with that could make his moods unpredictable. But he hadn't once taken any of his temper out on her, not even verbally. He was surprisingly funny, undeniably warm—and she'd never felt more sheltered and valued than when he'd wrapped his arms around her and snugged her close to his chest. Tonight, she'd seen more of the soldier and man than a patient, and there wasn't anything about the scruffy, tattooed warrior that she didn't find attractive. He'd pushed her out of her comfort zone more than once, and yet he'd also defended her right to be in that comfort zone where her shy sensibilities could gather the strength she needed to keep moving forward.

And Rocky? She had a feeling the dog had a better understanding of how alike he and Ben were. The dog probably thought he'd finally found the kindred spirit he'd been looking for. Fierce warrior. Forced to leave the job they loved and had trained for. Focused on the mission. Growly and grumpy with a clear idea of who and what he'd tolerate, and who he'd allow into his small circle of friends. Loyal and protective and willing to take a bite out of anyone he perceived as a threat to one of those friends.

She was glad that neither Ben nor Rocky had taken a shine to Austin Bukowski because she had a weird feeling about the man. She hadn't been thrilled to learn that Steph was seeing him again. She wouldn't trust anybody who was friends with a creep like Joker. And his whining grief over Steph's murder had a desperate quality to it that made Maeve wonder if he knew more about her friend's death than he let on. Or maybe Austin was cut from the same cloth as Ray Maddox had been, and dealing with a man who was controlling and slyly denigrating triggered some bad memories for her.

One moment, Maeve was smiling at the similarities between man and beast that she wasn't sure Ben was aware of. The next, she realized she was crying again—big, quiet tears that slowly trickled down her cheeks and dripped onto her pajamas.

"Enough, already." She angrily swiped away those tears and climbed out of bed.

She needed to *do* something to help Steph and the police, not just keep reacting. Although, she wasn't sure what she was qualified to do. As she pulled on a pair of fuzzy socks to keep her feet warm and closed the drawer on her dresser, she had an idea. Leaving her phone on the charger beside her bed, she picked up her roomy catchall bag off the floor and dug around in the bottom to find the tiny flashlight she carried. Her intent was to tiptoe down the hallway to Steph's room and straighten up the drawers that had been left in such a mess.

But the flicker of a memory, of something that might be important, stopped her in the doorway. She turned back to her bed and picked up the bag, hugging its weight against her chest. This was the purse Steph had been carrying at Shotz's bar. She'd borrowed it that Thursday morning because she said she had some things she'd hauled home from work that she needed to return, and her small handbag wouldn't hold it all. Maeve later found out her friend had also packed a box of condoms and a change of silky underwear. She'd been planning on finding and seducing Austin all along.

Maeve hadn't minded. She preferred wearing her smaller cross-body purse when she went out on the town, so she wouldn't have to set it down in case she was asked to dance.

And certainly, because it was much lighter and a lot harder for anyone to pick her pocket in a crowded bar with the small, zipped-up purse.

Maeve sank onto the edge of the bed and studied the catchall bag, begging it to share its secrets.

This was the same purse *she'd* been carrying when she'd been mugged in the parking garage. That day, she'd filled it with her walking shoes, an extra pair of socks and some snacks for work.

"Where is it?" The men had dumped it out, then kicked its contents aside before running away. She'd barely crawled between two parked cars to retrieve her phone and punch in 9-1-1 when she heard a car speeding away from the parking garage. Only when the police officer had arrived on the scene did she gather the rest of her things. Had she missed something that had been kicked beneath one of the cars?

Maeve eyed the cross-body wallet purse she'd worn over her shoulder again tonight. It held her phone, money, keys, ID and not much more, hopefully making her less of a target to any future mugger. Plus, she liked how it left her hands free to hold her morning cup of coffee, or now, she supposed, the can of pepper spray hooked to her keychain. On the days when she wasn't planning to walk during her lunch break, she didn't need to carry the big bag, anyway.

After leaving Shotz's, Steph had come back to pack an overnight bag to go to Austin's. She'd swapped out purses then. Yesterday, Maeve had grabbed it up and tossed her things into it without thinking. Had Steph left something in her bag the men were after? Her boss, Bertram Summerfield, had mentioned something about missing files. But why involve muggers when he could simply demand his employee return the files to the office?

Maeve shook her head in frustration. There were answers

here somewhere—her exhausted brain just couldn't figure them out. Rising to her feet, she dumped the big purse out onto the bed and rifled through the contents. Shoes, snacks, socks. But nothing out of place. Nothing worth stealing and nothing that wasn't hers.

"Oh, duh." Steph would have unloaded the bag in *her* bedroom. If there'd been anything of hers left in it, Steph would have put it away there.

Picking up her flashlight, Maeve hurried through the dark house. Inside Steph's room, she turned on the lamp beside the bed so that the bright overhead light wouldn't carry down the hall to wake Ben. She quickly glanced around. Steph was more of a pack rat than Maeve, but there was a method to her mess. Dirty clothes in or near the hamper. E-reader and a stack of print books on the floor beside her rumpled bed. Work clothes pressed at the cleaners and hanging in her closet. Shoes stuffed into an organizer hanging over her closet door.

Maeve checked every pocket in the organizer. She checked the dirty clothes and stuffed them all in the hamper. Then, she smoothed the covers on the bed, running her hands over every inch to see if she felt anything beneath the silky coverlet that didn't belong there. Finally, she turned her attention to Steph's dresser, where her friend stowed everything from lingerie to makeup to jewelry. Was there anything here that didn't belong?

Her eyes landed on the framed picture on top of the dresser. The image was from the previous summer of the two of them on a day trip they'd taken down to Ha Ha Tonka State Park. After a day of hiking the paths and shopping for souvenirs, they'd posed for a selfie in front of the ruins of a castle overlooking the Lake of the Ozarks.

Maeve ran her fingers along the front and back of the

frame to see if anything had been hidden there. But there was nothing. This was a wild goose chase. Nothing more than a hope that she could find some clue that would provide a reason for Steph's murder.

It wasn't as if finding answers would bring her friend back. Or ease her guilt that she could have done something more to help Steph than report her missing. Maybe she could have stood up more to Joker and Austin. Only Steph was the one who'd refused to listen. She'd been so certain of her love for Austin, and had the confidence they would make things work out between them this time around.

Maeve was sitting on the end of Steph's bed, staring at her friend's larger-than-life smile and remembering how fun that day in the Ozarks had been, when Ben knocked softly on the doorframe and came in.

She hadn't heard him walking through the house, but she wasn't surprised to see him, either. This man seemed to have a sixth sense about what she needed.

"I'm sorry. Did I wake you?" She studied him for a moment in the warm glow of light from the lamp. He wore his jeans and T-shirt and usual glower. His feet were bare. And he'd taken off his prosthetic arm, leaving his stump exposed beneath the sleeve of his shirt. She was happy he'd made himself comfortable for the night. She was happier to know that the more time she spent with him, the less self-conscious he seemed to be.

Rocky padded into the room behind him, stretching his back legs and yawning before sitting beside Ben. It was a little disconcerting to have both males staring at her so intently.

"Ben?" She tucked her loose hair behind her ear. Why wasn't he answering her? "Is something wrong?"

"You're not sleeping."

"That doesn't answer my question."

"If you're going to cry, you're not going to do it alone in your friend's bedroom after midnight."

She thought she'd been mourning quietly, but Special Forces man must have heard her soft sniffles. Maeve stood and carried the photograph back to the dresser. "I honestly thought I was cried out."

He moved to stand beside her. "If you need to cry, do it. You're grieving a friend you lost to violence. You think I didn't cry when I woke up on the medevac chopper and found out three of my teammates and Smitty didn't make it?"

She tilted her face up to his. "Who's Smitty?"

"My K-9 partner." He reached over and pulled up the sleeve of his shirt to reveal the tattoo of a German shepherd overlapping the three stripes of a sergeant's insignia. There were two lines of words below the dog—*Smitty* and *Bravest Dog Ever.*

"He was killed? Oh, Ben." Tears welled up in her eyes again as she brushed her fingers across the drawing, as if petting the dog. This man had lost so much. And the fact that he was still here, still fighting every day to come back from those losses was more a testament to his strength than all those muscles beneath her hand. She realized that was warm skin and hard muscle she was literally stroking, and she curled her fingers into her palm and turned away to straighten the picture. "I'm so sorry."

But Ben commented on neither her uninvited touch nor the sympathy she offered. "That's a good picture of you and Steph. I like how big you're smiling there. Lights up your whole face. I wish I could see that carefree smile." He turned off the lamp and handed her the flashlight. "Don't want you caught in the darkness. Come with me."

He extended his elbow to her, as had become their habit this evening. Even without the prosthetic device strapped to his stump, she didn't hesitate to take hold of him and let him lead her back down the hallway. When they passed her room, she pointed inside. "Um, I sleep there."

But Ben led her straight out to the kitchen to the sink, where he pulled away just long enough to pull a glass down from the cabinet, turn on the faucet and fill it with cool water. He cradled the glass in the crook of his arm for a moment to turn off the water before holding the glass out to her. "I don't want you to get dehydrated with all those tears over your friend or my dog or anything else. Drink."

Yep. This total badass, gruff and scarred and no doubt weary from being up so late and having to deal with so many people when he was more comfortable with dogs and solitude, was taking care of her. Again.

Maeve felt an unfamiliar heat squeezing around her heart and spreading though her. She was starting to crave the way this man made her feel. Unsettled, off-kilter, needy, but oh, so valued and cared for. With every interaction she grew more confident stepping out of her cautious comfort zone. It wasn't just that Ben Hunter made her feel safe. He made her feel, period. Feel a whole heck of a lot.

The attraction she felt must have been simmering between them for months now. But acknowledging those feelings seemed to make her even more aware of how every scent, every touch, every word he shared was precious to her.

And maybe that was dangerous emotional territory for this time of night in the quiet house with her thoughts reeling all over the place. She'd followed her heart once before and had made a horrible choice. But then, she couldn't imagine Ray ever going out of his way to make sure she got out of her head, stayed hydrated and got some rest. She'd never met any man who made her feel as important as the man standing in front of her and watching her with those intense blue eyes did.

"You gonna keep looking at me like that? Or are you going to drink your water?" Ben issued the order in a gentle tone that didn't sound much like an order.

Feeling her cheeks heat with embarrassment at her wandering thoughts, Maeve put the glass to her lips and drank down half of it. "That was smart. Thank you."

Satisfied that she was taking care of herself physically, at least, he took the glass and polished off the rest in one big gulp before turning it upside down on the drying rack beside the sink. A man drinking from the same glass shouldn't have looked so sexy or felt so intimate, but it did. "You keep staring at me like that, and I'm going to get self-conscious. Make me think I've got dinner stuck in my beard, or I'm missing a hand or something."

Maeve shook herself out of her momentary lust-induced stupor, shocked that he would think for even one second that she was uncomfortable with his disability. "I didn't mean to. And you don't. Have food in your beard, I mean. Drinking from the same glass was unexpectedly hot and… Of course, your injury—"

"No offense taken, Sweetcheeks." He cut off her rambling apology and reached for her hand. "I'm just giving you a hard time, trying to get you to stop overthinking all the troubles keeping you awake tonight. Come on." He turned her toward the living room and ushered Rocky out of the kitchen ahead of them. "I didn't tell you about Smitty to make you cry more. Sorry about that."

"Don't be sorry. I'm glad to know more about you and the things you care about."

"It wasn't right, comparing losing him to losing your friend. He was just a dog."

Maeve stopped in her tracks and tugged on Ben's arm, so that he stopped and faced her. "You have him tattooed on your arm, Ben. He was more than *just a dog*."

"Yeah. He was my brother in every way that mattered. Saved my butt and my team more than once. Made us laugh. Kept us warm on cold nights."

She nodded her agreement. "It's the depth of our feelings about the people and things most important to us that make us cry when we lose them. You don't grieve losing what you don't care about."

With a nod, he took her hand and pulled her over to the sofa. "Rocky, bed." While the dog pawed the blanket on the floor next to the couch into a nest and lay down, Ben sat near the pillow she'd put out for him earlier and pulled Maeve down to the seat cushion beside him. "I know you're talked out. But I think it would help the healing begin, and maybe you could get some sleep, if you tell me a good memory about Stephanie Ward."

"I will if you tell me a good memory about Smitty."

He glanced toward the sleek black dog curled up beside his feet. "I will. But not in front of Rocky. I don't want him to get jealous."

Maeve chuckled at the tough, wounded veteran making up such a silly excuse about his equally tough dog. She dutifully scooted back against the seat cushion and was amused to see them both sitting side by side, each looking straight ahead, as if they were polite strangers waiting on a bench at the doctor's office together. "I know what you're doing. If you wanted to have this little therapy session, why didn't you just sit on the bed and talk to me there?"

"I am not getting in bed with you," he snapped.

Maeve didn't mind his tone. There was no anger there. It was more like the military-speak she heard from many veterans at the clinic. Ben wasn't a man who minced words, and she appreciated not having to guess what he meant when he spoke to her. But the fact she could feel the heat emanating from his body, even with a few inches between them, did make her a little self-conscious, especially when she was already feeling those little zings of awareness after spending so much one-on-one time with him tonight. She reached for the quilt at the other end of the couch he hadn't yet unfolded and pulled it onto her lap. "I trust you, Ben. I wouldn't have invited you into my house if I didn't. I'm just saying the bed is more comfortable than my couch."

He finally turned and glared down at her. "Seriously? Sharing a bed with you makes me think of…things. Man-woman things. And that's not what you need tonight. So, we're sitting out here where my body understands the difference between *sort-of-friend* Maeve and itch-under-my-skin Maeve who's freakin' adorable in those mannish flannel pajamas that are too big for you, but only force me to imagine the curves I know are under there."

"Freakin' adorable?" she teased, surprised by the off-hand compliment but never doubting its sincerity. She was relieved to know he was feeling those zings of awareness, too. "I didn't think we did *cutesy*."

He shook his head and looked away. "Don't throw my words back at me, Sweetcheeks." He grabbed the pillow and set it in his lap as if he, too, needed something to keep his hand busy in lieu of touching any of those imagined curves.

But Maeve admitted that she didn't want *distant* and *polite* with this good man. She felt better, safer, more desirable—maybe even a little more outgoing—when Sergeant Ben Hunter was with her. She reached over to squeeze his hard, muscular thigh just above his knee. "That's a really sweet compliment. Thank you." She took a chance that he might reject her getting closer and leaned her cheek against the outside of his shoulder, right where the image of Smitty had been tattooed. When he didn't shift away from her, Maeve curled her feet beneath her and settled in against him. "And you're right. I'm attracted to you, too, but I'm not ready for *things*, either. But I do like that you're a furnace, and I appreciate everything you've done for me. So, we will sit here like *sort-of friends*, and I will use up the last of my words to tell you about Steph if that's what you want to hear."

"You good with that, Rocky?" The black shepherd answered him with a snore. Ben's beard tangled with her hair as he turned to her and nodded. "We're both good with that plan."

Maeve smiled and curled her fingers around the crook of his elbow. "Steph and I were complete opposites in high school. If you think I'm quiet now, you should have seen how shy and introverted I was back then. She was one of the most popular girls in school. Grangeport is a small town, so we went all through school together. But we were never friends who hung out. I didn't have the greatest reputation—"

"You?"

"I was trailer-park trash. I wore secondhand clothes. Walked everywhere because we didn't have a car. Never had a dad. My mom…slept around a lot. It's how she got things paid for that we needed. She'd stay with a guy for a few weeks, sometimes a few months. He'd pay the light bill or buy her new clothes or groceries. Sometimes they were married men, and they'd get caught and that would end it. Or she'd get too demanding, and they'd leave. Sometimes she'd blame me. She'd say that a man didn't want a woman who had a kid that wasn't his.'"

This time, Ben did shift his position on the couch, but only to wind his injured arm around her shoulders and pull her more snugly against his side. She felt his mouth settle at the crown of her hair. "This is a good story, right?"

Maeve shook open the throw quilt and tucked it around herself before reclaiming Ben's warmth. "In high school our paths finally crossed. Freshman algebra. She was failing the class, so the teacher assigned me to be Steph's tutor. It's not that she wasn't smart—she was just more interested in boys and parties and cheerleading and choir than she was in schoolwork. I, on the other hand, knew I had to get scholarships if I wanted to go to college. So, I worked hard to get A's."

"You helped her get her grade up, and she was eternally grateful."

Maeve giggled. "Not exactly. I mean yes, she passed the class so she could stay involved in school activities. But one night she stayed out after curfew with her boyfriend at the time. Didn't get home until morning. She was in so much trouble, about to get grounded and miss the Sadie Hawkins dance. So, she told her dad she'd been studying with me and lost track of the time. And it was so late she stayed the night. When her dad confronted me, I covered for her. He wasn't thrilled that she'd stayed in the trailer where the likes of Claudia Phillips lived, but it was better than sleeping with a boy. Steph got to go to the dance, and she said I was pretty cool for helping her out like that."

"You little rebel you."

"Yeah, I was a total bad girl in high school."

He snorted, knowing that was a lie. "Did you go to the dance?"

She shook her head. "No one asked me."

"It was a Sadie Hawkins dance. Girls are supposed to ask the boys."

"That's not how shyness works. I don't think I ever initiated a successful conversation with a boy back then. I either stuttered my way around what I wanted to say, and no one understood me, or I rattled on nervously and freaked them out, or I didn't say anything at all. People thought I was stuck-up or disinterested in what was going on around me." The quilt dropped off her shoulder when she sighed. Maeve folded up the edge of the patchwork material and smoothed it across her lap. "If only they knew all the turbulence going on in my head all the time. I never knew how to verbalize what I was thinking or feeling. I didn't get much practice at home. I was desperate to be included. All I needed was for one person to ask me a question. If someone else started the conversation, I could answer and become a part of what was going on. But start something on my own? Not so much. It wasn't until I took an assertiveness training course in college that I got a little better at voicing my thoughts and being confident that I had something interesting or important to say. There are little tricks I use now that help me speak. You probably don't notice them because they're pretty subtle."

He dropped his hand over hers on the quilt where she kept creasing and smoothing it out beneath her fingers. "Like always wearing clothes with pockets or working something with your hands? A chess piece, a pen, your purse strap, this quilt. It's a way to dispel that nervous energy, right?"

Maeve's mouth gaped open at his perception. "You noticed that?"

"I notice a lot of things about you. Not liking surprises. Needing time to think before you speak. The way you nibble on your bottom lip after you blurt something out because you're worried you've said the wrong thing?"

She continued to stare up into those knowing blue eyes. "You're scary sometimes. And I don't mean that whole tatted-up, muscled, scruffy bad boy look. You pay attention in a way most people don't."

He snorted at her description of him. "It's my former line of work. I was trained to notice the details."

She pulled the quilt up to her chest and curled into his warmth. "I'm just glad you noticed that I needed someone tonight."

He was a big enough man that even without his prosthesis on, his upper arm and elbow fit almost all the way across her shoulders. When he seemed to think better of holding her with his damaged arm, Maeve reached up to grasp his arm and keep him close. "Don't. I don't care if you hold me with your arm or your prosthetic hand—as long as you hold me."

"It's taking some getting used to, but I like holding you, too. I haven't been close to a woman since...before." He shrugged. "It's still not easy for me. I have to think about where I'm putting things now. Am I going to need both hands? Or can I do the task with one? If not, how do I compensate? My body used to be a well-trained fighting machine. I moved and reacted on instinct. I didn't have to plan two or three steps ahead before I moved."

"Your occupational therapy is doing just that. Training your body so those movements become instinctive again. Personally, I believe you're thinking too much. Trust your instincts, Ben."

"Your gentleness and patience make it easier." He leaned back into the sofa, pulling Maeve with him so that they were both half-reclined, with his head leaning against the cushion and hers resting on the pillow of his shoulder. "Now, will you tell me the happy ending part of this story?"

"Are you asking me a question?" she teased.

He'd taken the hint. "I am. How did you and Steph become friends? If she was only using you for alibis, then I don't think too much of her."

"There's more." She breathed in his spicy scent and felt herself relaxing into him. "After bailing her out with her dad, Steph said I was someone she knew she could count on. We still didn't socialize much outside of school. But if a mean girl picked on me or some guy was being a creep because he thought like mother, like daughter, and he expected me to put out for him, Steph would set them straight. One night, Mom threw me out of the trailer because she thought her date was paying more attention to me than to her. Steph let me stay at her house. She even warned me about Ray when I started dating him. But he was the first guy to ever show a real interest in me, and I wanted to belong to someone so badly that I didn't listen. He was popular, so it made it easier for others to accept me because I was with him. Steph had already moved to K.C. when I had to leave him and college in Columbia. She said I could call her if I ever wanted to move to the big city. Once I switched colleges and graduated, I did. We've lived together ever since."

She felt the rumble of his growl vibrating through his chest. "Do I want to know why you *had to leave* Ray and the University of Missouri behind?"

She didn't want to move from her comfy spot. "No. You'll get mad."

She rode his chest as it expanded with a deep breath. "Look me in the eye, Sweetcheeks. Do I need to protect you from him, too?"

Bracing her hand against his chest, Maeve leaned back to

meet his stoic gaze. Eye contact equaled truth to him. "Not anymore. He hasn't talked to me since I moved away from Columbia. I never gave him my new number or address. I'm sure he's found someone else he can control and steal money from and verbally abuse. The last time he scared me, I packed up everything and left."

Okay, that wasn't the right thing to say. Instead of easing his concern, tension radiated off Ben like static electricity. "He scared you?"

Instinctively, Maeve reached up and cupped the side of his jaw. She spared a moment to acknowledge the stubbly silk of his beard tickling her palm before stroking her thumb across his chin in an attempt to soothe him. "After I broke up with him, he'd follow me around on campus or on my walk to work or home to my apartment. He'd call at all hours of the night, wanting to know where I was, who I was with." She hoped he could read the sincerity in her eyes. Other than bad memories and hard lessons learned, she truly believed Ray was no longer a threat to her. "I reported him to both the campus police and the Columbia, Missouri, police. They wrote up reports on him and gave me tips on how to avoid him and stay safe. He hasn't bothered me since."

His nostrils flared with another deep breath. "Yeah, probably a good call that I don't meet him. I'm proud of you for being strong enough to walk away and start your life over." His gaze held hers for a moment longer before he tucked her back to his side and settled into the couch again. Maeve found that warm spot at the front of his shoulder where she rested her cheek. Her eyelids grew heavy as she felt his fingers sifting through her hair and tucking it behind her ear in a gently mesmerizing move. "So, you ditched that mess, graduated and moved to Kansas City. Steph took you in a second time when you needed a place to land. I like her better now."

Maeve nodded, ready to wrap up her story and get to bed. "Anyway, we pooled our money and bought this house and started fixing up what we could do ourselves or afford to hire out. And then…"

Maeve wasn't sure when the conversation ended. Or if she'd drifted off midsentence, surrounded by Ben's body heat, lulled to sleep by their quiet conversation and the steady beat of his heart beneath her ear.

Chapter Eight

Maeve's brain responded to some distant sound of alert, even as her body relaxed more fully into the delicious heat cocooning her. Music was playing in some remote part of the world, a favorite orchestral piece that made her smile in her drowsy state.

Moment by moment, she became more aware of her surroundings. A cool light peeked through the curtains—not the golden pink of sunrise yet, but the hazy gray illumination from the lights on her front porch. Why had the motion-activated lights come on? Did she really care? She preferred sleeping to speculation.

She idly wondered who was playing music at this hour. Not her alarm clock. She could tell she hadn't had a full seven or eight hours of sleep. Her brain was too fuzzy, and her body insisted on staying where it felt warm and secure.

But the intrusive melody continued. Maeve stretched out, willing the rest of her to wake up.

With that languid movement, her senses pinged with awareness. Her eyes opened wide, and she knew exactly where she was.

She was sleeping on her couch, and there was a long, hard body spooned behind hers. Ben. She'd fallen asleep on the couch—actually, more on top of him—talking and snuggling with him. Now she understood the divine warmth hugging her body, and the spicy scent filling her nose. Little frissons of electricity zinged across every nerve ending, some were excited while others were slightly alarmed. Talk about invading his personal space and taking advantage of the would-be loner. They'd fallen asleep with the throw quilt draped over both of them. Her pillow was Ben's bicep. The stump of his arm curled around her waist and rested beneath the weight of her breasts as he held her tightly against him on the narrow cushions.

She felt the small, even puffs of his breath stirring her hair. And yes, she could feel his arousal pressed against her bottom. But she was equally aware that he was lying perfectly still. The man was asleep, and it was a natural response for a man with her bottom nestled against his groin. It wasn't as if he was doing anything suggestive. He had on his jeans, and she wore her pajamas. But she couldn't help but feel the temptation of wishing he wasn't asleep, as well as the boost to her ego, knowing this virile man enjoyed holding her like this—just as much as she enjoyed being held. Maeve's lips softened with a serene smile.

Until a furry black head popped up right in front of her face. "Oh." Rocky must have sensed her waking up and wanted to check out whatever sound or disturbance she'd made. His dark brown, nearly black eyes were staring at her intensely enough. Did he remember who she was? She'd showered last night. Did she have enough of Ben's scent still on her for the dog to remember she was a friend? She pulled her hands into her body, not wanting to give the unpredictable dog anything he could nip at. "Um, good dog," she whispered. The dog angled his head as if making sure he'd heard her correctly. Maeve swallowed and strengthened her voice to a soft, but more confident tone. "Good boy, Rocky. You're making sure the new gal hasn't done anything to hurt your partner. That's a good boy."

"You need to get your phone?" She startled again when Ben's husky voice rumbled against her ear. His grip around her tightened or she would have fallen onto the floor and landed on the dog. "Easy, Sweetcheeks. It's mighty early for someone to be calling. I was going to let you sleep if you didn't hear it."

Either he woke up fast, or he'd been awake for some time. Or maybe these two males simply woke up already on alert. Of course, that was her phone ringing back in the bedroom where she'd left it last night. She forced her breathing to slow and spoke in a more normal tone. "What if it's the police? Maybe they found something."

"Better get it, then." Ben hooked his arm beneath the quilt and tossed it down toward their feet.

Maeve shivered at the sudden chill and hugged her arms around herself as she sat up. "Is Rocky okay if I step over him? I don't want to startle him."

"Rocky." Sitting up beside her, he snapped his fingers and pointed for the dog to move. Rocky moved back to his blanket, panting with a measure of excitement now that he had Ben's attention. "He'll be fine. I'll take him outside while you grab your phone. Better hurry."

He nudged Maeve off the couch, steadying her with his hand and stump at either side of her waist when she nearly ran into the coffee table. Then she darted down the hallway to her bedroom.

The ringtone ended before she could reach her phone and pull it off her charger. She held it in her hand a few seconds, waiting for the message tone to beep. But instead of leaving a voicemail, the phone rang again.

She didn't recognize the number, so her greeting was understandably cautious. "Hello?"

"Maevie! Oh-Maevie-baby-I-need-to-see-you." Austin Bukowski, weeping and apparently drunk, sniffled loudly and slurred his words together. "I mish Steph so much. Our relationship was a tempesh-tuous one, but we had passion. We burned it up in the sheets. You ever make love like that? I bet not. You're missin' out."

"Austin? Are you drunk?" She asked the obvious question, hoping he'd realize that the things he was saying to her made her uncomfortable. "I miss Steph, too, but I don't think this is—"

"She knew what I liked, and I loved her for it." He sniffed again. "Please let me come over. I need to see you."

"Me? Why?"

"Because you're all I have left of her. We can comfort each other. You have to let me come over. You're not so bad. You know, you're pretty in your own kind of way. Once we unbutton a few things..." This was awkward. Although she suspected Austin didn't know exactly what he was saying, his words and tone rang of Ray Maddox, burying insults inside his compliments, telling Maeve how badly he needed her each of the first few times she'd tried to walk away. Only, she doubted Austin was attracted to a mouse like her after he'd been with a firebrand like Steph. "I need to have something of Steph's," he went on. "A scarf, a piece of jewelry, a picture—something of hers I can keep to remind me of her. I'll be there in twenty minutes."

"What? No." She shook off her confusion—and gross-out meter at her friend's ex hitting on her—and sharpened her tone. "One, you shouldn't be driving in your condition, and two, just no."

"Please, baby, I need to see you."

"I said no." That should have been answer enough, but she made up an excuse to avoid him, anyway. "I'll be leaving shortly. I have to work."

"At this hour?" Why was he calling her now if it was too early to start their day? "Maevie, please. Don't be a buzzkill. Get off your prissy high horse for five minutes and help me. I need to be with someone who loved her as much as I did."

Buzzkill? The man was spending entirely too much time with Joker. He sounded just like one of those guys in high school who believed her shy sensibilities meant she thought she was too good for him and needed to be taken down a peg. "I can't do this right now, Austin. I'm sorry you're hurting. But I am, too. I need to deal with my grief in my own way. Maybe we can talk at the funeral. I'm sure Steph's dad will let us know the arrangements as soon as the ME releases her body. He's the one you should talk to if you want a keepsake of hers as a souvenir."

"The funeral." Austin muttered a curse. "I don't know if I can go through that by myself. I want you to go with me."

"You can't just say what you want and expect me to go along with it."

Austin didn't bother to muffle his slew of angry curses this time. She heard Rocky barking furiously in the backyard. She went to the window and opened the curtains and blind to peek outside. She glimpsed the dog charging across the yard and Ben running after him, shouting a command. Clearly on the trail of something, they disappeared into the shadows. "What in the world?"

The barking was drowned out by an engine roaring to life and tires squealing for traction on the pavement. But was she hearing the car peeling out over the phone? Or in her own neighborhood?

"Austin, are you driving?" she asked, more worried about

the jerk being a threat to someone else on the road than to himself. Wait. Oh, hell. "Are you at my house?"

The front porch lights. He'd been that close to her?

She dashed from her bedroom.

"Maeve!" She heard Ben shouting her name before the back door slammed shut. They met in the hallway. Before she could say a word, he grasped her by the shoulders and backed her into her bedroom. "Are you okay?"

With Rocky trotting along beside him, she had no choice but to go where he wanted. "Did you see a car out front?"

"Yeah. It peeled out of your neighborhood at about fifty miles over the speed limit. Rocky must have heard the car door shut when the driver got in. I couldn't get eyes on him, and it was too dark to read a plate number." He hunched down to look her straight in the eye. "Are. You. Okay?" he repeated. "Where were you running off to?"

Maeve started to explain when Austin shouted in her ear. "Is that a man's voice? Someone's there with you? Is it that cripple who took you to see the corpse last night?"

"Excuse me?" What happened to the grieving drunk who could barely string a coherent sentence together?

"He's taking advantage of your vulnerability right now. It may be the only way he can get a woman. Except for freaks who like gimps."

Anger bubbled up inside her. "That is insulting. To Ben and to me. Not that it's any business of yours, but I happen to like him. Ben is a bona fide military hero. He's more of a real man than you could even think about being. He'd never steal from me or strand me in a sketchy part of the city or sneak around my house or force me to do anything I don't want to. I'm not going to the funeral with you, and I'm done talking to you. Stay away from me, Austin. I'm sorry you're hurting, but I have to go. Goodbye."

She punched the disconnect button and tossed her phone onto the bed.

"That was Bukowski?" Ben asked. "What did he want?"

Maeve raked her fingers through her hair, overwhelmed by the fury erupting out of her every pore. "I can't believe the nerve of that guy." She pointed to the door. "I think he called me from right in front of my house. The porch lights were on when I woke up, and they're motion-activated. Then I heard the engine—"

"Stay put. Close those blinds and don't leave this room. Rocky, heel!"

Man and dog ran from the room, leaving Maeve shaking as fear and anger warred for supremacy inside her. She hugged her arms around her waist, then quickly unwound them to check the lock on her window and close the blind as Ben had told her to.

By the time they returned several minutes later, Maeve was pacing the room. The moment Ben appeared at her bedroom door, she ran to him. She locked her arms around his waist and held on tight. "Did you see him? Was it Austin?"

Ben's arms settled lightly around her, and she felt the light pressure of his lips at the crown of her hair. "He's long gone. The leaves have been disturbed around the front windows. Someone was trying to get a look inside."

She turned her cheek into his shoulder and rested her forehead against his neck. "I was already mad and afraid, and then you ran after him with no jacket and no gun to protect yourself. I don't know what I would have done if something had happened to you."

"Honey, I was armed. I had Rocky with me."

At that matter-of-fact statement, Maeve leaned back against his arms. She met the sincerity in his eyes, then looked and saw the dog lying a little ways away, nonchalantly licking some mud and leaf debris from between his toes, as though he had no clue that he was a trained fighting machine if need be. "I'm so glad you have Rocky." The dog glanced up at his name. "Good boy. Good boy, Rocky."

He yawned at her praise, then laid his head down over his front paws.

"Am I the only one who's frightened by all this?"

"You have reason to be." Ben pulled his arms away and stepped back when she wound her own around her waist again. "Bukowski or whoever it was may have been on your porch. Rocky picked up some kind of scent and followed it out to the curb where the guy had parked. Sorry, he must have jumped the curb when he left. His tires chewed up some of your grass."

"I don't care about that. I care that that creeper lied to me." Her anger was a lot easier to deal with than her fear for herself or for Ben confronting Austin. "He said he was coming over in twenty minutes, even though I told him not to, when all the time he was already here. Watching me. Spying on me. Probably trying to figure out if I was alone. But I don't know why. What does he want from me?"

"Easy, Sweetcheeks. He's gone now. I'll call Detective Kincaid or Grove myself. Just take a deep breath and tell me what Bukowski said."

"He was weird. Crying about missing Steph, then inviting me to go to the funeral with him. No, not inviting me—telling me we're going together. Plus, he wants to come to the house and get a memento, something that belonged to Steph, to remember her by. I didn't like him when he was dating her, and I definitely don't like him now. He called her a corpse, and you a…" She couldn't say the word, not when she didn't see Ben that way. Her eyes locked onto his steely blue gaze and her anger quickly waned as grief reared its head again. She gnawed on her bottom lip as she remembered she had more important things to worry about than complaining about Austin or even defending Ben from his insults. "Do I have to go through all Steph's things now and pack them up? Will her father do that?"

Ben cupped the side of her jaw with his callused fingers and stroked his thumb across her lip to soothe the place where she'd nipped it. "Take a breath. While I appreciated hearing you say those nice things about me, you need to worry about yourself right now. Don't let Bukowski bully you into doing anything you don't want to."

Every nerve ending in Maeve's body seemed to zero in on the spot where Ben caressed her lip, leaving her tingling with awareness from head to toe. His touch was as distracting as it was comforting, and, oh, how she wanted him to kiss her. She tried to remind herself that he'd agreed to be her bodyguard, not her boyfriend. Maybe she was so inexperienced at healthy relationships that she was mistaking his tenderness and protection for something more. "I won't."

"And I wouldn't let anyone go through your friend's things until KCPD clears it. There may be answers in something she's left behind."

His reminder snapped her out of her obsession with all things Sergeant Ben. Maeve gestured to the big purse and the mess she'd left on her bed when she'd searched through it. "That's what I was thinking last night, before I got sidetracked with grief. Steph and I had switched purses. When I was mugged, I was carrying this purse she had that night at Shotz's bar. They asked, *'Where is it?'*, and it finally made sense to me. Maybe she put something in that purse that whoever killed her was after."

"Did you find anything in the purse?"

Maeve shook her head. "No files. No flash drive. No wad

of cash or stash of drugs. I'd started looking in other places where she might have taken it out and hidden it when I got stuck looking at that picture, and you found me and…made things better." With her temper and grief finally in check, she tilted her chin to smile up at Ben. "Thank you for that, by the way. I was stuck in my own head and couldn't find my way out."

He scanned the items on the bed before he shrugged off her gratitude. "Glad I could help. I'll take you to the funeral if you want. Or I'll stand guard in the back of the church or wherever if you prefer. But you're not going with Bukowski, and he's not getting anywhere near you—unless you tell me that's what you want."

"I don't want that. I'd be happy for you to go with me. But I don't even know when it is yet. What if you have to work? And haven't you been to too many funerals already, with your friends and Smitty? Why would you want to go celebrate the life of someone you never even met?"

"I'd go for you, Sweetcheeks." He reached out to touch her hair, feathering his fingers through the curls before tucking them behind her ear. "Let's just get through one day, then the next. Find out what Kincaid and Grove have learned, if anything. Tell them about Bukowski's call and your purse idea and let them search through Steph's things. Until we know what's going on and who killed your friend, I think you need to be careful about spending time with someone who might be a suspect."

Maeve turned her cheek into the palm of his hand before he pulled away. "You think the police suspect Austin?"

"*I* do. One of the last people to see her? In a relationship with her? I'm sure they're looking at him. And I want to know what the hell he's doing at your house before sunup." She supposed Austin could be wracked with grief, but she did get a weird vibe from him that made him look suspicious. Although, she couldn't see any motive the man had for killing his lover. Ben was scowling when she met his gaze again. "If you're feeling sorry for him, don't. Bukowski has other friends or family he can call on for comfort."

She didn't mind the scowl. This man's honest emotions and protectiveness were gifts no other man had ever given her. "And I have you." She glanced down at the dog standing beside him. "And Rocky."

"Damn right you do."

It was that promise right there that made Maeve realize that she was in love with Ben Hunter.

Oblivious to her world-changing revelation, he reached down and patted the dog's flanks before scooting him toward the door. "Get dressed. We both need to get to work."

Chapter Nine

Later that morning, after Ben drove them through a take-out place for a delicious breakfast of coffee and doughnuts that were completely off Maeve's diet, he drove her to the PT/OT clinic. They'd taken a brief detour to her car to make sure it was still locked and untampered with. And now Ben and Rocky had walked her through the front door into the medical building's darkened lobby.

Ben had his arm, boots and camo jacket back on and was scanning the building's empty entryway with a scowl. "You're sure someone you know is here with you?"

Maeve reluctantly released her grip on Ben's elbow and nodded to the light shining through the caged front entrance to the clinic's waiting area. "Yes. No patients yet. But a couple of the PTs come in early to run on the treadmills and update their patient records. Probably some of the office staff, too, to get paperwork done before the place gets too busy." She pointed to the door marked *Employees Only* just behind her. "Staff goes through here. I have the code for the punch pad. It locks behind me. I'll be fine."

He took note of every access point and even glanced back out at the early morning traffic beginning to fill the street out front or turning into the parking garage before he looked back down at her. "I'll see you after work."

"You don't have to do that. I've already taken advantage of you agreeing to walk me to my car last night. I gave you a trip to the morgue and fell asleep on you—"

"I'll see you after work." He articulated his words quite precisely, as if she hadn't understood his promise. "Either I'll walk you to your car and follow you home, or I'll drive you there myself."

Maeve already felt more secure knowing she'd be seeing him again today. "Okay." She wrapped her fingers around the long strap of her cross-body wallet bag and stared at the faded letters on Ben's T-shirt. Then she bravely raised her gaze to his and asked, "Could I give you a kiss? To say thank you?"

"You don't have to." If she wasn't mistaken, the hint of a blush warmed his cheeks.

"But I want to." Her nerves made her feel warm in the lobby's cool air, too. If she thought about this too long, her nerves would get the better of her, and she'd lose out on the chance to show Ben at least a little of how not *sort-of friends* she was feeling about him. "I've never kissed a man with a beard before."

Her tongue darted out to nervously lick her bottom lip and his pupils dilated, turning his eyes a deep midnight blue.

"The parts are in all the same places. They're just warmer in wintertime."

His silly comment made her laugh, pushing her past any hesitation. Impulsively, she grabbed two handfuls of the front of his jacket and pulled herself up on tiptoe to kiss him full on the mouth.

His hand and prosthesis settled on either side of her waist, pulling her closer, and suddenly her thighs were pressed against the unyielding strength of his. She'd meant to give him a kiss on the cheek, but somehow her instincts had ignored her overthought plan and done exactly what she'd truly wanted. And Ben didn't seem to mind. He angled his mouth one way, then the other, over hers before she felt his warm, raspy tongue nudging at her lower lip. When her lips parted, his mouth claimed hers.

Maeve's body swirled with sensations. Ben's chest and legs were sturdy and strong, an unbending wall she could lean into with no fear of falling. His arms slid around to the small of her back, and even the poke of his titanium hook couldn't distract her from the pulse of his fingertips kneading against her spine. He tasted of the bitter black coffee he'd drunk with his breakfast, with a hint of mint from the toothpaste they'd shared. His long beard was softer than she'd expected, tickling her lips and chin like dozens of extra caresses against her skin. And his lips were firm and warm, commanding yet gentle. Her nipples tightened into sensitive pearls against the rough canvas of his jacket and his hard chest underneath as desire heated her from the inside out. She couldn't remember ever being kissed like this, ever wanting to be kissed like this, ever wanting to kiss a man with the same thoroughness and care of Ben's lips against hers.

She eased her grip on his jacket and slid her hands around his neck to palm the prickly buzz cut of hair at the back of his head and hold his mouth firmly against hers. Her mind blanked for a few seconds as her hunger for Ben overwhelmed her. That mindless desire frightened her a little— the discovery that her passion could go from zero to sixty in the span of a few seconds—and she abruptly tore her sensitized lips from his.

She was breathing hard and still clinging to him like a

lifeline as she sank back onto her heels. Ben's breaths stuttered in rhythm with her own as he eased his hold on her, settling his hands at her waist without pushing her away.

"You sure you're the shy girl?" he teased, his voice deep and gravelly. He rested his forehead against hers, his dark blue eyes boring straight down into hers. "You can kiss me like that anytime you want, and you don't have to ask."

Maeve touched her tongue to the stinging swell of her lips and pulled her hands down to rest on the more neutral position of his chest. "You don't think I'm a buzzkill, do you?"

He raised his head and frowned at her. "What does that mean?"

She smoothed the wrinkles she'd put in his jacket with her first needy grab. "Something rude that someone said to me. He was trying to rattle me. But I kind of believed that he could be right, that I was too cautious and damaged by my past to be any good at this."

"Whoever that jackass was didn't know what he was talking about. You're good. You're better than good." He dipped his head to press a chaste kiss to her mouth. "You taste delicious."

"I taste like coffee and doughnuts."

"And you. You taste like you." His nostrils flared with a deep breath before he lifted his fingers to her hair to brush a loose curl off her cheek and tuck it behind her ear. "Something is happening between us, Maeve. I don't know if I'm the best man for it—for you. But for the first time in months, since I gave up my stripes and moved back to Kansas City, I want to try. I want to be a man that you could care about."

"You are. I do."

He gently touched his thumb to the fading bruises that still marked her cheek and jaw, and she could see that her injuries, although healing, still upset him. "I'm not asking you to make any promises. I just want you to know that... I'm trying. I want to do better—I want to be better—for you."

"I want to do better, too. Not be so quiet and shy and stuck in my head or tongue-tied—"

"You be who you are. I think you're good for me. You're calming. You help me stay in the present and let me work through my fractured headspace when I can't. You're caring and warm and so damn sensual..." His gaze met hers and she believed the honesty shining there. "But I want to be good for you, too. I will protect you till my dying breath if I have to. But I don't want that to be the only reason you're with me."

She shook her head, trying to come up with the right words to say to make him understand that she hadn't developed some juvenile attachment to her bodyguard. She was attracted to the man—to his character, to his bravery, to his blue eyes and that tattoo of a dog he still grieved for stamped onto his shoulder.

But the words didn't immediately come, and Ben gently released her and stepped back. "I guess that speech will give you something else to think about."

She nodded and he grinned.

"I didn't mean you had to start thinking right now."

She tapped a finger to her temple. "Always thinking, remember?"

He picked up Rocky's leash. "We gotta go."

"Goodbye, Ben. I'll see you after work," she added, letting him know she'd heard what he'd said earlier. Then she looked down at the dog sitting beside him, no doubt bored with human conversation and the trading of affection that had nothing to do with him. Maeve held her fist out to Rocky the way Ben had taught her. When he stepped closer to sniff it and ran his tongue across her knuckles, she giggled and knelt in front of the big dog. "Good boy, Rocky." She petted him around the ears and neck the way he liked, sliding her fingers beneath his collar and service dog vest to scratch the black fur there. "Thank you for being such a good protector last night and this morning. You're my good boy. I'll see you later. Keep an eye on this guy for me today, okay?" The persnickety dog scooted closer as her words took on an indulgent baby-talk tone. Then he surprised her when he stretched his neck into her caress, giving her greater access to his favorite petting spots. "You like when I use my fingernails, huh?"

"Don't be turning my dog into some kind of softie," Ben chided.

Maeve tilted her face up to Ben, the warmth in her heart making her smile. "You called him *your* dog. You *do* want to keep him."

He reached down with his prosthetic hand to help her up, and she didn't hesitate to hold on to it. "We don't do cutesy stuff, remember? Now get inside, woman, so I can get to work. Mrs. Caldwell and the dogs are going to wonder where I am." She stood there smiling at him. Like Rocky, Ben was all bark and no bite, with her at least. "Maeve..." It sounded like a warning, but his gentle eyes said he wouldn't really hurt her or yell at her for trying his patience.

But she knew that he was a man who *did* struggle with patience, and she didn't want to make leaving difficult for him. "Be kind to yourself today, Ben. You've done more for me in the past twelve hours than you will ever know. Thank you."

"Thanks for asking me. It was good to feel useful again. It was good to be needed." He leaned in to kiss her once more. The press of his lips was chaste and brief and left her wanting more. His gaze captured hers before he pulled away. "I'm going to want to kiss you again."

"Okay."

He nodded, apparently liking her response. "Okay."

"Bye."

"Rocky, heel."

She was grinning like a happy fool as she punched in the security code and entered the clinic. She knew that he and Rocky were waiting at the glass doors until the steel door closed behind her, and Maeve had never felt so cherished.

She'd kissed Ben Hunter. And the grumpy sergeant had kissed her back. There was no *sort-of friends* connection between them anymore. The feelings were new, but she was certain she loved him. And he'd admitted he liked her as well. He'd shown her how much he liked her with that kiss and in so many other ways.

"I just want you to know that... I'm trying. I want to do better—I want to be better—for you." What goal was he working toward? Asking her out on a date? Making out with her? Building a relationship? She was okay with all of that. If anyone knew how to be patient, it was Maeve Phillips. She'd survived her mother, growing up a small-town pariah, Ray Maddox and her friend's murder. She could survive the ups and downs of a relationship with a wounded warrior with post-traumatic stress issues, too.

She just had to be patient, keep stepping out of her comfort zone to interact in a more personal way with Ben and show him— in whatever way he needed until he believed it—that he was perfect for her just as he was.

Maeve was still smiling at the end of the day as she powered down her work tablet and plugged it into the charger in her cubby in the staff locker room. She pulled out the flash drive with patient files and tucked it into the pocket of her scrubs so that she could finish the updates on her laptop at home. Then, she stowed her work sweater in her staff locker and pulled on the heavier gray cardigan she'd need for the chilly autumn air outside. She looped her purse over her neck and shoulder and closed her locker to find her friend and coworker Allie Malone standing there. Allie, a Navy veteran, was tall, athletic, deeply happy with the man she had recently married, and now she was smiling down at Maeve as though she had a juicy piece of gossip to share.

Allie winked. "You and Sergeant Hunter, huh?"

Maeve felt her cheeks heating with a blush. "Why do you say that?"

"You are the last person I would expect to play coy with me." Allie reached out to squeeze Maeve's hand to reassure her she was being supportive. "I saw you two kissing this morning. I waited to come in until after he left so I wouldn't embarrass you. And he smiled. I don't know if I've ever seen him smile."

Maeve acknowledged that Ben was more grump than gentleman. "He's a little abrupt and rough around the edges, but he's a good man."

"Obviously. But this is the guy who told me several months ago that he thought he scared you."

Maeve was surprised to hear that. "Ben doesn't scare me. He's sweet with me."

Her friend arched a blond eyebrow. "Really?"

Clearly, Allie was hoping for more information about the possibility of a new romance. And, frankly, Maeve wouldn't mind talking about some of what she was feeling with a friend she trusted. "He's not the world's greatest conversationalist, but then, neither am I. But he listens, probably more than any guy I've known. And he pays attention to everything. His eyes are as sharp as that dog of his."

"And he makes *you* smile."

"He does." Maeve started buttoning her sweater to give herself some time to think of how she wanted to phrase this. "It's just that, we both have some issues. What if I'm not the right kind of woman he needs? What if I'm not strong enough to deal with his PTSD? What if he decides I'm too much work to be with?"

Allie grabbed her running jacket out of her locker and shrugged into it. "You're a strong woman, Maeve. Quiet strength is just as powerful as the flashier kind. Sometimes, even more so. I have no doubt you can handle anything Ben is dealing with." She zipped up her jacket and smiled. "And believe me, once someone gets to know you, you are the easiest person in the world to get along with."

Maeve thanked her for the compliment. "He did say he thought I was good for him."

"See? He's a smart man." Allie pulled her long blond ponytail from the neckline of her jacket. "Look at me and Grayson. He thought I was with him because of that stalker I had, that I only needed him because he was my safe place to land when everything got to be too much. And he is that. But I had to convince him that he was the man I loved. He finally figured it out."

"Ben is pretty protective," Maeve conceded, finding hope in her friend's happily-ever-after story. "He's a veteran Special Forces soldier. I think it's in his DNA."

"I'm sure he is." Allie dropped the flash drive with her patient files on it into her purse and looped the bag over her shoulder before closing her locker. "But that's not why he watched you until the very last second the staff door closed behind you, and you were out of his sight."

"What do you mean? How was he looking at me?"

"The same way Grayson looks at me. I think the sergeant's got it bad for you."

Maeve couldn't hold back her smile. "I've got it bad for him. He said he wants to be better for me. He's already physically healthy after his injuries. But I think he's talking about being mentally healthy. I don't know if I can make him understand that I want to help him on his journey. I don't want Ben to think he has to be perfect before he can commit to a relationship."

"Then don't let it get stuck in his head that he's damaged goods and decide he's not good enough for you." Allie turned to link her arm with Maeve's as they headed out of the locker room to the front doors of the building. "You know that Grayson and I got married by a justice of the peace, but we've been planning a reception to celebrate with all our friends."

"Uh-huh."

"Well, Ben is a friend of Grayson's, so he's already getting an invitation to the reception. You're my friend, so you'll be invited, too. Please tell me you'll come together. I'm worried that Ben will be in an antisocial mood or claim he doesn't have a suit he can wear or use some other excuse. I promise we'll keep it casual. I don't care if he shows up in his Army fatigues. I just want him to come. I like seeing the two of you together."

Maeve pushed open the staff exit door. "I don't know if he likes big gatherings, but I can ask him."

"Great."

The conversation ended abruptly when Maeve looked through the lobby's glass doors and saw the black Dodge Charger parked in the clinic's circular drive, not ten yards from her. She froze in her tracks, tugging Allie to a halt beside her.

What were the chances of two black Dodge Chargers following her?

"Maeve? What's wrong?"

Even more frightening than the car itself was the man leaning against the passenger side door, smoking a brown cigarette. Although his offensive tattoos were hidden by the leather jacket he wore, there was no mistaking Joker's oily black hair or the sheer bulk of his body. Maeve shivered as the meanness in those soulless dark eyes reached out to her.

She was also aware of the darker gray smoke curling through the crack in the window beside Joker and drifting around him like a cloud. Someone else was in the car behind him, although she couldn't see any face through the tinted windows.

"Maeve?" Allie urged her for an explanation. "Do you know that guy?"

Had he followed her that night from Shotz's bar? Had he attacked her in the parking garage across the street? How did he know where she worked?

Maeve retreated a step, pulling Allie along with her. "We need to call the police."

"Who is he?"

"Nobody we want to talk to." She nudged Allie to pull out her phone. "Go on. Call 9-1-1. Ask for Detective Atticus Kincaid or Kevin Grove. Tell them Joker is here."

"Joker?"

"That's his name. It's stupid, but it's him. And he shouldn't be anywhere near me."

Allie pulled her phone from her bag. "Is he the guy who mugged you?"

"I don't know. But he might know something about my roommate's murder."

"Murder? I thought she was a missing person."

"She's not missing anymore. Last night…" She finally tore her gaze from Joker and the black car and looked up at Allie. "I had to identify her body at the ME's office. She was strangled to death."

Her friend's arm came around her shoulders. "Oh, my God, Maeve. I'm so sorry."

Maeve turned her focus back to the man outside, just standing there, smoking. Watching. Waiting. "I wonder what he wants."

"You are not talking to him."

"Don't plan to. But maybe I should stay here and make sure he leaves before any of the patients or staff run into him."

As if he'd read her lips or sensed her attempt at bravery, Joker flicked his cigarette to the pavement and stomped it out beneath his boot. She jerked when he took a step toward her. She heard his answering laughter through the panes of glass. Instead of approaching the clinic, though, he pointed two fingers at his eyes, then turned his hand to point one finger straight at her, sending a frightening message. *I'm watching you.*

"That's a threat." Allie pulled her closer to her side and moved toward the staff door. "Let's wait inside."

Knowing she was in no position to confront Joker and his friend or even stand in the vestibule to play his intimidation game, Maeve tore her gaze away from Joker's ominous eye contact and followed her friend back through the employees' entrance. Maeve pushed the door shut behind them as Allie's call to 9-1-1 picked up.

She identified herself and their location. "I'd like to report a suspicious person loitering outside our clinic. I believe he's a person of interest in a murder investigation. He may be trying to intimidate a witness who's here with me."

"Ask for Kincaid or Grove." Maeve whispered the reminder. "They're the detectives investigating Steph's murder."

"Could you patch me through to Detective Kincaid or Grove in homicide? They're working the case."

Maeve pulled her phone from the pocket of her scrubs and punched in another number.

The call picked up after two rings. "Maeve?"

Just hearing Ben's voice gave her a measure of calm. "Where are you?"

"I'm just loading Rocky into my truck, and we'll be on our way. Everything okay?" His guarded tone meant he'd picked up on her panic.

She wasn't about to deny it. "No. I need you."

Chapter Ten

Ben set speed records along 40 Highway into the city and darted in and out of rush-hour traffic to get to the woman he was falling in love with.

He couldn't even take the time to process that revelation. Months of longing and an intense night and morning where they'd shared so much and gotten intimately acquainted had pulled that long-buried truth out of the recesses of his brain. He wasn't sure he could handle this. He wasn't sure he could handle being all in with someone again, the way he'd been all in with his teammates and Smitty. He wasn't sure he could handle a deep connection like that and risk losing it again. Or worse, feel responsible for losing what might be the best thing that had ever happened to him.

But damn it, if his first instinct when Maeve said *"I need you"* was to dive behind the wheel of his truck and haul ass to get to her just as fast as a US Army Special Forces soldier could without a chopper to fly him to the scene—without even a plan of attack once he got there in mind—then he had a feeling he was well beyond guarding his heart and his psyche against the possibility of future losses.

Joker, Austin Bukowski's buddy who had creeped Maeve out at Shotz's bar, and whom KCPD had a long history with, was at the clinic with her. Although she'd assured him the police had been notified, he put through his own call to Kevin Grove.

The burly detective must have his name programmed into his phone. "Sergeant Hunter?"

Ben didn't mess with pleasantries, either. "Where are you? How the hell did someone like Joker get that close to Maeve?"

"We're en route," the detective reassured him. "One of our friends from the crime lab, Grayson Malone, is married to one of Ms. Phillips's coworkers. He's already on the scene."

"I know Malone." He tightened his fist on the steering wheel. He hated to ask this. "Is there a crime scene?"

"His wife called him. Malone's got eyes on your woman. What's your ETA?" *His woman*. Yeah, that was exactly what he was feeling right now. Thankfully, Grove didn't try to dissuade him from storming the clinic and getting in KCPD's way. Backing away from Maeve when she was scared and needed him wasn't going to happen.

"It's rush hour. I'm still maybe ten minutes out." The traffic light ahead of him turned yellow, and Ben raced through the intersection. Ten minutes felt like way too long. It had only taken ten minutes for his world to blow to hell in that Central American jungle. His pulse was racing. He needed to calm himself the hell down or he'd cause an accident and be too late to stop another tragedy from wrecking his life. "Get to her. Make sure she's safe."

"We will. You get here safely, too."

Ben disconnected the call.

Rocky must be picking up on the sense of emergency Ben felt because the big dog was pacing in the back seat, his breath huffing out in eager gasps. By the time Ben had whipped his truck into the parking garage across from the clinic and jerked to a stop in the handicapped parking spot he could find closest to the entrance, even though he usually avoided using them, the dog was whining in anticipation.

The truck was still rocking when Ben climbed out and reached for Rocky's leash. "Come on, boy. Let's go get our girl."

He muttered a curse at the line of cars he had to wait for before they could cross the street to the clinic. He didn't see any crime scene tape blocking off the entrance, but there was an unmarked police car with a magnetic siren stuck on the roof above the driver's side parked at the front doors. A black-and-white KCPD squad car blocked the entrance to the circular drive. And a van with a handicapped sign he recognized as his friend Grayson Malone's modified vehicle was parked at the exit.

Other than the two uniformed officers who were keeping the area clear of curious pedestrians and lookie-loos driving past, Ben recognized several familiar faces gathered on the sidewalk in front of the clinic. Ultra-serious detective Atticus Kincaid and his partner, Kevin Grove, with his omnipresent computer pad. His friend, Grayson, stood tall on his prosthetic legs and metal crutches, his CSI kit on the ground between him and his wife, Allie. The tall blonde had her arm linked through Maeve's, and all three of them were listening to whatever the detectives were saying.

From this distance, he couldn't make out details. But Maeve's dark hair was pulled back in its customary ponytail, with a few curly tendrils falling loose around her face and neck. He could see the fading bruise marring her pale cheek. But he couldn't see her expressive eyes. Was she hurt? Crying? Had something been forcibly taken from her, leaving her feeling helpless and violated again?

Ben knew he was wired right now. His tension must be traveling down the leash because Rocky barked at two young men who crossed into the parking garage behind them. They hurried past, joking about something he wasn't paying attention to.

But Rocky's bark echoing between the buildings caught Maeve's attention, and she swung her gaze toward him. She raised her hand and waved. "Ben!"

"Maeve!" Screw waiting for a light to change. He thrust his arm out, warning the next car that he was stepping into the street. The vehicle screeched to a stop, and he moved out with Rocky. A moment later, a light did change, and the break in the flow of traffic allowed them to hurry on across. They jogged past the squad car and group waiting to greet him and went straight to Maeve.

She stepped away from her friend and reached out to him. But a touch or a handhold wasn't going to do. He hugged his left arm around her and pulled her right into his chest before he dropped a kiss to the crown of her hair. He inhaled the innocence of her vanilla shampoo and the musk of stress and a long workday that clung to her skin.

"Are you okay?" He raised his head to the detectives. "What's going on?"

"Joker was here." Maeve mumbled the response against his jacket.

He knew he was holding on a little too tightly. "I know, Sweetcheeks. You told me."

Atticus Kincaid nodded. "We believe he's the driver who followed Maeve from the bar that first night. If she hadn't had the wherewithal to drive to the police station, and he'd followed her all the way home, we might be looking at a different crime."

"And now he shows up here?" Ben's vision filled with

fireworks. His pulse thundered in his ears. "What did he say to you? Did he touch you? Threaten you?"

Rocky bumped into his thigh, pacing back and forth beside him. He growled when one of Grayson's metal crutches got too close to him.

Ben shouldn't have been surprised when Maeve pushed against his chest and forced him to ease his hold on her. She tilted her face up to his. "Look at me." Eye contact. This was real. This was truth. "I'm okay, Ben. Take a couple of deep breaths and dial it back a notch. You're upsetting Rocky." She gently reached for Rocky's leash. "Here. Let me."

"You can't handle—"

"I can," she insisted, pulling the leash from his hand. Her voice was little more than a whisper, but her words brooked no argument, like so many OT sessions when he'd been stubborn about using his new hand. "Let go."

Ben swore, then turned away to do just as she'd asked. He fisted his hand on his thigh and bent over, sucking in deep gulps of air to try and clear his head. He counted each breath and focused on the light massage of Maeve's hand between his shoulder blades. He listened to the soft, even tone of her words. "I'm okay," she assured him. "Joker... threatened me. But he drove away as soon as we went back inside to call the police—and you. Thank you for being here. I feel better with you here. I'm okay."

"Okay." His nostrils flared with another deep breath, and his shoulders rose and fell as he calmed himself down. This wasn't some botched jungle mission. No one was dead. Her words, her scent, her touch, all muted the emotional flashback. After one more cleansing breath, he knelt down beside Rocky to pet him. He looked into those deep brown eyes that seemed to take every cue from him. This dog was a true partner. That's what Rocky was becoming. *His* partner. They thought alike, reacted the same way to stressors, needed to calm themselves when the stimuli of the world around them became too much. They both cared about the woman at their side. "She's okay, buddy." He needed to hear those words again himself. "She's okay."

When he straightened, he found Maeve standing right beside him, her concerned green-gray gaze watching him carefully. He gave her a nod to let her know that he had his act together again, that he was more in the present with her now than stuck in his head in the past.

She slipped Rocky's leash back into his grip as he turned to join the conversation. He was pleased to see that her presence had calmed Rocky down from five-alarm status, too. The dog now stood dutifully by Ben's right side. He wasn't sure if everyone here knew of his and Rocky's struggles with PTSD. But he saw Allie wink at Maeve and mouth the word *strong*. Whatever that interchange was about, Maeve's cheeks warmed with a blush and she gave her friend a quick smile. Everything settled back into place inside him when Maeve slipped her fingers through the crook of his elbow.

Thankfully, no one in the group mentioned his lapse in control. He was glad the detectives moved ahead as though this interview was all business as usual. Maeve was the one they needed to focus on. He didn't intend to be a problem they had to deal with, too.

Kevin Grove once again tapped on his computer pad while Detective Kincaid asked a question. "You want to walk us through what happened?"

Maeve clung to Ben's arm and pulled him along with her as she moved to the place where the Dodge Charger had been parked and proceeded to tell them about her interaction with Joker, and why the man had frightened her. While she discussed details and how an unspoken threat from the tattooed giant was every bit as intimidating as actual words or an unwanted touch, Ben watched Rocky sniffing the pavement around them. Ben gave the dog a little more leash as the black shepherd seemed to be more than curious about oil stains on the concrete and the gravel and debris that had collected against the curb. He snuffed loudly several times, indicating he was taking in every scent. Rocky had been trained to be a jack of all trades for the Marines, and certainly, scent detection was one of his many skills. But what was he tracking?

When the dog sat and looked back at Ben, he knew the dog had found something significant. "Whatcha got there, boy?"

"I see it," Grayson announced. "Is he trained to detect incendiary objects?"

"I'm not sure."

"Well, he's hit a target. Burnt ash." Grayson opened his CSI kit and pulled on a pair of sterile gloves before grabbing a large pair of tweezers and a small envelope. He inclined his head toward Rocky. "Will he let me approach?"

"Sure." Ben tugged on the dog's leash. "Rocky, heel." When the dog was at his side, he rubbed his flanks and praised him. "Good boy, Rocky. Good boy."

Grayson adjusted his crutches and lowered himself to the curb before reaching into the autumnal debris and picking up a brown cigarette butt.

Detective Grove leaned in to study the small piece of evidence. "I guess your dog knows that's a bad habit."

Maeve's fingers clenched a little more tightly around Ben's arm. "That's the cigarette Joker was smoking."

Allie Malone agreed. "That's right where he was standing."

Maeve continued. "Plus, I recognize the look of it—long, skinny and brown instead of white."

Grayson bagged the item and pushed himself to his feet. "I don't know if Joker's DNA is on file, but this will make it easy enough to add if it's not. Maybe the lab can tie this to the evidence they got off your friend's body."

Ben remembered an odd occurrence of Rocky following his nose the day before. "He had a similar hit around Maeve's car yesterday. Found a burn mark that looked like someone had put out his cigarette there. Do you think he recognizes Joker's scent? If we do a walk around the parking garage in the area where Maeve was attacked, could we prove that he was one of the guys who assaulted her?"

Detective Kincaid answered for the officials on the scene. "Rocky's not a registered scent-detection dog, so it wouldn't hold up in court. But if he hits on something, it'd be enough to call in someone from the K-9 unit who is official. You two willing to give it a try?"

"Yes, sir," Ben answered.

Maeve stopped Grayson before he could secure the envelope inside his kit. "Could I smell it? To see if it's the same scent I smelled when I was attacked?" Grayson moved his crutches to one hand and held the open envelope out to her. She curled her nose at the pungent scent even Ben could detect from beside her. He read the disappointment on her face when she pulled back. "I don't know. I can't tell if it's anything unique. Maybe all smokers smell like that." Then she perked up as she remembered something else. "There was another guy, I'm assuming it was a guy—I don't know why any sane woman would want to hang out with Joker—who stayed inside the car. He was smoking, too. It was thicker, heavier smoke."

"Maybe a cigar?"

"Possibly. Too bad the scent doesn't linger in the open air. Maybe that's the odor I'd recognize." He took a little of

Maeve's weight as she sagged against his arm. "Joker got in behind the wheel and they drove away almost as soon as we called you guys. We watched them on the security monitor in the office."

"And you never saw who was in the passenger seat?" Kincaid asked. Maeve shook her head. He shifted his gaze to Ben. "Maybe that John Doe is the scent Rocky keeps hitting on."

Ben nodded at the possibility. "Even if you identify your John Doe, what did he and Joker want?"

Maeve was the one who answered. "I think Joker wanted to scare me—to let me know he was watching me."

"Why?" Kincaid asked, thinking out loud. "Does he think you can tie him to your friend's murder?"

"Or to mugging you?" Grove speculated.

Maeve worked her bottom lip between her teeth, and Ben could tell she was pausing a moment to organize her thoughts before answering. "I've been thinking about this. I believe Steph must have taken something from them—maybe to blackmail Austin into getting back together with her or to incriminate her boss for sexual harassment. If Austin took something—files, a video, whatever—to help her, maybe he got in trouble with the firm and wants it back to save his job or even keep from being disbarred. It could be the missing files from work Mr. Summerfield mentioned at the ME's office. Maybe there's something there that could get *him* disbarred. Joker was part of the conversation that night at Shotz's, too. Maybe she took something to get rid of him. Maybe she even told him that she'd given it to me. And that's why he followed me from Shotz's that night."

Detective Kincaid nodded as if he had been thinking along the same lines. "It seems that he and whoever was in that car believe you have it."

"Or that I know where it is." Maeve shrugged. "Problem is, I don't. I have no idea what they're looking for."

Ben shook his head, not liking any of the possibilities that she'd suggested. "What did your roommate take that's put that lowlife on your tail?"

That was the million-dollar question that could solve a murder and end the threat to Maeve.

She asked the million-and-one-dollar question.

"And where is it?"

Chapter Eleven

Ben didn't mind Maeve's long silence as he drove them toward her neighborhood later that evening. He didn't need to be entertained with a lot of conversation, although he enjoyed their quiet chats, her intuitive strength and her sense of humor. Now that he understood a little better about her need to quietly recharge after interacting with a lot of people, he wanted to give her the time and space she needed to take the edge off her stress level.

But he didn't want her getting stuck in her head, overthinking all that had happened to her and imagining one worst-case scenario after another now that Bukowski, Joker and whoever the mystery man inside Joker's car might be had intruded on her life again. Was she worried about another attack? Ending up like her friend Steph? Was she regretting asking for his help now that they were spending so much time together?

"You hungry?" he asked, as they passed by a string of fast-food restaurants.

He was relieved that she looked across the cab of the truck at him and didn't hesitate to answer. "Yeah, but... I've got a frozen pizza at home I can doctor up for us. Or I could make a big salad. Or both. If you don't mind." She glanced back out the window at the lighted signs and drive-through lines and busy parking lots of the restaurants. "I'm peopled out."

Having Maeve all to himself? Avoiding the crowds? "I don't mind." He took his hand from the wheel to pat his stomach. "Eating something healthy sounds like a good plan. I don't get the exercise I used to back when we were training every day. I'm gettin' soft."

She laughed. "There's nothing soft on you, Sergeant."

A blush colored her cheeks when she realized the sexual innuendo in that comment, and she turned away. A smile curved his own lips. The woman wasn't lying. Other than when he'd been caught in the middle of that emotional flash-back, or they'd been talking over the investigation with Detectives Kincaid and Grove, he'd been half-hard with desire for the pretty brunette.

Those cruel classmates and jerk ex-boyfriend might have given her grief for being shy, but he knew the truth behind her quiet exterior. Maeve Phillips was observant and com-passionate and brave. She was a deep thinker who could carry on a meaningful conversation as easily as she could laugh at a joke. She was pretty and passionate and caring. She seemed to understand when he needed to be pushed, when he needed to be comforted and when he needed to be left alone. She didn't pity him because of his disability. She treated him as a friend, a confidant and a protector who just happened to have a stump and a hook on the end of his arm and a gnarly dog in his back seat.

Maeve treated him as a man.

She was a gift he hadn't realized he needed.

And he'd be damned if anyone was going to hurt her again or take her from him.

"Thank you for the compliment, Maeve. I owe any healthy response you may have detected entirely to you."

She shook her head and kept looking out the side window. "Are we there yet?"

Ben laughed out loud, loving her ability to make him feel like laughing again. He reached across the center console to wrap her hand in his and ask for her attention. When she turned and tilted her eyes to his without hesitation, he almost blurted out the truth in his heart. Instead, as she'd advised him earlier, he dialed it back a notch and made sure she was all right with his teasing. "I hope I'm not embarrassing you. But you have to know I'm extremely attracted to you. On a lot of levels. Not just physically. But I'm a guy and…" He shrugged. "That's just how we react."

She smiled and squeezed his hand before urging him to return his grip to the steering wheel. "I'm attracted to you, too. Not just physically. I'm just not used to flirting and being able to say whatever thought comes into my head. Especially if it's a little naughty."

His hand fisted around the wheel as he imagined whatever controlling crap her mother and ex must have used on her that made her think she had to edit everything that came out of her mouth. Ben inhaled a deep breath to calm himself and summoned what he hoped was a gentle smile for her. "I promised I'd always be honest, right? You and me? It's a nonjudgment zone. Say whatever you need to say. And feel free to practice your flirting skills on me anytime." He snorted. "You can't be any rustier at this relationship stuff than I am."

"Relationship?"

She wanted honest? "Yeah. That's where I see us heading. If you can put up with a beat-up old war horse like me."

"If *you* can put up with all the troubles I seem to be a magnet for lately," she countered.

He nodded, getting her point. "What's happening between us makes me think of the major my team used to report to in Special Forces. He always said our personalities and diverse skills and backgrounds made us a band of misfits—but together, we were the finest unit he'd ever worked with. We got the job done."

She settled back against the headrest. But her gaze stayed with him as he drove, and her serene smile stayed in place. "I like that analogy for us. A couple of misfits." She pointed to the cage behind her. "Three, if you throw in Rocky."

"You are not a misfit."

"Then neither are you." Rocky got up and whined, then circled around and plopped back down with a huff, as if he resented no one clearing him of the misfit label. Maeve chuckled and stuck her fingers through the cage links to invite Rocky to sniff her hand, which the big brute did. "You're not a misfit, either, Rocky. You're my good boy."

Ben shook his head at her indulgence. "He's a Marine, Sweetcheeks. Don't you be sweet-talking him."

"Oh, I don't know." She scratched the dog's muzzle when he stretched his nose into her touch. "I've heard that Marines—and Delta Force soldiers—like to cuddle. With the right woman." He felt his own cheeks heat up with anticipation when he felt her eyes on him. "Was that better flirting?"

"Lord help me." How was he supposed to resist her when she upped the innuendo and adorability factor like that? As much as he wanted to pull into one of these parking lots, tug her onto his lap and kiss her until they were both as turned-on as he was right now, he needed to feed her, make sure she got a good night's sleep and get control over his own demons before he took this relationship wish any further.

"I can't take much more of this conversation. We don't have to figure out anything tonight. Close your eyes and rest," he begged her. "I'll have you home in a few minutes."

The smile lingered on her lips as she dutifully closed her eyes and huddled inside the thick gray weave of her cardigan sweater. Not sure whether she was cold or snuggling in for comfort, Ben turned the heater up a notch and drove away from the commercial area into the residential neighborhood where Maeve lived.

He thought back through the events of the day—from that world-changing kiss at the clinic this morning to Maeve's panicked phone call to him. Needing *him*. He hadn't been the go-to guy for anybody since leaving the Army. And he'd never met another woman who seemed to get him and his moods like Maeve did. He glanced back at the dark brown eyes watching him from the back seat. Even his beast of a dog who preferred work to most people had fallen under Maeve's spell.

And yeah, Maeve was right. Ben wasn't sure what hoops he'd have to jump through with Jessie Caldwell and K-9 Ranch, but Rocky had quickly become *his* dog. He wanted to adopt the temperamental brute permanently and train him to help with his panic attacks. Since Rocky was such a hard charger, he'd also look into training him for scent-detection work. If he could get the dog certified, maybe they could consult with KCPD or the fire department. He seemed to have a knack for finding ash and accelerants and other remnants of incendiary devices. Not only could they expand Mrs. Caldwell's business, but it would give Ben a more specific role to play at the training center. It felt a little like the Army. He hadn't been content to be a regular soldier, so he'd worked hard to make the Special Forces teams.

He and Rocky, followed by Maeve and the detectives, had

tracked her path through the parking garage across from the clinic. The dog had picked up a scent at the spot where Maeve said she'd first been struck by the two men. While he didn't find another object like the cigarette butt, his low growl and deep huffs seemed to indicate that he was picking up the scent of someone or something he didn't like. Or maybe Rocky was responding to the tension running down the leash from Ben's temper brewing at the knowledge that this was the spot where a grown man had put his hands on Maeve. Possibly, the only reason she'd walked away from that assault was because she didn't have what the men were after, and they'd made sure she couldn't identify either of them. But if she'd seen one of their faces…

As his thoughts veered off into a dark place, he heard Rocky whining behind him and pawing at his cage. "I'm okay, boy," he whispered, not wanting to disturb Maeve in case she'd drifted off to sleep. He made a fist and pressed it to the cage behind his shoulder. He was surprised to feel Rocky's paw come up and tap the spot, giving him a canine high five. Ben smiled at the dog in the mirror. "You got my back, huh? Thanks, buddy."

Rocky was telling Ben that it wouldn't be hard at all to train him to be Ben's service dog—or anything else he wanted.

As Ben pulled his hand back to the steering wheel and turned onto Maeve's street, he caught her gray-green eyes watching the interchange from across the truck. "Told you he was your dog."

Ben thought his evening was about to improve once they got inside, got comfortable and ate some dinner. But the moment he and Rocky followed Maeve through the front door, he threw up what used to be his fist and gave an order. "Stop!"

"Oh my God."

As the color drained from Maeve's face, Ben linked his arm through hers and pulled her behind him.

He'd seen battlefields in better shape than the utter destruction of her entryway and living room. Every cushion on the sofa where they'd fallen asleep together had been cut open and tossed around the room. The quilt they'd slept under was shredded. The coffee table was smashed to the floor. And the few pictures on the walls had been knocked down, their broken glass and torn images scattered about like confetti. A bookshelf had been tipped over. A plant sat in a pile of soil and the broken pot that had once contained it. Through the doorway into the kitchen, he could see cabinet doors and the refrigerator propped open, with a carton of milk spilling its contents onto drawers that were overturned on the floor.

"They searched my house." Maeve barely breathed the words. "Is it always going to be like this?"

Fury raged through Ben at her defeated tone. He tugged her fist from the back of his jacket and turned to her. He tapped his prosthetic hand beneath her chin and urged her to look at him. Good. He read the fear stamped on her face, but he saw something else sparking in her eyes—anger. *That* he could work with. She needed the shot of adrenaline the fiery emotion would give her.

He briefly dipped his lips to press a kiss to her forehead before reaching behind her to shut the door and twist the dead bolt into place. He pushed her against the wall beside the door, knowing this small corner of the house was clear and she would be protected from anyone still hanging about outside. "Stay put. Call Kincaid and Grove to report the break-in. Rocky and I are going to check it out, make sure whoever did this isn't still on the premises. Rocky. Patrol."

With his ears up and nose down, Rocky headed out. Ben gave a few tugs on the leash to lead him into each room, then let the dog move where he needed to. Much as he had when he'd been clearing enemy safe houses and drug lord hideouts in the Army with Smitty, Ben yelled, "Clear!" as they left each room without any sign that the perp was still on the premises. Rocky was panting hard, more from his degree of focus than from the physical exertion. If Ben was a dog, he'd have been panting, too. In every room he took a mental snapshot of the details, trying to ignore the emotional blow this level of destruction would have on Maeve.

The rest of the house was much the same as the living room and kitchen. It looked as though whoever had broken in had forced a window open back in Steph's room, leaving the front of the house undisturbed, so that no one in the neighborhood would see and report them. Nothing had been left untouched in either bedroom. He had to wonder how much of this chaos was a search, and how much was some sick thug doing his damnedest to hurt Maeve by violating what should be her sanctuary.

Suddenly, Rocky's energy kicked up into the red zone, and the dog turned sharply into the bathroom across the hall from her bedroom. "Whatcha got, boy?"

Ben cursed when he saw the destruction there. He didn't need a dog's nose to smell the stench of smoke permeating the room. There'd been no signs of an intruder still in the house, but Rocky had followed his natural drive to discover the most important clue yet. The dog propped his front paws on the ledge of the tub and sniffed the charred remains of burnt household goods inside the tub. He barked once before he sat on his haunches and looked up at Ben. "I see it, too, boy." The message might be encoded, but the threat was as clear as anything else Maeve had described. Ben patted the dog's flank and scratched him around his muzzle, turning the job into a game, which Rocky had won. "Good job, Rocky. Good boy."

"Ben?" Too late he heard Maeve's footsteps running down the hall. She slammed into his chest as he turned to catch her and back her out of the room. "I heard Rocky. Do I smell smoke? I have a fire extinguisher in the kitch—"

"What part of *stay put* don't you understand?" He couldn't get her out of the small room before she saw what he and Rocky had discovered.

"I heard you clearing each room. I counted the number of times you said it, once for each room and knew that meant the intruder was gone. I'm safer with you than by myself. The detectives are on their way." Other than picking her up and carrying her out of here, the woman wasn't going to leave. She clung to the front of his jacket but leaned over to peek around his shoulder. "What's in the bathtub?"

Counting off the rooms. Smart. And he couldn't argue that he felt better with her within arm's reach, too.

He kept his arm around her waist and turned to face the tub again. "The perp burned some of your things. Looks like clothes, towels, the shower curtain, maybe a bedspread. The one in Steph's room has been shredded, and the one from your room is missing." He nodded to the charred piece of technology sitting in the middle of it all. "Is that your laptop?"

She nodded. "Steph had hers with her when she disappeared. Ben?"

"I bet they searched your laptop, then put it here with the other stuff to destroy the evidence. They would have taken it if it had what they were looking for. But they wanted you to find it. They ran water in the tub to put out—"

"Ben." Her fingers pinched the side of his waist. She

pointed to the letters scrawled across what had once been white tiles above the back of the tub.

Buzzkill.

"I saw it. What does it mean?"

"It's a message from Joker."

"How do you know?" He glanced down at her. Her cheeks had gone pale.

"It's what he calls me. I wasn't exactly friendly when I met him at Shotz's. He wanted to party, and I wasn't interested in what he offered to teach me. I just wanted to leave. He said that I was—"

"I know what the word means." Ben called Joker a name he should have been embarrassed to say in front of a lady. He could feel his blood pressure rising, and his pulse thundered in his ears. "What if you'd been here when they broke in? What message is he sending to you? That he intends to hurt you? That he wants to kill you?" Ben had been trained how to kill a man with his bare hands, and right now he really wanted to know if he could still do it with one hand. Judd—Joker—Lasko sure made him want to try. "He doesn't know you. He doesn't deserve to breathe the same air as you. Don't let him get in your head."

"Come on. What's done is done. Let's get out of here." She tugged on Ben's arm, and he followed her into the hallway. "Do you need to run around the block?"

Ah, hell. He was scaring her as badly as that burnt message had. "I'm not leaving you."

"I can feel you vibrating with tension. Do you need to punch something?" She tapped the wall. "There's some drywall here. It's not going to hurt the look of the place any if you go at it."

"I'll be fine," he ground out between his teeth. "You don't have to take care of me. I'm supposed to take care of…"

She stepped into his body and wrapped her arms around his waist, resting her forehead against the juncture of his neck and shoulder. Although he had no clue if he'd been swaddled as a baby, Maeve's gentle touch, the press of her body into his seemed to have the same effect. Ben didn't question the way his heart rate evened out and his breathing slowed to a more normal rhythm. He tightened his arms around her and rested his cheek against the crown of her hair. He felt the imprint of her fingers against his spine. The soft pillow of her breasts, the subtle perfume of her hair, the warmth of her body calmed him. He anchored himself to her, to her caring and heat and quiet strength and simply breathed.

He heard her snap her fingers behind him. Then her left hand dropped to his side. Was she petting the dog? Drawing him into this circle of serenity? Ben felt Rocky leaning against his thigh, adding his warmth and support to this healing embrace. "That's it, Rocky," she praised him. "Good boy."

Ben reached down and splayed his fingers over Maeve's hand on top of the dog's head. "That's my boy. You've got my back, don't you."

"We both do." Then Maeve straightened to rest her hands against Ben's chest and tilted her gaze up to his. "Are you better now?"

"Yeah. Thanks." Snapping out of his dark mood, he pulled her hand into the crook of his elbow, ordered Rocky to heel and led them all toward the front door. "You're not staying here tonight. These guys know where you live. If it's Joker, he also knows where you work."

"It's Joker," she said with utter certainty. "I don't understand why he thinks scaring me like this is going to get him whatever it is he wants. I mean, this is clearly him. He's leaving DNA all around me and personal messages now, so even the cops are going to know it's him. Does he think he's untouchable? That no one's going to arrest him? He acts like he has diplomatic immunity."

Ben paused at the front door as an idea occurred to him. "Maybe he does."

Maeve scoffed at the idea. "He's never been a politician or set foot in an embassy in his life."

"Maybe not. But something like it." This was worth discussing with the detectives. "Why is he such good friends with Bukowski? Clearly, they don't run in the same social circles. Does he supply him with drugs or women or whatever his vice is in exchange for some kind of legal magic to keep Joker out of jail? If Steph found evidence of that kind of complicity—bribes or blackmail or witness intimidation or ratting out someone else in exchange for his freedom— then neither Joker nor Bukowski would want anyone to get wind of that."

Maeve seemed to think his idea had merit. "Austin would be disbarred. Fired. Every client he ever defended would come under scrutiny."

"Joker would end up in prison."

"Mr. Summerfield asked about missing files, too—at the ME's office. Is he part of this?"

"No clue." He reached around her to unlock the dead bolt. "Maybe Joker is a predator of the worst kind—a bully who never grew up. He thinks you know what he's looking for and that you're just being stubborn and holding out on him, so he's trying to wear you down until you give him what he wants."

"If I knew what it was," she pointed out.

Ben looped Rocky's leash around his hook and reached out to cup the side of Maeve's face and neck with his hand.

"And maybe he gets off on terrorizing you and doesn't care who knows it."

She shivered as if that was a distinct possibility. "He has terrible tattoos on his arms. Violent images toward women." She wrapped her fingers around his wrist, keeping them connected. "Yours are beautiful. They're reminders of things you've loved. Even if they're sad, about things you've lost, they're still about pride and loyalty and love."

He vowed right then and there, that if this terror campaign didn't break her and she gave him the chance to make things work between them, he'd get her name inked onto his skin, too. It would be small and tasteful. Maybe pastel colors. Beautiful. The essence of Maeve herself.

But that future wasn't certain. He glanced around the room. Even though his darkness was under control now, his blood still simmered at this violation of everything she'd worked so hard for. Unable to resist her bravery and kindness a moment longer, and needing some of her strength for himself, Ben dipped his head and kissed her. Her lips instantly softened under his, then parted in welcome. Everything in him centered itself at the contact. And though the man in him wanted to pull her closer and deepen the kiss, he kept his touch gentle and far too brief.

"I could drink on those lips forever," he whispered as he pulled away. He grinned at the blush staining her cheeks. He was so far gone on this woman, he didn't think he'd recover if she decided a relationship with him was too big of a gamble for her to handle. "Come on, Sweetcheeks. I need to get you out of here. We'll wait in my truck for Grove and Kincaid."

Once he had her settled into the passenger seat with the heater running, he played a few rounds of fetch with Rocky and his rope tug to reward the dog for searching and clearing the house, and for reminding him that he was part of a team again. Rocky was a true working dog, never tiring of the game or his desire to please his partner. The exercise in the brisk air was good for Ben, too. As much as he wanted to take Maeve into his arms and hold her again, he needed to be thinking about her protection detail. As a Special Forces soldier, he would have had a plan B, C and D in mind, in case keeping his company wasn't security enough to keep her safe.

But the late autumn chill and the distance between him and Maeve made Ben anxious to get back to her. He urged Rocky up into the back seat and gave him a drink of water from the bottle he'd stashed behind the seat for him. Then he climbed into the front seat across from Maeve. "The detectives are on their way?"

She nodded. "They'll be here in a few minutes. Detective Grove said they wanted to get eyes on Joker and put a surveillance team on him." Her gaze dropped to the dashboard. "Oh, and I got a call from Steph's father. He's going to have Steph's body cremated. He plans a visitation and service all at the funeral home next Tuesday."

Ben reached across the seat to squeeze her hand. "I'm sorry, hon. You want me to go with you?"

Her gaze shot up to his. "Yes. Please."

"Done." He squeezed a little harder. "If Bukowski hassles you about going with you again, you tell him you have other plans."

"At least it's the weekend and I have a couple days off to clean up this mess. I don't know if there's anything in the house I can salvage for the service. One of her silly decorative pillows or some pictures that weren't completely trashed. I don't even have my laptop to reprint them."

"I've got a computer you can use," he offered. "If you've still got the SIM card from your camera or they're on your phone."

"Thank you." She arched her eyebrows in a wry expression and lifted the tiny purse strapped across her shoulder and chest. "That's about all I've got. My phone, credit card and access to my bank account, plus the flash drive I need for work. I can stay in a hotel for a couple of nights and come back here and work during the day—with you or someone else to help keep an eye on things."

"No."

"You can't help me this weekend?" She masked the disappointment in her voice by turning around to stick her fingers through the cage to pet the panting dog. Her sad smile nearly broke his heart. "You mean you *won't* help me. This turned out to be a lot more of a commitment than just walking me to my car."

"It's not that." He pulled her fingers away from the dog and squeezed them in his own hand. She should be getting her comfort and reassurance from him, not Rocky. "I'll help you once the cops clear the scene. I'm with you to the end on this. But you aren't staying in any hotel by yourself."

"I'm not staying here," she argued, hating the idea as much as he did.

"No, you're not." Plan B was finally taking shape in his head. "You're coming with me."

Chapter Twelve

Maeve dozed on the drive out to K-9 Ranch where Ben and Rocky lived. She was exhausted from the day, from her emotions, from everything that had happened over the past week.

She jerked awake when they turned onto the gravel road leading into the ranch.

"Easy, Sweetcheeks," Ben reassured her. "We're here."

They stopped briefly while Ben punched in a security code and the gate swung open. He saluted the camera she could see above the keypad and pulled in before the gate closed behind them.

"That's impressive," she commented, trying to get a sense of the beautiful autumn leaves and rich green of the oak and pine trees beyond the lights lining the access road.

Ben turned on his brights as they approached a two-story farmhouse with a wall-to-wall front porch, a barn and several outbuildings on the well-lit, well-maintained property. "Mrs. Caldwell had some trouble out here last year. *Mr.* Caldwell upgraded security after that."

"Is that why you feel I'll be safer out here than in the city?"

"Partly." They passed two long cinder-block buildings.

Even through the truck's closed windows, she could hear the symphony of dogs barking at their approach. Rocky jumped up in the back seat and joined the chorus.

Maeve covered her ears. "How many dogs are out here?"

"Rocky. Stand down." Ben shushed the shepherd, whose bark was deafening in the enclosed space of the truck, before answering her question. "Over twenty. That's counting the dogs who live here permanently, the rescues and a couple of trainees we're housing until their owners become certified handlers."

"Wow. I had no idea K-9 Ranch was this successful." She smiled back at Rocky, whose tail was thumping now that they were home. "You come from good stock." Then she turned to Ben. "Are they all guard dogs?"

"Hardly." Ben pulled into a parking spot next to the barn. "Even if they're a puppy or destined to be a pet, having all the dogs on the premises is the best alarm system in the Kansas City area. Nobody will show up here that we don't know about."

He proved his point when they got out of the truck, and a tan, long-legged Anatolian shepherd came out of the barn. Before Maeve could ask if he was friendly enough to be petted, Ben put Rocky into a sit and saluted the big dog. "It's just us, Rex." As if Ben's acknowledgment was all the confirmation the curious dog needed to prove they weren't intruders, he turned and trotted back inside the barn. "He's top dog around here," Ben explained. "Rex patrols the grounds and keeps an eye on things. He's not much for people, but do not trespass on the property or mess with his goats."

"Understood. You'll let me know which dogs are friendly and which ones aren't?"

"We'll do that tomorrow. The family dogs are probably in the house by now. The others are in their kennels." After pointing out his second-floor apartment and the stairs leading up to it on the south side of the barn, Ben tucked her hand in the crook of his elbow and grabbed Rocky's leash and walked them back to the house. Maeve willingly fell into step beside them. "We're not going to your place?"

"I need to have a conversation with my boss."

"About what?" She was seeing the soldier now because Ben was clearly on a mission. His strides were long and purposeful, though not so long that she couldn't keep up. His gaze was focused as they circled to the back of the house and climbed the steps onto a wide cedar deck. Maeve could see lights on in the kitchen through the small panes of glass in the steel back door, and several people seated around a long farm table, including two middle-aged women, four children and an older man. The adults were laughing and chatting, and except for the youngest preschool-aged child, the children were intent on the papers and books in front of them. Maeve halted in her tracks and pulled her hand from Ben's arm. "Are they having a party? I don't want to interrupt anything."

"It's all right, Sweetcheeks. Family gathering. I've met everyone here and can vouch for them, so there's no need for you to worry." He pressed a firm kiss to her temple before unhooking Rocky from his leash and harness. "At ease, Rocky. Guard the back door if you want, but you're off duty. Don't get on Rex's bad side while we're gone. We'll be back in a few minutes."

Rocky seemed aware of the white-muzzled German shepherd limping toward the back door and the black Lab that sprang to his feet and followed the other dog. A fluffy Australian shepherd lifted its head from the knee of a blond-haired girl, then put its head back down, as if content that the first two dogs had their arrival well in hand. Instead of reacting with any alarm, Ben's K-9 partner settled down in a sphinxlike position, surveying the backyard beyond the edge of the deck before resting his head on his front paws.

"Do you think he understands you when you talk to him like that?" Maeve asked.

"I don't know, but he seems to relax like he knows he's off duty when I have a conversation with him. As opposed to giving him commands." He settled his prosthetic arm at the small of Maeve's back and knocked on the door, even though the dogs had already alerted the family to their arrival.

Maeve wasn't sure what to expect when a large man with salt-and-pepper hair and a gun and badge strapped at his waist opened the door. It wasn't the friendly smile or welcoming handshake he extended to them, though. "Ben. Good to see you. Everything all right?"

A beautiful woman with sun-warmed cheeks and a long blond braid frosted with silver came up beside the man and smiled. "Hey, Ben. What's up?"

"Ma'am. Garrett. Could I talk to you for a few minutes?"

"Sure." The older woman nudged aside the man who must be her husband and ushered them into the kitchen and dining area. "If you'll introduce us to your friend first."

His arm tightened around Maeve's waist. "Maeve Phillips. My boss, Jessie Caldwell. Her husband, Garrett. Deputy sheriff," he added, explaining the badge and gun the other man wore.

"Ben has been a blessing since he started with us. One of the best trainers I've ever worked with." Jessie Caldwell extended her hand to Maeve and dropped her voice to a mock whisper. "But we're still working on his people skills."

Ben snorted at the teasing dig over forgetting to introduce her. Maeve hadn't minded, but she wasn't comfortable with the other woman thinking the slight had been on purpose. "I think his people skills are just fine."

"I can see that they're improving," the older woman answered cryptically, before ushering them into the dining area while her husband locked the door behind them and shooed the dogs back to their respective beds. "We're done with dinner and cleanup and were just sitting down for coffee and cocoa with our friends. May I offer you a cup of either one?"

"Ma'am, I just need to—"

Maeve interrupted. "I'd love anything hot. Thank you. My fingers are freezing."

Ben immediately reached for her hand and rubbed it against his stomach. "You didn't say anything."

Although she appreciated his abundant heat, she hadn't meant for him to worry. "It's not life or death."

A flash of midnight darkened his eyes. "Don't say things like that."

"Ben, I'm fine." She splayed her free hand against his chest and gave him a reassuring pat. "I'm running on fumes. I don't have my coat, and it was chilly outside."

"We should have packed more of your things." Before she could say anything else, he'd shrugged out of his camo jacket and draped it around her shoulders, rubbing his good hand up and down her right arm. "Better?"

Maeve couldn't hide her smile or blush at the tender, protective gesture. "Yes. Thank you."

He turned to the others in the room. "All right. We can stay for a bit." She was glad to see the flare of whatever dark emotion she'd glimpsed had vanished from his features. Ben Hunter might still look the part of a badass Special Forces operator with his beard and muscles and tats, but when that hint of a smile softened his expression, she saw the caring, protective man he'd been with her, time and again. He turned back to his boss and offered her a smile, too. "Coffee for me, please, ma'am."

"Two decafs coming right up." She moved around the kitchen island to pour two mugs of coffee. "What did I say about ma'am-ing me, Ben?"

"Military protocol is hard to break, ma'am. Um, Mrs. Caldwell. Jessie." Maeve almost chuckled at his flustered response. But she had no intention of embarrassing him further in front of the other people. Thankfully, he quickly recovered. "You are the boss. Technically, you outrank me."

"All right, then. I order you to stop calling me *ma'am*. It makes me feel old."

"Yes, m…" Ben stopped talking and the other woman winked at Maeve and smiled.

"Cream and sugar are on the table." Jessie Caldwell brought the mugs to the table and set them on the empty placemats before glancing up at Ben. "Have a seat. Please. What did you need to discuss?"

"Maeve's had some trouble that I'm helping her with. She's going to be staying at the ranch with me for a few days if that's all right. I didn't know what your rules were about having company."

The older woman touched Ben's shoulder. "It's your apartment, Ben. Unless you're doing something that threatens my children or dogs, you can invite over anyone you want. It's not our business."

"I appreciate that."

"Sit." The rather intimidating man pulled out a chair for Maeve. But he was all smiles when he moved to the dark-haired boy and beautiful blonde girl sitting at the table. "Our children, Nate and Abby."

Maeve smiled. "Hi."

Their father gave the children some sort of meaningful glare, and Nate piped up with a "Nice to meet you." The little girl echoed the same words in a much softer voice.

Jessie stepped behind the other woman's chair and squeezed her shoulders in a friendly gesture. "This is my friend and our fostering and adoption mentor, Stella Smith." She nodded to the freckle-faced boy and tiny, dark-eyed girl sitting on either side of the plump woman who had streaks of turquoise and lavender in the topknot of her blond hair. "Two of her current charges, Colby and Ana."

The red-haired boy leaned into Stella and whispered, pointing to the prosthesis Ben wore. "Is he a robot?"

Stella draped her arm around the boy's thin shoulders and hugged him. "Oh, no, sweetie. Mr. Hunter is the man who works with the dogs, remember?"

Instinctively wanting to protect Ben from the spotlight of the boy's curiosity, Maeve reached for Ben and wrapped her fingers around the titanium hook. "This is Ben's new hand."

Ben covered her hand with his. "It's okay. He's not the first kid to gawk at it."

"I want him to understand. He shouldn't be afraid of it. Or you." She continued her explanation, showing and telling the boy that it was a miracle of medicine and engineering, not anything to be whispered about or feared. "It's part of who he is. He got hurt very badly. Ben fought hard to get better. The best doctors took good care of him, and they gave him this hand to be a part of him. They made sure he stayed alive, and that makes me very happy. He can do a lot of things with it. He helps on the ranch. He drives his truck. He takes care of me. He gives the best hugs." The boy's green eyes widened at her words, and by the time she'd finished, all four children had set their mugs of cocoa aside and were paying close attention. "It's called a prosthesis. That's a big tongue-twister. Can you say that?"

The little red-haired boy tried to sound out the word. "Pwo-tee-tis."

"Protesis," Nate answered, coming a little closer to the right pronunciation.

Although the little dark-haired girl didn't say anything, Abby echoed what her brother had said. "Protesis."

Seeming more at ease with the attention, Ben pushed back his chair and turned. "You guys want to touch it?"

The boys were out of their chairs immediately and dashed around the table to check out Ben's prosthetic hand. Little Ana seemed as shy as Maeve had once been and stayed in her seat beside her foster mother. But Abby bravely stepped up to Ben to examine his hand and listen to him answer the boys' questions.

Then the blonde girl braced her hand on Ben's shoulder and said, "I'm glad you're not dead."

Maeve would have fantastic dreams remembering the way Ben smiled down at the little girl and patted her shoulder. "Me, too. Thank you, Abby."

"My old dad is dead. He hurted himself, too, but nobody helped him. Garrett's my new dad. He gives good hugs, too, and he had his own dog named Ace when he was little."

Then Abby leaned in closer to whisper a secret that everyone around the table could unfortunately hear. "She likes you. Are you going to marry her like Garrett married Jessie? I was the flower girl. I still have my dress if you need—"

"Okay, sweetheart. Let's give Ben a little space." Garrett scooped his daughter up in his arms and carried her back to her chair.

The grownups around the table chuckled.

"And on that overly personal note..." Stella pushed her

chair away from the table and stood. "Sounds like you all need to have a serious conversation. Why don't I take the children upstairs. I'll make sure their homework is done, and then we'll find a game we can play."

"Thank you, Stella." While the children ran ahead of them, Jessie followed the woman to the archway of the kitchen. "And I want to talk to you more about adopting one of our dogs. I have several that would be good with your foster kids."

"I'm sure you do."

Then Mrs. Caldwell came back to the kitchen. She looked from Ben to Maeve and back, then took a seat near the head of the table beside her husband. "I like how you defended Ben."

Ben turned back to Maeve and held his elbow out to her. "So do I." The moment she linked her fingers to his arm, he pulled her against his side and pressed a kiss to her temple. "Thank you for making that easier for me."

"I didn't want them to be afraid of you."

"They aren't. Not now, thanks to you."

"I'm not afraid of you, either, Ben," she whispered.

He nodded, kissed her again and let his lips linger against her hair. "One thing at a time, Sweetcheeks. Okay?"

She nodded.

They each doctored up their coffee and drank a few sips before Garrett pushed his mug aside. "Maybe you'd better explain what kind of trouble you're talking about."

With that command, Ben didn't waste any time jumping into the topic he'd wanted to discuss. "Maeve's roommate was murdered, and now the men who did it—or at least the guys KCPD suspects—are after Maeve." He drew the back of his knuckle along her jaw to point out the healing scrapes and bruises on her face. "They believe she has something

Maeve's roommate took from them. She was assaulted a few days ago. Harassing phone calls and texts. Someone broke into her house while she was at work today and tore it apart."

"Oh, my goodness," Mrs. Caldwell gasped. "Are you all right?"

"I'm fine," Maeve assured her. "I'm way out of my element stuck in the middle of an investigation like this, but Ben and Rocky have been helping me."

"Protection detail?" Garrett asked.

"Yes, sir."

"Friends," she answered at the same time, noting that Ben's military protocol was firmly in place when he addressed the older man.

"Yeah, we're *sort-of friends*."

"We are way past being *sort-of friends*," Maeve argued. She tried to explain their relationship to Jessie and Garrett. "I've worked with Ben at the veterans' occupational therapy clinic for several months now, so I've known him for a while. When I needed someone to make me feel safe, he stepped up to help. He's good for me. Brings me out of my shyness and puts up with me when I can't seem to get out of my head."

"It's not a chore, Maeve. Have I ever made you feel like it is?"

"No, of course not." She let her hand rest over the warmth of his forearm and the cords of muscle underneath. "I think I'm pretty good for him, too. Plus, now he has Rocky. By the way, he wants to adopt Rocky, if that's okay—but he might be too stubborn to ask you. Rocky's good for him, too."

Mrs. Caldwell's gaze darted back and forth between the two of them while they bantered, then she looked at her husband and winked. "I like that idea."

Garrett rolled his eyes at a secret message between husband and wife. "It's bad enough you're trying to set Stella up with my friend Joe. Now you see romance everywhere." His gentle reprimand wasn't really a reprimand at all because he squeezed Jessie's hand and she smiled. Keeping his fingers laced with Jessie's, he braced an elbow on the table and got serious again. "What kind of threat level are we talking about? Do I need to send my family away to stay with friends for a while?"

Maeve was horrified by the idea of Joker getting anywhere close to his happy family or those sweet children. "Oh, I don't want to cause that much trouble." She started to push her chair back. "I should go to a hotel, after all. I don't want anyone else to get hurt."

"No." Ben captured her hand and linked their fingers together in the same familiar claim the Caldwells shared across the table. "We discussed this. The Caldwells have security cameras all over the property." He nodded toward the man with the salt-and-pepper hair. "Deputy Caldwell is one of the best I've ever met. He's former military. We talk the same language. Plus, until Bukowski or Joker put a tracker on me, which will never happen, they don't know where I live."

Garrett nodded. "About the only place you'd be more secure is in a safe house." A shadow of emotion flickered over his wife's expression, and the big man reached over to caress Jessie's cheek and hold her gaze until she smiled again. "Our home has been used as a safe house in the past. I can't imagine anyone getting past Rocky or Ben, but if they do…" He looked back at Ben and gave him one of those curt nods Ben often used. "You'll have the backup you need. I'll give you the access codes to monitor the security camera feeds yourself. Who's working the investigation at KCPD?"

"Atticus Kincaid and Kevin Grove."

"I know the Kincaids. That's a family legacy of good cops. You're in excellent hands with him." He leaned back in his chair, keeping Jessie's hand securely in his grip. "Do you need me to call in an extra patrol unit to help stand watch?"

Ben shook his head. "I'm more comfortable with a covert operation. I don't want to draw any attention to the fact that Maeve is here if we can help it."

The conversation continued for several more minutes as Maeve told them about the investigation, Ben and Garrett strategized best practices to keep her safe, and Jessie made sure Ben had enough sheets and blankets for a guest, as well as plenty of food on hand. A half hour later, the Caldwells escorted them to the back door where Rocky was dancing back and forth in anticipation of seeing Ben and Maeve again.

"Are you sure?" Maeve asked one more time, uncertain how she felt about these strangers taking her in and keeping her safe. Her own mother had never done that. "I don't know how I can ever repay you."

She was surprised when the older woman pulled her in for a hug. "You made friends with Rocky." Jessie pulled away far enough to glance down to see Maeve's hand resting on top of Rocky's head. "You got that devil dog to like you and be calm around you, and this man to come out of his grumpy shell and care about something beyond everything he's lost. That's payment enough.

"Welcome to K-9 Ranch."

"THE ONLY REASON I'm letting you sleep on the couch is because Rocky's crate is between you and the front door." Ben gently lectured Maeve, needing to hear the words out loud one more time to convince himself that he'd made the right decision by agreeing to Maeve's insistence that he sleep in his own comfortable bed, and she take the couch. He pointed out each access point to his comfortably spacious one-bedroom apartment. "The windows are only accessible if someone puts a ladder up against the side of the barn, and Rocky will hear them long before they get inside. Dead bolt, chain and knob lock are secured on the door. The bathroom window is too narrow for a grown man to get through. And if they come in the backside by my bedroom, I'm there."

"Got it, Sergeant." Maeve lay at one end of the couch, huddling inside the sweatshirt she'd borrowed from him, and tucking the covers all around her. Then she shooed him away. "Good night, Ben."

"I don't expect any kind of incursion. But if you hear anything suspicious, the first thing you do is let Rocky out of his crate. If I'm not already awake, you come get me. I'll lock you in the bathroom, which is the most secure place in the apartment, while the two of us handle whatever's out here." He scraped his palm over the top of his short hair and down over the weary planes of his face before tugging it down his beard. He was exhausted. He really needed to get his arm off and rub some lotion onto the skin he felt chafing there, simply because he'd worn his prosthesis way too long without any break today. A hot shower would do him a world of good right now, but he knew he needed sleep more than the reviving stimulation of cleaning up. He breathed out a heavy sigh. "Any questions?"

"Go to bed, Ben," she insisted, sitting up. "You must be exhausted. You nodded off during the movie we watched."

He snorted. "Some protector I am."

"Even badasses need their sleep. I'll be fine. Now go." She responded to his grinching with a soft smile before snuggling under the blankets they'd spread over the gray tweed couch. Having left most of her clothing back at her house because so much of it had been touched and would be a horrible reminder of how her world had been violated since Steph's disappearance—not to mention it might be a potential source of evidence—she was wearing one of his T-shirts and a hoodie that swam on her small frame. Along with sweatpants rolled up at the waist and a thick pair of his socks, she should have looked like a child playing dress-up in his clothes.

Instead, she reminded him of a very grown-up teddy bear that he wanted to curl up with. Only, she was no toy, and he was definitely no child. His body remembered the sleek curves hidden beneath her clothes from holding her last night. He remembered her soothing scent and the heat the two of them had generated together. And it might be a little caveman of him, but he also liked the fact that they'd gotten close enough that wearing his clothes was no big deal. It felt like a claim. His clothes—his woman.

On that possessive note, Ben turned off the lamp beside the sofa, murmured a good-night to Rocky and headed to bed.

He wound up taking a shower, anyway, before slipping on a pair of sweats and a T-shirt. He made sure his service pistol was in easy reach of his right hand in the bedside table and his prosthesis was within arm's reach, ready to grab at a moment's notice. Even if he couldn't get it on quickly enough to make for an even fight with an intruder, he figured he could use the device as a club and rely on his military skills to even the odds. Once he was convinced he couldn't make the apartment any safer for Maeve without growing a new hand and having the rest of his team here to back him up, he climbed beneath the covers. He tried sitting up in bed and reading a book, but the World War II histori-cal tome couldn't hold his attention tonight.

Eventually, he found himself in his bedroom doorway, leaning against the jamb. Moonlight crept through the blinds to subtly illuminate the main living area. From the galley kitchen with its eating counter and stools to the sofa, re-cliner and big TV in the living room, to Rocky's crate where he could hear soft canine snoring, everything seemed to be as it should be.

Maybe he should have been startled when he saw Maeve's dark curls stir on the pillow where she slept. But when she sat up, turned and faced him, then threw back the covers and padded across the room toward him, something settled inside him instead of feeling alarmed.

She walked right up to him, wrapped her arms around his waist and briefly squeezed him in a hug. He'd barely dipped his nose to the crown of her hair when she pulled away, took him by the arm and led him to the bed. "Come on. You can't stay up all night watching me not sleep, ei-ther. Get in."

He let her push him down to sit on the edge of the bed. "You're not tucking me in and walking away," he warned her.

"No. You'll just get up again. Scoot over." He stretched out beneath the covers, and she climbed in beside him and snuggled close. "Could I stay with you?"

"Of course." He shifted so that he could wrap his arm around her back and pull her to his side. He liked it when she used him as a pillow. "You still cold?"

"Not especially." She turned onto her side, with her cheek resting on his shoulder and her fingers splayed across his chest. "I can't fall asleep. I could feel you watching me." She hushed him before he could apologize. "Knowing you're watching over me makes me feel safe. But my thoughts are racing, and I'm wired. I want to solve this mystery and find Steph's killer and make all this stress go away and have a normal life again with you still in it somehow. But I don't know how to make that all happen. It's a lot of mental energy to burn off when I'm lying still with nothing to do but think." She stroked her fingers over his beard before resting her hand on his chest again. "Why aren't *you* sleeping?"

"You were too far away from me."

"I was in the next room, Ben. You left the door open."

"Doesn't matter. You were too far away for me to touch you." He brought his stump up to lay it over her hand to do just that. "It's hard to know you're safe and lower my guard enough to sleep when I can't at least feel in my subconscious brain that you're okay."

"I feel safer when I have contact with you, too. And don't get me wrong, I'm all for cuddling with your body heat. But would you…? Since we both are wide awake… Do you think…? What I mean is…" Her cheeks blushed an adorable shade of pink and his body tightened in response to the decidedly feminine reaction to the sensuous turn of her thoughts.

He hoped he understood what she was asking. "I'm not a mind reader, Maeve. Tell me exactly what you mean."

Her eyes met his. "Would you make love to me? I mean, are you interested in that kind of intimacy? With me? Because I really want to. I figure it'd be a great rush of endorphins, and maybe just enough exercise to wear me out so my brain will shut down and I can relax."

"You want to be with me because it'll make you sleepy?"

She propped herself halfway on top of him, her legs tangling with his. "I want to be with you because I'm afraid if something happens to me, or this ends and you decide you don't need to protect me anymore, I'll never get the chance to hold you in my arms and feel you inside me and know that I had someone special in this world who was all mine— even if it's only for tonight."

Ah, hell. How was he supposed to be noble and say no to that beautiful invitation? "I will always protect you, Sweetcheeks." Since she was still partly lying on his good arm, he reached up with his stump to brush aside the hair that had fallen onto her face. She turned her cheek into the caress and that last little holdout of believing he wasn't enough anymore melted away. He was just a man with Maeve, not a washed-up vet or a cripple or anything else but the guy she wanted to be with. "I don't know that I'm anything special. But you are."

"*We* are. Together, *we* are special."

"Yeah." Not so eloquent, but he got what she was saying. He felt it, too. He palmed her hip to lift her and tugged with his elbow to pull her squarely on top of him. "What's happening between us is unexpected and precious. If you think you want me, I'm not going to turn you away. Because I *know* how badly I want you." She worked her bottom lip between her teeth, thinking of how she wanted to respond to that confession. He reached up and freed her lip, gently soothing it with the pad of his thumb. "You're going to have to help me with a couple of things since I only have one hand. I'll need to prop myself up over you, so I don't squish you. Or, if you're on top, I might want to touch those pretty breasts. I don't even know if I can get a condom on by myself. It kind of feels like the first time in some ways. Are you okay with all that?"

"I've never been the more experienced one in a relationship. I like being on a more equal footing. I feel a little less like a buzzkill and more like—"

Ben stopped that line of thinking with a kiss. "Those are someone else's words. Not yours, and certainly not mine. You're the one who marched into my bedroom and led me to bed," he reminded her. No way was that bold move anything like the prude her enemies suggested she might be. Shy didn't mean she wasn't brave. Quiet didn't mean she wasn't fascinating. Lacking experience didn't mean she wasn't the sexiest thing he'd ever held in his arms. "The way you cuddle and kiss and never hesitate to touch me is such a turn-on, I'm half-hard whenever I'm around you."

She adjusted her body against his, feeling his arousal, and smiled shyly. "Like now?"

This woman. He breathed in deeply and exhaled, trying to get control of his body's instinctive reaction to her. "Are you sure this is what you want?"

She simply nodded and pushed his T-shirt over his head. Once he'd tossed the shirt aside, she began to explore his tattoos. "What's this one?"

He glanced down at the starburst that covered his left shoulder and carried over to his chest and back. It represented the firefight from *that* day. "It's a memorial to the teammates I lost the same day I lost my hand."

"Lunchbox. Irish. Hornet." She touched each name that was woven into the artwork, then kissed it. She blinked away the tears that shone in her eyes and moved on to another tribal marking. "And this?"

He let her explore for a few minutes, enjoying every sweep of her fingers and warm touch of her lips against his skin. But he didn't want to talk about his ink. With her help, he pulled off her sweatshirt and the T-shirt underneath and let them fly into the shadows of the room to join his shirt. Ben touched one of her breasts and squeezed. The eager tip speared his palm and he desperately wanted to take that nipple into his mouth. "You'll be brave enough to tell me if I do something you don't like? Or if you really do like something?" She moaned, her eyes closed as she savored his touch. "Eyes, Sweetcheeks."

Her eyes snapped open. "Yes, I like that. You'll tell me, too?"

He loved this woman with every fiber of his being. She was his partner in every way that mattered. She defended him, just as he defended her. She made it easier for him to interact with the world and not be so self-conscious about his disability, just as he hoped he made it easier for her to be more outgoing and not overthink things when her shyness genes kicked in. Her strength made him feel stronger. Her kisses and clutching hands and unmistakable desire made him feel like a whole man again. She needed him. He needed her. She was gentle and brave and pretty and sexy and everything he'd ever wanted in a woman. He wanted a future with Maeve. But as she'd often admonished him, he'd focus on the present.

For this night, at least, Maeve was his.

He rolled her beneath him and wedged his thigh against the heated juncture of her legs. "Yeah, honey, I will. But I don't think there's anything you can do that I won't—" She silenced him with a kiss and a firm grab of his backside. The last of their clothes disappeared and they figured out the condom, together.

There were no more words between them. A giggle, perhaps. A sharp intake of breath as hands wandered and kisses consumed. His own moan of pleasure. And finally, his name on her lips, gasping with the power of her release that clutched him tightly inside her and carried him over the summit to his own bliss before they collapsed into each other's arms and truly, deeply slept.

Chapter Thirteen

The next two days and nights were more of the same for Maeve. Work at her house. Go back to Ben's apartment at K-9 Ranch and help with his evening chores. Eat, make love, and sleep the best sleep of her life beside him.

Those nights were a good thing, because her days had become a nightmare. Police interviews. Reclaiming what little hadn't been destroyed in her house. Going through every last thing she and Steph owned which hadn't been labeled and carted away as evidence, looking for the thing that was at the heart of her friend's murder and Joker's terror campaign against her. Dealing with Austin's harassing calls and texts. Falling deeply in love with a surly veteran Special Forces soldier who sometimes needed his space and sometimes needed her snuggled closely in his arms, but always kept her in his sight or had a friend watch over her twenty-four hours a day.

Tomorrow was Steph's funeral, and Steph's father had asked her to say something at the service. Public speaking was one of her worst nightmares, but she'd do it for Mr. Ward. She'd do it for Steph.

Today, Maeve stood in front of her locker in the staff room near the end of her shift. When her cell phone buzzed in her pocket, her shoulders sagged with fatigue. Ben had already texted that he was on his way to pick her up. Detectives Kincaid and Grove had promised not to call during work hours unless there was a major break on the case. That left only one person who'd be texting her now.

"Give it a rest, Austin." Maeve pulled her cell phone out of the pocket of her scrubs to read the message.

I'll pick you up for the funeral tomorrow at 9:30.

She typed in a quick reply and sent it.

No. I have other plans.

At the clinic, she kept her phone in silent mode so as not to disturb her sessions with patients. But her phone had been vibrating on and off all day long. A few had been legitimate calls—a doctor consulting on an OT patient, a call from Steph's father regarding tomorrow's funeral service and Ben checking in with her at lunch to see how her day was going. But the others?

Her phone vibrated again. She tipped her head back and blew out an impatient breath.

Instead of immediately answering, she opened her locker and pulled out her wallet purse. Since she still hadn't replaced the laptop that had been trashed and burned in her bathtub, she needed to use one of the computers at work to update her patient files. She butted the door closed with her hip and unzipped the side pocket of the purse to retrieve her clinic flash drive. She carried everything over to the long countertop that ran the length of one wall in the staff locker room. The counter was fitted with chairs and two computers that staff could use in lieu of private office space.

She woke the closest computer and looped her bag over the back of the chair before sliding the flash drive into its port and waiting for the files to boot up. Only then did she pull out her phone again to read Austin's text.

Maevie, please. I know I'm going to lose it tomorrow. But you're sensible and calm. I know you can help me keep my act together. No one knew Steph like us. If we could spend that half hour together before the service, I'll feel better. I bet you would, too.

She seriously doubted that. She typed in a quick response.

It's okay to lose it. You're grieving the woman you loved. But my answer is still no.

Her phone vibrated almost instantly with a call. When she saw Austin's name, she dismissed it and turned her cell completely off. She set it on the counter next to the computer.

Austin Bukowski didn't help with her stress level any. Just like a few minutes ago, he'd called or texted her every day, begging her to go to the funeral with him and insisting that she let him come over to the house to select something of Steph's to keep as a memento. He had to be looking for something. Austin was too much of a self-absorbed jerk to care about a sentimental trinket from his late girlfriend. Even if her home hadn't been a crime scene and wasn't temporarily under surveillance by KCPD to see if the intruder returned, she didn't want Austin there. She wasn't even sure she wanted to be there herself anymore with the way all of her and Steph's belongings had been violated.

Despite its spartan decor, she loved Ben's apartment. The location out in the countryside was perfect for fresh air and long walks and finding quiet time away from the city. His kitchen was small but state-of-the-art, and she'd enjoyed cooking dinner with him the past couple of nights. The Caldwells were super nice neighbors, and Jessie was even becoming a friend, inviting Maeve over for a cup of tea and a sample of the delicious banana bread she'd baked. Garrett Caldwell was still a bit intimidating to her, but he'd never been anything but polite, and he and Ben seemed to have hit it off as friends. Their children were sweet. And the dogs? Although Rocky was still her favorite, she'd never been surrounded by so many childhood wishes come true. K-9 Ranch housed numerous purebreds and mixed breeds, from an energetic Jack Russell terrier to a lumbering big black Newfoundland. She helped Ben with his evening chores when they got home from the clinic. She knew the dogs by name now. Some were friendlier than others, but none were threatening, especially with Ben or Jessie there to command them.

She'd been given a taste of the life she wanted. But the dark specter of Steph's unsolved murder made her think her newfound happiness was temporary. That Ben wouldn't be as interested in her once the responsibility for keeping her safe had passed. That shy and quiet wouldn't be interesting enough for him, or he'd be so self-conscious about his PTSD issues that he'd just want to be sort-of friends again.

The screen on the computer monitor had gone dark by the time she shut down her thoughts. She moved the mouse to bring up the icons again, then frowned and sat back in her chair.

These weren't her patient files.

What exactly was she looking at?

There was a list of folders on the menu, yes, but she didn't recognize any of the names. Chad Meade. Roman Hess. Edward Di Salvo. The names sounded vaguely familiar, but she didn't think they belonged to anyone she knew personally.

She scrolled down the list and stopped at a name she'd become very familiar with. She pulled her hand off the mouse as if the man who belonged to that name could somehow reach her through the electronic connection. A shiver ran down her spine.

Judd Lasko.

Joker.

"Oh my God." Why was this in her purse? She glanced around at the lockers. Had she gotten her own flash drive mixed up with someone else's patient list?

But... Joker? He'd never been a patient here.

Needing answers as much as she needed her next breath, Maeve pulled her bag from the back of her chair. She always kept her flash drive in the outside zipper pocket. She quickly opened it and turned it upside down, dumping its meager contents onto the counter. Lip balm. Pen.

A second flash drive.

Without pausing to repack her bag, she closed the files on her screen and removed the strange flash drive. Then she inserted the second one from her purse and booted it up to read a slew of familiar names. Her patient list. This was what she always carried.

She removed it, tucked it back into her purse and reinserted the unknown flash drive. This was the extra. But how...?

Maeve closed her eyes at the memory of the unexpected hug Steph had given her that night at Shotz's. She'd held on to Maeve longer than usual, as if she knew it would be the last time they'd see each other. Her hand had gotten tangled in Maeve's purse strap when she'd pulled away.

"I've taken precautions this time. I've got the upper

hand," Steph had whispered before pulling away. *"He's not going to hurt me again."*

The upper hand.

Blackmail.

Steph had copied whatever this was that could implicate Austin and then had slipped it into Maeve's purse that night at Shotz's. Insurance. A way to force Austin to take her back, in case love and lust weren't enough. This had been tucked away in the one place Maeve hadn't looked. Her little purse had been with her the evening Joker and the mystery man had come to the clinic and her house had been ransacked. She hadn't been carrying it the day she'd been mugged because she'd needed the big bag for her walking shoes. Austin or Joker or whoever had been looking for something in the big purse Steph had borrowed and used that night at Shotz's. But it had never been in that bag at all.

Maeve had been carrying the evidence with her this entire time.

Tears of frustration stung her eyes, but she swiped them away. She plugged in the flash drive and pulled up the files again. This time she clicked on the one name she was certain she knew. Judd Lasko.

She wasn't sure what she was looking at as what seemed to be a ledger or invoice filled her screen. But there were no monetary amounts listed. Only words. Dates. Names. And chunks of gibberish that were probably some kind of code.

1 February 2024. AB. PO. = TS. / BS. SA. D126. PD.

"Blood type?" she mused out loud. "Assault and battery? Post Office? Police officer?" She could guess what the BS might stand for, but why curse in the middle of a coded document? "Bertram Summerfield? South America?" She shook her head, wishing this discovery made sense. "Police department? Paid?"

There were several more lines that were similarly cryptic. Dated entries with equal signs. She opened another file and found more dates and gibberish. Was this Steph's coding system? Had her friend copied someone else's files from work? She wondered if the detectives working the case could make sense of the dates and what the letters and D126 might stand for.

Maeve's hands were fisted on either side of the lip she was chewing as she wracked her brain for answers when she heard her friend Allie in the hallway outside the staff locker room door. "Yeah. Don't worry. She's okay. She's in there. Go on in."

She looked over her shoulder to see Ben striding across the room. "I just tried to call, and your phone went straight to voicemail."

"I turned it off."

Of course, he was worried when he'd been unable to reach her. "Was Bukowski harassing you again? What did he want?"

"We exchanged some texts about the funeral. When I repeated that I wasn't going with him, he called."

"And that's when you shut it off. Honey, if I can't reach you, you know I'm going to think the worst." When he saw she was transfixed by her computer screen, Ben knelt beside her and brushed her hair away from her cheek and tucked it behind her ear. "Talk to me, Sweetcheeks. What's going on?"

Maeve spoke her thoughts out loud. "Docket 126. Time served. Assault and Battery pled down to time served in exchange for whatever happened in Docket 126. His debt is paid. Joker's debt was paid."

"What are you talking about?"

"I think I broke part of the code."

"What code?"

"I found a flash drive in my purse. I think it's from Steph." She pointed to her screen. "Are those what I think they are?"

He swore. "Evidence of crimes?"

"That's why she's dead." The tears she'd held back finally spilled over. "I'm not sure what this means, but it has to be what everyone's been looking for. She died for a bunch of gibberish."

"Gibberish that someone doesn't want anyone else to see." Ben hooked his phone into his prosthetic hand and put it to his ear as he wrapped his good arm around her and pulled her close.

She heard the burly detective's voice pick up the call. "Sergeant Hunter. What's up?"

"Grove." It was acknowledgment enough. "She found it."

"YOU'RE GOOD PEOPLE, MAEVE. I appreciate all the kind, funny things you said about Steph. She did have a big heart, didn't she?" Russell Ward met her at the podium at the front of the funeral chapel and swallowed her up in a hug that lifted Maeve off her toes. His voice was rough from tears, but he smiled as he released her. "Thank you."

"I owed her a lot. I'm so sorry for your loss."

"The world's loss." Spoken like a true father. He walked with her until he reached his wife in the front row and sat again.

Maeve continued on down the aisle. She was shaking by the time she got back to her seat and linked her arm around Ben's. He reached over to squeeze her knee and pressed a kiss to her forehead. "Easy, Sweetcheeks. You gave a good speech. I feel like I knew Steph, too, now. It was a nice tribute to your friend."

She nodded her thanks, rubbing her cheek against the textured canvas of the camo jacket he wore with a crisp white shirt, a tie, and khaki slacks. "I miss her."

"I know you do." He shifted his arm free and wrapped it around her shoulders, pulling her flush against his side and his comforting warmth. "I know you do."

They sat like that through the rest of the service, and if anyone noticed or whispered about the titanium hook resting on her shoulder, Maeve neither heard nor cared. She was feeling a little weak and vulnerable right now. But Ben had her. He'd had her from the moment she'd asked him to walk her to her car last Thursday. He'd stepped up in a way no one in her life ever had before.

But there was another man, sitting in the pew across the aisle from them, who made her feel very differently.

Austin Bukowski's red-rimmed eyes hadn't blinked as he'd watched her walk down the aisle after the eulogy. But she didn't believe those were tears, at least not for Steph.

She could feel his dark gaze on her even now, watching, hating. She'd said no to him—more than once—and his glare made it clear that that wasn't a word he was used to hearing. Despite his tailored suit and designer shoes, Austin was looking a little rough around the edges. He wore an immobilizing brace and bandage around his left hand, and he looked as though he hadn't slept in days. She shivered against Ben, wondering if Steph had told Austin no, too. No, she didn't have the files she'd stolen. No, she wasn't going to kowtow and do whatever Austin wanted—she had terms to their relationship that she expected him to meet. No, she wasn't going to let their sexual harasser boss control her career because she had files that could implicate them both in illegal activities.

If Ben wasn't here with her, Maeve would have left the

service long ago, just to get away from the hate and blame condemning her in Austin's eyes.

"Ignore him," Ben whispered against her hair. He'd spent a good deal of the service glaring right back at Austin. And she had a feeling that if this wasn't such a solemn occasion, he would have been up and across the aisle, telling Austin what he could do with his intimidation campaign and that if he didn't give it up, then Ben would make him stop. "Man, I wish I had Rocky with me right now."

She'd been so wrapped up in her grief that she hadn't noticed the tension radiating through Ben. "Are you all right?" she whispered, her concern evident. "Is this reminding you of your teammates' funerals? Do you need to step outside?"

"Dial it back a notch, Sweetcheeks," he answered, using words that had become a catchphrase between them whenever one of them got too caught up in their thoughts and emotions. "I'm okay. Rocky wouldn't tolerate anyone staring at us as long and hard as Bukowski is. We'd have a strong case of provocation if Rocky decided to take a chunk out of him."

Maeve squelched the urge to giggle as the minister invited them to stand and sing the closing hymn. It often surprised her how Ben could lighten her mood and make her laugh, even when she suspected he was dead serious, like now.

For Ben's sake, as well as hers, she was anxious for all this stress to end soon. He'd done an admirable job of protecting her, but she knew their time together was costing him. Stirring up bad memories. Sometimes feeling inadequate or second-guessing himself. Sometimes filling him with a cold, calculating intensity that must be a carryover from his time in Special Forces. She wondered just how long he could keep his mood swings in check and not erupt into the explosive kind of violence she imagined he was still quite capable of.

She prayed for Detectives Kincaid and Grove to work quickly to connect all the evidence and draw up arrest warrants. There were plenty of reasons for Austin to want to cover up the information in those files. Grove and Kincaid had recognized several of the names as high-profile criminals. Kevin Grove had done a quick check on his laptop and discovered a case of sexual assault filed against Bertram Summerfield. More research indicated that the charges had been dropped because the star witness for the prosecution—the alleged victim herself—had disappeared. They had yet to determine if she'd been paid off or if something more sinister had befallen her. And in February 2024, Joker had received nothing more than time served and community service in a trial where he'd been accused of assaulting a police officer. Had Joker done a deadly favor for Summerfield in exchange for representation by one of the most successful criminal law firms in the city?

Grove had matched up other docket numbers with cases related to Bertram Summerfield and his clients. Witnesses disappeared or recanted their testimony. Evidence was destroyed or went missing. Apparently, a significant number of Summerfield and Associates' clientele were pro bono cases. But those clients hadn't really gotten free, powerful representation. They'd paid in other ways. A favor to clear one case in exchange for a top-notch attorney who could get charges pled down or dismissed altogether.

Steph had gotten her hands on a truckload of illegal activities being conducted by Austin's law firm in the name of winning cases and making a ton of money. Joker and others like him apparently did the work that a lawyer who wanted to win an unwinnable case without getting his hands dirty needed to have done. It still didn't tell the detectives who had actually put his hands around Steph's neck and ended her life, but it provided crystal clear motivation. Stephanie Ward had tried to blackmail Austin with the information, and he was either covering his own ass or protecting his firm by getting her out of the way, so she couldn't say anything to the authorities and ruin their little racket. But had Austin killed Steph? Had Joker? Mr. Summerfield? Had some other client paid his fee by silencing the firm's traitor? How deep did this racket go, and who had taken it upon themselves to end Steph's life?

After the service ended, the guests filed out to the reception area on the far side of the lobby or out to the parking lot to have a smoke or head to their cars. When Ben turned them toward the front doors, he asked, "You ready to go? I'd like to check on Rocky."

She tugged on his arm to stop him. "I think I should stay and talk to Mr. Ward for a few minutes. I promise I won't go outside until you get back."

"I can wait."

"No." She nudged him toward the doors. "Rocky needs you. I'll be fine for the ten minutes or so it takes."

"If Bukowski tries to talk to you, walk away. Then text me. I'll come back in with Rocky, no matter what the funeral home's policy is on dogs." He seemed to be reconsidering his agreement to leave her at the reception when he leaned in and kissed her. "Ten minutes."

She watched him stride outside into the sunny autumn afternoon that Steph would have loved. Maeve straightened the new gray dress and black tights she wore as she searched the lingering groups of guests chatting and commiserating in the lobby and reception room, looking for Mr. Ward. She spotted the grieving father at a display of pictures and headed toward him. She was close enough to hear him talking about Steph's activities in high school when furtive movement several feet beyond him caught her attention.

"Oh, my God." Big, crude man, oily black hair. What was Judd Lasko doing here, lurking near the kitchen area? Joker was the last person Steph or her family would want to see.

The moment she started backing away, his dark gaze found her, drilled into her. When he ran his tongue around the rim of his lips, Maeve nearly gagged. She pulled her phone from her pocket and typed in a quick text to Ben.

Joker is here. I'm heading to the front to meet you.

She sent the text and spun toward the front doors. And slammed right into the wall of Austin Bukowski's chest. Before she could protest, he ripped her phone from her grasp and tossed it into the trash can beside the kitchen entrance. "You won't be needing that." With the fingers of his bandaged hand, he lightly gripped her arm and turned her to the door where Joker had just exited. "Come with me, Maevie."

"I don't think so." She easily twisted free from his injured grasp and elbowed him in the gut.

"Raise a stink, and I'll start shooting." She froze when she felt the hard steel barrel of a gun poking her in the back. "The old man will be the second target I hit. Now smile pretty and move."

"You're late." Joker was at the far end of the kitchen, looking out the back door.

"I didn't think that cripple would ever leave her alone," Austin argued.

Whatever Joker had been checking for, the pathway must have been clear. "Car's right out here."

"Isn't this enough of a tragedy already?" Maeve found

her voice despite her fear. "You're the last people Steph and her family would want here."

Austin handed her off to Joker, who hustled her out the door toward the waiting black Dodge Charger. The grip on her upper arm was bruising enough to make her fingers tingle and go numb. "We're not here to see that snitch off to the afterlife, Buzzkill. We're here for you."

Chapter Fourteen

Ben cursed ninety ways to Sunday at what he'd just seen behind the funeral home. Walking Rocky through the park across the street was too damn far away to stop it.

The creep who had to be twice the size of Maeve dragged her out to the black car, Bukowski hot on their heels, carrying a gun down at his side. Joker opened the back door, shoved Maeve inside and jogged around to climb in behind the wheel. Before Bukowski could get in behind her, Maeve grabbed the door handle and slammed the door shut on Bukowski's bandaged hand. The jerk screeched in a high-pitched, unnatural sound of pain. But when she pushed the door open again and scrambled out of the car, Bukowski furiously slammed the gun against her head, and she crumpled like a sack of potatoes.

"Maeve!"

While Bukowski scooped her up and dumped her into the back seat, Joker gunned the engine. The dirty lawyer fell into the seat behind her and pulled the door shut as the powerful car sped out of the parking lot.

Ben didn't bother giving chase. He'd never catch them. Instead, he changed directions and ran toward his truck. "Heel, Rocky! Move it!"

He and his partner broke into a dead run and quickly reached his truck. He didn't bother loading Rocky into his cage. He swung open the driver's side door and lifted the dog inside, pushing him into the passenger seat while he started the engine and pulled out his phone and hit the number he wanted before setting his phone on speaker and dropping it into the cup holder on the center console. Ben backed out, shifted into Drive, then floored it to get out to the street before he lost sight of the Dodge Charger.

When the call picked up, a calm voice answered. "Detective Grove."

Ben couldn't do calm right now. "They took her!"

"What are you talking about?"

"Bukowski and Joker. They stuffed her in a black Dodge Charger. I'm in pursuit."

"Don't get yourself in trouble, Sergeant," the detective warned.

"It's Maeve! I'm not going to give them the chance to kill her like they did her friend."

He heard Grove snapping his fingers to get someone's attention. "Give us your location. I'm rolling black-and-whites—"

"No! She's outnumbered and outgunned. I don't want to spook these guys. They've got no problem hurting women."

Grove cursed. "These guys think they're untouchable. They'll have no problem hurting you, either. Where are you right now?" Ben rattled off the street and cross-street as he flew through the intersection, heading toward the downtown area. "Kincaid and I are on the way. Keep the phone line open and update us on your location."

"Copy that."

"And Sergeant?"

"Yeah?"

"I like you. Don't get yourself killed."

"The only person I can guarantee isn't dying today is Maeve. Hunter out." With the indication that he was done talking, Ben darted in and out of traffic to get closer to the speeding car. He glanced across the cab to see Rocky sitting at attention, his gaze glued on the world zipping past outside the window. Ben nodded, appreciating having a teammate by his side as he went into battle again. "Let's go get our girl."

MAEVE GRADUALLY WOKE to the nauseatingly potent odors of stale beer, sweat and cigar smoke. Her cheek rested against something hard and cold and tacky, and she tried not to imagine what that might be. She was loathe to open her eyes, not only because her head was throbbing, but because she wanted to get a sense of where she was and what was happening before she revealed that she was aware.

When she finally slitted her eyes open, she wasn't surprised to find herself sitting in the back booth at Shotz's bar. Joker stood over by the bar, his head on a swivel as he watched both the front and back entrances, which she assumed would be locked at this time of day. Austin sat in the booth across from her. The stub of a cigar in an ashtray, a bottle of whiskey, a shot glass and the gun sat on the table in front of him as he struggled to rewrap his injured hand.

What was this place? A branch office of Summerfield and Associates?

Without lifting her head from the table, she tried to assess her own injuries. Did she have a concussion? How long had she been unconscious? Was the sticky stuff on the table her own blood oozing from a head wound? She wondered how quickly she could grab that gun and get herself out of here before Austin or Joker could react.

Something about her internal planning must have reflected in her expression because Austin pushed to his feet. "There she is." He downed the shot of whiskey, pulled her out of the booth and dropped her onto a hard chair beside it. Before she could grab the armrests and stand, he slapped her across the face. "Where are the files, Maevie? And you'd better not say with the cops."

It wasn't the hardest she'd ever been hit, but it was enough to make the bar spin around her and her stomach turn queasy. A moment later, she'd swallowed the bile in her throat and lifted her gaze to Austin. Since Kincaid and Grove *did* have the flash drive, she wasn't about to answer that question. Was this how Steph had met her death? Had she and Austin ever shared their romantic reunion? Or had kidnapping and torture and a demand to return the incriminating evidence been the last conversation she'd had?

"Which one of you strangled her to death?" Maeve demanded, even though she knew she had no power here. If this was to be her last conversation, she intended to die knowing the truth.

Austin poured himself another shot of whiskey and downed it. "We had fun together. That should have been enough. But she wanted the ring and the happily-ever-after. I had to shut her up so she wouldn't blab to the police or anyone else. The people I work with don't play games, Maevie. They demanded I eliminate the problem, or they'd eliminate me." He held up his injured hand before resting it against his chest. He looked pale. "This is just a reminder of what they'll do to me if I don't shut this mess down."

Joker chuckled from his spot across the bar. "And I'm here in case he messes anything else up. I'll take you both out. But I'll have a little fun with you first, Buzzkill."

Austin seemed more rattled by the threat than she was.

But Maeve had stopped caring about his pain long ago. "Is Mr. Summerfield part of this scheme, too?"

A cloud of stinky cigar smoke filled the air in the booth next to where she'd been dumped. She fisted her hands around the arms of the chair as Bertram Summerfield stood, buttoned his suit jacket and pushed Austin aside to stand right in front of her.

Austin might be drunk and desperate, Joker might be cruel and creepy. But the white-haired *gentleman* standing in front of her was absolutely terrifying. There was no emotion on his face, merely a curious tilt of his head as he puffed his cigar and studied her. "You and your friend have been a lot of trouble to me, Ms. Phillips. The police didn't even know crimes were being committed until you started talking to them." He puffed harder on his cigar until the end of it was nearly white-hot. Maeve's breath stuttered in her chest as he pulled the cigar from his lips and held it close to her cheek. Even without it touching her, she could feel the heat of the cigar searing her skin. She turned her face away and leaned back in the chair. "Where are my files? You're the only one Steph had an opportunity to give them to. There's too much money at stake, too many favors owed one way or the other to let this go." Austin grabbed the back of her neck and held her still so she couldn't twist away from the burning cigar hovering above her cheek. "Where. Are. My. Files?"

Joker turned toward the door. "Did you hear that?"

"You locked the doors, right?" Summerfield asked.

"Of course."

The door swung open. She heard the scrabble of claws on the wood floor a split second before she heard the deep-pitched command. "Rocky! Attack!"

A furry black bullet shot past Joker and Austin and leaped

at the imminent threat. With a furious snarl, Rocky knocked Summerfield to the floor. He clamped his jaw around the white-haired man's wrist and shook it hard until the older man screamed in pain and the cigar flew from his hand.

A split second later, in a similar blur of movement, Ben charged the distracted Joker, hitting the bigger man square in the gut. He lifted him off his feet and rammed Joker's back into the edge of the bar. She heard the loud *oof,* followed by a curse, then saw Joker raise his big fists and bring them down on Ben's shoulders. Ben crashed to the floor, but it seemed to be a strategic maneuver instead of a painful blow. He flipped onto his back and twisted his legs like a helicopter, catching Joker in the kneecap and then the crotch, bending the big man over. Ben kicked him in the face, then somehow got to his feet and jumped on Joker's back, wrapping his good arm around the man's neck.

Amidst the din of vicious snarls, grunts of pain, shouts and cursing, Maeve never forgot the killer in the room. When she saw Austin running for the back door, she pushed to her feet. "Rocky!" she yelled, hoping she had enough authority to command the canine protector as well. "Stand down!" Summerfield groaned as the dog released him and Rocky swung his head back to face her. She pointed to the man running down the back hallway as he cradled his broken hand. "Get him!" No, that wasn't the right command. What had Ben said? "Rocky! Attack!"

Poor Austin didn't stand a chance. He was curled up on the floor in a ball, trying to shield his face as Rocky pinned him beneath his paws and barked and bit at whatever he could reach, as two familiar detectives stormed into the front of the bar with their guns drawn.

Maeve had picked up her chair and set the legs down on

either side of Summerfield's torso, trapping the man on the floor. She looked across the room to Ben. He was breathing hard. There was blood at the corner of his mouth, his prosthetic hand was dangling from the harness around his shoulders and Joker hung limply in the chokehold of his arms.

Ben didn't release his grip around Joker's neck until the detectives got out their handcuffs and lowered him to the floor. While they cuffed the unconscious man, Ben commanded Rocky to return to his side. "Rocky! Stand down! Good boy. Good boy." He reached down to pet the dog around the ears and chest, then hurried over to Maeve. He tugged her away from the chair she was still holding and pulled her in for a hard hug before leaning back to examine her face. "You got an ambulance on the way? She's hurt."

"They're a few minutes out." With Joker subdued, the two detectives cuffed Austin and Bertram Summerfield. Atticus Kincaid pulled the white-haired attorney to his feet. "We'll take it from here, Sergeant."

Grove walked up with a whimpering Austin limping beside him. "Didn't I tell you to leave the confrontation to us, Sergeant?"

"They were hurting Maeve. I couldn't let that happen. I picked the lock and sent Rocky in first to clear the scene." A pair of uniformed officers came in to take the two prisoners from the detectives. "We're the strike force. You two are the officers who get to mop things up in here and write the reports."

Atticus Kincaid actually grinned. "We can manage that. Are you all right, Ms. Phillips?"

Maeve clung to the crook of Ben's elbow and nodded. "Austin hit me. I may have a mild concussion." When Ben started to go after him again, she tightened her grip and pulled him back. "I think I re-broke his hand."

"Good. I'll break the other one if he touches you ever again."

"I don't think that'll be an issue." Maeve watched him reach down and pet Rocky. When he met her gaze again, she could see that he had calmed a fraction. She paused a minute to help Ben get his prosthesis back on. Fortunately, it didn't look as if it had been damaged in the fight. Then she turned to the detectives. "You decoded everything on the flash drive?"

Detective Kincaid nodded. "Enough for at least three warrants. That's in addition to kidnapping and assaulting you."

"Good. Austin told me he's the one who killed Steph. I don't think he wanted to, but he was afraid for his own life if he didn't."

The paramedics now on the scene lifted Austin onto a gurney where he was handcuffed to the apparatus itself. Detective Grove interrupted them to ask, "Is that true, Mr. Bukowski?"

Austin grunted, refusing to answer the question. "I want my attorney."

The big detective shrugged. "I don't recommend anyone from Summerfield and Associates. I hear they're under investigation."

Ben nodded as the paramedics wheeled Austin away. "Nice one, Grove."

Maeve sat in the chair Ben pulled over for her as the paramedics checked her over next. "In all seriousness, if my testimony isn't enough, I imagine any of those three gentlemen will turn on the other in exchange for a lighter sentence. They like to wheel and deal like that."

Kincaid answered. "Those interviews are on my to-do list, ma'am."

She winced as the paramedic pressed a gauze bandage into place on her forehead. "You're putting them away, and they won't come after me again?"

"Yes, ma'am, and I don't think so. If, somehow, they do get out on bail before their trials, we'll be sure to notify you and get you into a safe house."

"*We're* her safe house." Ben linked her hand through his elbow and held Rocky by his leash at his side. "Any heads-up on a possible threat would be appreciated, though."

"Will do, Sergeant. We'll get complete statements from you two later. Good working with you both." The detectives exchanged handshakes with Ben and Maeve, then followed the entourage of prisoners being loaded into a squad car and ambulances outside the bar.

Once she'd been cleared by the paramedics and given a list of warning signs to look for if her mild concussion got any worse, Maeve turned to Ben. "I really do want to get out of this place."

"Yes, ma'am. Rocky, heel."

Maeve tilted her face to the waning sunshine, trusting Ben to lead her safely to his truck. She waited patiently as he cleaned up Rocky's muzzle and loaded the dog into the back of the truck where the warrior shepherd curled up into a ball like a contented puppy and promptly fell asleep.

Ben peeled off his camo jacket and draped it around Maeve's shoulders before opening the passenger side door. Instead of climbing in, Maeve pushed Ben back against the side of the truck and nestled herself square within his arms. "You know what I want to do right now?"

She felt him smile against her hair. "Enlighten me."

She leaned back against his arms and took in the bruise at the side of his mouth and the scrape along his cheekbone before tilting her gaze to his. "I want to take you home— back to your apartment at K-9 Ranch. I'm going to clean up your injuries, look you straight in the eye and tell you that I have fallen in love with you, and then I'm going to kiss you as thoroughly as I know how, and then I'm going to seduce you. I don't know if I'll be any good at it, but I'm going to get lots of points for enthusiasm, and you will never call me your *sort-of friend* again."

"Been thinking about that speech for a while, have you?" he teased.

She nodded and his stance shifted so that his fingers tunneled into her hair and cradled the back of her head, and those deep blue eyes were gazing down straight into hers. "One, I'm down with everything you just said." He dipped his head to claim her mouth. "And two, I already know you're going to rock my world and that I will never love any other woman the way I love you."

What? Had she heard that right? She wedged her hand between their chins and pushed his kiss aside. "You love me?"

"Heart and soul, Sweetcheeks. I'm a better man with you in my life. I have a purpose. I'm calmer. I'm happy. My dog likes you—and he has very discriminating taste in people. You see *me*. Not the hand. Not the tats or the beard. Not the soldier. Not the guy who's not quite right in the head. They're all part of me, but you see in here…" He touched his heart. "And up here…" He tapped the side of his head. "And it's healing me. I'm yours for as long as you want me."

Maeve beamed him a smile that came all the way from her heart. "Then I guess you'll be mine forever."

This time, when he leaned in for a kiss, she rose onto her tiptoes and met him halfway.

* * * * *

COMING SOON!

We really hope you enjoyed reading this book.
If you're looking for more romance
be sure to head to the shops when
new books are available on

Thursday 27th
February

To see which titles are coming soon, please visit

millsandboon.co.uk/nextmonth

MILLS & BOON

LET'S TALK

Romance

For exclusive extracts, competitions
and special offers, find us online:

📘 MillsandBoon

𝕏 @MillsandBoon

📷 @MillsandBoonUK

♪ @MillsandBoonUK

Get in touch on 01413 063 232

For all the latest titles coming soon, visit
millsandboon.co.uk/nextmonth

afterglow BOOKS

Afterglow Books is a trend-led, trope-filled list of books with diverse, authentic and relatable characters, a wide array of voices and representations, plus real world trials and tribulations. Featuring all the tropes you could possibly want (think small-town settings, fake relationships, grumpy vs sunshine, enemies to lovers) and all with a generous dose of spice in every story.

♪ @millsandboonuk
◎ @millsandboonuk
afterglowbooks.co.uk
#AfterglowBooks

For all the latest book news, exclusive content and giveaways scan the QR code below to sign up to the Afterglow newsletter:

SCAN ME